NAKED PREY

ALSO BY JOHN SANDFORD

Chosen Prey
Mortal Prey
The Fool's Run
The Empress File
The Devil's Code

Published by Simon & Schuster UK

John Sandford is the pseudonym of Pulitzer-prize winning journalist John Camp. He is the author of fifteen PREY novels, and three KIDD novels. He lives in Minnesota.

NAKED PREY

John Sandford

SIMON &
SCHUSTER

London · New York · Sydney · Tokyo · Singapore · Toronto · Dublin

A VIACOM COMPANY

First published in Great Britain by Simon & Schuster UK Ltd, 2003
A Viacom company

1 3 5 7 9 10 8 6 4 2

Simon & Schuster UK Ltd
Africa House
64–78 Kingsway
London WC2B 6AH

Simon & Schuster Australia
Sydney

A CIP catalogue record for this book is
available from the British Library

ISBN Trade Paperback 0-7432-4007-3
ISBN Hardback 0-7432-4826-0

Book design by Amanda Dewey

Printed and bound in Great Britain by
The Bath Press, Bath

For Deborah Howell,
there at the beginning

1

THURSDAY NIGHT, pitch black, blowing snow. Heavy clouds, no moon behind them.

The Buick disappeared into the garage and the door started down. The big man, rolling down the highway in a battered Cherokee, killed his lights, pulled into the driveway, and took the shotgun off the car seat. The snow crunched underfoot as he stepped out; the snow was coming down in pellets, rather than flakes, and they stung as they slapped his warm face.

He loped up the driveway, fully exposed for a moment, and stopped just at the corner of the garage, in a shadow beneath the security light.

Jane Warr opened the side door and stepped through, her back turned to him as she pulled the door closed behind her.

He said, "Jane."

She jumped, her hand at her throat, choking down a scream as she pivoted, and shrank against the door. Taking in the muzzle of the shotgun, and the large man with the beard and the stocking cap, she screeched: "What? Who're you? Get away . . ." A jumble of panic words.

He stayed with her, tracking her with the shotgun, and he said, slowly, as if speaking to a child, "Jane, this is a shotgun. If you scream, I will blow your heart out."

She looked, and it was a shotgun all right, a twelve-gauge pump, and it was pointing at her heart. She made herself be still, thought of Deon in the house. If Deon looked out and saw them . . . Deon would take care of himself. "What do you want?"

"Joe Kelly."

They stood for two or three seconds, the snow pellets peppering the garage, the big man's beard going white with it. Then, "Joe's not here." A hint of assertion in her voice—this didn't involve her, this shotgun.

"Bullshit," the big man said. He twitched the muzzle to the left, toward the house. "We're going inside to talk to him, and he's gonna pay me some money. I don't want to hurt you or anybody else, but I'm gonna talk to Joe. If I have to hurt the whole bunch of you, I will."

He sounded familiar, she thought. Maybe one of the guys from Missouri, from Kansas City? "Are you one of the Kansas City people? Because we're not . . ."

"Shut up," the big man said. "Get your ass up the steps and into the house. Keep your mouth shut."

She did what he told her. This was not the first time she'd been present when an unfriendly man flashed a gun—not even the second or third time—but she was worried. On the other hand, he said he was looking for Joe. When he found out Joe wasn't here, he'd go. Maybe.

"Joe's not here," she said, as she went up the steps.

"Quiet!" The man's voice dropped. "One thing I learned down in Kansas City—I'll share this with you—is that when trouble starts, you pull the trigger. Don't figure anything out, just pull the trigger. If Joe or Deon try anything on me, you can kiss your butt good-bye."

"All right," she said. Her voice had dropped with his. Now she was on the stranger's side. She'd be okay, she told herself, as long as Deon didn't do anything. But there was something too weird about this guy. *I'll share this with you?*—she'd heard a serious asshole say anything like that.

They went up the stairs onto a back porch, then through the porch into a mudroom, then through another door into the kitchen. None of the doors was locked. Broderick was a small town, and it doesn't take long to pick up small-town habits. As they clunked into the kitchen, which smelled like microwave popcorn and week-old carrot peels, Deon Cash called from the living room, "Hey," and they heard his feet hit the floor. A second later he stepped into the kitchen, scowling about something, a thin, five-foot-ten-inch black man in an Indian-print fleece pullover and jeans, with a can of Budweiser in one hand.

He saw Warr, the big man behind her, and then, an instant later, registered the shotgun. By that time, the big man had shifted the barrel of the shotgun and it was pointing at Cash's head. "Don't even think about moving."

"Easy," Cash said. He put the can of Budweiser on a kitchen counter, freeing his hands.

"Call Joe."

Cash looked puzzled for a second, then said, "Joe ain't here."

"Call him," the big man said. He'd thought about this, about all the calling.

Cash shrugged. "HEY JOE," he shouted.

Nothing. After a long moment, the man with the shotgun said, "Goddamnit, where is he?"

"He went away last month. He ain't been back. We don't know where he is," Warr said. "Told you he wasn't here."

"Go stand next to Deon." Warr stepped over next to Cash, and the big man dipped his left hand into his parka pocket and pulled out a clump of chain. Handcuffs. He tossed them on the floor and looked at Warr. "Put them on Deon. Deon, turn around."

"Aw, man . . ."

"It's up to you," the big man said. "I don't want to hurt you two, but I will. We're gonna wait for him if it takes all night."

"He ain't *here*," Warr said in exasperation. "He ain't coming back."

"Cuffs," the big man said. "I know what it sounds like when cuffs lock up."

"Aw man . . ."

"C'mon." The shotgun moved to Cash's head, and Warr bent over and picked up one set of cuffs and the big man said, "Turn around so I can see it," and Warr clicked the cuffs in place, pinning Cash's hands behind him.

The big man dipped his hand into his pocket again and came up with a roll of strapping tape. "Tape his feet together."

"Man, you startin' to piss me off," Cash said. Even with his hands cuffed, he managed to look stupidly fierce.

"Better'n being dead. Sit down and stick your feet out so she can tape you up."

Still grumbling, Cash sat down and Warr crouched beside him and said, "I'm pretty scared," and Cash said, "We gonna be all right. The masked man can go look at Joe's stuff, see he ain't here."

The big man made her take eight tight winds of tape around Cash's ankles. Then he ordered Warr to take off her parka and cuff her own hands. She got one cuff, but fumbled with the other, and the man with the shotgun told her to turn and back toward him, and when she did, clicked the second cuff in place. He then ordered both of them to lie on their stomachs, and with the shotgun pointed at them, he checked Cash's cuffs and then Warr's, just to make sure. When he was satisfied, he pulled on a pair of cotton gloves, knelt beside Warr, and taped her ankles, then moved over to Cash and put the rest of the roll of tape around his.

When he was done, Cash said, "So go look. Joe ain't here."

"I believe you," the big man said, standing up. They looked so helpless that he almost backed out. He steadied himself. "I know where Joe is."

After a moment's silence, Cash asked, "Where is he?"

"In a hole in the ground, a couple miles south of Terrebonne. Don't think I could find it myself, anymore," the big man said. "I just asked you about him so you'd think that . . ." He shrugged. "That you had a chance."

Another moment's silence, and then Warr said, "Aw, God, Deon. Listen to his voice."

Cash put the pieces together, then said, loud, croaking, but not yet screaming, "We didn't do nothin', man. We didn't do *nothin'*."

"I *know* what you did," the big man said.

"Don't hurt us," Warr said. She flopped against the vinyl, tried to get over on her back. "Please don't hurt us. I'll tell the cops whatever you want."

"We *get* a trial," Cash said. He twisted around, the better to see the man's face, and to test the tape on his legs. "We innocent until we proved guilty."

"*Innocent.*" The big man spat it out.

"We didn't do nothin'," Cash screamed at him.

"I know what you did." The crust on his wounds had broken, and the big man began kicking Cash in the back, in the kidneys, in the butt and the back of his head, and Cash rolled around the narrow kitchen floor trying to escape, screaming, the big man wailing like a man dying of a knife wound, like a man watching the blood running out of his neck, and he kicked and booted Cash in the back, and when Cash flopped over, in the face; Cash's nose broke with the sound of a saltine cracker being stepped on and he sputtered blood out over the floor. Across the kitchen, Warr struggled against the tape and the handcuffs and half-rolled under the kitchen table and got tangled up in the chairs, and their wooden legs clunked and pounded and clattered on the floor as she tried to inchworm through them, Cash screaming all the while, sputtering blood.

Cash finally stopped rolling, exhausted, blood pouring out of his nose, smearing in arcs across the vinyl floor. The big man backed away from him, wiped his mouth on his sleeve, then took a utility knife out of his pocket and stalked across the room to Warr, grabbed the tape around her ankles, and pulled her out from under the table. Warr cried, "Jesus, don't cut me!"

He didn't. He began slicing though her clothing, pulling it away in rags. She began to cry as he cut the clothing away. The big man closed his mind to it, finished, leaving her nude on the floor, except for the rags under the tape on her ankles, and began cutting the clothing off Cash.

"What're you doing, man? What're you doing?" Cash began flopping again, rolling. Finally, frustrated with Cash's struggles, the big man backed away and again kicked him in the face. Cash moaned, and the big man rolled him onto his stomach and knelt between his shoulder blades and patiently sliced at Cash's shirt and jeans until he was as naked as Warr.

"What're you doing?" Warr asked. Now there was a note of curiosity in her voice, showing through the fear.

"Public relations."

"Fuckin' kill ya," Cash groaned, still bubbling blood from his broken nose. "Fuckin' cut ya fuckin' head off . . ."

The big man ignored him. He closed the knife, caught Cash by the ankles, and dragged him toward the door. Cash, nearly exhausted from flopping on the floor, began flopping again, but it did no good. He was dragged flopping through the mudroom, leaving a trail of blood, onto the porch, and then down the steps to the lawn, his head banging on the steps as they went down. "Mother, mother," Cash said. "God . . . mother."

There wasn't much snow on the ground—hadn't been much snow

all winter—but Cash's head cut a groove in the inch or so that there was, spotted with more blood. When they got to the Jeep, the big man popped open the back, lifted Cash by the neck and hips, and threw him inside.

Back in the house, he picked up Warr and carried her out to the truck like a sack of flour and tossed her on top of Cash and slammed the lid.

Before leaving, he carefully scanned the house for anything that he might have touched that would carry a fingerprint. Finding nothing, he picked up the shotgun and went back outside.

"WHERE'RE WE GOING?" Warr shouted at him. "I'm freezing."

The big man paid no attention. A quarter-mile north of town, he began looking for the West Ditch Road, a dirt track that led off to the east. He almost missed it in the snow, stopped, backed up on the dark roadway, and turned down the track. He passed an old farmhouse that he'd thought abandoned, but now, as he went by, he saw a single light glowing in a first-floor window, but no other sign of life. Too late to change plans now, he thought; besides, with this night . . .

The wind had picked up, ripping the snow off the ground. He'd be far enough from the farmhouse that he couldn't be seen. He kept moving, the light in the farmhouse window fading away behind him. In the dark, in the snow, there were no distinctive landmarks at all.

He concentrated on the track and the odometer. Four-tenths of a mile after he turned off Highway 36, he slowed, looking out the left-side window. At first, he saw nothing but snow. After a hundred feet or so, the tree loomed, and he pulled over, then carefully backed, pulled forward, and backed again until he was parked across the road.

"What?" Cash groaned, from the back. "What?"

The big man went around to the back of the truck, opened it, grabbed the thick wad of tape around Cash's legs, and pulled him off the truck as if he were unloading lumber. Cash's shoulders hit the frozen earth with a meaty impact. The big man got him by the tape and dragged him past the first tree into what had been, from the car, in the dark, an invisible grove of trees.

One of the trees, a pin oak, loomed at the very edge of the illumination thrown by the car's headlights. Ropes were slung over a heavy branch fifteen feet above the ground. The big man, staggering under Cash's weight, dropped him by one of the ropes, then went back for Warr. When he got her to the hanging tree, struggling and kicking against him, he dropped her beside Cash.

"Can't do this, man," Cash screamed. "This is *murder*." The storm around them quieted for a moment, but the snow pellets still whipped through the trees, stinging like so many BBs.

"Please help me," Warr called to Cash. "Please, please . . ."

"Murder?" The big man shouted back at Cash, raising his voice above the wind. He broke away from them, toward a tree branch that was sticking up out of the snow, ripped it off the frozen ground and staggered back to Cash. *"Murder?"* He began beating Cash with the long stick, ripping strips of skin off Cash's back and legs, as the black man thrashed on the ground, gophering through the snow, trying to get away. "Murder, you fuckin' animal, murder . . ."

He stopped after a while, too tired to continue, threw the stick back into the trees. "Murder," he said to Cash. "I'll show you murder."

The big man led one of the ropes over to Cash, tied a single loop around his neck, tight, with strong knots. He did the same with the second rope, around Warr's neck. She was now shivering violently in the cold.

When he was done, the big man stood back, looked at the two of them, said, "God damn your immortal souls," and began hauling on the rope tied to Cash. Cash stopped screaming as the rope bit into his neck. He was heavy, and the big man had to struggle against his weight, and against the raw friction of the rope over the tree limb. Finally, unable to get him in the air, the big man lifted him and pulled the rope at the same time, and Cash's feet cleared the ground by a meager six inches. He didn't struggle. He simply hung. The big man tied the lower end of the rope around the tree trunk, and tested it for weight. It held.

Warr pleaded, but the big man couldn't hear her—later couldn't remember anything she said, except that there were a lot of whispered *Pleases.* Didn't do her any good. Didn't do her any good when she fought him, either, though it might have given her a brief thirty seconds of satisfaction.

He couldn't get her high enough to get her feet off the ground, and as he struggled to do it, a space opened between the bottom of his coat sleeve and the glove on his right hand. The space, the warm flesh, bumped against her face, and quick as a cat, she sank her teeth into his arm, biting ferociously, twisting her head against his arm. He let go of the rope and she fell, holding on with her teeth, pulling him down, and he hammered at the side of her head until she let go.

She was groaning when he boosted her back up, and she ground out, "We're not the only ones."

That stopped him for a moment: "What?"

"They'll be coming for you, you cocksucker." She spat at him, from three inches away, and hit him in the face. He flinched, grabbed her around the waist and boosted her higher, his gloves slippery with blood, and then he had her high enough and he stepped away, holding tight to the rope, and she swung free and her groaning stopped. He managed to pull her up another four inches, then tied the rope off on the trunk.

He watched them for a few minutes, swinging in the snow, in the dim light, their heads bent, their bodies violently elongated like martyrs in an El Greco painting . . .

Then he turned and left them.

They may have been dead then, or it might have taken a few minutes. He didn't care, and it didn't matter. He rolled slowly, carefully, out of the side road, down through Broderick and on south. He was miles away before he became aware of the pain in his wrist, and the blood flowing down his sleeve toward his elbow. When he turned his arm over in the dim light of the car, he found that she'd bitten a chunk of flesh out of his wrist, a lemon-wedge that was still bleeding profusely.

If a cop stopped him and saw it . . .

He pulled over in the dark, wrapped his wrist with a pad of paper towels and a length of duct tape, stepped out of the truck, washed his hand and arm in snow, tossed the bloody jacket in the back of the truck and dug out a lighter coat from the bag in back.

Get home, he thought. *Burn the coat, dump the truck.*

Get home.

2

WEATHER DAVENPORT crawled sleepily out of bed. The kid was squalling, hungry in his bedroom down the hall, and she started that. Lucas woke up as the housekeeper called, "I got him, Weather. I'm up."

"Ah, great," Weather said. She came back to the bed, sat down, looked at the clock.

"Getting up?" Lucas asked.

"Alarm's going off in fifteen minutes anyway," she said. She yawned, inhaled, exhaled, pushed herself off the bed and headed for the bathroom, pulling off her cotton nightgown as she went. Lucas, lying half awake under the crazy quilt, could see nothing but darkness on the other side of the wood slats that covered the window. January in Minnesota: the sun came up at 11:45 and went down at noon, he thought.

He shifted his head around on the pillow, tried to get comfortable, tried to get back to sleep. Sleep was unlikely: He'd been feeling down for a month or more, and depression was the enemy of decent sleep.

JOHN SANDFORD

The marriage was fine, the new kid was great. Nothing to do with that—his sense of the blue was a chemical thing, but the chemicals made sleep impossible. If he went down further, he'd check with the doc. On the other hand, it might just be the winter, which this year had started in October.

He heard the shower start, and then Ellen, the housekeeper, banging down the stairs with the kid. The kid was named Samuel Kalle Davenport, the "Kalle" a Finnish name, for Weather's late father. The housekeeper was a fifty-five-year-old ex-nurse who loved kids. The four of them together had a deal they all liked.

After a few minutes, the shower stopped and Lucas sat up. He was awake now, no point in struggling against it. He climbed out of bed, remembered the clock, picked it up and turned off the alarm. As he did, Weather came out of the bathroom, rubbing her hair with a towel.

"You getting up?" she asked cheerfully. She was a small woman, and an early bird. She liked nothing better than getting up before the sun, to begin the hunt for worms.

"Uh," Lucas said. He started for the bathroom, but she smelled so warm and good as he passed her that he slipped an arm around her waist and picked her up and gave her a warm sucking kiss on the tummy below her navel.

She squirmed around, laughed once, and then said, severely, "Put me down, you oaf."

"Mad rapist attacks naked housewife in bedroom." Lucas carried her back to the bed and threw her on it and landed on the bed next to her, hands running around where they shouldn't be.

"Get away from me," she said, rolling away. "Come on, Lucas, goddamnit." She whacked him on the ear, and it hurt, and he collapsed on the bed. She got out and started scrubbing at her hair again and said, "You men get hard-ons in the morning and you're so proud of them, just swishing around in the air. You can't help showing off."

"Try not to use the word *swish*," Lucas said.

"Sex in the morning is for teenagers, and we aren't," she said.

Lucas rolled over on his stomach. "Now you've offended me."

"Offend this," she said. She'd spun her towel into a whip, and snapped him on the ass with it. That hurt, too, more than the whack on the ear, and he rolled off the bed and said, "Arrgh, naked housewife attacks sleeping man."

Weather, laughing, backed away from him, rewinding the towel, said, "Sleeping man snapped in the balls with wet towel."

Then Ellen, the housekeeper, called from the stairs, "You guys up?"

They both stopped in their tracks, and Weather whispered, "Well, you are. What do you want me to tell her?"

WEATHER WAS A SURGEON, and she was cutting on somebody almost every morning. This morning, she had three separate jobs, all at Regions, all involving burns—two separate skin grafts, and a scalp expansion on the head of a former electric lineman, trying to stretch what hair he had left over the burn scars he'd taken from a hot line.

She was bustling around the kitchen, in full imperial surgeon mode, when Lucas finally made it down the stairs. Ellen had the kid in a high chair, and was pushing orange vegetable mush into his face.

"I'll be home by three o'clock, Ellen, but I'll be out of touch from seven-thirty to at least ten," Weather was saying. "If there's a problem, you know what to do. The man from Harper's is coming over this morning to look at the front steps . . ."

The phone rang, and they all looked at it. Maybe a canceled operation? Lucas picked it up: "Hello?"

"Lucas? Rose Marie." The new head of the state's Department of Public Safety.

"Uh-oh."

"You got that right. How soon can you get in?"

"Fifteen minutes," Lucas said. "What's up?"

"Tell you when you get here. Hurry. Oh—is Weather still there?"

"Just getting ready to leave."

"Let me talk to her."

Lucas handed the phone to Weather and at the same time said, "Rose Marie. Something happened, I gotta run."

Weather took the phone, said, "Hello," listened for a moment, and then said, "Yes, Lucas gave it to me. I think we'll start tonight. Uh-huh. Uh-huh. I don't think we'll skip any of it, I was listening to the Japanese flute last night . . ."

While they were talking, Lucas went to the front closet and got his overcoat and briefcase. He took his .45 out of the briefcase and clipped it on his belt, and pulled the coat on, listening to Weather talk to his boss. Rose Marie subscribed to a theory that children became smarter if they were exposed to classical music as fetuses, continuing until they were, say, forty-five. She'd found a set of records made specifically for infants. Weather had swallowed the whole thing, and was about to start the program.

"I'm going," Lucas called to her, when he had his coat on.

Weather said, "Wait, wait . . ." and then, to the phone, "I've got to say good-bye to Lucas. Talk to you tonight." She hung up and came over to Lucas and stood on tiptoe to kiss him on the lips. "She said you'd be going out of town. So . . ."

"Oh, boy," Lucas said. He kissed her again, and then went over and kissed Sam on the top of his head. "See you all."

RUNNING A FEW MINUTES later than the fifteen he'd promised, Lucas Davenport walked a long block down St. Paul's Wabasha Street, toward the former store that housed the state Department of Public Safety. Lucas's own office was a mile or so away, at the main Bureau of Criminal Apprehension office on University Avenue, so he'd had to find a space in one of the commercial parking garages. Around him, feather-like flakes of snow settled on the sidewalks, on the shoulders of passers-by, and drifted into the traffic, slowing and softening the usual hustle of the morning rush.

LUCAS WAS A TALL, athletic man, hatless, in a blue suit and gray cashmere overcoat, swinging a black Coach briefcase with no thought of the North, of dead people hanging in a frozen stand of oaks. Both coat and case were Christmas gifts from Weather, and though he'd taken some grief about them—they were a little too fey for a cop, he'd been told—he liked them. The coat was soft and warm and dramatic, and the briefcase had that aristocratic thump that impressed people who were impressed by aristocratic thumps. That included almost all bureaucrats.

He was surrounded by bureaucrats, as the result of a political cluster-fuck that had stretched across three or four different sets of politicians. When the dust had settled, the former Minneapolis chief of police was the Minnesota Public Safety Commissioner, and Lucas had a new job fixing crime for the governor.

Lucas's job was officially designated "Director, Office of Regional Studies." The ORS had been planted within the state Bureau of Criminal Apprehension, and drew its budget and support from the BCA—but Lucas reported directly to Rose Marie Roux and through her to the governor. The governor had already been burned by a couple of outstate murder cases that had gone unsolved, and he'd had enough of that.

In both cases, the local sheriff's departments had investigated the murders, before calling in the BCA. When the cases proved too complicated or politically touchy, they started screaming for help—and blamed the BCA, and the state, when the cases went unsolved.

That the cases had been mucked up by the locals hadn't cut any ice with the hometown newspapers. Where was all the scientific investigation stuff they kept seeing on the Discovery Channel? Why were they sending all that taxpayer money to St. Paul? What was the governor doing, sitting on his ass?

Questions that a 44 percent governor didn't appreciate.

So the governor created the Office of Regional Studies in consultation with Roux. The office was intended, as the insiders all knew, to "fix shit." The BCA director, John McCord, hated the idea. Nobody above him really cared. They just wanted shit fixed. Lucas smiled at the thought. He hadn't fixed anything big yet, but this call sounded like others he'd gotten from Roux over the years.

Lucas smiled often enough—he liked his job and his life—but the years had given him a hard face and French-Canadian genes had left him with crystal-blue eyes. His hair was dark, with flecks of gray, and a white scar ran across his forehead and one eyebrow onto the cheek below. Another scar dimpled his throat, a nasty round white spot with a slashing tail. He'd been shot by a little girl and had been choking on his tongue and on the blood from the wound, passing out, and a surgeon—the same one he'd later married—had opened his throat and airway with a jackknife.

That had all been years ago.

Now, he thought, he spent too much time in a chair. In an effort to fight what he saw as sloth, he'd been playing winter basketball with a group of aging jocks from Minneapolis. He was broad-shouldered, quick-moving, and not quite gaunt.

HE BRUSHED BY a redheaded woman who was leading a muffin-sized red dog in a muffin-sized red Christmas sweater down the sidewalk. The woman smiled and said, "Hi, Lucas," as they passed. He half-turned and blurted, "Hey. How ya doin'?" and smiled and kept going. Where'd he know her from? Somewhere. He was up the steps, inside the shopping mall that led to the DPS, in an elevator: *A bartender,* he thought. She used to be a bartender. Where? O'Brien's? Maybe . . .

ROSE MARIE ROUX'S office was a twenty-foot square that she'd furnished with her own money: a good cherrywood desk, two comfortable visitors' chairs in green leather, a couch, a few prints and photographs of politicians, a bookcase full of reference books and state procedure manuals.

Rose Marie was sprawled in a chair behind her desk, an overweight woman with improbably blond-tinted fly-away hair, wearing a rumpled blue dress, with an unlit cigarette hanging from the corner of her mouth. Word around town was that when she took the job, she'd moved the commissioner's office across the building so she could get a window that opened. At any time of day, you were likely to see her head sticking out the window, it was said, with a plume of smoke hanging over it.

"What?" Lucas asked.

"Sit down," she said. She pointed at a green leather chair. "The governor's a couple of minutes out, but I can give you an outline." She took a breath. "Well . . ."

"What?"

"We've had a lynching." The statement hung in the air like an oral Goodyear blimp.

"Tell me," Lucas said after a moment.

"Up north, a few miles outside of Armstrong. You know where that is?"

"By Thief River, somewhere."

"Very good. A black man and a white woman were found hanging from a tree out in the countryside. They were naked. Handcuffed, legs taped with strapping tape. They'd been living together in some flyspeck town north of Armstrong."

"Lynched," Lucas said. He thought about it for a few seconds, then said slowly, "Lynched means that somebody is suspected of a crime. The townspeople take justice into their own hands and the law doesn't do anything about it. Is that—?"

"No. What actually happened is that they were murdered," Rose Marie said, twisting in her chair. "Sometime last night. But it's a black man and a blond woman and they're hanging from trees, naked. When the word gets out, the shit's gonna hit the fan, and we can say *murder* all we want, and the movie people are going to be screaming *lynching*. We need to get some shit up there."

"Does Bemidji know?" Lucas asked. The BCA's Bemidji office handled investigations in the northern part of the state.

"I don't know—they don't know from me. What we've got is an informal contact with Ray Zahn, the state patrolman out of Armstrong," Rose Marie said. "He called in about forty-five minutes ago, and had the call switched to me, at home. He seems to be a smart guy. He was first on the scene, a couple of minutes ahead of the first sheriff's deputies."

"Maybe the sheriff'll handle it," Lucas suggested.

"Zahn says no. He says the sheriff is a new guy who's scared of his own shadow. Zahn says the sheriff'll call us as soon as he looks at the scene."

"And I'm going."

"Absolutely. That's the first thing the governor said when I called him. We've got a National Guard chopper getting ready. You can fly right into the scene."

"That's all we know?" Lucas asked.

"That's everything," Roux said.

"Then I'll get going," Lucas said, pushing up from the green chair. He felt a hum, a little spear of pleasure breaking through the blue. An evil bastard to hunt: nothing like it to cheer a guy up. "You can call me in the air if anything changes."

"Wait for the governor. He's only a minute or two away."

———

WHILE THEY WAITED, Lucas got on his cell phone and called Del: "Where are you?"

"In bed." Del Capslock had come over from Minneapolis with Lucas.

"Get up. I'll pick you up in fifteen or twenty minutes. Bring some clothes for a couple of days. Bring some boots, too. We're going up north. We're gonna be outside."

"Uh-oh."

"Yeah. Exactly right. I'll tell you when I see you."

ROSE MARIE'S TELEPHONE RANG, and she picked it up, listened for one second, then dropped it back on the hook. "Governor just came through the front door."

GOVERNOR ELMER HENDERSON was six feet tall and willowy, with lightly gelled blond hair fading to gray, long expressive hands, and watery blue eyes. He wore narrow, gold-rimmed glasses that gave him a scholarly look, and conservative gray, blue, or black suits handmade in London, over handmade English shoes.

Henderson's clan had money and a history in Minnesota politics, but Elmer hadn't been expected to carry the family banner. He had, in fact, always been the family weenie, with a whiff of sexual *difference* hanging around him from his college and law-school days.

He'd been expected to spend his life as a second-stringer in the boardrooms of large Minnesota corporations, while his two brothers grew up to be governors and senators and maybe presidents. But one of the brothers turned to cocaine and multiple divorce, and the other got drunk and powered his antique wooden Chris Craft under a dock and made a quadriplegic of himself. Elmer, by default, was chosen to soldier on.

As it happened, he'd found in his soul a taste for power and a talent for intrigue. He'd created a cabal of conservative Democratic state legislators that had decapitated the Democratic Party machine, and then had taken it over. He'd maneuvered that victory into a nomination for governor. A little more than a year into his first term, he looked good for a second.

Henderson was also a northern Catholic conservative Democrat, in his mid-forties, nice-looking, with an attractive wife and two handsome if slightly robotic children, one of each gender, who never smoked dope or rode skateboards or got tattooed or visibly pierced—although a local talk show host had publicly alleged that Henderson's eighteen-year-old daughter had two clitorises. That, even if true, could hardly be held against Henderson. If the party should choose a southern Protestant liberal for president, and needed some balance on the ticket . . . well, who knew what might happen?

HENDERSON CAME IN IN A RUSH, banging into Roux's office without knocking, trailed by the odor of Bay Rum and his executive assistant, who smelled like badly metabolized garlic. They were an odd couple, almost always together, the slender aristocrat and his Igor, Neil Mitford. Mitford was short, burly, dark-haired, badly dressed, and constantly worried. He looked like a bartender and, in his college days, had been a good one—he had a near-photographic memory for faces and names.

"Has Custer County called yet?" Henderson asked Roux, without preamble.

"Not yet. We're not officially in it," Roux said.

The governor turned to Lucas: "This is what you were hired for. Fix this. Get up there, let the regular BCA guys do their thing, let the sheriff do his thing, but I'm going to lean on you. All right?"

Lucas nodded. "Yes."

"Just so that everybody is on the same page," Mitford said. He'd picked up a crystal paperweight from one of Rose Marie's trophy shelves, and was tossing it in the air like a baseball. "This is a murder, not a lynching. We'll challenge the word *lynching* as soon as anybody says it."

"They're going to say it," Roux said from behind her desk.

"We know that," Henderson said. "But we need to kill it, the use of the word."

"Not a lynching," Mitford repeated. To Lucas: "The sooner we can find anything that supports that view, the better off we'll be. Any little shred. Get it through to me, and I'll spin it out to the TV folks."

"Gotta knock it down quick," Henderson said. "Can't let it grow."

Lucas nodded again. "I better take off," he said. "The quicker we get up there—"

"Go," said Henderson. "Knock it down, the word, then the crime."

Roux added, "I'll call you in the air, as soon as Custer County calls in. I'll get the BCA down here to coordinate you with the guys out of Bemidji."

"All right," Lucas said. "See ya."

And as Lucas was going out the door, Henderson called after him, "Great briefcase."

ON HIS WAY TO DEL'S HOUSE, Lucas called Weather at the hospital, was told that she'd just gone down to the locker room. He left a message with her secretary: he'd call with a motel number when he was on the ground.

Del lived a mile east and north of Lucas, in a neighborhood of postwar ramblers and cottages, all modified and remodified so many times that the area had taken on some of the charm of an English village. Del was waiting under the eaves of his garage, wearing a parka and blue corduroy pants pulled down over nylon-and-plastic running shoes. He had a duffel bag slung over his shoulder.

"Running shoes?" Lucas asked, as Del climbed into the car.

"Got boots in the bag," Del grunted. He hadn't bothered to shave, but his breath was minty-fresh. He was nut-tough, smaller than Lucas, street-weathered, shifty, a guy who could pass as a junkie or as homeless or almost anything else that didn't involve a white collar. "Does Weather know about this?"

"Left a message. How about Cheryl?" Lucas asked. Del's wife was a nurse.

"Yeah, called her. She's working the first shift—I told her probably two or three days. What happened?"

"Interesting problem," Lucas said. He outlined what he knew about the hangings as they headed to Lucas's house to pack.

"A fuckin' lynching, and we gotta fix it. For our own sakes, along with everything else," Del said, when Lucas had finished.

"Not a lynching."

"Walks likes a lynching, quacks like a lynching . . ." They sat silently for a moment, watching the snow come down around a red light. Then, "Could be a good time, you know?"

LUCAS CHANGED CLOTHES and packed in ten minutes, stuffing underwear, jeans, a laptop, and a cell-phone charger into a black nylon bag. He said good-bye to the housekeeper; kissed the kid, who was taking a nap and who, with a beige blanket folded around him, looked a little like a submarine sandwich; and collected Del, who'd called a cab.

The cab driver got lost for a while, trying to find the entrance to the National Guard site at Minneapolis–St. Paul International. When they finally arrived, the pilot and copilot, who had become impatient, briskly packed them into the back of the chopper.

THE FLIGHT WAS UNCOMFORTABLE: the old military chopper had been built for utility rather than comfort. Conversation was difficult, so they gave it up. Even *thinking* was hard, and eventually they huddled, nylon-and-fleece-clad lumps, on the bad canvas seats, closed up in the stink of hot oil and military creosote, heads down, fighting off incipient nausea.

After an eternity, the chopper beat got deeper and they felt the beginning of a turn. Del unbuckled, half-stood, looked forward and then patted Lucas on the shoulder and shouted, "There it is."

Lucas pressed his forehead to the icy plastic window of the National Guard helicopter and tried to look forward.

A THOUSAND FEET BELOW, the Red River plains of northern Minnesota stretched north and west, toward Canada and the Dakotas. Though it was January, and the temperature outside the chopper registered at six degrees below zero, the ground below them was only dappled with snow. The few roads resembled lines on a drafting pad, dead straight across the paper-flat farmscape.

To the southeast, along the route they'd just flown, the country had been rougher and the snow deeper. Dozens of frozen-over lakes and ponds had been strung like rosary beads on the snowmobile trails; jigsaw-puzzle farm fields, red barns, and vertical streams of chimney smoke had given the land a homier personality.

Straight east, out of the helicopter's right window, was a wilderness of peat bog punctuated by the hairy texture of trash willow. To the west, they could just see a shadowy hint of the line of the Red River, rolling north toward Winnipeg.

They'd overflown the hamlet of Broderick, in Custer County, and were now closing on a line of cop cars parked on what Lucas had been told was West Ditch Road. The roof racks were flashing on two of the cars. To the north of them, in one of the bigger patches of snow, they could see a stand of leafless trees.

The copilot leaned into the passenger compartment and shouted over the beat of the blades, "We're gonna put you down on the highway—they don't want the rotor blast blowing dirt over the crime scene. A state patrol car will come out to get you."

Lucas gave him a thumbs-up and the copilot pulled his head back into the cockpit. Del pulled off the Nikes, stuffed them in his duffel bag, and began lacing up high-topped hiking boots. Lucas looked at his watch: 11:15. The flight to Broderick had taken better than two hours. Minnesota was a tall state, and Custer County was about as far from St. Paul as it was possible to get, without crossing into North Dakota or Canada.

Now the pilot dropped the chopper in a circle, to look at the highway where they'd land. At the same time, a state patrol car, followed by a sheriff's car, rolled down the side road and, at the intersection, blocked the main highway north and south.

"Better button up tight," the copilot called back to them. "It's gonna be chilly."

The chopper put down on the tarmac between the two cop cars, and the copilot came back to slide the door. Lucas and Del climbed out into the downdraft of the rotors.

The air was bitterly cold. Dirt and ice crystals scoured them like a sandblaster, and, unconsciously ducking away from the rotors, they ran with their bags back to the state patrol car, their pants plastered to their legs, the icy air lashing their exposed skin. The patrolman popped the back and passenger doors, and as they climbed in, the chopper took off in another cloud of ice crystals.

"That really sucked," the patrolman said as they settled in. He was in his late forties, with white eyebrows and graying hair, his face as weathered as a barn board. "Didn't even think about the goddamned prop wash, or whatever it is."

He buckled up and looked back at Del, nodded, then held out a hand to Lucas and said, "Ray Zahn. Sorry to get you up so early."

"Lucas Davenport, that's Del Capslock in the back," Lucas said, as they shook hands. "They haven't taken the bodies out yet?"

"No. They've been waiting for the ME. Couldn't find him for a while, but he's on his way now." Zahn did a U-turn and they bumped off the highway onto the gravel road, and the sheriff's car fell in behind them.

"You know the people? The ones that got hanged?" Del asked.

Zahn got the car straight and caught up with Lucas's question. "Yeah. It's a couple from down in Broderick. We've IDed them as a Jane Warr and a Deon Cash. They were living in an old farmhouse down there."

"Cash is black?"

"Yup." Zahn grinned. "Only black dude in the entire county and somebody went and hung him."

"That could piss you off," Del ventured.

"Got that straight," Zahn said with a straight face. "Our cultural diversity just went back to zero."

3

WEST DITCH ROAD was frozen solid, but sometime during the winter there'd been a thaw, and a tractor had cut ruts in the thinly graveled surface. As they bumped through the ruts, now frozen as hard as basalt, Zahn pointed to a house across the ditch and said, "That's where the girl's from."

"What girl?" Lucas asked. He and Del looked out the windows. A thirty-foot-wide drainage ditch ran parallel to the road and showed a steely streak of ice at the bottom. A narrow, two-story farmhouse, its white paint gone gray and peeling, sat on the other side of the ditch. The house faced the highway, but was a hundred feet back from it. A rusting Jeep Cherokee squatted in the yard in front of the sagging porch.

Zahn glanced over at him. "How much you know about this? Any-thing?"

"Nothing," Lucas said. "They threw us on the chopper and that's about it."

"Okay," Zahn said. "To give it to you quick, a girl named Letty West lives in that house with her mother. She's this little twerp." He thought that over for a second, then rubbed an eyebrow with the back of his left hand. "Naw, that's not right. She's like a little Annie Oakley. She wanders around with an old .22 and a machete and a bunch of traps. Caught her driving her mother's Jeep a couple of times. Got a mouth on her. Anyway, last night—she looked at her clock when she woke up, and she says it was right after midnight—she saw some car lights down the road here, and wondered what was going on. There's nothing down here, and it was blowin' like hell. This morning, about dawn, she was walking her trapline along the ditch, and went up on top to look at that grove of trees. That's how she found them. If she hadn't, they might've hung there until spring."

THEY WERE ALL LOOKING out the windows at the girl's house. The place might have been abandoned, but for a light glowing from a window at the front door, and foot tracks that led on and off the porch to the Jeep. The yard hadn't been cut in recent years and clumps of dead yellow prairie grass stuck up through the thin snow. A rusting swing-set sat at the side of the house, not square to anything, as though it'd been dumped there. A single swing hung from the left side of the two-swing bar. On the far back end of the property, a forties-era outhouse crumbled into the dirt.

Lucas noticed a line of green-paper Christmas trees taped in an upstairs window.

"How old's the girl?" Del asked.

"Eleven or twelve, I guess."

"What's the machete for?" Lucas asked.

"Something to do with the trapping," Zahn said.

"She down at the scene, or . . . ?"

"They took her into town with her mother, to make a statement."

Lucas asked, "Who'd know about this road? Have to be local, you think?"

Zahn shrugged: "Maybe, but I think it's probably the first road the killer came to that led off the highway, outside of Broderick. First place he could do his business with a little peace and quiet."

"Must have scouted it, though," Lucas said. The road was only slightly wider than the patrol car, with no shoulder on the left, and on the right, six feet of frozen dirt and then an abrupt slope into the ditch. "That ditch would be dangerous as hell. How'd he turn around?"

"There are some tracks, you'll see them up ahead. What's left of them, anyway. He just jockeyed her around, and got straight. But you're right; he must've scouted it."

"If this kid could see him, why'd he think he was out of sight?" Del asked.

"We had a good wind through here last night, a nice little ground blizzard," Zahn said. "From the grove of trees, on the ground, he might not be able to see the farmhouse, but from up on the second floor of the farmhouse, you could see his lights down in the grove. Anyway, Letty said she could, and there's no reason to think she was lying. She never turned her room light on."

"Mmm." Lucas nodded. He'd once been in a ground blizzard where he couldn't see more than three feet in any direction, but if he looked straight up, he could see a fine blue sky with puffy, white fair-weather clouds. "So the victims lived back in Broderick?"

"Yeah, down there in another old farmhouse. That's how we iden-tified them so quick. Took one look and knew who the guy was. Him being black."

"How long did he live here?"

"Year and a half. He was in jail down in Kansas City, showed up here in July a year ago, and moved in with Warr. Warr was working at the casino in Armstrong, dealing blackjack. We just found out about the jail thing this morning."

"The Warr woman—she was from here?" Del asked.

"Nope. She was from Kansas City, herself," Zahn said. "Got into Broderick about a month before Cash, so we think she must've been his girlfriend, and came up here when he was about to get out of jail, to nail down the job. But to tell you the truth, we don't really know the details yet."

"Okay."

"What about Broderick?" Del asked. "Anything there? What do they do? Farmers?"

"Well, it was mostly a ghost town until Gene Calb got his truck rehab business going. There was always a gas station and a store, and a bar off and on, servicing the local farm folks. Just a crossroads. Then some people moved up here, to be close to work at Calb's—houses are really cheap—and now, there must be twenty or thirty people around the place."

"So what the hell was an interracial couple from Kansas City doing there?" Lucas asked.

"That seems to be a question," Zahn agreed. They'd come up on the line of cop cars, which were parked on both sides of the narrow lane. A half-dozen cops were standing around, backs to the wind, ducking their heads briefly to see who Zahn was bringing in. Zahn threaded between them, slowed, pointed to a tall white-haired man in sunglasses, a camo hunting jacket, and nylon wind pants, who stood with his hands in his pockets talking to two other men. Zahn said, "That's the sheriff, Dick Anderson. I'll let you out here. I'm gonna find someplace to get turned around. I get claustrophobic when I'm pointed the wrong way."

LUCAS AND DEL climbed out, and the sheriff and the two men he was talking to looked down at them, and the sheriff said something to the other two and they both smiled. Del, who was coming up behind Lucas, muttered, "We're city slickers."

"For a while, anyway," Lucas agreed. He smiled as he came up to the sheriff. Lucas's blue eyes were happy enough, but his smile sometimes made people nervous. "Sheriff Anderson? Lucas Davenport and Del Capslock with the BCA. We understand you've got a situation."

"If that's what you'd call it," the sheriff said. The sheriff was about forty, Lucas thought, with a pale pinkish complexion; he ran to fat, like a clerk, but wasn't fat yet. His hands stayed in his pockets. A statement of some kind, Lucas thought.

Anderson nodded to the two men with him: "These are deputies Braun and Schnurr. We understood that Hank Dickerson was coming up from Bemidji with a crime scene crew."

Lucas nodded, still smiling. "Yes. They should be here anytime. Del and I were sent by the governor to make sure everything was handled right."

"The governor knows about this?" Anderson asked doubtfully.

"Yes. I talked to him this morning before I left. He said to say hello and that he hoped we could get this cleared away in a hurry."

"Maybe I should give him a call," Anderson suggested.

"I'm sure he'd be happy to hear from you," Lucas said. He looked around. "Where are the victims?"

Anderson turned toward the stand of trees north of the road, took a hand out of his jacket pocket, and pointed. "Back in there, where the guys in the orange hats are."

Lucas said to Del. "Let's go take a look."

"Are you running this, or Hank?" Anderson asked.

"Both of us, in a way," Lucas said. "I report directly to the commissioner of Public Safety and to the governor. Hank reports up through the BCA chain of command."

"So what exactly do *you* do?" Deputy Schnurr asked. "Handle the politics or what?"

"I kick people's asses," Lucas said. His eyes flicked over Schnurr and the other deputy, then went back to the sheriff. "When they need to be kicked."

He and Del both stepped away at the same time, toward the men in the orange caps. The sheriff and his two deputies hesitated, and Del and Lucas got a few steps away and Del said, "That was cool."

"Hey, the guy didn't even shake hands."

"Yeah." They pushed through a tangle of brush and caught a glimpse of the bodies hanging from the ropes; passed a few more trees and then saw them fully, in the clear. Lucas focused on them, got careless, pushed back a springy branch and got snapped in the face by a twig. His cheek stinging, he said, "Careful," to Del, and went back to staring at the bodies.

They looked like paintings, he thought, or maybe an old fading color photo from the 1930s, two gray, stretched-out bodies dangling from a tree, half facing each other, ropes cutting into their necks, with four white men not looking at them—desperately not looking at them.

As they came up, Del asked, quietly, "You ever noticed how hanged people sort of all look alike—like they lose their race or something? They all look like they're made out of clay."

Lucas nodded. He *had* noticed that. "Except redheads," he added. "They always look like they came from a different planet."

Del said, "You're right. Except for redheads. They just get paler."

The four orange-hatted men were spaced around the bodies at the cardinal points, as though they might be rushed from any direction. A short stepladder was set up beside the bodies, and the snow had been thoroughly trampled down for fifty feet around. Two of the men were doing the cold-weather tap dance, a slow shuffle that said they were freezing. When Lucas and Del came up, one of the orange-hats turned and asked, "Who're you?"

"BCA," Lucas said. "Who're you?"

"Dave Payton." The man turned back to the bodies and shivered. "D-Deputy sheriff."

"What're you doing?" Del asked.

"K-Keeping everybody out of a circle around the bodies. You guys are supposed to have a crime crew coming. You don't look like them."

"They'll be a bit," Lucas said. His voice had turned friendly. "You get here early?"

"I was the first car in, after the state patrol. Ass is freezin' solid."

"Where's the line they were brought in on . . . tracks or anything?"

Payton jerked his arm toward the road. "Back that way, I guess. Pretty trampled down, now."

Lucas looked, and could see the kind of snaky break in the brush that often meant a game trail. If the bodies had been brought in along it, then the hangman had known exactly where he was going.

Del had taken a couple steps closer to the dangling bodies. "Woman's got blood on her face," he said.

"G-Guy's pretty messed up, too," Payton said. "Looks like somebody beat the heck out of him before he did . . . this."

"I don't think it's her blood," Del said. "Some of it's off to the side, and on her upper lip and nose."

"We'll get the lab to check," Lucas said. "That'd be a break, if it's the killer's."

Payton said, "D-D-D-DNA. We did a DNA in a rape last year."

"Catch the guy?"

"N-N-No," Payton said.

Lucas said, "Look, why don't you go sit in a car for a while and get warmed up, for Christ's sakes? You're shaking like a leaf."

" 'Cause Anderson'd have a cow," Payton said.

"We're taking over the crime scene," Lucas said. "The BCA is. I'm *ordering* you to leave, okay?" He looked at the other guys, who were watching him, some hope in their eyes. "All of you. Get some place warm. Get some coffee."

Payton bobbed his head, said, "Aye aye, cap'n." The four men hurried in a wide circle around the hanging bodies, another of them muttered, "Thanks," and then they all scuttled off through the naked trees toward the cars.

"ANDERSON COULD BE a problem," Del said, conversationally, when the deputies were out of earshot. He and Lucas were still looking at the dead people. The ghastly fact was that Cash and Warr hung only a few inches off the ground, and neither one had been tall—Lucas and Del were looking almost straight into their dead, half-open eyes, at their purplish faces, and the two bodies swayed together as though dancing on the same floor where the two cops were standing. "He doesn't know what he's doing," Del continued. "Half the goddamn crime scene is stuck to the bottoms of the deputies' boots. Then he left them out here to freeze."

"Yeah." Lucas decided that they were gawking at the bodies. "We're gawking," he said.

"I know," Del said, looking at Warr. "How many dead people we seen in our lives? You think a thousand?"

"Maybe not a thousand," Lucas said, still looking.

"I don't dream about any of them, except maybe one burned guy I saw, all black and crispy but still alive . . . died while we were waiting for the ambulance. And a little kid who drowned in a creek, she was my first one right after I went on patrol."

"I remember my first kid."

"Everybody does," Del said. He did the cold-weather tap dance, and blew some steam. "I'm gonna remember this one for a while."

"THEY'RE ON DISPLAY," Lucas said after a while. "You think it could be a biker thing? Bikers do this kind of shit, sometimes."

"I've never seen it," Del said doubtfully. A gust of wind came through, and both of the bodies slowly rotated toward them.

"Neither have I, but I've read about it," Lucas said.

"Read about it, or seen it in the movies?"

"Maybe the movies," Lucas admitted. "The thing is, the guy who did this *wanted* everybody to freak out. This isn't just a murder. This is something else. The guy was making a point."

"No clothes around," Del said. "Must've pulled the clothes off somewhere else, or took them with him."

"Somewhere else. This was all planned," Lucas said. "The killer wasn't struggling around in the dark, pulling their clothes off. He didn't have to look for this place, off the top of his head. He knew what he was going to do. He worked it all out ahead of time."

THEY WERE TALKING about the line the killer took through the trees, and the angle down to the kid's house and the distance from the town, and more about the *display* of the bodies, when they heard people coming in. Anderson was pushing through the brush with Braun and Schnurr, followed by three more men in bulky uniform parkas and insulated pants. "Must be the guys from Bemidji," Del said.

They were. Dickerson, a tall man in a tan parka, with straw-colored hair and gold-rimmed glasses, introduced himself and the other two agents, Barin and Woods. All of them gawked at the bodies as they talked. "The crime scene and special operations guys are about five minutes behind us," Dickerson said. "The ME's out on the road right now. The special ops guys'll get it on film and we'll process the scene, then we'll get those folks out of the trees."

"We need a careful sweep," Lucas said. "I mean like, crazy careful."

"Pretty screwed up already," Dickerson said. Then he second-thought himself, with the sheriff right there, and diplomatically added, "We're getting set up now. We're bringing in a propane heater, and after we get finished crawling the place, we'll melt out the snow and make sure nothing was trampled down into it."

"Excellent."

"You and I ought to go off somewhere, and decide who's going to do what." Again, a bureaucratic wariness.

"Del and I don't have anything to do with crime scene stuff," Lucas said. "That's all yours—but make sure the ME takes a close look at the woman's mouth. That blood on her face looks likes it might not be hers. We'll want a DNA on it and we'll want her mouth cleaned out."

"Sure."

"Otherwise, we can chat if you want, but basically, Del and I just go around and talk to people." Lucas said. "Your guys should do the same thing—interview whoever you want. Duplicate us. No problem."

"So we're not . . . one investigation." Dickerson looked skeptical.

"Nope." Lucas shook his head. "Del and I have done this a lot, in Minneapolis. We find it's handy, with the hard ones, to have two investigations running side by side, if you can do it without a lot of infighting. You get different ideas going."

Dickerson shrugged. "It's all right with me. These two guys"—he turned a thumb to Barin and Woods—"will be doing all the work. I'm going to get us set up, hang around today and maybe tomorrow, and then I'll be on call down in Bemidji. I understand the governor's taken an interest."

Lucas said, "He has. He's worried about the image. Two people hanged, naked, the man's black."

"Got a pretty good dick on him, too," said Schnurr, the sheriff's deputy.

Lucas turned on him, his teeth showing. "Shut the fuck up. Honest to Christ, if I hear anybody talking like that, I'll personally slap the shit out of him."

"Didn't mean nothin'," Schnurr said. He shuffled his feet like a child who'd been bad in class; but he had mean eyes.

"If a reporter heard that, or even heard you'd said it, sheriff's deputies making cracks like that, we'd have twice as much trouble as we do now. So keep your fuckin' mouth shut," Lucas finished. To Anderson: "I don't know how much you like your job, but your whole goddamn county is about to get smeared in the national media. Do you understand that?"

"I . . . don't know," Anderson said, uncertainly.

"Believe me, it's gonna happen. And one asshole making comments like this guy, it could mean that you don't only lose your job, but you gotta move to Arizona and change your name."

Anderson glanced nervously at Schnurr and said, "We'll keep a lid on it."

Dickerson was peering up at the bodies, embarrassed, Lucas thought, to be from the same agency as Lucas. "You better," Lucas snarled. He looked again at Schnurr, nailing him in place, then asked Anderson, "The little girl who found the bodies—is she in town?"

"Giving a statement," Anderson said.

"We'd appreciate it if you'd have somebody call in, tell them to keep her there until Del and I have a chance to talk to her."

Anderson nodded.

Lucas said to Dickerson, "Good luck. You guys got it."

"We got it," Dickerson said.

"NEED TO GET TO that little girl," Lucas said, as they walked back out to the line of cars. "If the sheriff's crew is as bad as it looks, we need to talk to her before somebody fucks her up."

"Gotta get some wheels," Del said.

"Get them at a car dealer, probably, if we get there fast," Lucas said. "Tomorrow morning, you won't be able to rent a car anywhere north of Fargo."

"Zahn oughta know."

———

ZAHN DID KNOW. "Holme's Motors in Armstrong," he said. "Fix you right up. How many do you want?"

"Two?"

As they bounced slowly down the dirt road, past the girl's house to the highway, Zahn fumbled out a cell phone, pushed a speed-dial button, and said, "This is Ray Zahn. Let me talk to Carl." And a moment later, "Hey. I gotta couple of cops in town from St. Paul. They need two cars, good shape. Uh-huh." He turned to Lucas: "What kind of credit card?"

"American Express or Visa, whatever they take," Lucas said.

"American Express or Visa . . . yeah. Yeah. Ten minutes. Yeah, see you then." He hung up. "All fixed," he said. "One of you gets a loaded three-year-old Oldsmobile, the other one gets a six-year-old five-liter Mustang."

"I'll take the one with the best heater," Del said.

"We need to get over to the sheriff's department, quick as we can," Lucas said. "Is that the courthouse?"

"Law Enforcement Center," Zahn said. "Three years old, state-of-the-art, behind the courthouse and right across the street from Holme's car lot. The LEC is the reason Dick Anderson's the sheriff."

"He built it?" Lucas asked.

"No. The last sheriff did. Bobby Carter," Zahn said. He grinned at Lucas and pumped his eyebrows. "Don't tell anybody I said so—Bobby's a friend of mine—but he got a little too close to the construction process. Nobody went to jail, but people around here figure that a good chunk of money stuck to his fingers. He's back to farming."

"What was Anderson? Not a deputy?"

"He was a lawyer, private practice. Real estate, mostly. He worked with the county attorney, sometimes. When Bobby got into trouble and figured he better get out, he put up one of his good old boys to run. That pissed people off. Anderson jumped in at the last minute and got elected."

"A political wizard, huh?" Del said.

Zahn smiled into his steering wheel as they bumped over the last set of ruts onto the highway, and turned south toward Broderick and Armstrong. "Never heard anybody use the word *wizard* around him," he said. "He's pretty much wholly owned by Barry Wilson, who's the head of the county commission. That's okay, most of the time. Doesn't work too well when there's an actual crime, or something."

THE TOWN OF BRODERICK was a few hundred yards down the highway, and Zahn took them through it at a crawl.

The town was built along two streets that intersected the highway at right angles. A big four-square farmhouse sat on the north edge of town, on the west side of the highway. A sheriff's car sat in the driveway, in front of the garage, and Zahn said, "That's the victims' place."

"Okay." It looked like a rural murder scene on a CNN report, a lonely white farmhouse surrounded by snow, with a cop car in the yard.

Farther south, still on the west side of the highway, they passed Wolf's Cafe, which looked like a shingle-sided rambler; the Night Owl Club; and a building with a wooden cross fixed above the door and a bare spot where a sign had been pulled down. "That used to be the Holy Spirit Pentecostal Church—holy rollers," Zahn said. "They eventually rolled out of town. Now a bunch of women work there. Like religious women, do-gooders, I guess. Some Catholics and some Lutheran women from Lutheran Social Services, and I heard one of them's a Quaker. One of the Catholics is a looker. The other ones are the blue-tights kind."

Scattered among the buildings were a half-dozen small houses, a couple of trailer homes, a corrugated-steel corn silo with a cone-shaped roof, and a red barn.

The east side of the highway was sparser: a Handy Mart gas station and convenience store; Calb's Body Shop & Tow, in a long yellow metal-sided pole barn; Gene's 18, an over-the-road truck rehab place; and two more houses.

"That's it?"

"That's it, that's the town," Zahn said, as they rolled out into the countryside.

Del asked, "What's all the truck places, the body shops? Isn't that pretty heavy industry for a place like this?"

"Naw . . . I don't know. Would you drive your car nine miles to get it fixed? We're nine miles from Armstrong."

"I guess I would," Del admitted. "Actually, I know I would, 'cause I have."

"And it was an inheritance deal. Gene inherited the body shop from his old man, and then he added the truck rehab business. Truck rehab, you can do anywhere. He does pretty good. He's why the town started coming back. Most everybody who lives here works for him. Not a bad guy."

"A long way out," Del said.

"Some people like it lonely," Zahn said. "Some people don't."

Then they were out of town, out in the countryside. A crow or a raven was flying south, parallel to the highway, a fluttering black speck against the overcast sky, the only thing besides themselves that was moving. Del said, "Jesus Christ, it's flat."

They rode in silence for a couple of minutes, then Zahn started a low, unconscious whistling. Lucas recognized the tune, probably from an elevator somewhere. "What's that song you're whistling?"

"Didn't realize I was whistling," Zahn said. He thought a minute. "It's that thing from *Phantom of the Opera.*"

"That's right." After a second, "You don't seem to be too upset, you know, by the bodies."

"Well, you're with the Patrol, you learn not to be a pussy, like a homicide cop or something," Zahn said.

"All right, pussy," Del drawled from the back seat.

Zahn glanced over the seat and said, "Every time I go out to an accident and there are a couple of high school kids bleeding to death right in front of my face, and screaming for their dad or their mom, I know them. They're kids from down the street. You do that for a few years and a couple strangers up in a tree won't bother you much. Unlike some homicide pussies."

4

KATINA LEWIS GOT OUT of bed at one minute to ten o'clock in the morning, the goose bumps like oranges in the chilly morning air. She padded barefoot across the cold wooden floor, into the bathroom. She was a round woman who no longer fought the roundness, thirty-six years old, five years divorced. With her dark brown hair, she was a rarity in this corner of the country, where it seemed everybody was blond or towheaded. She had good English skin from her father, a short nose and a bow lip from her German mother, and she had her hopes and her religion.

She desperately hoped for children, though she felt the time running out. She prayed to the Lord to help her, and had faith. More than faith: she had fine discriminating morals—she could run drugs for God, knowing that she was on a mission of love, knowing that God *was* love.

Katina Lewis wasn't silly about love, didn't walk around with a moony glow on her face, and she could get as cranky as the next woman.

She simply thought of love as something real and tangible and everyday, like crackers or soap, that she simply hadn't been able to acquire. But if you looked for love long enough, she believed, if you kept the idea in your heart, if you had faith, you would surely find it. God *would not* keep it from you.

Now she'd found it in this unlikely place—this bleak, gray, flat prairie. As she headed for the bathroom, she glanced back at the bed and the top of Loren Singleton's towhead.

She loved him, she thought.

He'd make a good father, if he let himself go. If he loosened up. But she wouldn't want him to loosen up too much. She loved that cowboy thing, that sandpaper jaw in the morning, those bitten-off words, the stoicism that rode on his face. She loved the look of him, lounging with a shoulder against a wall, feet crossed, showing his boots, a Marlboro hanging from the corner of his mouth.

She'd begun to talk to him about it. She'd talk more, maybe today, or someday soon. Time passed—that was one thing she'd learned in her twenties, and in her first marriage. Time passed and was gone and you couldn't get it back.

LEWIS HAD SET HER alarm clock for ten. In her urgency to make it to the bathroom, she'd forgotten about it. At ten o'clock exactly, the hourly livestock report trickled out of the two-inch speaker, five feet from Loren Singleton's ear.

Quietly.

As though a strange man had stolen into his house, to whisper in his ear, "*. . . slaughter steers, choice two to three, 1,125 to 1,637 pounds, sixty-one dollars to sixty-two seventy-five. Select and choice two to three, 1,213 to 1,340 pounds, sixty-one to sixty-one ten . . .*"

The voice took a minute to penetrate, and then Singleton stirred, squeezed his pillow around and cocked an eye at the clock, and the man said, "That's the South St. Paul stockyard report. Ed Wein will have up-dates through the day, right here on your feeder-cattle central. Now, from our news bureau, we have a report here from Broderick, Min-nesota, where two people have been found hanged in a grove of trees just north of Broderick. The first reports said that two people, a black man and a white woman, were found hanging . . ."

The words were so flat and so unbelievable that they took a few sec-onds to connect. When they did, Singleton's head popped up: "What?"

Lewis called from the bathroom, "Did you say something?"

"Shut up," he shouted back.

The man on the radio said, ". . . Anderson confirmed that two peo-ple were dead, but deferred further comment until the medical exam-iner could reach the scene. We will follow this story during the day, so keep your dial set here to North Dakota's All-News Central . . ."

The voice was both tinny and tiny. Singleton rolled across the bed, grabbed the clock, tried to find the volume control, heard the weather-man come up and say, "You never know what life's gonna bring, Dick . . ." and then his voice was lost in the noise of the flushing toilet.

LEWIS CAME OUT of the bathroom, pulling her cotton night-gown down over her hips, her heavy legs jiggling at him: she was an-noyed. She didn't like being shouted at, being told to *shut up*.

She opened her mouth to say so, when Singleton, still staring at the radio, said, "Did you hear that?"

"I heard you *shouting* at me," she said, letting a little of the annoy-ance seep into her voice.

"Somebody killed Deon and Jane," Singleton blurted.

The irritability vanished. *"What?"*

"Gotta call . . ." he said. Over his shoulder he added, "They were found *hanged in a tree.*"

He trotted naked out of the bedroom and down the hall. Nothing bounced or bobbled when he moved: he was solid. Lewis looked at the radio, which was now firmly into the weather. More gloom. That was the essence of it. Cold and gray and maybe, if we were unlucky, a lot of snow, followed by more cold and gray.

Jane and Deon? She called after him, "What did the radio say? What did they mean, *hanged?*"

Then she heard him talking on the phone, and turned around, like a dog in its bed, looking for her jeans, couldn't find them, and heard the phone clatter back on the hook. A moment later, Singleton came back. "Deon and Jane were found hanging in a tree across the Nine Mile Ditch. That Letty kid found them. This morning, about two minutes after I went off duty. They were naked and dead. Somebody beat the shit out of them before they were hanged."

"No." She was astonished, but not distraught.

"Yup. People are coming in from all over. State police are flying in from St. Paul. They might already be here. Ray Zahn's going up to meet them, take them around." He had a few more details, but not much.

"I've got to go," Lewis said. She turned her back, stepped toward the bathroom and he said, "You smell like vanilla," and she said, absently, "That perfume . . . I wonder if your mom knows anything?"

"Don't know."

Katina hadn't known Cash or Warr very well, and hadn't liked either one, but their deaths could create problems. "I've got to get down to the church. We had some sisters getting ready to make a run. I better call Ruth right now."

She disappeared, half-dressed, down the hallway, and Singleton stood there, puzzling over it, staring at the very expensive cowboy boots that sat at the end of his bed. Deon and Jane?

Lewis came thundering back. "She already heard, five minutes ago. I gotta get down there. What're you doing, cowboy?"

"I don't know. Still gotta get some sleep. Then maybe see what's going on."

———

SINGLETON SAT DOWN on the edge of the bed and ran his hands through his hair, worried. What the hell had happened? Hanged? He couldn't get past that part. Maybe he should go look, but too much curiosity . . . who exactly knew that he'd spent time with Jane and Deon?

Katina knew some of it, of course. Calb knew some of it, knew that he'd been at their house a few times. Maybe some of the other body shop people—the shop was just down the highway, and they may have seen him turning in Deon's driveway.

But he'd taken a little care *not* to be seen. When he was there, he'd always parked on the slab beside the garage, where you really couldn't see the car. That hadn't been a matter of foreboding, but just common sense. Now the common-sense care might pay off.

WHAT'RE YOU DOING, COWBOY? Lewis had asked.

Loren Singleton was a cowboy, though without a horse or a ranch. He wanted to like horses, but horses always tried to bite him, sooner or later, and he'd quit trying to ride. Besides, Cadillacs were even better—old, over-the-top, seventies and eighties Cadillacs, which, for a cowboy, was close enough.

In his own mind, Singleton was a cowboy and an artist with automotive lacquer, and only in a secondary, unimportant way, a sheriff's deputy and a lookout for a band of car thieves. He knew, though, that something was missing in his life. He felt that all the details were there, but not the color. He felt like a black-and-white photograph—only when he met Katina did a little color begin to bleed into his life.

In other people's minds, Loren Singleton was, when they thought of him at all, a loner, a familiar outsider, a man always standing on the edges. A few women had tried to talk with him—he wasn't bad looking, and the cowboy clothes seemed to give him some kind of personality—

but they'd found him unresponsive, emotionally stunted. As a deputy, he had a reputation for casual brutality that seemed to go with his essential coldness. Even his cars, his Caddys, tended to cold, brilliant colors that could set your teeth on edge.

Everybody nodded to him on the street; almost nobody spoke to him.

THEN KATINA LEWIS had arrived to work with the nuns. Singleton wasn't sure that he'd ever loved anyone before he met Lewis. He thought about it sometimes. He probably loved Lewis, he thought—there was no other explanation for the way he felt when he was around her—but did he love his mother? Had he ever? She was the only other possibility for love in his life, and everyone was supposed to love his mother. People got "Mom" tattooed on their arms. People ate at places called "Mom's," because Mom would never hurt you, would always have that extra piece of pie for her little boy.

But Singleton's mom had whacked the shit out of him for years; had beat him up so badly when he was six months old that an uncle had taken him to the hospital, told the doctor that he'd crawled out of his playpen and had fallen down the stairs.

His father, Edgar Singleton, had died in a live-steam accident at the chipboard plant when Loren was two years old. Singleton had heard his mother telling stories, with some relish, about "poached Eg," how his father had been poached from the neck down when a steam line broke in a processing tank, and how he lay in the hospital, burned over 95 percent of his body, waiting to die, without pain, but also without a mind: he'd rambled on for seven days about haying on the old farm, then he'd died.

When Eg was gone, Mom began dressing Singleton in girl's clothes. She'd wanted a girl; girls were more manageable. She did her damnedest to make Singleton into one—would have done better if the nosy old school principal hadn't gotten a restraining order against her, requiring her to dress her kindergartener in gender-appropriate clothing.

Singleton vaguely remembered all of that. After the court order, she still made him put on a dress, occasionally, and serve tea at one of her ladies' poker parties. That ended when he was eleven, big for his age. She'd ordered him into a dress, and he'd refused. She'd begun to hit him with a broomstick that she'd used to beat him in the past, and he'd fled into the winter darkness.

When he came back, she was in the bathtub. He'd gone into the bathroom, and she'd screamed at him and tried to cover her nakedness, but he didn't care about that. He, a big, tough, abused eleven-year-old, had grabbed her hair and shoved her head under water. She'd thrashed and fought and clawed at him, but he'd held her under until she quit struggling.

Then he held her under for another fifteen seconds. When he finally let her up, she lay back against the end of the tub, apparently without breath. Then, she breathed in, a small breath, and then another one. In five minutes, still weak, she tried to climb out of the tub. Singleton heard her, came back in, shoved her head under water again, until she passed out a second time.

The second time she revived, she was quiet about it: crept over the edge of the tub and crawled to the bathroom door and managed to get it locked. She lay there, naked, until the next morning, when she heard him whistling out the door on his way to school.

When he came home that night, he found she'd locked him out. He kicked the back door until the lock broke, found her crouched inside with a baseball bat. He pointed a finger at her, the eleven-year-old did, and said, "Don't fuck with me anymore."

They spent their next seven years together, with the bedroom doors locked at night.

AFTER HE GRADUATED from high school, Singleton had en-
listed in the Air Force, had been trained for the Air Police, and had been
sent to Eielson Air Force Base outside of Fairbanks, Alaska. All he could
remember of the place were the clouds and the cold: better than two
hundred days of cloudy skies every year, bone-chilling for seven months,
cold for another three, mosquitoes for the final two.

Just like home.

Out of the Air Force, he worked in East Grand Forks for a while,
moving lumber around a home improvement warehouse, then heard
about a deputy sheriff's job in Custer County. His AP background got
him in. But he didn't try very hard, at anything, and after two years was
assigned to permanent Sunday-through-Thursday night shift. If he'd
take it, he could stay, the sheriff said. Otherwise, it was the highway. He
took it.

There was almost nothing to do at night in Custer. In twelve years,
there'd been three house fires that started on his shift, and maybe once
a month he'd get a medical emergency, which only required that he
show up. He'd stop a few speeders on country roads, jail a few drunks,
break up the occasional barroom fight with his casual brutality.

Given his work hours, he didn't have a social life. He followed no
sports teams, didn't hunt or fish or ride ATVs or snowmobiles, didn't
garden or read or pay attention to music or go to movies. Didn't even
watch much TV.

His only real interest were the old Cadillacs. He'd get one in his
garage, do the mechanical work that would bring it back to life, and then
lovingly and carefully strip it down to bare metal. After months of prepa-
ration, he'd move it to Gene Calb's auto-body shop, where he rented the
equipment to do the paint. He changed cars every year or so, driving one
while he rehabbed a second one. His current ride was an '82 Eldorado

Biarritz with a custom Rolls Royce grille. The finish was a hand-polished flame-orange flake over a deep mocha base.

That was it. Other than the Caddys, it was all about taking numbers, passing the years.

Then, four years earlier, Gene Calb had offered to expand their relationship—an expansion that would give Singleton free working space for his cars and a thousand dollars a week, with an up-front payment of ten thousand dollars.

Ten thousand down, and a thousand dollars, cash money, no taxes, every Friday. All he had to do was keep an eye out . . .

The money had changed everything. For one thing, his mother had begun to take an interest in him. Then, one night up at the casino, he'd introduced her to Deon Cash and Jane Warr.

And then Katina had shown up.

SINGLETON HEARD KATINA coming out of the shower, heard her clumping around, getting into her pants and shoes. She came out of the bathroom like a rocket, kissed him quick, once on the mouth, once on the penis, gave him a quick suck and then said, "Wally's gonna have to wait."

"C'mon, thirty seconds," he said.

"Fifteen seconds." She sucked on Wally for fifteen seconds, and then hurried away, laughing, and was gone.

SINGLETON AND KATINA LEWIS had fallen in bed a couple of months after they met, which was at Calb's. Katina came in with her sister, Ruth, who was showing her around before Katina made her first run across the border. Ruth didn't care for Singleton, but Katina was immediately attracted. Their daddy liked to work on old cars, she told

Singleton later. Ruth didn't care about that—she was closer to her mother, and to Jesus.

Katina saw a relationship with Singleton. She'd already mentioned love, that she might be falling into it, with him. She'd told him over dinner at the Bird, and then peered over the little red votive candle on the table.

Singleton had felt something blossoming within him, as he looked across the table at the woman. After all this time, a woman really cared for him? Somebody who would hang out with him, and cook and make babies? How did that happen?

He'd reached across the table, and had taken her hand; tears rolled down his face, and she said something like, "It's okay."

Later, feeling a little unmanly about the whole thing, about the tears, he'd started to apologize for himself and she'd laughed and squeezed him and said, "Loren, you did just perfect. Just *perfect*."

Somehow, he thought, he had.

SINGLETON HAD WORKED until seven that morning and had come home to find Katina in his bed. He'd crawled in with her, though he hadn't been too tired. Now, at ten o'clock, he was sleepy; he closed his eyes and tried to go back to sleep.

Deon and Jane, he thought. *Hanged.*

Fear tickled through his chest. He tried to shut it out, flopped this way and that, wrestling with his pillow. Maybe somebody was coming for him, he thought.

A hangman.

Katina didn't know anything about that.

RUTH AND KATINA LEWIS stepped inside the body shop's overheated office, took off their mittens, and Ruth pulled the door shut behind her. Gene Calb was working behind his desk. He was a balding, heavyset man in his mid-forties, with a weathered face and thick, scarred mechanic's hands. A pair of reading glasses perched on his thick nose. He looked over the glasses and said, "Guys. You musta heard."

"A little while ago, in town," Ruth said. "Jane and Deon, but people said they were hanged?" Ruth stuffed her mittens in her coat pocket, and unzipped the parka. Ruth Lewis *felt* like her sister, but didn't look like her. She was a slender woman, where Katina was round, and she had flinty green eyes behind steel-colored, wire-rimmed glasses, while Katina's eyes were softer, paler. Ruth's hair was close-cropped, an ascetic's 'do; Katina wore her hair full. Ruth's cheeks were rosy from the cold, like her sister's, but unlike Katina, she wore no lipstick or jewelry—a pretty woman determined to do nothing with her looks.

Ruth was the older sister and the boss, Katina the subordinate.

Calb said, "Hung in a grove off the ditch road. That Letty kid found them this morning." He looked at the clock. It was just 11:45. It seemed like the morning had stretched on forever, since he'd heard the news at ten.

"So what are we doing?" Katina asked. She always reminded Calb of a clucking hen, a busy, mildly overweight woman, but with a sensuous underlip. She was supposedly a member of some Catholic religious group, but apparently one that didn't have anything against sex: Katina had been sleeping with Loren Singleton, and Singleton was looking as happy as he ever did, if a little peaked. "Do we do *anything?*"

"I'm closing down," Calb said. "For the time being. Until we find out what's going on."

"That's not acceptable," Ruth said.

"I . . ." A car went by on the highway, and Ruth and Katina and Calb all turned their heads that way—you always looked at a car on the highway in Broderick. A Highway Patrol car with extra passengers.

"Ray Zahn," Ruth said.

"Loren told me that a couple of big shots flew in from St. Paul, and Zahn's driving them around," Katina said.

Calb shook his head. "I'll tell you what, guys; they're gonna hook Deon up with me, and I don't know what I'm going to tell them."

"Tell them as much of the truth as you can," Ruth suggested. "That you hired Deon to drive for you, on the recommendation of an old army buddy in Kansas City, that you rehab trucks from all over the Midwest, and that he picks them up."

"That's not exactly . . ."

"He does that," Ruth interrupted. "You could give references."

"Yeah. He's done that," Calb said. "What about you guys?"

"We can't stop," Ruth said. Her chin was set, tough, square. "We need to keep working."

"I'm sorry, but we *gotta* stop, until we find out what's going on," Calb objected. "This may be coming out of Kansas City. If that's what it is, maybe we can give some stuff to the cops, and they can settle it, but before then . . ."

"Ray, we can't," Ruth said urgently. "We haven't made enough runs lately. The Ontario net just came back up, since Jeanette died."

"I can't help that," Calb said. "I talked to Sister Mary Ann yesterday, when she came in—she seemed pretty happy."

"She did fine, but the mix wasn't that good. We can't stop," Ruth said.

"Hey—I'm shipping a load of junkers out right now. George is on his way in with his truck and we're getting them the fuck outa . . . excuse the language. I'm sorry." He was genuinely worried that they might be offended. Ruth had once been a nun.

"I don't care about the language," Ruth said. She switched a smile on, and then off. "All I care about is that we keep working—and we *won't* stop. If we have to pile up the junkers on your doorstep, that's what we'll do."

"Ah, Jesus Christ on a crutch," Calb said, forgetting himself again.

———

THE DEAL WAS complicated, but profitable for everyone.

A man named Shawn Davis from Kansas City, Missouri, working with old drug-dealing friends in St. Louis, Des Moines, and Omaha, would spot and steal late-model Toyota Land Cruisers, 4Runners, and Tacoma pickups. No Nissans, no Fords, no Chevys. Nothing but Toyotas. That kept parts and paint supply simple.

The stolen vehicles would be driven, individually, from Davis's place in Kansas City to Calb's body shop, in Broderick. Calb had been in the Army with Davis, and they'd done some chickenshit black market stuff in Turkey, selling U.S. government meat. They trusted each other, to a point. The stolen cars were driven north by Deon Cash, who was Davis's cousin, or Joe Kelly, a friend of Cash's.

As Cash or Kelly was driving north, one of a group of religious women—as a group they were called the "nuns" by the Custer County people, and some of them were—would pick up a late-model, but high-mileage, last-legs Toyota in Canada, usually from a dealer auction. The nun would nurse the wreck across the border into Minnesota, and deliver it to the body shop.

In the shop, the stolen car would be repainted to match the beater. Some of the parts and trim—the dashboard graphics indicating kilometers per hour, instead of miles—the ID numbers, and papers of the high-mileage Toyota would be transferred to the low-mileage machine.

A nun would then drive the truck back across the border, where it would be resold. The remnants of the beater would be shipped to a junkyard, where it would be crushed into a cube and sent to a smelter.

The money was great: a battered, busted-up two- or three-year-old Toyota Land Cruiser, often owned by the kind of long-distance salesman who'd put fifty thousand rough miles a year on his car, would be purchased at a used-car auction for a few thousand dollars Canadian. Three weeks later, it would turn up on a working ranch in Saskatchewan or Alberta, in near-new condition, with all the right papers. The buyer would pay the equivalent of $50,000 American for a $20,000 machine.

After all the work was done, and the employees paid, and the investment in the vanishing truck was accounted for, Calb and Shawn Davis would split $5,000 on each Toyota sale, give or take. Two trucks a week added up to a quarter-million tax-free dollars a year, each. Hiding the cash was almost as much trouble as making it, but they found ways.

THERE WERE A few flies in the ointment.

The nuns made everybody nervous. They weren't paid anything, which meant that Davis and Calb didn't have a good hold on them. The women were using the trucks and the body shop's expertise to smuggle drugs south across the border. Although they had no economic hold on the women, Calb believed that they were safe. The women were, he thought, the next thing to fanatics. Nice fanatics, like Ruth Lewis, but they would go to prison before they talked about the deal.

Another fly was Deon Cash, and his old lady, Jane Warr. Cash wasn't quite right. Shawn Davis had given him a job reluctantly, paid him $432 per delivery, because he was a cousin, and because he had shown in jail that he could keep his mouth shut. But Cash was a bad man; and worse, he was stupid.

A third fly, and lately a big juicy one, was Cash's friend, Joe Kelly. Kelly stayed with Cash and Warr between runs. Then, a month earlier, he'd disappeared. Nobody knew where. Everybody wanted to know. Calb had begun to suspect that Kelly had made a move on Jane Warr, and that Cash had buried him out in the woods.

Now this.

―――――

CALB WASN'T LISTENING to Ruth Lewis's appeal. He was staring past her, out into the shop, thinking about the whole mess, and calculating. He had to have something going out there when the cops arrived. Maybe he could haul one of his own trucks in, tear it down, start repainting it. The place couldn't be empty, with a bunch of guys sitting around staring at the walls . . .

"Gene! Gene!"

Calb looked back at Ruth: "Sorry—I was thinking about . . . getting something going out in the shop. Before the cops get here. It looks weird, being empty."

"Give us the cash to buy a truck," Ruth said. "One truck."

"Listen. Guys. We've got to figure out what's going on here. You have to figure it out, too—I mean, you're doing the driving. I thought maybe Joe Kelly just took off, but there was no sign he was going and Deon said all his clothes are still hanging in his closet . . ."

"You think Joe's dead, too?" Katina asked.

"Well, where is he?" Calb asked. "Nobody in Kansas City has heard from him."

"There's an auction Saturday morning in Edmundston that's got the perfect truck," Ruth said. "Three years old, two hundred and fifty thousand kilometers, runs good enough to get across."

"I gotta talk to my Kansas City guy . . ."

"Gene, we've got to do this," Ruth said urgently. "We've got a load waiting. We're desperate."

"Let me talk to my guy." He looked around the office. "You know, if this doesn't get settled quick, we might have to start worrying about where we talk. What we say."

"You could always come over to the church to talk," Katina said. "I don't think they'd have the guts to bug the church."

"Maybe . . ." Calb looked out the window. "I wonder what happened? I heard they were just hanging there, like icicles, all . . . messed up."

"Jane Warr. She was not a nice woman. Deon was worse," Katina said. She turned to Ruth. "The Witch used to hang around with Jane. I hope she's not involved with this somehow."

"Ask Loren," Ruth suggested.

"I will. But Jane and Deon . . ."

"May God have mercy on their souls," said Ruth, and she crossed herself.

5

ARMSTRONG, THE COUNTY SEAT, came over the horizon as a hundred-foot-tall yellow concrete chimney with a plume of steam hanging over the prairie, then as a couple of radio towers with red blinking lights, then as a row of corrugated steel-sided grain elevators along a double set of railroad tracks. They followed the tracks past the elevators, past a few broken-down shacks on what had once been the bad side of town, into a quiet neighborhood of aging Cape Cod houses, all painted either white or a dirty pastel pink or blue, over a bridge labeled CROSS RIVER, and into the business district.

"What's that smell?" Del asked, as they came into town.

Zahn looked at him. "What smell?"

"Paper plant, or chipboard plant," Lucas said.

"Chipboard," Zahn said. "I don't smell it anymore."

"Jesus. It smells like somebody's roasting a wet chicken, with the feathers on," Del said.

"Ain't that bad," said Zahn.

"Yes, it is," Del said.

The downtown was a flat grid, mostly brick, yellow and red, with meterless curbs along blacktopped streets, three or four stoplights. Lucas could see both a Motel 6 and a Best Western, Conoco and BP stations on opposite corners with competing convenience stores, a Fran's Diner followed by a Fran's Bakery followed by a Fran's Rapid Oil Change, a McDonald's on one corner and a Pizza Hut halfway down the block, a sports bar called the Dugout.

At the heart of the town was a scratchy piece of brown grass, patched with gray snow, with a two-story, fifties-ish red-brick courthouse in the middle of it. A newer red-brick Law Enforcement Center hung on to the back of the courthouse, with a fire station even farther back.

Three cops and a couple of firefighters were outside in the cold, leaning against the walls of their buildings, smoking.

Holme's Motors was across the street from the LEC, in a metal building with a single plate-glass window looking out at a dozen used American cars. Red, white, and blue plastic pennants hung down from a wire stretched above the lot; there was just enough wind to keep them nervously twitching. Zahn pulled into the lot, and through the window they could see a man poking numbers into a desk calculator. "That's Carl," Zahn said.

Carl Holme was broad and bald-headed, with a cheerful smile. "Heard about the Negro getting hung," he said to Zahn, when they pushed through the door. "That's gonna dust things up, huh?"

"I'd raise your prices before the TV people get here," Zahn said.

"Really? You think?"

Five minutes after they walked in, they walked back out into the cold. Lucas took the Olds and Del cranked up the Mustang and they trundled behind Zahn, a three-car caravan, sixty feet across the street to the Law Enforcement Center.

The smoking cops said hello to Zahn, looked with flat curiosity at Lucas and Del. Zahn took them inside, was buzzed through a bullet-proof-glass door to a reception area, where he introduced them to Zelda Holme, the car dealer's wife, a pretty, round-faced woman who was also secretary to the sheriff.

"Sheriff Anderson called and said you wanted to talk to Letty. We've got her back in the lounge," Holme said, smiling and friendly. "Come right along."

"I'm gonna take off," Zahn said to Lucas, lifting a hand. "You've got my number. Call if you need anything."

"See you later," Lucas said. "Thanks." He and Del fell in behind Holme, and as they followed her along a cream-painted concrete-block hallway, Lucas mentioned that they'd just rented cars from her husband.

"I hope you counted your fingers after you shook hands with him," she said cheerfully. "Carl can be a sharp one."

The lounge was the last door on the right, a pale yellow concrete cubicle with Office Max waiting-room chairs, vending machines, and a slender girl in jeans who had her face in an *Outdoor Life* magazine.

"Letty, dear?" Holme said. "You've got visitors."

LETTY WEST TURNED her head and took them in.

She was blond, her hair pulled back tight in a short ponytail. She had warm blue eyes that Lucas thought, for an instant, he recognized from somewhere else, some other time; and an almost oval face, but with a squared jaw and freckles. She wore jeans and a blue sweatshirt and dirt-colored gym shoes that had once been white nylon. A Coke can sat on an end table at her right hand. She might have been a female Huckleberry Finn, except for a cast of sadness about her eyes—a Pietà-like sadness, strange for a girl so young. Lucas had seen it before, usually in a woman who'd lost a child.

A good-looking kid, Lucas thought, except for the weathering. Her face and hands were rough, and if you hadn't been able to see her pre-teen figure, you might have thought she was a twenty-year-old farmer's daughter, with too much time hoeing beans.

"These gentlemen are here to see you from St. Paul," Holme said. She was stooping over like older women did when they approached younger children, her voice too kindly.

"Cops?" Letty asked.

"State policemen from St. Paul," Holme said.

"Cops," Letty said.

Lucas looked at the kid and said, "Hi," and then to Holme, "We can take it from here."

"Okay," she said. Holme looked once at Del, as though he might be carrying a flea, and went back out the door. Lucas had the impression that she might have stopped just outside, so he said to Del, "Did I see a water fountain in the hallway?"

"Let me check," Del said, smiling. He stuck his head out, looked both ways, and then said, "Nope. Nothing there." More quietly, "She's going."

THE LOUNGE HAD two candy machines and two soda machines—one Coke, one Pepsi—and smelled like floor wax and spilled coffee, with a hint of flatulence. Lucas asked the girl, "You want another Coke?"

"This one wasn't mine," she said, indicating the Coke with her elbow.

"Well, you want a first one then?"

"If you're buying," she said.

He had to smile—something about her dead-seriousness made him smile—and he got a Diet Coke for himself, tossed a can of sugared Coke to Del, and she said, "I'll take a Pepsi, if that's okay."

"That's fine." He slipped a dollar into the machine and pushed the Pepsi button.

"Where's your mother?" Del asked, as he popped the top on his Coke.

"Probably down at the Duck Inn," Letty said. "We figured I could handle this on my own."

"Yeah?" Del's eyebrows went up.

"She gets a little out of control sometimes," Letty said.

Lucas asked, "She's still your mother. We could call her."

"Not much point," Letty said. "She's probably pretty drunk by now. She's been at it since ten o'clock."

"She drinks a little, huh?" Del asked. Del had dropped onto a couch next to the door.

Letty took a delicate sip of her Pepsi, and then said, "No, she drinks a *lot*. Almost all the time."

"Where's your father?"

She shrugged. "Who knows? Last anybody heard, he was in Phoenix. That was when I was a little kid."

"Ah," Lucas said. "That's tough . . . Listen, did you talk to some sheriff's deputies this morning? Make a statement?"

"Yeah."

"So what'd you tell them?"

Her face went dark and her blue eyes skittered away from his. "About the bodies."

"Let's start right from the beginning. Last night you were in your house . . ."

THE NIGHT BEFORE, Letty said, she had been in bed on the second floor of the house, just across the drainage ditch from West Ditch Road. Although the windows on the north and west sides of the house had been boarded up, and the rooms closed to cut heating bills, she had her own room on the east side of the house, and still had a window.

She was in bed, asleep, when a vehicle went past the house on West Ditch Road. That never happened in the winter. The road was used by a local farmer as back access to a couple of fields, but was used mostly for ditch maintenance, and the strangeness of a passing vehicle was enough to wake her up.

"When I heard the car, I was afraid it was Mom," she said. "She was out last night and it was windy and there was a little snow and if she missed the driveway . . . sometimes . . . I don't know. If she was drinking and she tried to turn around on that ditch road, she could roll the car into the ditch or something. So I got up and looked out the window and was watching the car and it stopped up the road a way, and I thought it was starting to turn around, and I was really worried, but then I heard my mom coughing downstairs and I went and called her. She came to the bottom of the stairs and I told her somebody just went by on the ditch road and they might be lost. She came up and looked out the window and we watched it, and it stayed there for a while, and then it drove out."

"This was about midnight?"

"Two minutes after. When I woke up I looked at my clock, and it said twelve-zero-two."

"You didn't see the people?" Lucas asked.

"I didn't even see the truck, except for the lights. The wind was blowing and all I could see was snow and the lights."

"How long did you watch the lights?" Del asked.

"Quite a while. I don't know, exactly. I didn't look at the clock before I went to bed."

"You didn't see it again, after it drove out?"

"Nope. Never saw it again."

In the morning, she told them, she'd gotten up to run her trap line. She ran thirty traps up the ditch, and in the surrounding marshes, for muskrat. She'd get up at five in the morning, collect the day's catch of 'rats, reset the traps, dump the 'rats into a garbage bag, and haul them back to the house by seven. Since it didn't get light until seven-thirty or so, she'd do it all by the light of a rechargeable flash.

This morning, after she'd run the traps, she'd climbed the bank onto the ditch road to walk back to her house. She hadn't been all that curious about the car from the night before, until she saw the tracks in the snow, and the lines in the snow where somebody had dragged something back into the trees.

"What'd you think they were?" Lucas asked.

"What I thought of was bodies," Letty said, holding his eyes. "That's the first thing I thought of. It scared me in the dark—but when people throw their garbage away out here, they don't haul it down the ditch road. They just stop on the side of the highway and heave it into the ditch. They don't hide it. So I couldn't think of anything else but . . . bodies."

"So then . . ."

"WELL, I WENT BACK THERE, and I didn't see them at first, because it was still dark." Her eyes were wide now, fixed on Lucas, as she remembered and relived it. "I came to this place where there was a big square of messed-up snow with nothing in it. I just, I don't know, I guess I saw a dark thing, hanging, and I lifted up the light, and there they were. The black guy's eyes were open. Scared me really bad. I ran back out to the road and got my 'rats and ran all the way back to the house and woke up my mom. She didn't believe me at first, but then she did, and we called the cops."

"That was it?"

"Yup." She nodded and took a hit of the Pepsi.

"Did your mom go down to the trees to look?"

"No. She was afraid to. She doesn't like dead things. She doesn't even like to drop off my 'rats for me, and they're inside a bag and everything."

"What do you, uh, do with the 'rats?" Del asked.

"Sell them to Joan Wickery. She's the fur-buyer in these parts," Letty said.

"How much do you get?" Lucas asked. He'd never met a trapper.

"Depends on what it is," Letty said. "She gives me $1.75 for average 'rats, and six dollars for 'coon. Problem with 'coon is, they're smart and they catch on when you're trapping them. I have to drive over to the dump to get them. So I only go over about two days a week, get maybe two or three at the most. I can get twenty 'rats out of the ditch, and the marsh across the road, and be done before school."

"You don't have to skin them out or . . . whatever?" Lucas asked.

"Nope. Joan's boys do all of that. I just bring in the carcasses."

Del was fascinated. "What do they do with all the muskrat bodies?"

"Grind them up. Turn them into feed. I don't get paid for that, though. I only get paid for the fur. Joan says the carcasses pay her to keep the doors open, and the fur's her profit."

Del asked, "Feed for what?"

"Mink. Joan's got a mink farm."

THEY SAT AND LOOKED at her for a minute, then Lucas asked, "Anything else you can tell us?"

"I hope I don't die by getting hung," she said. They all thought about that for a moment, then she added, "They twisted. Hanging there. They twisted." She made a twisting motion with her fingers.

They thought about that some more, Lucas groping for something to say that might comfort her, but he couldn't think of anything. After a moment, he asked, "Listen, why'd you think it was your mom's car going down the road?" Lucas asked. "Anything about it?"

She thought for a second, then nodded. "Yeah. It was a Jeep. I think it was. A Jeep Cherokee's got this big square red taillight . . ." She drew a big square taillight in the air. "And then a big square yellow light under that, that's your turn signal. Then there's a little white light which is the backup light, inside the yellow light. That's what I saw on the road. Those red taillights like my mom's, and then, when he was backing around down there, when I was afraid she'd go in the ditch, it had those white lights inside the big square yellow light—the yellow lights didn't come on, but you could see them because of the white light inside them."

"Jeep Cherokee," Lucas said.

"Yup. I didn't think of it this morning, when I was talking to the other cops."

They talked for a few more minutes, and Lucas finally smiled at her and said, "Okay. I'm out of questions."

"I got one," Del said. "I'm a city guy. How do you trap muskrats?"

She told them quickly, about the difference between feeding platforms and houses. "The houses look like little tepees made out of sticks and cattails and stuff. You see them all over on marshes. Little piles. I went down to the Cities once with my mom and I saw a place by the airport that had more houses and feeders than I ever saw in my life."

"Really." Del was charmed. "By the airport?"

"Yup. Anyway, after freeze-up, you can open the houses and some of the big feeders with a machete or a hay knife and slip a trap right inside; there's a whole bunch of rooms in a big house. So you put the trap inside, and there's a chain off the trap, and you pin that down outside the house. Then you patch the hole in the house, so it's dark in there, and they'll walk right into the trap. Then, there's a hole in the bottom of the house that leads under the ice—that's how they get around after freeze-up—and when the trap snaps, they jump through the hole to try to get away, and they drown. I use mostly Number 1 jump traps."

"So, what do you do, pull on the trap to see if there's a body . . . ?"

She shook her head, groped in her pocket, found a pencil stub, and got a napkin. "The chain comes out of the house like this . . ." She drew a chain with a bigger circular link at the end. "Then you put your pin through this circle, so that the 'rat can't pull it free. But you keep the pin in the middle of the circle, when you set it, so if something hits the trap inside, it'll pull the circle against the pin. That way, you can walk up to a house and see right away if anything has hit the trap."

"Huh."

"You can usually get four or five of them out of a house. You always got to leave some breeders."

"How much do you make during a winter?" Lucas asked.

She grinned at him and shook her head. "That's not polite."

"You're a kid," he said.

"Tell that to the feds when they want their taxes."

"THINK YOU COULD give me a ride home?" Letty asked. She crushed the empty Pepsi can in her hands, and tossed it into a waste basket.

"What about your mom?" Lucas asked.

"She can always get a ride from one of her friends," Letty said. "I don't want to hang around all day."

Lucas nodded. "Okay. But let's go check with Mrs. Holme, see if they had anything else set up."

"I'd rather ride with you," Letty said. "I don't like the deputies. They give me a hard time."

"You get in trouble?"

"Mostly about driving my mom's car. But I got no other way to get around, and it's too far to walk to town."

"How old are you?" Del asked.

"Twelve," she said.

"That's a little young to be driving, don't you think?"

"Might be for some people," she said. Then, "If you give me a ride, I could show you around Broderick. I know every house in the place."

"Sounds like a deal," Lucas said.

HOLME WAS HAPPY ENOUGH to let Lucas take Letty home. Outside, in the parking lot, they decided that Del would hit the local motels, and ask about strangers driving Jeeps. Lucas would take a look at the victims' house in Broderick. Later on, they'd hook up for an afternoon snack, and then go out to the casino and talk with Warr's coworkers.

Letty listened to them talk, then told Del, "There's four motels. You want to know where they're at?"

Del said yes, and Letty started to explain the layout of the town, drawing with a piece of gravel on the blacktop, her hands rough, red, but apparently impervious to the cold. Halfway through the explanation, Lucas cut her off, and they walked over to the courthouse, found the county clerk, and bought maps of both the town and the county. Letty read the maps well enough and, with the clerk, pinpointed the motels. .

Outside again, Del took off in the Mustang, and Lucas and Letty headed back toward Broderick. As they crossed the river, Lucas noticed a dense spread of ice-fishing shacks at a bend to the north. A few were simply flat-topped boxes with doors, while others were more elaborate, with pitched roofs and American flags on door poles. Then the river was behind them and they followed the railroad tracks past the pastel Cape Cods and the dwindling businesses and quickly were back on the prairie.

"You ever been out here before?" Letty asked after a while.

"Not exactly here," Lucas said. "Been over to Oxford."

"You got a gun with you?"

"Yes."

"You ever shoot anybody?"

"Maybe," Lucas said.

"What's that supposed to mean?"

"It means you should mind your own business," Lucas said.

He tried not to be mean about it, but Letty stayed on top of him. "Don't want to talk about it?" Letty asked.

He looked at her. "Why don't we change the subject?"

She shrugged. "Okay, if you don't want to talk about it."

AFTER A WHILE, "You got any kids?"

"Two," Lucas said. "A daughter, and my wife just had a baby boy."

"What's your wife do?"

"She's a doctor."

"I'd like to be a doctor," Letty said, looking out at the countryside. The countryside reminded Lucas of a modern painting he'd once seen at the Walker Art Center as a young cop, out on a sexual assault call. The painting had been done in two colors—a narrow band of black on the bottom, a wider band of gray above it. He still remembered the name: *Whistler in the Dark: Composition in White and Gray.* If the artist had known about it, he could have called it *Winter Landscape, Broderick, Minnesota.*

"Or maybe run a beauty salon," Letty was saying. "We've got three beauty salons in Armstrong, two good ones and one bad one."

"Mmm," Lucas said.

"If I was a cop, I'd put secret agents in every beauty shop in town. Teach them to be hairdressers, but, y'know, they'd all have tape recorders and cameras hidden away. Like spies."

"Take a lot of cops," Lucas said.

"Yeah, but you'd know everything. I go to Harriet's Mane Line with my mom, and the salon ladies know everything that's going on. *Everything.* That'd be pretty good for a cop."

Lucas looked at her again, more carefully. "You're right. That's absolutely right. Maybe you'll grow up to be a cop."

"I could do that," she said comfortably. "Wouldn't mind carrying a gun. If I'd had a real gun this morning, I wouldn't have been scared at all. All I had was that crappy .22."

THE THING THAT MADE traveling across the land so strange, Lucas realized, was that you did nothing: you simply sat in the car and time passed. Driving almost anywhere else, the road moved: you went up and down hills and around curves and past houses, speed zones came and went, cars and trucks went by, and something new was always popping up. Out here, the road was dead straight, with hardly anything on it, or at the sides. Rather than whipping around a curve over the crest of a hill, and finding a town tucked away, surprising you, here the towns came up as a slowly growing lump on the horizon; you could see them, it seemed, for hours before you arrived.

Though Broderick arrived quickly enough: Lucas slowed as they came into town. "So what's where?"

"Okay. So there's the church," she said, pointing across the highway. "It used to be run by Don Sanders. He's kinda crazy and I stay away from him. For the last, I don't know, maybe two or three years, there are a bunch of women living there. People call them the nuns."

"Are they nuns?"

"A couple of them are. They wear old-fashioned dresses."

"Okay. You know them?"

"I talk to them in the diner, when I see them, but my mom says I should stay away from them because they might be lesbians. They claim that they're church people, and say that they take food and clothes to poor people."

"Do they?"

She nodded: "I guess. I got some jeans from them once. Chics. I know a couple of them, the nuns, and one of them, Ruth Lewis . . . I really like her. She doesn't take any shit from anyone. She says I'm as good as anybody and I should remember that."

"How about the Sanders guy? Why do you say he's crazy?"

"I just don't like the way he looks at me. I get a bad feeling."

"Like what? Like he might hurt you?"

"Like he might try to make me do something with him," she said.

"Okay." He didn't comment; he simply filed it until he knew her better. Young girls, in his experience, were sometimes psychic in their ability to pick out predators. At other times, they were capable of straight-faced accusations against the absolutely innocent. "He's been re-placed by lesbians?"

"That's just my mom," Letty said. "I know that Ruth's sister is going out with a guy in town. The word is, she's no lesbian."

Lucas said, "Huh," and took another look at her, and thought she might have blushed. She hurried on, pointing over the dashboard. "Those two big yellow buildings belong to Gene Calb, he fixes up cars and trucks. He's a real good guy. If I'm out with my traps, he'll let me come in and warm up. I can't go into the bar or the cafe because some-times I'm a little stinky, but he doesn't care. I think Mom had a crush on him once, but he's married. I heard that sometimes the lesbians drive for him, like when he needs a car delivered somewhere. I could do that, if I had a license."

"And you probably ought to wait for the license," Lucas said.

"Yeah-yeah." She pointed: "That's the bar, the guy who runs it is named Pete. Mom used to go there when Randy Pearce ran it, but she says she doesn't feel welcome anymore. She says it's a dive now, a bunch of paint sniffers from the body shop. She says they're all jailbirds."

"Are they?"

She shrugged. "Some of them been in jail, I guess, but they seem like pretty good guys."

On the other side of the highway: "The diner is run by Sandra Wolf, she's pretty nice, and John McGuire has the gas station, he's okay. And down there, right across from the barn . . ." She pointed down a side street, where a low rambling house sat across a graveled street from a small white barn. ". . . I don't know what those guys do, but if I was a cop, I'd take a close look at them."

"Yeah? Why?"

"I was walking through there, taking a shortcut back from the lake, and the guy came out of the house and yelled at me to get off his property. I was only about ten feet on it. And he's got dogs, big black-and-brown ones. He had these little paper flags around his property for a while. They said, 'Dog Training, Invisible Fence,' but I think if he sicced one of those dogs on you, that invisible fence wouldn't do any good. They'd go through it like it was, you know, *invisible*."

"But all he did was yell at you."

"I thought it was pretty suspicious. I mean, he's got ten acres there, and I was about three steps on it."

"What's the guy do for a living?"

"Works at Calb's. Sometimes he's got a woman in there. I've seen a couple of them, different ones. He sure does keep you off his property."

They were coming to the north end of town, and the house where Jane Warr and Deon Cash had lived. Two sheriff's cars were parked outside now, along with one of the BCA cars from Bemidji.

"If you want to stop, I can wait," Letty said. "You might want to ask me some more questions after you look inside."

HE WAS BEING STEERED, Lucas thought—she'd shown signs of the female steering gene during the interview at the LEC, and even more on the way to Broderick. On the other hand, she was right. He pulled in and parked. A sheriff's deputy stepped off the porch and walked toward them. Lucas got out, said, "I'm Davenport, with the BCA."

The deputy nodded. "Okay. One of your guys is inside."

Lucas stuck his head back inside the car and said "Wait," shut the door, and followed the deputy up to the porch.

"Where'd you get the kid?" the deputy asked, bending down a bit to get a look at Letty. She lifted a hand to him.

"She was downtown making a statement. You know her?"

"Sure. I know everybody around here. She's a pretty interesting kid. Don't let no grass grow under her feet, that's for sure. Gonna wind up rich."

"Got a nice line of bullshit," Lucas said.

"First thing you notice," the deputy said. He pushed the door open and Lucas stepped into the house, into an entry with a coat closet to one side. He continued into a living room, where one of the BCA guys he'd been introduced to that morning was standing at the bottom of a double-wide staircase, talking on a cell phone. He saw Lucas and held up a finger. Lucas nodded and looked around.

The place smelled of macaroni, cheese, marijuana, and blood, not a new smell in the few hundred houses he'd been through on homicide cases. To his right, in the corner, was a wide-screen Panasonic television, and on a table next to it, a big Sony. A game console was plugged into the Sony, while the Panasonic had boxes for a DVD and satellite dish. A love seat and a leather chair faced the TVs.

Straight ahead, behind the BCA guy, on the other side of the staircase landing, a hallway led to the kitchen. Lucas could see a breadmaker sitting on a counter next to a microwave.

To the right, an archway led into another room, with a dining table in the center of it. The table was stacked with boxes, most of them from small electric appliances. Fifty or sixty magazines, mostly on sex,

European cars, or travel, were in heaps along one wall. A Bose Wave Radio sat upside down under the table, as though it had fallen off; it was still plugged into a wall socket. A set of earphones, one earmuff broken off, lay on the other side of the table, along with a generic-brand bottle of ibuprofen. A box of Wheat Thins sat on top of the litter of boxes on the table.

The generally upset state didn't have the look of deliberation, of a search—it simply looked like bad housekeeping.

"Hey . . ." The BCA guy came up behind him. "Look at this." He led the way to the kitchen. On the way he said, "I'm Joe Barin, by the way, we were introduced . . ."

"This morning," Lucas said.

"Here," Barin said. "Be careful where you put your feet. We've got some blood spatter."

He was pointing into a wastebasket on the floor by the kitchen door. When Lucas looked inside, he saw two tiny Ziploc-type bags, the kind used by hardware stores to hold small collections of screws, washers, cotter pins, and the like, and by dope dealers to parcel out measured amounts of cocaine, heroin, and crystal methadrine. There were no cotter pins in sight.

"You pull one out?"

"Not yet. You can see there's some residue. I wouldn't stake my child's life on it, but it's coke."

"They were dealing?"

"We looked around, can't find any more baggies. So maybe just using. Or maybe we'll find more stuff later . . . and then, we've got these clothes." He pointed to another corner, at a heap of clothing. "It's all cut to shreds. This is where the killer cut the clothes off them."

"So he comes in with a gun, cuffs them up, tapes them up, then cuts the clothes off them."

"Beats the shit out of the guy, of Cash."

"Beats the shit out of Cash, and then drags them both out the door, and throws them into his truck, and takes them down the road, and hangs them."

"Yeah."

"Tough guy."

"Fruitcake."

LUCAS LOOKED AROUND the kitchen for a few more seconds: nothing for him here, that he could see. The crew might get something. "What's upstairs?"

"Three bedrooms and two bathrooms," Barin said. "One of the bedrooms doesn't look too used. One of the other ones has a double bed, and there's some clothes hanging in a closet, a man's clothes, and some stuff in the bathroom, but it doesn't look like it's been used lately. The clothes are not Cash's, they're for a bigger guy. The third bedroom, the big one, was their regular bedroom. Clothes for both Warr and Cash. Lots of clothes. Lots of cashmere."

"Let's get the crime scene crew over quick as we can," Lucas said. "Tear this place apart. If they were dealing, that would explain a lot. Could be punishment killings."

"Okay." Barin hesitated. "I don't exactly understand the chain-of-command here . . ."

"Where's Dickerson?"

"Still out at the scene, I guess."

"He's in charge on your side, I'm running my own thing. What I just suggested was . . . a suggestion." Lucas grinned at him. "Of course, I *do* talk to the commissioner five or six times a day."

Barin shrugged. "I'm not big on bureaucracy. Tearing the place up is the right thing to do."

"The guy with me, Del, knows every drug hideout invented by modern man. I'll bring him by later on."

"Good enough."

The deputy came to the door. "This young lady . . ." Lucas and Barin turned. Letty was standing behind the deputy, looking around with interest. ". . . says she has to use the bathroom."

"Uh . . . not here. I'll run you home," Lucas said. To Barin: "So you know what you're doing. I'll get Del up here."

"Okay." Barin was looking curiously at Letty. "Is this the young lady who found . . ." He tipped his head to the north.

"Yeah," Lucas said.

Barin said, "For a second, I thought she might be your daughter. She's got exactly your eyes."

"I CAN WALK BACK to the cafe," Letty said to Lucas. "It's only two blocks."

"I'll take you," Lucas said. "C'mon."

On the way out, Letty pointed at the wide-screen Panasonic television in the corner. "That used to be in the window at Lute's. You know how much that cost?"

"Thousand, fifteen-hundred?"

Letty snorted. "It was on *sale* for nine-thousand, nine-ninety-nine. Ten thousand bucks. High-definition TV. Sat there for six weeks, and then one day, it was outa there. Didn't know it came here, though."

Lucas looked at Barin, raised his eyebrows. Barin nodded—he'd check. A ten-thousand-dollar television would give weight to the drug-dealing proposition.

"So let's go," Lucas said to Letty.

But outside, Letty said, "I don't really have to pee. I just wanted to get a look around."

"Well, Jesus Christ," Lucas said, irritated.

"I'm trying to help. You need all you can get," she said. Then, "Why couldn't I pee here?"

"They have to process the whole place. Crime scene process. Like the shows on television. Bathrooms are good places to process, because they have good surfaces for fingerprints and so on. You can sometimes get DNA out of them."

"Okay." She nodded. "Good reason."

"Let's get you home," Lucas said.

6

LETTY'S HOUSE WAS VISIBLE from Cash's: a gray spot on the bowl-rim of the horizon.

"What the heck are they doing?" Letty asked, peering out the passenger window, as they drove out of town.

"What?" Lucas ducked his head to look through her window. Out over one of the farm fields, directly south of the line of cop cars at the crime scene, two helicopters were hovering thirty feet above the ground, kicking up a small storm of ice crystals and dirt as they moved slowly sideways, in line, toward the ditch and the police cars.

"Television," Lucas said. He looked at his watch: not yet two o'clock. The newsies had been quick. "Taking pictures." He glanced over at her. "You really don't have to use the bathroom?"

"Not really."

"Okay. You better stick with me for a while."

———

A SHERIFF'S CAR was parked across the side road, and Lucas held his ID out the window as he turned in. The deputy stopped to look through the windshield—it was one of the guys who Lucas had released from the hanging site—and waved them through. They continued down the track toward the cop cars.

There were fewer cars now, but as they pulled up, they saw three men carrying a black body bag through the trees.

"Are those the dead people?" Letty asked, peering out over the dashboard.

"One of them," Lucas said. He popped the door and was about to get out of the car when his cell phone rang. He swiveled back into the car and punched the phone: "Yeah?"

"Lucas. Neil Mitford." The governor's aide. There was electronic noise in his voice. Again, Lucas remembered, they were on the edge of nowhere. "Anything yet?"

"One of the victims, the black guy, was in jail down in Missouri until he moved up here. That was probably a year and a half ago. The guys from Bemidji are running that down. And at the house where they lived, there're a couple of baggies in the wastebasket, small ones like the kind used for street drugs, that show some white residue—probably cocaine."

"Excellent," Mitford said. "Is it too early to start spinning out a dope story?"

"Don't let the governor do it. You want to be able to deny it if you have to," Lucas said. "But I think it'll hold up. They're just bringing the bodies out of the woods now."

"Any film?"

Lucas told him about the helicopters: "I don't know what they could see from out there. They'll be able to get pictures of the bodies coming out in the body bags."

"But nothing of the trees?"

"I don't know. I'll ask and get back to you."

"We're pretty anxious," Mitford said.

"I'll get back," Lucas said. He rang off and turned to Letty: "This time, you *stay* in the car."

"It's a free country," she said.

"You step out on the crime scene, which this is, and I'll put you in a sheriff's car and send you back to Armstrong to sit in the sheriff's office and think about it for a few hours," he said.

"Not fair," she said.

"So take a couple aspirins and lie down," Lucas said.

As he started climbing out again, Letty said, "Ex-con with bags of cocaine, huh? That's a pretty picture."

"*Stay,*" Lucas said.

AS HE GOT OUT OF the car, Lucas spotted Ray Zahn leaning on the fender of his patrol car at the far end of the line. Zahn was watching the body bag being loaded into a Suburban. Lucas walked toward him. Zahn turned his head, nodded, and called, "Bringing them out."

"ME still in there?"

"Yeah, he helped take them down. He had them cut the rope so they could keep it around their necks to make sure that this rope was what killed them."

"You think any of the TV helicopters got pictures?" Lucas asked as he turned into the trees. Zahn trailed behind.

Zahn said, "Yeah. I don't know how much they could see, but if you go over there diagonally, look out over toward the field, there was an open line into the hanging tree. You don't see it right away because of the brush, but if you're up fifteen or twenty feet, looking down at an angle . . . that's exactly where the choppers were. They kept moving in and out of that hole."

"Shit."

"Maybe couldn't see too much."

"Anything was too much." They could see the hanging tree and a group of men around it. "The ME's the guy in the black coat?"

"Yeah. Henry Ford."

"Really? Henry Ford?"

"Yeah. He's out of Thief River. Good guy. Doesn't know shit about cars."

ANDERSON, THE SHERIFF, Dickerson, the BCA supervisor, and a few other men were huddled to the left of the second black bag, cigarette smoke streaming away from them.

"Cold," Zahn mumbled from behind him. "Radio says it's two below."

"I heard," Lucas said. "But it's gonna warm up tonight. Then maybe snow."

"We could use it," Zahn said.

Anderson had spotted them coming through the trees and turned to the ME, who had what looked like an unfiltered cigarette hanging from one lip, and said something, and Ford looked toward them. He was a white-haired man, hardly old enough to be so white—thirty-five, Lucas thought—with round gold grandpa glasses. Lucas came up, with Zahn a step behind, nodded and said, "Dr. Ford? Lucas Davenport." They shook gloved hands, and Lucas said, "Anything useful?"

"They almost certainly died here, if that's useful," Ford said, talking around the cigarette. "Cash's neck was cut by the rope and he bled down the length of his body and there were a few drips on the ground, in the snow under his right foot, so he was alive when they hung him up. I assume the same was true with Warr, but we'll know for sure later. The blood on Warr's face—I don't believe it's hers. I was worried about jarring anything loose, taking her down, so I took some swabs on the spot. We've got three short blond hairs, not hers, not Cash's."

"Good. Excellent. Any signs of drug use?"

Ford took the cigarette out of his mouth. "Both of them were raw around the nostrils, like they might be if they used cocaine. Cash had some scars on both of his forearms and Warr on her right forearm and both feet, that could be from needles. I couldn't swear to the cocaine because we haven't seen much of that here lately. We'll need a few hours to verify all of this. We'll do the full range of toxicology, of course."

"Okay. Quicker is better, though." He looked out toward the choppers, still hanging south of the crime scene. He could see them clearly, just above the brush. They would have had a straight shot of the bodies hanging from the tree. To Dickerson: "There's no chance that you had the bodies down before the choppers arrived?"

"No." The BCA man shook his head. "If they've got the right cameras, they got the shot. If we'd had another twenty minutes . . ."

"They tried to come right in and we waved them off," Anderson said. "Not much more we could do."

"Spilled milk," Lucas said.

THE BCA CRIME SCENE CREW was already working the site, and Lucas drifted over and spoke for a moment to the supervisor. "Nothing. No good footprints—everything is frozen, and the snow didn't hold anything," the man said. "The length of stride and the size of the foot would make the killer a male, but hell . . . we didn't think a woman dragged them back there anyway. Looks like just one guy, if that means anything."

"Yeah, it does," Lucas said.

"So it's one guy. Not much else—we're gonna clean the whole place out, though, right down to the dirt."

LUCAS TURNED TO GO BACK to Dickerson, but the phone rang again and he pulled it out and punched it up.

"You're not going to believe it," Del said. "There was a guy staying at the Motel 6 the night before last, driving a '95 Jeep Cherokee, paid with cash. I've got his registration card, he shows Minnesota plates, including the tag number. I'm gonna run it, see what happens. The night clerk says he saw the guy again last night—that he pulled into the parking lot as if he were going to check in again, but he didn't. He just sat in the lot for a few seconds, then pulled away. The clerk says he was a white guy with a short beard, big guy, well-spoken. He was wearing a dark blue parka and a watch cap. If Letty's right on the time, he would have been in the motel parking lot about an hour earlier. Maybe a little less."

"Huh. Anybody else stay in the room since him?"

"One guy last night, who already checked out, and the room's been cleaned. We've got a credit card on the guy who checked out, so we should be able to get him for some prints. I locked up the room and put some duct tape on the doors."

"What else?"

"If I don't get something to eat in the next twelve minutes, my ass is gonna fall off."

"Got a place?"

"There's a cafe called the Red Red Robin. It comes reluctantly recommended."

"See you there in fifteen," Lucas said.

He went back to Dickerson and they stepped away from the crowd to talk. Lucas told him about the dope baggies at the Cash farmhouse. "I was just heading back down there," Dickerson said. "Anything else?"

"We interviewed the kid and she thinks the killer's car was a Jeep

Cherokee," Lucas explained and outlined the conversation with Del. "So the guy at the motel saw the Jeep not long before Letty saw the lights out here on the road. It makes me nervous to say it, but it fits."

"Gotta process the room," Dickerson said. He was interested now. "Priority one."

"It's sealed with official duct tape," Lucas said. "Feel free."

"Do any good for us to talk with the kid?"

"I don't think so. She mostly just found them," Lucas said. "You can take a crack at her if you want."

"We got other stuff to do, if you think you got it all."

"I'm taking her back downtown, to see if I can keep her away from the reporters for a while," Lucas said. "We'll talk to her some more."

LETTY WAS SITTING on the hood of the Oldsmobile, apparently impervious to the cold, when Lucas got back to the road. "Couldn't breathe inside the car," she said. "But I stayed right here." She hopped off the passenger side, popped the door, and climbed in. "The bodies in the bags looked stiff, like bags full of boards," she said, as Lucas got in and fumbled out the key.

"Uh. You know a place called the Red Red Robin?"

"The Bird. Downtown. Nice place. My mom and I went there once for Thanksgiving."

"I'm going in to get a bite to eat with Del. I hate to leave you without your mother." He didn't mention that he hated even more to leave her with a pack of reporters outside her door. "Want to come?"

"Sounds good to me," Letty said. "If you're buying."

"I'm buying."

On the way, Letty asked, "They were stiff in the bags. Is that like, rigor mortis?"

Lucas shook his head. "No. They were frozen. Like Popsicles."

———

THE RED RED ROBIN was a storefront cafe with a robin painted on a swinging wooden sign outside the door, like the sign on an English pub. Inside, a dozen red-topped stools ran straight down a coffee bar, and behind those, and behind a sign that read, PLEASE SEAT YOURSELF, were sixteen booths covered with the same red leatherette as the stools. The place smelled of fried eggs, fried onions, fried potatoes, and fried beef. Eight other customers sat in three groups down the booths. They seemed to be arranged to keep an eye on Del, who sat halfway down the right-hand wall.

"Anything?" Lucas asked Del, as he and Letty slid into the booth.

"Ran the numbers. No such tag," Del said.

"Shit." He glanced at Letty. "Shoot."

"But it occurs to me that a guy who's gonna come up here and do something like hang two people would have to be pretty weird to do it in a small town, in his own car. He's gotta know he's gonna be *somewhat* noticed."

"You'd think."

"So maybe he wouldn't lie about the Minnesota part of the plates, in case the clerk might notice. Maybe he just jumbled the numbers. I got the guys in St. Paul to look for recent title transfers on older Jeep Cherokees. Turns out the new ones don't have those taillights. The motel clerk thought that it might be an older model, too."

"Maybe get lucky," Lucas said.

Letty asked, "Can you guys talk while you eat? Or is that too complicated?"

Del lifted an eyebrow at her. "My daughter is only three years younger than this kid," Lucas told him. "Do you think I could lock her in a freezer? I mean, what if she grew a mouth like this one?"

"Ha ha," Letty said. She handed a slightly greasy menu to Lucas. "You're buying."

———————

LETTY STUFFED HERSELF. Del and Lucas went out of their way to prove that they could talk while they ate. The food struggled toward mediocrity, but, Lucas realized as he sampled the potatoes, wasn't going to make it. Half of the meatloaf was refrigerator cold; the other half, microwave hot. As they were finishing, a tall man in tan Carhartt coveralls came in, stamping his feet and snuffing with the cold. Letty called, "Hey, Bud."

The man looked around until he spotted Letty, then stepped over. He was about fifty, Lucas thought, and as thin and hard-looking as an oak rail, with a bulbous red nose and flinty white eyes.

"Hey, Letty," he said, his eyes bouncing off Lucas and Del. "Been working hard, or hardly working?"

"Doin' okay," she said. "I heard you been shootin' beaver again."

"Yeah, over to Spike. What's this about you finding those people? I heard about it at Jerry's."

"Yep." Letty puffed up a little. "They were *nude.*"

"All right," Lucas said dryly. "Let's finish the meatloaf."

"Bud's a trapper, like me," Letty told them. To Bud: "These guys are state agents. They're taking me around."

Bud nodded. "I thought Jane might come to a bad end," he said.

"Why was that?" Lucas asked.

"Not good people," he said. "She thought we were a bunch of hicks. She was always laughing at people behind their backs, and she used to talk about Las Vegas all the time, like that was the navel of the universe. Every time she opened her mouth she'd start off by saying, 'In Las Vegas we used to . . . whatever.'"

"Sounds like you knew her pretty well," Del said.

"Just to play blackjack," the trapper dude said. "She was the main dealer up at Moose Bay." He hesitated, then said, dropping his voice, "You know what you ought to do when you get up to the casino, is talk to a guy named Terry Anderson. He knew Warr *real* well." He leaned on *real* just enough.

Lucas nodded and said, "I'll do that. Thanks. Terry Anderson."

"Any relation to the sheriff?" Del asked.

The trapper was puzzled, looked at Letty and then back to Del. "Terry? Why would he be?"

"Both Andersons?" Del suggested.

The trapper cackled: "Shit, buddy, half the people up here are Andersons."

They talked for another fifteen seconds, then Bud retreated to the counter and got a menu.

"Heck of a trapper, and he's supposed to be an unbelievable hunter, too. He knows more about animals than they know themselves," Letty said. "He's been number one around here for years."

"Taught you everything you know?"

She shook her head: "He doesn't teach anything to anybody. He's got his secrets and he keeps them."

Lucas dropped his voice to match hers: "Think he might have had anything going with Jane?"

"No." Now she was almost whispering. "Don't look at him, he'll know we're talking about him. But, uh, everybody says Bud's a little . . . gay."

WHEN THEY'D FINISHED the meal, Lucas sent Del to Broderick, to look for dope hideouts. "We're gonna pick up Letty's mother," Lucas said. "Then, I'll see you up there."

As he and Letty were about to get in the car, he remembered Mitford. "Damnit . . . why don't you go look in a store window for a minute?" he suggested to Letty, and pulled out his phone.

Mitford picked up on the first ring, and Lucas gave him the bad news: "They've got pictures. I don't know how good, because they were a couple hundred yards away, but they've got something."

"Aw, man. That's terrible. Anything on the dope?"

"Not yet. My partner's on the way up to the house. If there's anything, he'll find it. What about Cash, and the jail business?"

"We're getting that now, through Rose Marie," Mitford said. "We got a summary: he's had a whole list of minor stuff, some drug-related, disorderly conduct, like that. Then this last one, he was originally charged with ag assault. He beat on some other guy with a steel coat tree in a hotel. They pled it down and he took a year in the county lockup on some lower-level assault. Served nine months."

"Doesn't sound like something you get hanged for."

"I got Missouri trying to figure that out. They said they'd get back to us this afternoon, with whatever they can find," Mitford said. "Oh, and I got two more words for you."

"What words?"

"Washington Fowler."

"You're joking." Washington Fowler was a civil rights attorney from Chicago, who'd mostly given up the law in favor of incitation to riot.

"I'm not," Mitford said. "He's having a press conference here, at the airport, in an hour, and he's flying out to Fargo in a private plane in an hour and a half. The governor invited him over to the mansion for a conference, but he told us to go fuck ourselves. You should see him up there tonight."

"Aw, jeez."

"Yeah. Lucas—we need to hit Cash hard. The woman, too. Before the news. Before that film gets down here. Before Fowler gets up there."

"We're looking."

WHEN LUCAS GOT OFF the phone, Letty suggested that they might find her mother at the Duck Inn, two blocks over. They ambled over, Lucas looking in the storefronts. Small towns, he'd realized a long time ago, were a little like spaceships, or ordinary ships, for that matter—

they generally had to have one of everything: one McDonald's or Burger King (couldn't support one of each), a department store, a quick oil change, a hardware store, a feed store, a satellite-TV outlet, a bar or two. Everything needed for survival. Armstrong was like that, a lifeboat, one of everything necessary for life, all packaged in yellow-brick and red-brick two-story buildings. About one in four of the storefronts was empty, and the owners hadn't bothered to put "For Rent" signs in the windows.

The Duck Inn was a cliché, a plastic faux-hunter's haven smelling of beer, with a fake old-fashioned jukebox that played CDs next to the twin coin-op pool tables. A cliché, and Letty's mother wasn't there. "Cop came and got her. I think they went over to the courthouse," the bartender said.

The courthouse was just down the block, and they found Martha West leaving the Law Enforcement Center. She was a natural blond, like Letty, but her hair had been tinted an improbable rust color. She wasn't weathered like Letty, but there were explosions of tiny red veins on her cheeks, so that she would always look rosy-cheeked. She wore a parka and khaki slacks, with pointed boots, and was carrying a beaten-up guitar case. She saw Letty and Lucas, and called to Letty, "Where you been? I been looking all over for you."

"Cops have been taking me around," Letty said, jerking a thumb at Lucas. "This is Agent Davenport."

"Lucas Davenport," Lucas said.

"Martha West." West's eyes were moving slowly, and then jerking back, like a drunk drifting out of his lane, then jerking the car back straight. She was loaded, but controlling it.

"I was about to drop Letty at your place, but I didn't want to leave her alone," Lucas said.

"We ate at the Bird," Letty said, with a slight sophisticated depre-cation in her voice.

"Really?" The mother looked at Lucas like he might have done something incorrect.

"She had an open-faced meatloaf sandwich, mashed potatoes, green beans, and apple pie," Lucas said. "And about six Cokes."

"Two," Letty said, "They were free refills."

They loaded Martha and her guitar into the back seat of Lucas's car, and on the way north, he caught her eyes in his rearview mirror and said, "There'll be some reporters who want to talk with you. If I were you, I'd get in the house, get your heads straight, clean up a little bit. I can get a guy from the Bureau of Criminal Apprehension to talk with you about your statement. About what you should or shouldn't say or about whether you should talk at all. You could always tell them to go away."

"TV?" asked Martha. She straightened, touched her hair.

"For sure," Lucas said. "But they can be aaa . . ." He changed directions. ". . . jerks. Be a good idea if you talked with a BCA guy who knows how to deal with the media."

"All right. I'll talk to him," Martha said. "But I've been on TV many times."

"Okay. Then you know how to handle it."

"I used to work with the Chamber of Commerce, and the TV would come to me for comment." Her eyes rolled toward the westside ditch. "And I've always been a singer. So I've been around."

"Okay."

"But I'll talk to your person. That wouldn't hurt."

As they went through Broderick, they saw a collection of media trucks at the cafe, and, just down the highway, Lucas saw Del's Mustang at the victims' house, next to Dickerson's car. He slowed, did a U-turn, and said, "The guy I'm going to introduce you to is Hank Dickerson, who is the head of the whole Bureau for the northern part of the state. He'll help you out."

HE LEFT THEM in the car, and as he crossed the yard, the cop outside said, "You won't believe what they found."

"Yeah?"

Joe Barin, the BCA agent, was standing at the bottom of the stairs, and when he saw Lucas, pointed up. "Take a look," he said.

Lucas went up the creaky stairs, and found Del with Dickerson and one of Dickerson's crime scene crew in the main bedroom. The bedroom smelled of makeup and after-shave; a framed Michael Jordan poster hung on one wall, opposite a fake antique beer sign. The cops turned to Lucas when he walked in, and Dickerson said, "Del found their hidey-hole."

The hidey-hole was in the bedroom closet, and was custom-made. What appeared to be a cross-brace for the closet pole was, in fact, a cover for a four-foot-long, six-inch-high wall cache. Inside the cache, Lucas could see what appeared to be a one-kilo bag of cocaine, separated into dozens of smaller baggies; a Colt Magnum Carry Revolver, like one he had in his gun safe at home; and cash. The cash was wrapped in paper bands and took up three running feet of the cache between the bag of cocaine and the back wall.

"Holy cats. How much?"

"We don't want to take it out until we get pictures, but I figure something upward of three hundred thousand, if it's all hundreds," Del said. "All the top bundles are hundreds—and all used. Not a single new bill, as far as you can tell from looking at the sides."

Lucas said to Dickerson, "You need to have three guys here with the money all the time, until it's counted. Make sure one or two of them are sheriff's deputies. You want both agencies involved. People are gonna ask how much of the money went into cops' pockets."

Dickerson nodded. "Right, we'll do that. Another thing. I walked across the highway and talked to Gene Calb, at the truck place. He was

Cash's boss. He said he had no idea what was going on, but he said there was another guy living here, part time, named Joe Kelly. He said Kelly disappeared a month ago and nobody's heard from him since. The clothes in the other bedroom are Kelly's. We got a couple charge-card receipts with his name on them."

"Check the companies for new activity."

"Under way," Dickerson said.

"We got another thing," Del said. "Maybe."

"What?"

"I want you to look at it," Del said. "Then you tell me."

Lucas followed him, Dickerson trailing, down through the house to the basement. On the way down, he told Dickerson about Washington Fowler. Dickerson was unmoved.

"You're pretty calm about it," Lucas said. "The guy goes around starting fires."

Dickerson smiled. "That's your problem, general, not mine. You're the guy who's supposed to fix shit."

THE BASEMENT WAS unfinished concrete block and exposed joists, but with a new-looking furnace, a new hot-water heater, and new wiring and fluorescent lights. In one corner, a new bathroom had been built in a beige-painted cubicle, with a standard toilet and a sink, and a fiberglass shower booth with sliding glass doors.

Del said, "Well?"

"Well, they just remodeled it," Lucas said. He looked around, saw nothing of obvious interest. Del had to be thinking about the bathroom, and Lucas went that way. The bathroom was bare, and smelled of disinfectant. Large, lots of room to move around. Lucas swung the entrance door, then knocked on it. Looked like wood, sounded like a metal fire door. Knocked on the walls: not drywall, as he'd expected, but painted plywood. And heavy, probably three-quarter inch. Yale keyhole lock with a bolt, lockable from the outside. No keyhole on the inside . . .

He stepped back and said to Del and Dickerson, "It's a goddamn cell."

Del turned to Dickerson. "You heard it here first."

TWENTY MINUTES LATER, Lucas, Del, and Dickerson walked through the gathering collection of cop cars in the yard. Letty was sitting on the hood of the car again, while her mother waited inside. When she saw them coming, she climbed out, and Lucas introduced Dickerson. "Hank will help you with the TV commentary. And he'll get you home."

"Cops say you found a bundle of money in there," Letty said to Del. "That right?"

"Just a rumor," Del said.

Dickerson, looking from Lucas to Del, asked, "What're you guys doing next?"

"Gonna talk to St. Paul, and maybe wander around some more," Lucas said. He looked back at the house. "This thing is getting interesting."

7

FREE OF LETTY and her mother, Lucas and Del caucused at the cars. "Moose Bay?" Del asked.

"That's a big topic," Lucas said. "Why don't we talk to this Calb guy?"

They both looked across the highway at the yellow metal buildings with the trucks parked out front, and Del nodded.

Calb had two buildings, an auto-body and tow building, and a truck-rehab building, connected by an unheated shed-like walkway. They went into the auto-body building, which consisted of a small office and a series of repair bays at the back; a woman in the office directed them through the walkway to the truck-rehab wing. The truck area was bigger and more open, forty feet long and thirty wide, with a thirty-foot ceiling; it smelled of diesel and welding fumes. A row of red toolboxes sat at the back, and an electric heater was mounted high on one wall and glowed down over a burgundy Peterbilt. Three men were clustered around the open door of the truck, peering inside, and one of them asked, "What the fuck were they carrying in there? You think there was some acid dripping in there?"

"I don't know . . ." Then one of the men saw Lucas and Del, and nudged the heavyset man who was deepest into the truck. He backed up, saw them, stood upright, and asked, "Can we help you fellas?"

"We're with the state Bureau of Criminal Apprehension," Lucas said. Del held up an ID case. "We need to talk to Gene Calb."

"That's me . . . I'll be with you in just a second." He turned to one of the other men. "I don't know, Larry. I'd go after it with a grinder, and if you don't get good metal . . . we'll cut another piece off a wreck and weld 'er in. There's a hulk down in Worthington, out of a fire, oughta work."

"Looks like it's rotten all the way to the bottom. I could push a nail through it," said an emaciated man in oil-stained Mr. Goodwrench coveralls.

"Well, cut through it and find out."

Calb shook his head as he turned to Lucas and Del. "The whole floor of the passenger side is eaten away. Not the driver's side, just the passenger side. It's not rust, exactly, but it's rotten. Like they spilled acid on it or something and then let it soak for a few years."

One of the other men said, "Cat pee? Cat pee'll rot holes in hardwood floors."

"Well, Jesus, how could he stand the smell?" Calb shook his head once more. "If I were you, Larry, I'd keep my hands out of it."

"You sure as shit can count on that," said the man called Larry.

To Lucas and Del, Calb said, "C'mon this way, fellas. We'll go back to my office. You want to know about Deon? I already talked to some of you guys. With the BCA, right?"

"We're doing a little back-checking," Lucas said. "How well did you know Mr. Cash?"

They pushed through a door into another small office and Calb gestured at a couple of guest chairs, then settled behind his desk as he answered. A caution flag signed by Richard Petty, and a Snap-on tools calendar from the 1980s hung on a wall. Everything else was parts books.

"He worked for me," Calb said earnestly, leaning across the desk to Lucas. He had a big head and a blunt nose and square, mildly green teeth the size of Chiclets—the face of a plumber or a carpenter or a character actor playing a hardworking joe. "We weren't friends. An old Army buddy down in KC asked me if I could get him a driver's job. I knew he was just out of jail and, tell you the truth, I'm not sure he was that much reformed. With what's happened, it looks like he wasn't."

"What do you think happened?" Del asked.

Calb said, "Well—you know. Somebody took him out and hung him. I know it wasn't none of my boys, because none of my boys could do that. Jane too, killing both of them. I think it's gotta come out of KC. He was in jail, that's what it's gotta be. Somebody back there."

"How about Jane Warr?" Lucas asked. "How well did you know her?"

"Not real well. She didn't hang around or anything. She came up with Deon, from KC. She wasn't much—she was a card dealer up at Moose Bay, I'm sure you know."

"So . . . were they renting that house? Own it? What was the situation there?"

"They bought it, cheap—thirty-six thousand, I think. Then they fixed it up. Joe Kelly did some of the work, he'd once worked as a handyman, and they had a couple guys in from town, they did some of it."

"There are rumors around town that she might have had a relationship with a guy up at the casino," Del said.

"I wouldn't know about that," Calb said, shaking his head. "Like I said, she wasn't that bright, but I don't think she'd be dumb enough to play around on Deon. Deon had a mean streak. That's why he was in jail. If he'd found out something like that, he would have beat on her like a big bass drum."

"Mmm."

Calb picked up a piece of paper from his desk, something with a printed IRS seal, looked at it, flicked it off to the side. "Then there's the whole thing about Joe. Joe's gone—and nobody knows where he went. Never said a word to anyone. One day he was here, and the next day, he wasn't. He was from KC, too."

"You think it might be possible that Joe did this? That there was some kind of an argument, and for some reason'. . . "

Calb shook his head. "Nah. To tell you the truth, Joe just didn't have the *grit* to do this. Not hanging them, where he had to look them in the face."

"So maybe he just took off," Del said. "Or maybe . . ."

"Something else I thought of, after the other BCA boys was here," Calb continued. "If this whole thing didn't come out of the Kansas City jail—and that's gotta be it, in my opinion, but if it didn't—then you oughta get up to Moose Bay. That would be the place to look, along with KC."

"Why?" Del asked.

"The word around town is that Letty West saw them out there at the stroke of midnight," Calb said. "Is that right?"

Lucas nodded. "Close to that."

"Jane worked the three-to-eleven shift. She couldn't have got home much before half-past eleven, and last night, with that ground blizzard, it was probably later. If he took them up there to hang them at midnight, he must have grabbed her the minute she got home. So he was waiting for her—or followed her home."

Lucas and Del both nodded. They talked for another five minutes, and Lucas got the impression that Calb was genuinely confused by the killings. Cash had had some words from time to time with coworkers, but never anything serious, nothing that had even led to a confrontation. "Just that, you know, mechanics and guys like Deon don't mix. He thought he was a basketball star. One of those bad gangsta dudes, whatever they call them. That's what he thought."

OUTSIDE, WALKING BACK across the highway, Lucas said, "I thought about her getting off at eleven, and being hanged at twelve."

"I did too," Del said. "I was saving it up."

"Pig's ass," Lucas said. "Anyway, somebody thought of it."

"Maybe Warr was the target," Del said. "We've been doing nothing but talking about Cash."

"Got to get on her, get some background going. I'll talk to Dickerson."

"Gotta get up to Moose Bay," Del said. "How's the heater in the Olds?"

"Fine."

"Then let's take your car. Mustang heater wouldn't soften up butter."

MOOSE BAY WAS RUN by the Black River band of the Chippewa, on the banks of a river whose water was stained so absolutely black by decomposing vegetation that when it froze over, even the ice looked black. From Cash's house to the res was twenty-four minutes, nine minutes down to Armstrong, then another fifteen minutes through Armstrong and out the county road to the casino.

"Tell me your theories," Del said, on the way out. "You give good theory."

"I'm thinking . . . drug deal," Lucas said. "Calb was probably right both ways: it's connected with Kansas City and Cash's jail contacts, and it's probably connected with the casino. The casino Indians don't have much truck with drugs, but the people who come in to gamble, have a good time . . . they'd do a little coke."

"So the money's drug money," Del said. "All in cash, all bundled up, but not fresh bricks. Cash makes the wholesale contacts, driving for Calb back and forth. Warr has the contacts up here, delivers it out to the individual dealers. Or deals it herself."

"Then they fuck with somebody. Or, somebody knows they've got that money, and they come looking for it."

"But then they'd just shoot them—they wouldn't hang them," Del said.

"Trying to get them to talk?"

"More likely they fucked with somebody and got made an example of," Del said. "A bigger network that's still up and running, where they need an occasional example."

"Maybe," Lucas said. "Where does Calb come in?"

"He doesn't. Not necessarily."

"Look at the farmhouse—there was a lot of work done in there, new work, and it cost a bundle. Believe me, I know." The Big New House back in St. Paul had cost $870,000. "If Calb knows Cash is only getting paid for driving, and if Warr is just dealing cards, where'd he think they got the money to fix that place up? There's a hundred grand in work in there, minimum, and a ten-thousand-dollar television set."

"Tell you what—if the total's a hundred and thirty-five thousand dollars, that's not much for a house, with two incomes, and a guy upstairs who might be paying rent," Del said.

"C'mon," Lucas scoffed. "How many drug dealers do you know who have a mortgage? How many have bought a house?"

"Jimmy Szuza bought a house for his mother."

"Jimmy Szuza was working for his mother, the treacherous old bitch. He was fronting for her."

"Still." After a couple of minutes: "And what about the cell?"

"Beats the shit outa me."

"CALB WAS RIGHT about the travel time," Lucas said, glancing at his watch as they rolled into the casino's parking lot.

The casino looked like a larger version of Calb's truck shop, but a truck shop on steroids: a huge, rambling, two-story yellow-and-green metal building with a prism-shaped glass entry built to resemble a crystal tepee. "Liquor in the front, poker in the rear," Del said.

"Bumper sticker," Lucas said. "But I don't think they sell booze."

THE MOOSE BAY security chief was a cheerful Chippewa man named Clark Hoffman, who hurried down to meet them after a call from the reception desk. "Figured you'd get here sooner or later," he said, shaking their hands. He looked closely at Del. "Did you hang out at Meat's in the Cities?"

"Yeah, I'd go in there before it closed," Del said.

"It closed? Shit."

"Couple years back."

Hoffman thought about that for a moment, then said, "I used to kick your ass at shuffleboard. I thought you were a wino."

Del grinned and shrugged. "I remember. You told me you were at Wounded Knee."

"That's me," Hoffman said. "Sneaking through the weeds with a hundred pounds of frozen brats in a backpack. Fuckin' FBI—no offense. C'mon this way."

They followed him upstairs to his office, Del filling him in about Meat's. "Trouble with the health inspectors," Del told him. "You name it, they had it: mice, rats, roaches, disease. The only thing that kept you from dyin' was the alcohol."

"Everything did have a . . . particular flavor," Hoffman said. "Ever notice that?"

"Yeah."

"I always sorta liked it. What happened to Meat?"

"He moved to San Clemente and opened a porno store."

"Not much money in retail porno anymore," Hoffman said, shaking his head. "Not since they started piping it into every motel room in the country."

JANE WARR'S EMPLOYMENT file sat in the center of Hoffman's desk. He pushed it across at Lucas and said, "Not much there. She learned to deal at a school in Vegas, held a couple of jobs there, worked at a Wal-Mart for a while, outside of Kansas City, then came up here."

"We heard a rumor that she might have had a relationship here with a guy named Terry Anderson."

Hoffman frowned. "Where'd you hear that?"

"Downtown. Can't tell you exactly who mentioned it," Lucas said.

"I'll check, and I'll find out. I hadn't heard anything, but then—I might not have. About anyone else, but not about Terry."

"Why not Terry?" Del asked.

"He's my brother-in-law," Hoffman said. He grinned at Lucas, but it wasn't a happy face. "He's married to my sister."

"Aw, shit," Lucas said. "Listen, all we heard was one guy, who didn't like Warr, but maybe got turned down by her and knew we'd be up here talking to you. Maybe just a wise guy."

"One way or the other, I'll know in the next half hour," Hoffman said. He interlinked his fingers, stretched his arms out in front of him, and cracked his knuckles. "I'll let you know."

"Take it easy," Del said.

"I'll take it easy," Hoffman said. "My sister, on the other hand, might kill his ass. If it's true."

"Tell her to take it easy, too," Del said. "I mean, Jesus."

"You have any cocaine going through here?" Lucas asked after an awkward pause.

Hoffman spread his hands. "Sure. On the res, and some of the customers bring it in. We try to keep it out—we make so much money that we try to keep everything spotless. We don't need to give some asshole state senator an excuse to build state-run casinos. When we see it, we call the cops. Anybody caught with it is banned, no matter what the cops do."

"Any chance Warr was dealing?" Del asked.

"Not in here," Hoffman said. "We watch the dealers, and they know it. We tape them every minute they're working."

"Really? Do you still have last night's tapes?" Lucas asked.

"Sure do. We've got tapes for the last month, and tapes of anything that might ever come up in the future. Catch people stealing, they'll be on tape until the next glacier comes through."

Del said, "We don't have a line on who did this, but we'd sort of like to see a guy, big guy, new beard, dark watch cap or ski cap, dark parka and jeans, drives a Jeep Cherokee."

"I don't know about the Cherokee, but I know who you're talking about. We've got him on tape," Hoffman said.

"You know him?" Lucas asked. "Who he is?"

"Not who he is, but I looked at him pretty good. He'd be on the tapes, though most of what you'd see is the top of his head. The camera coverage on the slots isn't as good as it is on the tables, because the slots aren't as much of a problem."

"When can we see them?" Lucas asked. And, "How do you know it was him?"

"Right now. And I know who you're talking about, because some people don't act right, and you tend to notice them. This guy wasn't interested in gambling. I couldn't *tell* what he was interested in. I noticed him the night before last, and then he came in again last night," Hoffman said. "He was plugging dollar tokens into the slots, but slow, and he hardly paid attention when he won, like he didn't care. People don't act like that in casinos. They're always walking around counting their coins and looking at machines, or they get perched up on a chair and they start pounding away. One thing they don't do, is they *don't* not give a shit."

Del looked at Lucas. "Hell of a long thread, from the motel guy to here."

"Gotta pull it," Lucas said. To Hoffman: "Let's go see the tapes."

Hoffman took them to a surveillance room—on the way, he asked, "You really think your info on Terry might be good?" and Lucas said, "Jeez, I hope not"—where a half-dozen women roamed along twenty monitors, watching the activity on the floor below. There were good overhead shots of all the blackjack tables, but most of the cameras over the slots looked straight down. Only a few looked at the slots from shallow angles, and those were farther back.

"The main problem with the machines is theft—guys dipping coins out of other people's coin buckets," Hoffman explained. He pointed at a monitor showing a woman who was sitting in front of a machine feeding in quarters. All they could see was the top of her head, her shoulders, and her arms. "See, like this lady, she's pushed her coin bucket halfway around the machine. If you're on the next aisle over, you can reach across and dip her. We get one of those a week, guys who never think about cameras. Dumb guys. But you can't see them dipping from the side. You can only see them reach from the overheads."

He led them to a cubicle at the back of the room, where an Indian man with two careful red-ribbon-tied braids was poking at a computer. "Les, are we still on last night's tapes on Number Twelve?"

"Yeah. That's good for another couple of days." The man looked curiously at Lucas and Del.

"State police," Hoffman said. "Looking into the Jane Warr thing."

"Hanged," Les said. He toyed with the end of one of his braids. "That sort of freaked me out when I heard it. She won't be on Twelve, though . . ."

"We're looking for another fella. Go to ten o'clock. Start there."

The computer guy typed in a group of codes, and they waited, fifteen seconds, then twenty, and finally a wide-angled color film came up. The people in the film moved in a herky-jerky motion, indicating that the camera was shooting at a super-slow rate. "There he is," Hoffman said, tapping the camera.

The camera was looking down a long row of slots from slightly above. Two-thirds of the way down the row, a tall man in a dark coat, watch cap, and glasses was playing one of the machines.

"Can we get a closer shot of him?" Lucas asked.

"Not from that camera—we could have zoomed in if we thought he was up to something, but he never did anything," Hoffman said. "I just noticed him when I was down there because he didn't seem right. I forgot about his glasses, though."

"How about another camera?"

"The overhead won't help, but we've got a camera coming across from the side, but it's gonna be partly blocked by the machines."

"Number twenty-eight," Les said. "I can get it if you want it."

"Get it," Lucas said.

Number twenty-eight showed slices of the man's face, only marginally more clearly than the first camera. "Is that the best there is?"

"Probably got him walking in or out on number thirty-six, but I don't know when he arrived. Leaving, we'd only get the back of his head . . . It'd take some time. I don't know how much better the shot would be," Hoffman said.

"We could take the flashes we got of him on twenty-eight, freeze the shots, and then stitch them together and we'd have his whole face," Les said. "I could do it in Photoshop."

"How long would that take?"

"I don't know. I've never done it, but I think I could. I could print the best partial shots, too."

"Let's try it all," Lucas said to Hoffman. "We can get a subpoena to make it all legal."

"That'd be good," Hoffman said. "It'd help publicity-wise, if somebody asks—but we could get started right away. Look, look where he keeps looking."

"What?"

Hoffman tapped the monitor. "See, he keeps looking over the top of the machine, sideways. That's where Jane is. She's out of the picture, but he keeps looking over there. Here comes Small Bear . . ."

A woman pushing a change cart moved into the picture. When she got to the man, she stopped and spoke to him. He nodded, took out his wallet and gave her a bill. She gave him a stack of coins, said a couple more words, then pushed on down the aisle.

"Who's that?"

"JoAnne Small Bear. Been working here since we opened."

"We need to talk to her," Lucas said. "We're gonna need all the tape you've got of this guy. Even the overheads. He might be wearing a ring or a watch, and that could be a good thing to know."

Hoffman nodded. "Sure. I'll have Les pull out everything we've got. You're a hundred percent sure it's him?"

"No. Only about ninety percent," Lucas said. "Ninety and climbing."

"How about this Small Bear?" Del asked. "Where can we get her?"

Hoffman looked at his watch. "She's gotta be checked in by now— she works the three-to-eleven. Let's go find her."

JoAnne Small Bear looked nothing at all like a bear—she looked more like a raspberry. Barely five feet tall, she was jolly and fat, with black eyes and brilliant white teeth; she wore boot-cut jeans with a western shirt and a turquoise necklace. She remembered the man in the watch cap. "He looked lonely and sad," she said. "Pretty good-looking, though. Polite."

"Any particular characteristics that might tell us about him?" Del asked.

"Maybe," she said. "You think he killed Jane Warr?"

"We need to talk to him," Lucas said.

"Jane was a big pain in the ass," Small Bear said.

"You don't hang people for being a pain in the ass," Del said. "You wouldn't have wanted to see her this morning when they cut her down."

Small Bear exhaled and said, "I know one thing that might be important. When he opened his billfold to give me some bills, I saw that he had a black card. One of those American Express black cards."

Del looked at Lucas and Lucas shrugged.

Small Bear looked from Lucas to Del to Lucas and said, "You don't know about the black cards?"

"I don't know what you're talking about," Lucas said.

"We get every card in the world in here," Hoffman said. "The black card is called the Centurion Card. To get one, you gotta spend a hundred and fifty thousand bucks a year with American Express. I bet there aren't a hundred of them in Minnesota."

"You're kidding me," Lucas said. "A hundred and fifty thousand a year?"

"That's what I hear."

Del said to Lucas, "That ought to narrow the list."

LUCAS STEPPED AWAY, took out his cell phone, found a slip of paper with Neil Mitford's personal cell-phone number and punched it in. Mitford answered on the second ring: "This is Davenport. Things are moving here. We could have a photo and maybe a name pretty quick—but we need some help."

"What?"

"We need somebody to get to American Express. Maybe there's a local office or a local official we can give a subpoena to, but we need all the names of all the Centurion Card members from Minnesota and the Kansas City area. Maybe somebody could feed them a list of ZIP codes. We need it quick as we can."

"Wait a minute, let me jot this down." After a second of silence, Mitford said, "What the fuck is a Centurion Card?"

"Some kind of exclusive card," Lucas said. "The casino people say they're pretty rare."

"I'll find out the fastest way to do it, and get it to you."

"See if you can get a printable list from them, and fax it to the sheriff's office here. And tell them, you know, it involves a multiple murder. Put a little heat on them."

"I can *do* heat," Mitford said. "I'll call you."

HOFFMAN HAD WALKED away while Lucas was talking; when he got off the phone, Del said, "Hoffman's gone to get Anderson. His brother-in-law."

"Damnit. I would have liked to have been there, see how the guy takes it."

"He went over there . . . he said he'd be right back, maybe we could catch him."

THEY FOUND HOFFMAN and Anderson just outside an employee's canteen off the main floor. Anderson was a thin, dark-haired white man with big crooked teeth and a small narrow mustache. He was waving his arms around, his face harsh and urgent, as he talked to Hoffman, who leaned against a wall with his arms crossed. Lucas heard, "Goddamnit, Clark, you know me better than that, I just ate lunch . . ."

Lucas came up, with Del trailing, and said, "There you are."

Hoffman turned and pushed away from the wall. To Anderson he said, "These are the cops."

Anderson pushed a finger at Lucas: "What the hell are you doing, telling Clark that I've been cheating on Suzie?"

"Didn't exactly say that," Lucas said. "We heard from a guy in town that you were pretty friendly with Jane Warr."

"What guy?"

"Can't tell you, unless we bust you. Then you'd have a right to know," Lucas said, hardening up. "Your lawyer could get the name."

Anderson shriveled back. "My lawyer? What the hell is going on?"

Del edged in, the beat-up good guy. "Listen: just tell us—how well did you know her?"

"I wasn't screwing her, if that's what you mean."

"How well?" Del pressed.

Anderson took a step back, and the stress in his voice dropped a notch. "A little bit. She used to deal in Vegas and I worked out there for a while, years ago. I didn't know her then—we weren't even there at the same time—but you know, working in Vegas was sort of a big deal for both of us. When we were both off at the same time, we'd eat lunch together, here in the canteen, sometimes. But most of the time, just in a group, only once or twice, when there was just the two of us." He looked at Hoffman: "Clark, I wouldn't bullshit you."

"All right," Hoffman said.

Del said, "Did you ever meet any of her friends, Deon Cash or Joe Kelly?"

"I didn't really meet them, but I knew who they were, because they were black," Anderson said. To Hoffman: "That's another reason I wouldn't do it, Clark. Even if I'd wanted to. You ever see her boyfriend? The guy was like some kind of ghetto killer or something."

"All right," Hoffman said again.

"She ever say anything about them?" Lucas asked. "Or was she worried about anything? Did she seem apprehensive, or scared?"

"A few weeks back, I don't know, three or four weeks, the Joe guy took off. Or disappeared. She didn't know where he went, she said he just vanished. She was pretty worried about him, but that's all I know. She never did say if he ever showed up."

"She seemed scared about it?"

Anderson dipped his chin, thinking, scratched his head, straightened his hair—a little relieved grooming, Lucas thought—and said, "Maybe scared. Sort of more *freaked out,* like when you find out something weird about someone. Like if somebody told you your best friend was a child molester, or something."

"Did you see a guy watching her last night? A big guy."

"Wasn't here last night. I was out with my *wife,*" Anderson said, leaning on the *wife.*

"Okay," Lucas said. "Tell me this: how much coke was she pushing out on the floor here?"

"*What?*"

"Cocaine," Del said.

Anderson looked at them like they were crazy. "She wasn't dealing cocaine. No way. I woulda known about that. You get a bunch of dealers and one of them is pushing, everybody knows. There was nothing like that about Jane."

"She use it?" Lucas asked.

Anderson's eyes flicked away. "Maybe . . . I never saw her use it." He unconsciously rubbed his nose with the back of his hand. "But she used to get a little cranked, and once or twice I thought she might've gone back to the ladies' can and done something."

"You didn't tell us," Hoffman said.

"I didn't *know*," Anderson said. "Hell, you even hint at something like that around here, and the next thing you know, somebody's looking for a job. And I kinda liked her."

"But not too much," Hoffman said.

"No. Jesus, Clark." Then his eyes narrowed, and he turned to Lucas. "Did that asshole Bud Larson put you on me?"

Lucas kept his face straight and shook his head. "Haven't heard any Larsons mentioned," he said. "Why?"

"Nothin'," Anderson said. To Hoffman: "He was the guy who complained that we cold-decked him. Last week? Mean-looking guy?"

Del looked at Lucas and shook his head.

WHEN THEY WERE finished with Anderson—still a worried man, despite Hoffman's assurances that he believed him—they went looking for other employees who remembered the big man. Les, the computer operator, brought down the first printout of the man's face: it was fuzzy, but would be recognizable in context.

Nobody else remembered talking to him.

By the time they finished talking with other employees, Les had saved a dozen shots of the man, and two stitched-together composites, to a CD that could be opened on any PC with the Imaging program, which he said was most of them.

"We still need the actual tapes," Lucas told him.

"We're pulling them; we'll hang on to them," he said.

THEY'D BEEN IN the casino for an hour and a half when Mitford called back. "We're running with Amex. They accepted a faxed subpoena and they're putting the list together now. They say they'll have it in half an hour. I'm having copies faxed to the sheriff's office up there, and another one down here. They say there might be a couple hundred names."

"We'll head downtown," Lucas said. "I've got a CD with some photos on it."

"We'd like to see some down here."

"I'll e-mail them to you. You gonna be there?"

"Until you guys go to bed," Mitford said. "Washington just had a press conference in Grand Forks and he says the law enforcement agencies must be complicit in this crime—I'm reading this—either actually or morally. Then . . . ah, blah blah blah. I think he's on his way up there to have a rally."

"Yeah? In Armstrong? Who's gonna rally?"

"I don't know. I'm just telling you what he says."

"I'll get back to you," Lucas said.

On the way out, they thanked Hoffman, agreed that Anderson probably hadn't been playing around on his sister, and made arrangements to have the videotapes picked up by a BCA crime scene man.

"SO WE GOT A face and a few hundred names," Del said. He looked at his watch. "You think we'll get him by midnight?"

"We're rolling," Lucas said. "And I'll tell you what: he left enough stuff on the bodies that when we identify him, we've got him. I'd bet that hair was his, I bet that blood on Warr's face was his."

"Could be Cash's."

"Not dripping down like that. It was fresh when she was hanging."

"God bless DNA," Del said.

ON THE WAY BACK to town, Lucas called Dickerson and filled him in. Then, "Did you get anything out of that motel room? Fingerprints, hair, anything?"

"We've got an ocean of fingerprints, but we've also got some places that appear to have been wiped," Dickerson said. "I wouldn't get your hopes up."

"Did you hear anything from St. Paul about tracking down the Cherokee?"

"If you go back a month, you can find maybe thirty Cherokee transactions in Minnesota. We've got the names on those, and we're working with North and South Dakota, Missouri and Iowa. I think Iowa's in, haven't gotten word from the others yet. I'm not sure South Dakota is computerized enough to get what we need that quick."

"Let's get what we can."

A BUNCH OF COPS were leaning on the wall outside the Law Enforcement Center, smoking, when Lucas and Del pulled into the parking lot. Lucas had just gotten out of the car when his cell phone rang.

"Yeah?"

"Lucas, it's Neil. I got the list on those cards down here, and it'll be up there in the next couple of minutes. I don't think you have to waste a lot of time checking it out."

"Why not?"

" 'Cause I think I know who it is."

"*What?*"

"There's a guy on the list named Hale Sorrell. You remember him?"

"Sorrell? He's . . . oh, *shit.*"

Del said, "What?"

Lucas ignored him, and asked Mitford, "Do you know him?"

"Yeah. I once tried to get him to give some money to our guy, on the basis that our guy was a rational conservative Democrat. Sorrell wasn't buying; he's a dyed-in-the-wool Republican. Seemed like an okay guy. Shitload of money from Medlux."

"Big guy, but not fat, big shoulders, dark hair, middle forties, glasses, this guy had a recent beard . . ."

"I don't know if he wears glasses, but he's at an age where he might. He's forty-six. He could grow the beard. Everything else is right on."

"I'm gonna e-mail you a photo. Maybe a couple of them," Lucas said. "Gimme an address."

"WHAT?" DEL ASKED, when Lucas rang off. "We got him?"

"Maybe," Lucas said. "Hale Sorrell? You remember?"

Del thought for a moment, then a light flared behind his eyes. "Oh, *shit.*"

"That's what I said. Let's get this list. Maybe they got a T1 or a DSL line out of here, we can send the photos from here."

THEY CROSSED THE parking lot at a half-trot. One of the deputies pushed away from the wall and said, "Chief Davenport . . . you remember me?"

Lucas slowed down. He *did* remember the deputy, more or less. He'd beaten up the guy's partner a few years before, in a different county, but not too far away. "Yeah, I do," Lucas said. "What happened, you take a transfer?"

"Moved over here when Sheriff Mason retired. My folks live over here. Anyway, have you seen the TV? The news?"

"No. Bad?"

"Pretty bad. That little girl, Letty, she was terrific, but man, they took some pictures of those people hanging in the trees, and they're everywhere. They were on the CBS and ABC and NBC evening news, and they're on CNN almost full-time. They got video of the bodies sort of swinging in the wind."

"Aw, Christ."

"Then that Washington guy gave a talk down in Grand Forks and they had this video picture behind him with the bodies hanging, and it looked like he was standing in there with them, and he was screaming about lynching."

"Maybe we better figure this out in a hurry."

"I'm pretty sure you can do it," the deputy said. "I been telling the guys about you."

"Not too much, I hope," Lucas said.

"Yeah, I told them that part," the deputy said. "That's the best part. Uh, whatever happened to the girl? The girl that come up with you?"

"Marcy Sherrill. She's a lieutenant in Minneapolis, now. She runs the Intelligence unit."

"Really . . . jeez." The deputy was impressed.

"Gotta go," Lucas said. "Nice talking to you again."

As he and Del went inside, he heard the deputy's voice, ". . . got a pair of knockers on her like muskmelons and . . ."

"You got groupies," Del said.

"Groupie with a good eye for knockers," Lucas said, amused. "Muskmelons . . . those are cantaloupes, right?"

THE SHERIFF'S DEPARTMENT had a fast line out. Anderson and a dozen other cops were in the building when Lucas and Del arrived, and came out to meet them. "Something happen?"

"We might have a name," Lucas said. "We need to send some pictures to St. Paul, right now."

Anderson's jaw dropped. He stood like that for a moment, looked at a deputy who'd trailed him in, and then said, "Well, Jiminy, who is it? You mean a name for the killer?"

"Possibly. Know in a minute, if I can get an Internet connection on a computer with a CD drive."

"I got one in my office."

Lucas followed him back to a big wood-paneled office with a blue high-pile carpet, seven-foot mahogany desk and a wall full of photographs. The sheriff with local politicians, his wife, his children, other sheriffs, cops. A computer sat on a side-table with an Aeron chair in front of it. Lucas dropped into the chair, brought up the computer, slipped the CD into the CD tray, and called up a Qwest connection. Ten seconds later, the best of the stitched photos was on its way to St. Paul; a minute later, another was on its way. Six deputies were crowded into the office now, and Lucas thought about the other BCA crew. He punched in Dickerson's number.

"Dickerson . . ."

"This is Davenport. Where are you?"

"Just outside of Armstrong. Thinking about heading home."

"We got a name. We're down at the sheriff's office. If the name is good, it ties together a lot of stuff. The money, the cell in the basement."

"What's the name?"

"Hale Sorrell."

Long pause. "Oh, *shit.*"

"HALE SORRELL?" Anderson demanded when Lucas rang off. "You mean the Rochester guy?"

Lucas nodded, leaned back in the chair, crossed his legs. "Daughter was kidnapped last month and never came back," he said. "We're not sure yet, but it's a possibility."

"You got pictures of him?" one of the deputies asked.

"We've got these pictures," Lucas said, tapping a photograph on the monitor screen. "They're not good, but they might be good enough. Once we get a solid maybe, and some DNA returns back from the medical examiner, then we'll know."

"That means his kid is out at . . . might have been at . . . her . . ."

"She might still be out there, somewhere, at the house," Lucas said.

"Did you know Sorrell was from up here, originally?" one of the deputies asked. "I mean, not right here, but down to Red Lake Falls? His father still lives down there, somewhere. He's in a nursing home or something."

Lucas said: "That's interesting. Maybe somebody around here set him up?"

"Could be, I guess."

Another deputy said, "Maybe he was fooling around with somebody. Red Lake Falls is pretty much known for its beautiful women."

"That's always a useful piece of information."

LUCAS'S CELL PHONE rang and the governor was there. "Lucas. Neil brought me up to date on this Hale Sorrell thing. I know him pretty well, I looked at the pictures."

"What do you think?"

"Neil and I agree. It sure looks like him. Not positive, but boy, it sure looks like him."

"We have a lot of DNA, sir. If we can get somebody to officially point the finger, we could get a warrant for some DNA samples and settle it."

"The devil's gonna be in the details. We don't want to be wrong. If we had to, is there any way you could hang this on the sheriff up there?"

"The sheriff's a pretty sharp guy, sir," Lucas said, looking up at Anderson, who appeared confused, and mouthed at Lucas, *Who is it?* Lucas went back to the phone. "I think we could probably work something out, if we had to—but before we do anything official, I'd like to get some good photos of Sorrell, put them in a photo spread and show them to a woman up here who actually talked to him. If she IDs him, we'd be on solid ground asking for the DNA."

"That sounds good. I'll get McCord on it right now. There've got to be some publicity shots around. He's served on committees and so forth. Can we transmit them up to you?"

"I think so. You'll have to talk to the local people, I don't know exactly what the printing facilities are here . . . hang on." He took the phone down and asked, "Do we have a photo printer of some kind?"

One of the deputies said, "Sure. We've got two or three different kinds. Standard stuff."

Back to the phone: "We're good, sir. When your guys find a photo, send it up here to the sheriff's department."

"We can do that," Henderson said. "Man, you moved fast—this is exactly what I wanted. That asshole Washington hasn't even gotten out of Grand Forks yet. He's supposedly going up to the hanging tree to make a speech."

"Sir, we can't let that happen. It's really a bleak place—it looks like it was invented for a hanging. The image'll be so strong that nothing else will make any difference, nothing we say. Maybe we could keep him out of there on the grounds that it's a crime scene."

"Can we blame that on the sheriff, too?"

"I think it could be worked out, sir."

"Is he right there, listening?"

"Yes, sir."

"Let me talk to him. Say something that would lead to me talking to him."

Lucas nodded. "I think you should talk to Sheriff Anderson about that, sir."

"Good. Give him the phone."

Lucas passed the phone to Anderson, saying, "The governor. He needs to speak with you."

Anderson took the phone. "Uh, Governor Henderson . . ."

As Anderson talked, Lucas said to the group of deputies, "Is there somebody here who usually handles photo spreads? We'll need a half-dozen pictures of white men with dark hair, probably in business suits, looking charming. Like a political picture." He looked around at the pictures on the walls. "Like these. Like that one." He pointed a finger at a smiling head.

One of the deputies said, "We got that."

The rest of it took an hour and a half. Lucas was in a semi-frenzy, driven by the momentum of the day, and Dickerson arrived, running hot with lights and siren, wanting to be there if it all cracked open. Forty minutes after Lucas talked to the governor, the sheriff's ID division took the transmission of two recent photos of Hale Sorrell, one a formal portrait, the other taken at a press conference after the disappearance of his daughter.

A deputy put together two different photo spreads: one of dark-haired white men in informal situations, another of dark-haired white men in formal poses. Then he retransmitted all the dummy photos to himself, so they'd be printed on the same paper and have the same general look.

Hoffman was still on the job at the casino. Small Bear was on the floor, he said, pushing her change cart.

"Keep her there," Lucas said. "We're on the way."

LUCAS, DEL, AND DICKERSON went with Anderson in a sheriff's truck, a comfortable GMC Yukon XL with a big heater. At the casino, Hoffman met them at the door. "Small Bear's upstairs," he said. "How're we doing?"

"Gonna find out," Lucas said.

Small Bear was sitting at a table in a conference room, her hands folded in front of her, looking a little frightened. Lucas explained quickly: "We have two sets of photos. We're gonna show you one set, then ask if you see the man who was here last night, and then we'll show you the other set. Okay?"

She nodded. Lucas spread the informal photos in front of her. She looked at them, slowly, slowly, pushing one after another away from her, until finally she was left only with Sorrell's. "I think this might be him. Not a very good picture."

"Okay." Lucas scooped up the deck of photos, put them back in the brown envelope they came in, opened a second envelope, and took out the formal shots. This time, Small Bear didn't hesitate.

"I'm pretty sure this is him," she said, tapping the photograph of Sorrell.

They all stood in silence, nobody moving, nothing audible but some breathing, and then Anderson groaned, "Jiminy," and Lucas turned and looked at Del.

Del nodded. "Got him."

8

MARGERY SINGLETON LOOKED like a green heron—a sharp-billed stalking bird with a mouth like a rip in a piece of rawhide, an arrowhead nose, rattlesnake eyes; her eyebrows plucked naked and re-drawn with a green pencil. She worked the first shift at Elysian Manor, pushing patients to and fro, cleaning up after them, rolling pills when a registered nurse wasn't available. Her best friend, Flo Anderson, *was* a reg-istered nurse, having put in her two years at Fargo, and they'd worked out a system where, if somebody needed a shot or to get blood taken, Margery could do it and Flo could sign. The patients, most of whom had Alzheimer's, didn't know one way or the other.

Margery heard about the hanging of Warr and Cash from a breath-less young nurse's aide who came back from lunch bright eyed with a tale she'd heard from a sheriff's deputy at the minimart.

"They're *hanging* down there, naked as jaybirds, all purple and frozen. The woman's tongue was sticking out like this:" She tilted her head, hung her tongue out of the side of her mouth and crossed her eyes. Straightening, she added in a lower voice, "They said that the black guy had a penis that was about ten inches long."

"That's bullshit," Margery said, her rattlesnake eyes fixing the young woman. "I seen two thousand dicks since I been in this place and there ain't been one of them more than seven."

"How many black men have been in here?" the nurse asked, an eyebrow going up. Had the old bat there.

"Hanged in a tree?"

"That's what they say. Do you think Loren might know more about it?"

"I'll find out," Margery said. She looked at her watch. She had another two hours before she could get off.

A supervisor named Burt stuck his head into the station where they were talking. "Old man Barrows got shit all over the couch. Clean it up, okay?"

Burt continued down the hall and Margery muttered, "Clean it up yourself, asshole." But she went to get her spray bottle and sponge, and the nurse's aide said, as she left, "If you hear anything from Loren, let me know. I mean, jeez."

LOREN SINGLETON FINALLY rolled out of bed at two o'clock. He'd been unable to sleep much, dozing off only to see, in his dreams, Deon and Jane hanging from a tree. He stretched, scratched, went into the bathroom. As he shaved, looking in the mirror, he started thinking about his latest Cadillac restoration. The car was at Calb's, and that could be inconvenient. The more he shaved, the more inconvenient it seemed. He finished shaving, showered, brushed his teeth, got dressed, and called Gene Calb.

Calb came on the phone and said, "Katina said you'd heard."

"Woke me up on the clock radio this morning," Singleton said. "I thought it might be a good idea to move the Caddy outa there, you know, until things quiet down."

Calb nodded. "Yes. Right away. Where do you want it?"

"My garage. You got somebody who could drive it down for me? I'll drive them back."

"I'll get Sherm, he isn't doing anything. So—what do you think?"

Singleton shook his head. "I don't know. I wonder if it has anything to do with Joe? You think they were fighting? I mean, Deon never said anything."

"I'm completely confused," Calb said. "If you told me shit was Shinola, I'd just nod my head and agree."

"Same with me. When can you move the car?"

"Right now. We're closing everything down, moving everything out. Sherm'll be there in fifteen minutes."

"I'll be outside waiting."

"Listen, Loren—we're really counting on you. You gotta keep an eye out. This is why you got the job."

"I understand. You can count on me."

THE CAR SHUFFLE took forty minutes. When it was done, Singleton went downtown, probed for information, got small pieces, and one essential fact: nobody knew anything. He called Calb, told him that. At three-thirty, he was back home. As he always did, when he first got home, he checked his money. He kept it in the basement, inside the holes in a row of concrete blocks. Maybe, he thought, he ought to move it. Get a bank box far away, maybe in Minot, or somewhere. If anybody looked at him seriously, the BCA people, they'd find the money and then the cat would be out of the bag.

The money. He didn't know what to do with it. He'd bought some expensive boots, another old Caddy, some good breather gear for painting his cars.

When he got his first lump-sum payment from Calb, he'd made the mistake of showing it to his mom. She'd claimed it, most of it, and had come back every week since, demanding more. Then he'd introduced her to Jane, and they'd gotten their heads together, and when the big money came in, she'd taken most of *that*.

Singleton had stood up to her—a little bit, anyway—and claimed fifty thousand. Fifty thousand would almost get him a small shop some-where. A Morton building, maybe, with space to work on a couple of Caddys at once, and maybe even space to rig up a paint booth.

Big dreams . . .

W H A M !

The back door banged open. Only one person entered like that, without warning. Singleton had a few hundred dollars in his hand, and he hastily shoved it into his pocket, pulled the string on the overhead light, and headed up the stairs.

Margery was waiting in the kitchen. She was a small, thin, wrinkled woman; a woman who was to other women what a raisin was to a grape. Her eyes were pale blue, and her hair, once blond, looked gray at first glance, but was actually almost colorless, translucent, like ice on a window. Her lips were thin, her chin was pointed; Katina called her the Witch.

"What the hell have you been doing?" she demanded. "Why'n the hell didn't you call me about Deon and Jane?" She turned her nose up, sniffed, stepped close to him. "You've had that whore in here, haven't you? I can smell her juice."

"Not a whore, Mom . . ."

She slapped him, hard, a full-handed slap. "She's a whore if I say she's a whore," she shouted. "She's a *whore.*"

Singleton stepped away from her, a hand to his face, furiously angry.

His mom had a thin neck, and sometimes he thought about snapping it. Take that goddamn little cornstalk neck and snap it off. He bared his teeth at her, ground them, felt his heart pumping.

Margery hadn't forgotten about the bathtub. She stepped farther away, took the tone down. "Whoever did this, they might be coming for us," she said. "That fuckin' nigger would sell us for a quarter, and you know it."

"Mom, what can I do?" He heard the plaintive whine in his voice. He didn't hate the whine, only because it had always been there when he was dealing with Mom and he didn't recognize it.

"You coulda called me," she shouted. "But you were up here with your whore when you coulda been callin' me. I gotta think about this." She looked around, eyes narrowing. "What're you doing here, anyway? You oughta be downtown, seeing what you can see."

"I was already down there for a while, and I didn't hear hardly anything. The cops found Deon's money. It was stuffed away in his house, somewhere. They got it all."

"Goddamnit," Margery said. "They got it all? Goddamnit."

"That's what I heard. There're state cops in town, and they're supposed to be really good. I think we better lie low."

"Nothing they can connect to us."

"Not unless . . . I mean, what if they've got Joe?"

"Joe's dead," Margery said. "We all agree."

"But what if he's not?"

"Then we are," she said. She pointed a trembling finger at him. "You get back down there, you find out what's going on. And you call me. Dumb shit."

They both turned to the sound of a car in the driveway. Singleton looked. "Katina," he said.

"I'm getting out of here," Margery said. "I'm not talking to that whore."

Margery and Katina met at the door, and Margery went on by with a sideways glance and not a single word. Katina, on the other hand, smiled and said, "Hi, Mom."

When she was inside, with the door closed, she asked, "What'd the Witch want?"

"Borrow money," Singleton said. That was always good for an excuse, because his mother genuinely did love money.

Katina bustled around, getting some coffee together. "What's the word on Deon and Jane?" she asked.

"Nobody knows what happened, but the BCA guys found a big pile of money and a bunch of dope up in Deon's bedroom," Singleton said. "They're gonna be all over the dope angle."

"Sheriff Anderson's out? Completely out?"

Singleton dipped his head. "He's out. He's smart enough to know that he was over his head—and if he wasn't smart enough, half the county commission went over to his office to tell him. Harvey Benschneider stood right over him while he made the call to St. Paul."

"Ah, boy," Katina said. She pulled off her gloves, parka, and ski hat, shook her hair out. "I can't believe they're dead. Gene's going crazy. You talk to him?"

"Yeah. He thinks maybe Jane was dealing cocaine at the casino," Singleton said. "Could they be that stupid?"

"Deon was a stupid man, and Jane wasn't much smarter," Katina said. She took cups out of a dish rack in the sink. "My question is, what do *we* tell the police?"

"*You* don't tell them *anything*," Singleton said. "Let Gene do the talking. No reason for any of us to get involved. Deon worked for Gene, not for us. If Gene's smart, he'll point the state cops at the casino. There's so much shit going on up there, they could investigate the place for the rest of their lives and not get to the bottom of it."

"Only one problem with that idea," Katina said.

"What?"

"Joe. Where's Joe? Jane told me that all of his stuff was still in the house. If Joe's dead, then it wasn't the casino."

"Could be. Could be if it's coke they were dealing. Can't tell with dopers. The other thing is—what if Joe came back and did this? What if he was looking for that money?"

"Hmm." They sat silently for a moment as Katina struggled with all the conflicting possibilities. Finally, she looked up at him and said, "Whatever happened to all three, we've really got to worry about our own positions."

"That's right. We *all* ought to stay away. If the state guys find one string, and pull it hard enough, the whole sweater's gonna unravel."

They talked for a while over their coffee, a middle-aged couple who got along. Singleton wasn't like the men she'd met in the Cities, Katina thought. He had some steel in him, some flint. Some Ugly.

She liked it—a man who'd stand up.

She just didn't know.

THE PARTY at the West house started when two newspaper reporters, accompanied by two photographers, showed up at the front door and asked for interviews. Letty was pleased to do it, though Martha was a bit embarrassed by the mess the house was in. That didn't seem to bother the photographers, who got a couple of shots of Letty sitting in her mother's old rocker. Then the first TV truck showed up. The newspaper people were okay, but compared to the TV people, they were mongrels at a dog show. The TV people were *stars*—Letty'd even seen some of them on her own TV.

The TV people agreed on one set of lights, and set them up around the living room, while Martha scurried around moving all of her best furniture into place, moving the worst of it into the kitchen. A guy came in with a couple of sacks of black-corn chips, cheese dip, and Coke, and then somebody else brought in a twelve-pack of Bud Light.

They asked Letty to get some traps, and she did, and they put them on the floor by her feet, and some of the cameramen crawled in close to get a shot of the traps, using the lights on top of their cameras. Somebody else challenged the cameramen to snap their fingers in the traps, and being cameramen, they did, although none of the on-air talent would do it. Then somebody else asked Martha about her singing career, and she got out her guitar and sang an old Pete Seeger song called "Where Have All the Flowers Gone," and then the main lights came up, and were adjusted, and the first interviewer, a blonde with a foxy face and feathery crimson scarf, said, "Letty, tell me about yesterday."

"I was up in my bedroom . . ." she began. Letty told them about the traps and the 'rats and the .22 and the bodies hanging in the dark. Then she told a dark-haired Italian-looking guy from Fox, and did it again for CNN, and as many times as they wanted, she stayed on top of it, fresh.

The TV liked her: the kid had this face, a face that looked like it ought to have a smear of dirt on it, though it had been scrubbed clean—a wild face with just a hint of feral, preteen sexuality.

They made her demonstrate the traps, her gun, explain the machete. She cradled the rifle in the notch of her left arm as she talked, and the reporters fluttered around her like sparrows over a spilled patch of Quaker oats. They could *smell* the connection between the kid and the tube . . .

"You're gonna be a star, honey," the foxy blonde said. She was a beautiful, smart woman whose socks cost more than Letty's wardrobe, and Letty believed her.

THE BCA GUY, DICKERSON, finally chased the TV reporters away. Several asked if they could come back the next morning. Martha said, "Of course." And Martha, as animated as Letty had ever seen her, began to plan for the next day.

"I look like a troll," she said, looking in the kitchen mirror. The house, suddenly silent, seemed cold and lonely and isolated from the world. "I've got to get a different coat, and my hair—ah, baby, I wonder if I can get into Harriet's. What time is it?"

While her mother called Harriet's Mane Line, Letty went up the stairs and threw herself on her bed and closed her eyes. Closing her eyes was almost as good as television.

When she'd been on TV, she'd felt *normal*. She was surprised by that. She could feel what the TV people wanted, and reflected it back at them: chin up, a little grim, a little tight, the .22 in the crook of her arm. But a smile now and then, too.

She felt she could *move* them. She'd grown up with TV, and knew how it worked.

Letty got up and closed the door. On the back of the door, she'd mounted a mirror that she'd found at the Goodwill store. She looked pretty tough, she thought, trying to turn so she could catch her own profile. She was weather-smudged from the wind and the ice, but she couldn't help that. But maybe . . .

She lay down again and closed her eyes. Maybe some lipstick. Just a little teeny hint of lipstick. She should definitely clean up her shoes. She'd seen a girl in a John Wayne movie, a spunky kid just a little older than herself, maybe, and that was the *look* she wanted. That was the *attitude*.

Martha West ran up the stairs. "Dick's here, he's gonna take me," she said. Dick was her on-and-off boyfriend; he'd heard about the press conference. "Are you okay? Harriet's gonna give me a quick wash and set, and then Dick and me might go out after. You know, just for a while."

"I'll be okay. I gotta get some traps out, for when the reporters come back tomorrow. And maybe clean up my room—one lady said they might want to look out my window, if they decide to do a reenactment."

"Okay. Maybe catch the kitchen, too, okay? And just run the vacuum around the living room. Spray some of the lemon Pledge around, okay?"

"Okay. Don't be too late. We gotta get up early tomorrow," Letty said.

"We're just gonna go out for a few minutes, see what people are saying."

Martha ran back down the stairs, and Letty sat on the bed and pulled on her knee-high gum boots and got her coat and gloves: going to set some traps. Her mom yelled back up, "Don't miss the six o'clock news. They said maybe five o'clock and for sure at six."

"Okay."

This was like paradise.

Ten minutes later, visions of MTV still dancing in her head, she was out the door with her trap sack. She carried the .22, though she didn't need it, and the machete in the green jungle sheath, which she did need. But who knew? Maybe the TV would come back, and the TV people liked the gun. She looked over her shoulder, and she trudged across the road and then into the frozen marsh on the north side, wishing them back.

She spent an hour with the traps, the sun dropping out of sight as she worked. Back at the house, in the light of the single bulb in her room, she looked at herself in the mirror, again, and thought about the men who'd come in from St. Paul, Davenport and Del, and how they carried an air of the city with them. She'd told Davenport she might like to be a surgeon, or a hairdresser, or even a cop. Maybe she could do those jobs, but she no longer thought that was what she wanted.

She liked the lights. She was going to be a reporter. A star.

She went downstairs, got one of the two remaining Cokes, and saw the keys to the Jeep on the kitchen table. She had a hundred and twenty-seven dollars hidden in an old metal Thermos jug under her bed. Maybe just a piece of pie down at Wolf's. After a day like this, she deserved it.

THE HOLY ROLLER CHURCH in Broderick had been converted into a rough-and-ready dormitory. Wooden screens divided the former prayer space into nine rooms, to provide privacy. Each cubicle contained a folding bed, a bureau, a night table, a fire extinguisher, and a curtain across the doorway, in the long tradition of the flophouse.

A Christian electrician from Bemidji had laid some cable between the rooms, so each room had one electric outlet to power a lamp. Personal radios and televisions were forbidden, not for religious reasons but because the noise might annoy others. Most of the women had Walkman radios or CD players, for personal use, and most had small bookcases jammed with mystery novels and spiritual how-to's.

The women who lived at the church usually ate communally, cooking out of the church kitchen, although there was no rule about that. A side room had a pile of bean-bag chairs, a television connected to a satellite dish, a DVD player and sixty or seventy slowly accumulated chick flicks. A balcony in the back, once an organ loft, had been set aside as a quiet place, for someone who needed a moment's peace and separation.

Two of the women at the church were nuns. None, or maybe just one—nobody was certain—was a lesbian. Absolutely none of them cared what the people in town said.

Ruth Lewis was the leader. She worked out schedules and tactics with Calb, for the dope operation, and coordinated through Catholic Charities and Lutheran Social Services for the food and clothing distribution work. The food and clothing distribution might have helped a few people, but Minnesota was a socialist state, and much of that was done more efficiently by the local state agencies. The women didn't care about that, either; a decent cover was worth maintaining.

After briefing the other women on the murders of Jane Warr and Deon Cash, Ruth listened to worries and arguments for an hour, but most of them were self-reliant, not given to panic. After an hour of talk, they agreed there was nothing to do but wait—to work the drug transport as well as they could, to work the rural food program, and to keep their heads down.

Afterward, Katina Lewis took her sister aside and said, "Loren will keep us posted about the police. There's a good chance that if something happens . . . if they find out about the drug runs, we'll have some warning before they do anything."

"If they know about you guys, about your relationship, we might pull Loren down with us," Ruth said. She smiled her cool smile. She didn't like Loren Singleton, and Katina knew it.

"He's willing to take the chance," Katina said. "The only problem might be, he's always been under his mother's thumb. If she knew what was happening out here, she'd sell us to the highest bidder. The old witch."

"Warn him."

"I am, sorta. What I'm really doing is . . ." She smiled; her older sister was always so solemn that she made Katina giggle.

"What?" Ruth asked solemnly.

"We're sorta changing thumbs," Katina said. "The old witch's for mine."

LATER, RUTH WALKED UP the highway in the afternoon darkness to get a salty fried-egg-and-onion sandwich at Wolf's Cafe. Ruth always felt guilty about the egg sandwiches—they were greasy, probably put an extra millimeter of cholesterol in her veins every time she ate one, the salt probably pushed her blood pressure, and the raw onion gave her bad breath that lasted for hours. On the other hand, she had no heart problems, her blood pressure was perfect, and the sandwiches tasted wonderful, a break from the gloom of winter and the glum healthy food of the communal kitchen.

The cafe had a double door, and always smelled of grease, and was fifteen degrees too warm, and Sandy Wolf called out, "Hey, baby Ruth."

"Hi." Ruth nodded shyly. She wasn't a hail-fellow, like Wolf, but she enjoyed the other woman's heartiness. Another woman sat halfway down the counter . . . not a woman, though, Ruth thought, but a girl, eating a piece of pie. Letty West.

"Letty?" Ruth stepped down the bar, smiling. She'd liked the girl the first time they met, and had talked to her a dozen times since. "How are you?"

Letty returned the smile, waved her fork. "I'm fine. Had a press conference this afternoon."

"Oh, I heard." Ruth went solemn, looked for the right words. "Heard that you found the . . . people."

"We was just talking about it," Wolf said. "Letty says they was frozen like Popsicles."

"They put them in the black bags to carry them out, and they were in there like a sackful of boards," Letty said.

"Do the police have any ideas who did it?" Ruth asked.

Letty shook her head. "Nah. They know a heck of a lot less than I do. They don't know anything about Broderick—I been filling them in. There's these guys, Lucas and Del, I'm helping them out. We ate up at the Bird this afternoon."

"What . . . did you actually see? At the murder scene?"

Sandy Wolf leaned on the counter and Ruth plopped on the stool next to the girl, and Letty went through the whole story, as she'd told it to the television cameras that afternoon. When she finished the story about finding the bodies, she added that the cameras were coming back the next day for a feature story. "They're gonna come along and run my traps with me. I had to go out this afternoon and put some traps in, just so I'll have some 'rats for the feature story tomorrow."

"Are they paying you?" Wolf asked.

"Maybe," Letty said. She wasn't sure—she hadn't thought of that angle.

"They oughta," Wolf said. "I mean, you got a product to sell. You could go on *Oprah*."

"You think?" Letty liked *Oprah*.

"You can't tell where this kind of thing will lead. You could be in Hollywood. Stranger things have happened," Wolf said.

"I don't know about Hollywood," Ruth said. She felt a tickle of concern. "Letty, do you have anybody staying with you out there, with you and your mom? I mean, a policeman?"

"No . . . You think we should?"

"Well." She nibbled at a lip.

"Okay. Now I'm scared," Letty said. She'd seen all the cop dramas. The killers always came back. "All I got is that piece-of-shit .22."

"The guy isn't coming back," Wolf said disdainfully. She'd been cleaning up the grill and she flapped her cleaning rag at Letty. "The guy who did this is a million miles from here. He's probably on Miami Beach by now."

"I hope," Ruth said. To Wolf: "Egg sandwich with raw onions?"

"Fried hard? Coming up," Wolf said. She asked Letty, "Another piece of pie? Short piece?"

"If you're buying," Letty said. She grinned at Ruth. "Got a free piece of pie for the story?"

"You'll get a free ride to jail if the state patrol sees that truck parked out back," Wolf grunted. To Ruth: "She's driving her mom's truck again. Little goddamn juvenile delinquent."

"Little goddamn juvenile delinquent who's gonna be on *Oprah*," Letty said. She looked at the wall clock. "Four-thirty. I gotta be out of here in ten minutes. They're telling me that we'll be on at five."

"Movie star," Wolf cackled, sliding a half-slice of cherry pie down the countertop.

WHEN RUTH GOT BACK to the church, she told Katina about Letty, smiling as she recounted the girl's enthusiasm. Katina wasn't so amused. "That kid's all over the place. If she's talking to the police, I hope she doesn't talk about us. Or about Gene's place."

"Not really much for her to know," Ruth said. "Bunch of cars getting fixed."

"I suppose. Just the way that she's always hanging around. I mean, Ruth—we're criminals. We should act like criminals, at least part of the time."

"She's having a good time. I don't think she's a danger to us," Ruth said. "She's a kid."

"If you say so," Katina said, letting her skepticism show.

"Besides—we've talked about this—sooner or later, one of us is going to get caught crossing the border. Or somebody will tell some ambitious little creep prosecutor what we're doing, and they'll come get all of us. We could go to jail, Katina. It's a fact of life."

Katina shook her head. "I never believed that. If we're careful. If we're really, really psychopathically careful, I don't think we will."

THE DISCUSSION HAD NOT quite been an argument, and nothing was resolved. Later on, Katina crossed the highway when she saw Singleton pull into Calb's parking lot. Singleton had a remote that worked the overhead door, and the door went up, and he pulled inside—to get the car out of sight, Katina supposed. There were still two cop cars and a state van at Cash's house, though it was so cold, all the cops had gone inside the house. Singleton saw Katina coming across the highway and held the door up for her, dropping it when she was inside.

"Gene's in the back," Singleton said.

Calb was in his cubbyhole, staring at an aging Dell computer. He looked up and said, "Loren," when Singleton came in, leaned back to look around him and said, "Hey, Katina."

"Talk to the state guys yet?" Singleton asked.

"Two sets of them. This afternoon. One set was okay and they were here for an hour, taking notes. The other set was just two guys who stood around with their hands in their pockets. Like the fuckin' gestapo."

"Davenport and Capslock," Singleton said. "Supposed to be heavy hitters. What'd you tell them?"

"The truth," Calb said. "I talked to Shawn down in Kansas City before they came in, told him what I was going to do, which was, tell the truth. That I knew Shawn in the Army and knew he had this troubled cousin and when the cousin got out of jail, I hired him as a favor. Then I told them I was about to fire him because he was a screw-up, and I suspected he used the drugs, but not that he sold them. I told them I thought the trouble might be coming from Jane's casino job . . ."

"Good," Singleton said. "I was going to suggest that. We've gotta reinforce it now that you got them thinking about it."

Katina pulled at her lip. "I'm worried about Letty West. She's spending a lot of time with the police, and she hangs around here."

Calb shook his head. "Nothing to worry about. She comes in to get warm, and I don't let her go in the shop because I don't want her getting hurt, all the shit laying around here. I don't believe she ever talked to Deon."

THEY CHATTED FOR a few more minutes, then, as they left, Singleton deflected a hint from Katina—she could have used some comforting in these troubled times—and headed back to Armstrong. He stopped at Peske's market to pick up a six-pack of caffeinated Coke, and ran into Roger Elroy, who was also looking into the cooler at the back of the store. "Anything happening?"

"They got him," Elroy said quietly.

"They *got* him?"

Elroy was young and eager and full of news. "They know who it is—those two BCA guys figured it out up at the casino," Elroy said. Singleton thought, *the casino,* and a wave of relief washed through him, and he leaned into the cooler for a six-pack. "It was that guy whose kid was kidnapped, Hale Sorrell, that guy from Rochester. Remember, last month?"

Singleton almost gave it away then. Might have, if Elroy had seen his face, but his face was in the cooler, as he reached deep inside. He stopped, got a grip both on himself and the six-pack, backed out, and said, "Where'd they come up with that?"

Elroy told him, briefly, then shook his head. "Anderson talked to the governor. They think the Sorrell girl's body might be out there at Deon Cash's place. You knew those guys, right?"

"Knew who they were," Singleton said. "Talked to Cash a couple of times . . . Jeez. So have they grabbed Sorrell yet?"

"Not until tomorrow. They're trying to run some stuff down—they've got a line on the car he used, they're running some pictures by a witness. They don't want to tip him off."

"Jesus."

"These BCA guys, they're heavy duty," Elroy said. "I met Davenport a couple of years ago, when he was on another job. I'm telling you, he's the smartest cop in the state. He's the guy who set up that ambush on that assassin woman down in Minneapolis. If he thinks it's Sorrell, then it is."

"Maybe not so smart. Maybe just lucky."

"You haven't met him," Elroy said. "He is something else. When I met him, he was up here with this policewoman, fuckin' her, she had a set of knockers . . ."

SINGLETON HAD A LOT to think about, and he prowled down the streets of Armstrong, doing just that. Thought about Letty West. Thought about her for five minutes, tried to remember exactly where he'd seen her around the farmhouse. He knew he'd seen her out around the dump, but not when . . .

He sat on a street corner for a while, tapping a Marlboro into his hand, lit it with an ice-cold Zippo. Thought about Hale Sorrell. Finally, disturbed and a bit angry at the unfairness of it, he drove over to Logan's Fancy Meats, used the phone on the outside wall, dialing a number from memory.

A man answered, "Hello?"

He hung up, walked back to his car. Unraveling sweaters. He lit another Marlboro, thought about it.

SINGLETON DIDN'T THINK of himself as a killer, because he'd never actually killed anyone—not that the law cared. The law would say he was a killer, because he was there when the girls were killed. It was all really gentle: Mom had gone into the room with them, and told them that they were being taken back home, but that they weren't allowed to see it. So she'd give them a shot, and when they woke up, they'd be back with their mom and dad.

They never woke up, of course. Singleton had carried them out in a black plastic garbage bag, still warm, out through the night, the burial spade rattling in the back of the truck. They'd gone quickly, quietly, mercifully. They never felt a thing.

He'd like to go like that. In a way, they'd been lucky.

NOW THEY HAD the Sorrell problem. It wasn't Joe; it was Sorrell. And there was only one way, as far as he could see, that Sorrell could possibly have found out about Deon and Jane, and that was through Joe. Sorrell had gotten him.

Had Joe given up his name as well? Or Mom's? Had Deon or Jane given them up?

Damn. Like a sweater unraveling. He thought about it for a few more minutes, and then called Mom.

9

DEL HAD GOTTEN THEM rooms in a Motel 6, but after Small Bear identified Sorrell with the photos, they decided to head back to the Cities. The helicopter had already gone, so they'd be driving.

"We have to put together an approach," Lucas told Dickerson, as they rode back to Armstrong in Anderson's truck. "You gotta stay right on top of the DNA samples. The lab'll want to take three or four days, but you can get them in two days if you push. Also: we need that formal statement from Small Bear. Get her while she's hot."

"You gonna bust him?"

"I'll talk to the governor," Lucas said. "I'd rather have the DNA done first, so we know that what we've got is good. But there's some politics in this, so—I dunno. If the DNA's good, we'll have him cold, and what I'd like to do is talk to him without any lawyers around. Find out what the hell happened. How did he pin them down? What was the sequence? Were there more people involved?"

Dickerson nodded. "All right. He was in the Army, so he'll have prints on file. I'll get them and run them against everything we're taking out of his hotel room, so we'll have that, too. I'll get *all* the tapes from Moose Bay, see if we can get him following her out of the casino . . ."

"Need statements from everybody . . ."

"I wish you'd stay around for when Washington gets up here," Anderson said to Lucas. Anderson was behind the wheel. "I don't know exactly what to do with him."

"Don't talk to the guy," Lucas said. "Be too busy solving the crime. This guy makes a living with confrontation, and you *cannot win.* Have somebody designated to handle your information and to deal with him— a woman would be best, somebody a little older and motherly, so if he really ripped on her, he'd seem like an asshole. But you oughta stay away."

"I gotta say something," Anderson protested. "It's my town."

"Man, I'm telling you, if you go out there and meet him, he's gonna fuck you," Lucas said. "If you want to be on TV, that's okay. Have somebody keep an eye on Washington, and talk to the TV people while he's taking a nap, or eating. Be really polite about him—welcome him to the community—but *do not* talk to him."

Anderson looked at Dickerson. "What do you think?"

"Lucas is right. If you talk to him with a TV camera around, he'll hand you your ass. If you gotta talk to him, do it privately, in your office. Don't let the cameras in."

"If you can hold him off until the day after tomorrow, then the whole thing may be moot," Lucas said. "We'll jump on Sorrell, and leak the story like crazy. Washington probably won't want to be identified as defending people who kidnapped and murdered a little girl."

"All right, all right," Anderson said. He muttered something under his breath, then said, "You guys are treating me like the village idiot."

After a moment of silence, Lucas asked, "Think you could do pretty good surgery?"

"What?" Anderson said.

"Surgery. You think you could do a heart bypass tomorrow if you had to?"

Now Anderson was pissed. "Is this leading to something?"

"Yeah. This: Washington is to confrontation and publicity what a heart surgeon is to bypass surgery. You shouldn't be embarrassed if you're not as good at it as he is. None of us are. It's his specialty. He's not interested in getting to know you, or understanding the problem, or solving the crime. He's here to fuck somebody and raise some money for himself. If you give him a target, he'll fuck you. Nothing personal— it's just his job."

They rode in silence for a while, then Dickerson said, "I'm seeing stars, I think."

"Supposed to clear off just long enough to get really cold, then to-morrow, we got more clouds coming," Anderson said.

DEL CALLED THE MOTEL 6 from the Law Enforcement Center and canceled their rooms, and Lucas talked to the car dealer, Holme, about taking the Oldsmobile south to the Cities. "It's a good run-ner," Holme said. "No problem about that. But how you gettin' it back?"

"I'll find somebody to bring it back, or bring it back myself," Lucas said. "Give me a week." He thought about the possibility of a body out at the Cash house: he'd be back.

And he called Mitford, who was still in his office. "We got a solid ID," Lucas said. "I'm coming back tonight, we ought to arrive sometime after two in the morning, so I can be in early tomorrow. If you talk to the governor tonight, our next question is: When do we take him?"

He explained about the DNA processing time. "The thing is, if we really nail him down right at the start, before he has a chance to get into some long strategy sessions with his lawyers . . . maybe we can find out what happened. At least what happened with the kidnapping."

"A two-fer," Mitford said. "Clean up the kidnappings and the lynchings—the hanging. I'll talk with the governor tonight. You'll be on your cell phone?"

"Yeah, but there are some big holes in the cell phone net. You might not be able to get me for a couple hours, unless I'm going through a town. Once I get on I-94 going south, we could probably hook up."

"If I don't get you, we meet tomorrow for sure. How about seven o'clock?"

"You got a life, Neil?"

"What?"

ON THE WAY OUT of the Law Enforcement Center, Lucas said good-bye to Anderson and Dickerson, the sheriff shaking hands with him this time. Lucas had the feeling that he wouldn't stay away from Washington, but that was Anderson's problem. "Guys, we kicked some ass today," Lucas said.

They consolidated their bags in the Olds, and Lucas took the wheel. As they passed the front of the courthouse, they saw the glow of TV lights on the front steps.

"Getting set up for Washington," Del said.

"Like a flame for a moth," Lucas said. "I'll bet you ten bucks that Anderson winds up out there."

"No bet."

THE TWIN CITIES were southeast from Armstrong, but the fastest way home was on a state highway that went directly west for almost forty miles, where they would hook up with the north-south I-29 in North Dakota. They'd take I-29 to Fargo, where they'd catch I-94 east into the Cities. It was a long way around, but both Anderson and Dickerson said it was the quickest way, by at least an hour.

On the way out of town, they called home to tell their wives that they were on the way. The housekeeper told Lucas that Weather was at the supermarket on Ford Parkway, but she'd pass the message on. Lucas put the speedometer on ninety and they headed through the moonless dark toward the North Dakota border.

"Ought to bring the Porsche up here, let her out," Lucas said. "Dead straight, not another car in sight, and we know where all the cops are."

" 'Course, we could hit a cow," Del said.

They rode along for a few minutes, then Lucas said, "You know, I didn't see any cows."

"Come to think of it, neither did I."

Another minute, and Lucas said, "They must've named Moose Bay after something. Maybe we'll hit a moose."

Del didn't answer. Lucas glanced over at him, found him staring out the window.

"What?"

"My God. Look at the lights. Northern lights."

Lucas couldn't see them from the south side of the car, so he stopped, and they both got out and stood next to the idling Olds. The stars were so close that they looked like headlights on a city highway, but the real show was to the north, where a rippling curtain of pale yellow and even paler violet hung from the vault of the sky. The curtain moved, swayed, brightened and then faded, and then exploded in another sector. They stood on the highway watching, until the cold began to seep into their shoulders, and then they got back in the Olds and took off.

Del still watched from his window, and finally he sighed and said, "Too much light to see them in the Cities. I mean, you can *see* them, but not like this."

"I can see them pretty good from my cabin," Lucas said.

"So goddamn bright that you don't need your headlights," Del said.

"Yeah?" Lucas reached out and turned off the headlights. They were immediately hurtling through a darkness so intense that it should have had Elvis paintings on it.

"Turn the fuckin' lights back on," Del said after a few seconds. "There might be a curve somewhere."

"No curves," Lucas said. "I could tie the wheel down, crawl in the back seat and go to sleep." But he turned the lights on, and they crossed the Red River into North Dakota thirty-three minutes after blowing out of Armstrong.

L U C A S   D R O V E   T H E   first two hours, then Del took two, and Lucas took them into the Cities six hours after leaving the Law Enforcement Center. He dropped Del at his house, then drove through the quiet streets to Mississippi River Boulevard and the Big New House. He left the Olds in the driveway, got his bag from the trunk, fumbled his house keys out of his pocket, and trudged inside.

Weather woke when he tiptoed into the bedroom by the light from the hallway. "That you?"

"No. It's a crazed rapist."

"How'd it go?"

"We cracked it." He started to undress.

"What?" She pushed herself up. "You can turn on a light. Here . . ."

Her bedstand light came on. "Are you working tomorrow morning?" Lucas asked. Weather operated almost daily.

"No. I might do a palate in the afternoon, but they've got to finish some tests on the kid, so it's not a sure thing. What happened with the lynching?"

"Not a lynching," Lucas said. "It was a revenge killing. You remember that Hale Sorrell who was in the paper a month ago, his kid got kidnapped?"

"Yeah?"

"It was him."

She was amazed, and a little entertained. "Lucas, you're joking."

"No. We haven't made an arrest, but the bodies were really clogged up with somebody else's DNA, and I'll tell you what: it's gonna be Sorrell's. He found out who killed his kid, he tracked them down and he hanged them. I don't know the details, but we're gonna find out."

"Oh, God. That poor family. That poor family."

"You don't really go around hanging people," Lucas said.

"What would you do if somebody kidnapped Sam and killed him?"

Lucas got in bed but didn't answer.

She pressed him: "What would you do?"

"I don't know."

"Oh, bullshit, Lucas, I know what you'd do and so do you," she said. "You'd wait until the police weren't looking, then you'd find them and kill them."

"All right," Lucas said. Then, after a while, "Make a spoon."

She rolled away from him, and Lucas snuggled up behind her, arm around her waist. "See anything about it on TV?"

"Yeah. That Washington man and the sheriff had a press conference, and Washington lost it and started screaming at the sheriff about being a redneck bigot and the sheriff kept apologizing. It was like he admitted it, or something."

"Aw, man, we told him . . ."

"It was pretty funny, if you like assassinations," Weather said. "And this little girl was on. She had this amazing face, like in those pictures from the Dust Bowl."

"Letty West. I'll tell you about her in the morning," Lucas said. They snuggled for a while, and then Lucas rolled away and said, "I gotta sleep. I'm supposed to be downtown at seven o'clock or some fuckin' thing."

"Set your clock," Weather said. "Are you going to arrest him? Sorrell?"

"No, no. It's just that the goddamn governor's aide is a maniac. He wants an early meeting. Nothing's gonna happen with Sorrell for a day or two."

LOREN SINGLETON AND his mother, unaffected by the crystal clarity of the night and the rippling northern lights, were passing through Fargo as Lucas snuggled up against Weather's butt. And as Lucas stirred under the drone of the alarm clock, and Weather kicked him and he groaned, and thrashed toward the snooze button, they were rolling up the long landscaped driveway at Hale Sorrell's house in the countryside east of Rochester.

Sorrell himself, wearing blue silk pajamas, let them in the house. Singleton, in his deputy sheriff's uniform, asked, "Is your wife up yet?"

"Oh, God. Oh, my God, you found her?" Sorrell asked, his eyes wide. They clicked over to Margery, but didn't ask the question: maybe she was some kind of social worker. He turned and shouted, "Mary! Mary!"

From up the stairs: "Who is it?"

"You better come down."

"You have any relatives in the house?" Singleton asked. "Any help, any friends?"

"No, no—Mary could call her mother . . ." Mary Sorrell came down the stairs and said, "Is it Tammy?"

"No, it's not Tammy," Singleton said. He thought about the warm bundle he'd carried outside.

"Then what . . . ?" Sorrell asked.

Was there fear in his eyes? Did he think Singleton was here because of the hangings? Better get it done with.

"It's just . . ." Singleton said, digging in his coat pocket. He glanced at his mother: they'd worked this out. "It's just . . ." The Sorrells were looking at his pocket, as though he were about to produce a paper or a photograph. Instead, Singleton produced a snubby .38 caliber revolver, pushed it toward Sorrell's eyes and pulled the trigger.

At the last moment, Sorrell flinched. Even at the short distance, Singleton might have missed—but Singleton flinched the same way, and the bullet struck Sorrell between the eyes and he fell backward. After a second of stunning gun-smoked silence in the aftermath of the blast, Mary Sorrell backed a step away, and began to scream, looking at her husband's body, and then, realizing, up at Singleton.

The gun was pointing at her head and Singleton pulled the trigger and flinched again, just as Mary Sorrell flinched the opposite way, and, though he was four feet from her, the bullet clipped only the corner of her ear, and she staggered away and turned and tried to run.

"Goddamn you," Margery shrilled, and to Singleton: "Shoot her. Shoot her."

She was now six feet away, and Singleton, shaking badly, shot her in the back and she went down, hurt but still able to scramble, weakly, to her hands and knees. She made a coughing noise, like a lion, coughing from the blood in her lungs and crawled away from him, trailing brilliant red lung-shot blood now. Still shaking, he stepped carefully around it and shot her in the back of the head and she went down for good.

Then Singleton and Mom both stood there until Singleton groaned, "Oh, God."

"Shut up, dumb shit," his mother said. "Just listen."

They listened together. For running feet, for a call, for a question. All they heard was the crinkling silence of the big house. They knew from Tammy that the Sorrells had no live-in servants, although there was a housekeeper who would be arriving after eight o'clock.

"We ought to check around," Margery said, looking up and down the entry hall. "There's money in this place. I can smell it."

"Mom, we gotta get out of here," Sorrell said. "We can't touch anything. I told you. They got microscopes, they got all kinds of shit. Don't touch *anything.*"

So they left, in the wan light of the predawn, locking the door behind them. They had at least a couple of hours before the housekeeper showed up. Not enough time to get back to Armstrong, but certainly enough time to arrive early in the day, to be astonished if Singleton was called upon to be astonished.

"Left some money back there," Margery said as they rolled out of the driveway. "Left some goddamned money on the table."

10

LUCAS SLEPT FOR four hours. Then the alarm buzzer went, and he groaned, and Weather kicked him and said, "The clock, the clock," and he groaned again and swatted the clock hard enough to trigger the snooze feature for the next thirty years. Weather said, "Get up, you'll go back to sleep, get up."

"No, just give me a minute."

"Get up, c'mon, you're keeping me awake."

"Jeez . . ." He rolled out of bed, stunned by the early hour, staggered to the window, looked at the indoor-outdoor thermometer—it was stuck at −2°F—then parted the wooden slats of the shade and peered out at a surly, pitch-dark morning. The sun wasn't due up for a while, but a streetlight provided enough illumination that he could see the bare branches moving on a lilac bush. Not only bitterly cold, but windy. Good.

He turned back to the bed, but Weather said, "Go in the bathroom."

"Miserable bitch," he muttered, and heard her cruel laugh as he tottered off.

Lucas didn't care for mornings, unless he came on them from behind. He liked the dawn hours, if he could go home and go to bed after the sun came up. But getting up before the sun wasn't natural. Science had proven that early birds weren't as intelligent, sexually vigorous, or good-looking as night owls, although he couldn't tell Weather—she cheerfully got up every workday morning at five-thirty, and was often cutting somebody open by seven o'clock.

THE GOVERNOR WAS an early bird. He was dressed in a crisp white shirt, sleeves rolled two careful turns—a concession to the fact that it was Saturday—dark gray slacks and black loafers. A pale gray jacket hung from an antique coat tree in a corner of his office. He looked fine, but Lucas could take some thin comfort from Neil Mitford, who looked like a bad car-train accident. He was wearing jeans and a tattered tweed jacket over a black-and-gold Iowa Hawkeyes sweatshirt, and had lost his shoes somewhere—he wore gray-and-red woolen hunting socks. John McCord, the BCA superintendent, huddled in a corner in khakis and a sweater with a red-nosed reindeer on the chest. Rose Marie Roux was still among the missing.

"Coffee?" Henderson asked cheerfully. "Wonder where Rose Marie is?"

"Probably killed by the cold," Lucas grumped. "Or run over by a car in the dark. Gimme about six sugars."

"Good to get up at this time, get going," Henderson said. "You get a four-hour jump on everybody. You're on them before they know what hit them."

"Unless you have a heart attack and die," Lucas said.

McCord had a sixteen-ounce Diet Pepsi in his coat pocket, his own source of caffeine. Mitford drained one cup of coffee in fifteen seconds, and poured another. The governor settled behind his desk and sipped. "What's going on, and what do we do about it?"

Lucas outlined the theory, upon which everyone agreed—that Sorrell had somehow learned who had killed his child, and had killed them in return.

"That'd take some brass balls," McCord said.

"He might be like that," Mitford said. "I did some research . . ."

Rose Marie slipped into the room, said, "Sorry—it was just so damn cold and dark," and found a chair. Henderson gave her a one-minute update, and then turned back to Mitford. "You were saying?"

"I pulled everything I could find on the guy. After he graduated from Cal Tech, he turned down a bunch of heavy-duty jobs and enlisted in the Army. He spent six years as an infantry and then a Special Forces officer. There are some hints that he had combat decorations, but there wasn't a war going on, so . . ."

"So he did snoop-and-poops and maybe cut a few throats," Henderson said. He seemed pleased with the snoop-and-poops and the throat cutting.

"That's what I think," Mitford said.

"So." Henderson picked up a ballpoint pen and toyed with it, leaned way back, and asked the ceiling, "When do we take him? We have enough, I think."

"We should get the DNA back tomorrow morning," Lucas said. "We could go tomorrow, but if anything else comes up, it wouldn't hurt to wait until Monday."

Mitford seemed startled. "Monday?" He looked at Henderson. "We can't wait until Monday."

Henderson was shaking his head and said, "Lucas, when I said *when* . . . I meant before breakfast, or after? We can't wait until tonight, or tomorrow. Washington is killing us. *Fifty states,* you know, CBS . . ."

"Yeah, yeah, I know it."

"They want me to go over to Channel Three and do a segment at eleven o'clock," Henderson said. "Then they're switching out to Fargo for a segment with Washington. I want to be able to say that we've made an arrest, and I want to say something about what we think happened. If I do that, we'll fuck the guy. Washington. I'd love to fuck him. Love it." He turned in his chair, once all the way around, and then again, his pink tongue stuck on his bottom lip as if tasting the word *fuck,* his glasses glittering from the overhead lights. "Love to fuck him."

"It'd be good," Mitford said. "And it'd be national."

Lucas began, "If we're trying to build a case . . ."

"It doesn't matter. Look, we've got X amount of information to arrest him with, and to get a DNA sample from him. Then we've got to wait a day or two to process his sample. So . . . why not grab him now?"

"Just . . ." Lucas looked at Rose Marie. "Doesn't seem orderly."

"Can I get some of that coffee?" Rose Marie asked. "I talk better when I can see."

"Of course," Henderson said. "Let me . . ."

"Lucas, everybody else is right and you're wrong," Rose Marie said as Henderson poured her a cup. "We've got two things going: a big crime and a big publicity problem. We can strangle the publicity problem before it gets out of control, and not do much harm to the criminal case."

"If we do hurt the criminal case," Mitford said, "what we've done is, we've fucked up a case against a bright, hard-working guy who employs hundreds of Minnesotans, and who killed a couple of thugs who kidnapped and presumably cold-bloodedly murdered his daughter. So fuckin' what?"

Lucas said to Mitford, "Don't get your shorts in a knot," and then, to the governor, "You say take him, we'll take him. It's seven-thirty now, I can kick Del out of bed, we'll go down and get him. We can have him by, say, ten at the latest, and you can make your announcement. I've got Neil's cell-phone number, if he'll be with you."

"I will," Mitford said. He jumped up and rubbed his hands together like a cold man in front of a fire. "Hot damn. We came, we saw, *we kicked ass*. And . . . he's a Republican."

"Poor bastard," said Rose Marie.

"You making the call?" Lucas asked, looking at Henderson.

"Get him," Henderson said.

DEL WAS AS MUCH a night owl as Lucas, and was not happy when Lucas shook him out of bed. Del's wife, Cheryl, was already awake and writing bills in the kitchen when Lucas arrived, and she sent Lucas back to the bedroom to do the dirty work. Lucas stuck his head in the door and cooed, "Get up, sleepyhead. Time to work."

Nothing.

"Sleepyhead, get up . . ."

"I hope you die of leprosy," Del moaned. He pushed himself up on his elbows. "What do you want?"

"It's not what I want," Lucas said. "It's what the governor and Rose Marie and McCord want. They want Sorrell busted at ten o'clock this morning, and you and I are going down, with a couple of BCA guys in another car, and we're gonna drag him kicking and screaming out of his mansion."

"Can't you do it by yourself?"

"I could, but then I'd feel bad, knowing that you were up here in a nice warm bed sleeping late while I was dragging my ass all the way down to Rochester."

"All right." He dropped back on the pillow. "Just give me one more minute."

Lucas wasn't buying that routine.

———

JENKINS AND SHRAKE were the BCA's official flatfeet. Most of the other agents had degrees in psychology or social work or accounting or computer science, and worked out for two hours a day in the gym. Jenkins and Shrake had graduated from Hennepin Community College with Law Enforcement Certificates, and, as far as anyone knew, that was the last time either had cracked a book that didn't have Tom Clancy's name on the cover. Both of them smoked and drank too much, both had been divorced a couple of times, and Lucas knew for sure that they both carried saps. They were the pair most often sent to arrest people because, they admitted, they liked the work.

Lucas and Del were eating scrambled eggs at a Bakers Square restaurant on Ford Parkway, six blocks from Lucas's house, when the other two arrived. Jenkins was a heavyset man, unshaven, with gray hair and suspicious eyes. Shrake was tall and lean, closely shaven with a pencil-thin white mustache, also gray-haired with suspicious eyes. They both wore hats and buttoned-up woolen overcoats and Shrake had an unlit cigarette pasted to his lower lip. They didn't sit, they stood outside the booth looking down, their hands in their coat pockets, like a couple of wandering East German *Stasi* thugs. They finished each other's sentences.

Jenkins: "If we can bust this asshole at ten . . ."

Shrake: "We can get back up here in time to watch the playoff game."

Jenkins: "If you guys don't fuck something up."

Shrake: "In which case, we'll miss the game."

Jenkins: "Then we'll tell everybody in the BCA that you guys are queer."

Shrake: "And that Davenport is the girlie."

Lucas continued to chew and Del put a piece of bacon in his mouth, and stared out the window at the Ford plant across the street.

"I think we can get it done by ten," Lucas said, after swallowing. "But you guys oughta know—Del actually *is* gay, and you've probably violated about six diversity guidelines."

Del turned and stared steadily at the pair, unsmiling, until Jenkins said, "Not that it really matters," and they all tried to laugh, but it was too early in the morning and too cold, and Shrake's hoarse laughter trailed away into a spasm of tobacco coughs. The sun was just up, and the car exhausts were melting the frost on the streets, leaving behind nasty little streaks of black ice. Too fuckin' early.

THE TRIP THROUGH the frozen countryside took an hour and a half, with an orange sun finally groaning up over the horizon. There was more snow around the Cities than in the northwest, and for twenty minutes, they ran down the highway alongside a snowmobile rally in the adjoining ditches, a couple of dozen sleds making a fast run south.

"Canadians call them snow machines," Del said, shaking himself out of a slumber, and looking out the window at the riders. They were in Lucas's new Acura SUV, which Lucas had begun to suspect was a disguised minivan.

"What?"

"They call them snow machines, instead of snowmobiles. Or sleds."

"Fuckin' Canadians."

"They are the spawn of the devil," Del agreed, yawning. "Want me to drive for a while?"

"If we stop, those goddamn flatfeet are gonna pull that Dodge off the road, and then they're gonna get stuck, and then it'll take another half hour to get down there, and we'll all be freezing and our socks will be wet."

"Good. I didn't want to drive. Wake me up when we get there."

———

SORRELL'S HOME WAS eight miles outside of Rochester on a rolling piece of country that might have made a decent golf course. Though the driveway was open, Lucas had the feeling that they'd triggered security sensors when they crossed between the two stone pillars that marked its entrance. The driveway leading to the hilltop house was blacktopped, carefully plowed, and though it seemed to pass through a woodlot, the trees were too aesthetically pleasing to be natural.

The house itself seemed modest enough from the bottom of the drive, a kind of Pasadena bungalow of redwood and brick, with a wing. Only when they got closer did Lucas realize how big the place was, and that what looked like a wing was a garage.

"I could put the Big New House in the garage," Lucas said, as they neared the crest of the hill.

"You paid what, a million-five for that?" Del said. Del had been trying to worm the price out of him.

"Nothing near that," Lucas said. "But this place—this place would go for a million-five."

"Or maybe six million-five . . ."

The driveway disappeared around the corner of the wing, apparently to hide the utilitarian commonness of garage doors. They stopped in front of the house, got out, waited until Jenkins and Shrake joined them. Jenkins parked his car beside Lucas's SUV, effectively blocking the driveway. They walked as a group, blowing steam in the cold air, up the steps of the low front porch. The porch had a swing, as did Lucas's Big New House, and a stone walkway along the front, under an overhanging eave.

Lucas looked at Jenkins and Shrake, said, "Ready," and Jenkins said, "Unless you want me around back." Lucas shook his head. "Let's everybody be polite," he said.

"Probably at work anyway," Shrake said. "The place feels empty."

Lucas pushed the doorbell and heard the empty echo. Shrake was right: there was something weird about houses—they felt either occupied or empty, and even without looking inside, most street cops could feel whether there were people inside.

One of Lucas's old friends with the Minneapolis police force, Harrison Sloan, theorized that people who were tiptoeing, or even breathing, gave off vibrations that the house amplified, and that you could subconsciously feel the vibrations. Lucas told him he was full of shit, but secretly thought he might be onto something.

He pushed the doorbell again, and then a third time. Jenkins moved down the walkway to a line of windows, and tried to see inside, trying one window after another. Halfway down, he stopped and moved his head up and down, his hand against the glass of the storm window, blocking reflections. Then he shook his head and said, "I'll be right back."

He went out to the Dodge, popped the trunk, and fished out a twenty-pound, yellow-handled maul. As he climbed back up the porch, Lucas said, "What are you doing?"

"Gonna knock the door down," Jenkins said.

"What are you talking about?" Del asked.

Jenkins sighed, as if instructing a slow student. "If you look through that window, you'll see a hand and an arm. Just a hand and an arm, sticking out of a hallway into the kitchen. It looks to me like a dead hand, but I can't be sure. It might still be a live hand, that dies while we stand here bullshitting. So if you'll stand back . . ."

Lucas turned to Del who said, "Oh, boy," and to Shrake, who said, gloomily, "There goes the fuckin' playoff game."

JENKINS HAD A NICE smooth wood-chopping swing, and the edge of the maul hit just above the doorknob, blowing the door open. Jenkins stepped back, and Lucas slipped his .45 out of its holster and pushed the door open with his knuckles. Del, to one side, with his Glock pointed overhead, said, "I'm going . . ." and then he was inside, with Lucas two steps behind, and Jenkins behind him. Shrake had jogged around to the back, just in case.

"Guy down here," Del said, and Lucas moved forward, and then Del said, "Another one," and Lucas saw the first body sprawled in the hallway, one arm sticking like a chicken claw into the kitchen. *Sorrell.* Lucas recognized him from the photographs, except that the photographs didn't have a bullet hole in the face.

Del was moving, and Lucas moved with him, and Lucas saw the woman, facedown in a puddle of blood. Like Sorrell, she was wearing a bathrobe, and one leg stuck out toward Lucas. As he'd done with the door, he stooped and touched her leg with his knuckles. Not cold; still some warmth.

"Not long ago," Lucas said.

"Let's clear the first floor," Del said.

Lucas spoke over his shoulder to Jenkins. "Put a gun on the stairs. We're gonna clear the floor."

"Gotcha," Jenkins said. He moved to the base of a curling stairway with a blond-wood railing, his pistol pointed generally up the stairs. Lucas and Del took two minutes clearing the first floor, slowing to pop the back door and let Shrake in. When the floor was clear, Shrake and Jenkins took the basement and Lucas and Del took the second floor, although all four believed the house was empty, except for themselves and the bodies.

And it was.

Lucas came back down the stairs, tucking the gun away, and said, "Let's move it out on the porch . . . make some calls."

The first call went to the Olmsted County sheriff's office. Lucas identified himself, gave the dispatcher a quick summary of the situation for the recording tape, and got the sheriff's cell phone. The sheriff took the call on the second ring, listened for a moment, then said, "Oh, my God. I'm on my way."

"Bring the ME and tell him we're gonna need some fast body temps."

Then he called the governor, through Mitford. "Neil. Get me a number for the governor. Like right now."

Mitford said, "He's next door. Hang on, I'll walk the phone over. Did you get him?"

"Not exactly," Lucas said.

Henderson took the line. "Get him?"

"We busted down the door of his house and found Sorrell and a woman who I expect is his wife, dead in the front hallway. Shot to death. Looks like executions. Looks like they'd just come down in their bathrobes and were shot. Like somebody got them out of bed. Bodies aren't quite cold."

"Good lord. Did you . . . touch them?"

"Yeah. The sheriff's on the way with the ME," Lucas said. He was standing on the porch, and down at the bottom of the hill, he could see a patrol car flying down the approach road, slowing for the driveway. "We've got one coming in right now."

"What do you think?"

"I don't know. I'm a little stunned. But I'd say that either Joe's not dead, and he came back, or that there's another player."

"What do I do with the CBS interview?"

"You got what, an hour? I'll talk to the sheriff about notifying the next of kin, tell them that it's critical to move fast. If we can get that done, you could make the announcement. I wouldn't make the announcement, though, before the next-of-kin notification. Not unless we get some media out here, or something, as cover. If you do, it'll come back to bite you on the ass—some relative talking to TV about how he heard it first from you, and how awful it was."

"Let me think about that," Henderson said. "In the meantime, get the sheriff to find the next of kin."

"Okay," Lucas said.

"Take down a number," Henderson said. He read off a phone number, and Lucas jotted it in the palm of his hand. "That's the red cell
phone. About ten people have the number, so don't call it too often. But
call me on this."

"Okay."

"You know, if you look at this one way . . . our problem was solved
pretty quickly."

"I wouldn't look at it that way," Lucas said. "Not in public, anyway."

"Call me back," Henderson said, and he was gone.

THE SHERIFF'S CAR reached the top of the hill and pulled
around Jenkins's Dodge, slid to a stop in the snow. An apple-cheeked
deputy jumped out of the driver's side, and, staying behind his car, hand
on his holstered six-gun, the other hand pointed at the cops on the
porch, shouted, "All right. All right."

"Jesus Christ, calm down," Shrake said, from where he was leaning
on the porch rail. He blew a stream of cigarette smoke at the kid. "We're
really important state cops and you're just a kid who's not important
at all."

That confused the deputy, and slowed him down. "Where are the
casualties?" he asked, no longer shouting.

"There are two dead bodies inside: Hale Sorrell and, we think, his
wife," Lucas said.

"Oh, God." The kid jumped back inside the car and they could see
him calling in.

Lucas's cell phone rang, and Rose Marie was on the line. "You gotta
be kidding me."

He moved down the walkway under the eaves. "We're not. We don't
know anything except that there's probably nobody inside the house, except the dead people. I haven't had a chance to think about anything."

"Sorrell for sure?"

"Yeah. You ever meet his wife?"

"A time or two—Sorrell's age, mid-forties, probably, dark hair, a little heavy, short."

"That's her, ninety-nine percent," Lucas said.

"Do I need to be there?"

"No. The locals are arriving, and I've got Henderson's direct line. If I were you, I'd get next to the governor and guide his footsteps, so as to avoid the dogshit."

"I'll do that. Call if you need anything," she said, and was gone.

THE SHERIFF'S NAME was Brad Wilson, and he arrived ten minutes after the first car came in. By that time, there were four sheriff's deputies on the scene, two of them on the porch, two more sent around to "cover the back—just in case," but mostly to get them out of Lucas's hair.

The sheriff was an older, barrel-chested man wearing a pearl-handled .45 on a gunbelt. He and Lucas had met once, when Lucas was working with Minneapolis. Lucas thought him competent, and maybe better than that. "You attract more goddamned trouble, Davenport," the sheriff said as he came up. "Hale's dead? And Mary?"

"Come on and take a look. We've been keeping everybody out so the crime scene guys'll have a chance."

The sheriff nodded and followed Lucas inside, stepping carefully. They stood back, but the sheriff, leaning over Sorrell, said, "That's Hale. And that's Mary. God bless me. How'd you come to find them?"

"We came up here to arrest him on murder charges," Lucas said. "Sorrell's the guy who hanged those two people up north."

The sheriff's mouth dropped open, then snapped close. After a moment, he said, "You wouldn't be pulling my leg, would you?"

"No. The two people he hanged were probably the people who kidnapped his daughter."

"You better tell me," the sheriff said. He looked a last time at the two figures on the floor. "Holy mackerel." And, "I got to call the feds. They are going to wet their pants."

AFTER THE SHERIFF called the FBI, Lucas got him to dispatch pairs of deputies to local homeowners. "We want to know if anybody saw a car or any other kind of vehicle here, this morning or late last night. Or anything else, for that matter. Ask them if they ever saw Sorrell in a red Jeep Cherokee."

The first media trucks from Rochester began arriving fifteen minutes later. Twenty minutes after that, a Twin Cities media helicopter flew over. Hale Sorrell's parents and Mary Sorrell's mother were notified of the deaths by the sheriff's chaplain, and said that they would notify other family members. Lucas called Henderson. "You're good to go. Next of kin are notified."

"Excellent. How are things down there?"

"We're just mostly standing around, waiting for the medical examiner. He was off somewhere, but he's on his way now."

AT ELEVEN O'CLOCK, still waiting for the medical examiner, they filed into a home theater, turned on the fifty-inch flat-panel television, and watched Henderson do the interview with CBS. Somebody—Mitford, probably—had roughed him up. His hair wasn't quite as smooth as it usually was, and a fat brown file envelope sat on the table in front of him. He looked like the harried executive with bad news, and he delivered it straight ahead, no punches pulled.

"Jesus, he looks almost . . . tough," Del said.

Washington came on, a moon-faced black man with a dark suit and white shirt, a man who knew he'd been seriously one-upped. The dead people were dope dealers and kidnappers? The hangman and his wife had been executed in their hallway?

"I feel there were some serious investigative shortcomings in Custer County, and I'm calling on the federal government to blahblahblah-blah . . ."

"Bullshit bullshit bullshit," Del said. "It ain't workin'."

Fifteen minutes after they were off the air, Henderson called. "Anything new?"

"No. You looked pretty good."

"Thanks. We heard Washington is on his way home to Chicago."

"God bless him."

JENKINS AND SHRAKE were in the media room, watching the playoff from premium leather–paneled theater seats. Del was prowling the house, checking desks and bureaus and calendars and computer files. Twenty minutes after he began, he handed Lucas a piece of paper: an Iowa title transfer application from a Curtis Frank, of Des Moines, to a Larry Smith, of Oelwein, Iowa, on the purchase of a 1996 Jeep Cherokee, dated three weeks earlier.

"Check the Oelwein address?" Lucas asked.

"No, but I will. Bet you a buck it's fake."

THE ME HAD ARRIVED, and after fussing around, checked the blood puddles and body temps. Sorrell and his wife had certainly been killed sometime after midnight, he said, and after he got some weights and checked the accuracy of the house thermostat and the floor-level temperatures, he said he could probably do better than that.

"Off the top of my head, I'd say they were killed this morning," he said. "They're a little too warm to have lain on the floor all night, and the blood is a little too liquid. But we'll have to do the numbers before we know for sure."

Sheriff Wilson was standing by the door and said, "Here come the feds. Just what we needed."

"Who?"

"Lanny Cole and Jim Green. Pretty good guys, actually."

"Mmm. I know Cole, I don't know Green."

Del came back and said, "There's no such address in Oelwein. It's fake. There is a Curtis Frank, and he says he sold the truck for cash. I talked to Des Moines homicide cops and they'll take a picture of Sorrell down to his house for an ID." He saw the men in suits coming up to the door and said, "Feebs."

COLE, THE FBI AGENT, shook hands with the sheriff and said, "How ya doing, Brad?" and nodded at Lucas and asked, "They got any more jobs over there at the BCA?"

"I got a slot for a female investigator," Lucas said.

"I can investigate females," Cole said. "So what happened here?"

Wilson and Lucas took him through it, Lucas connecting Sorrell with the hangings in Custer County. "I gotta call in on that," Cole said, squatting next to Sorrell. "We got civil rights guys on the way to take a look at it. You say Hale did it?"

"Most likely."

Cole nodded, and looked at his partner who said, "We knew something was seriously screwed up."

"Didn't know it was *that* screwed up," Cole said. He looked down at the body again and said, "Goddamnit, Hale. What'd you do?"

"You guys want in on this act?" Lucas asked.

Cole shook his head. "We're gonna want to know all about it, if you could forward your findings . . . but we're not going to get directly involved. We just don't have the manpower, what with discovering Arab terror plots at the Washington County courthouse."

Sheriff Wilson looked at Lucas and said, "Doesn't make any sense for us to do it—it doesn't sound like the killer's from around here. So you got it. I'll call John McCord right now, and ask you in."

"Good enough," Lucas said. "If your guys come up with anything, they can pass it up to me, and I'll coordinate with Lanny and Jim." To the feds: "Any problem getting your files on the kidnapping?"

"I'll talk to the SAC from here. We should be able to give you the file this afternoon."

Back to Wilson: "Can you handle the press down here?"

"I can do that."

"So we're set."

THE FBI AGENTS VISITED, nothing more, and at noon they left. A BCA crime scene crew arrived from the Twin Cities, and Lucas eventually joined Del in turning over the house, looking at pieces of paper. They found nothing of interest, but couldn't get into three of the Sorrells' four computers.

The two desk-top machines, one in a library and another in a home office, and a laptop in Sorrell's briefcase, were password-protected, and would have to be cracked by computer people. A fourth laptop, apparently belonging to Mary Sorrell, was not protected, but contained nothing but letters, a personal calendar, and a few documents relating to a heart disease research foundation.

Lucas was returning Sorrell's machine to the briefcase when he found an envelope with a bank letterhead. Inside were twenty separate receipts for bank drafts, each for $50,000, with each check made to a different, major Las Vegas hotel.

"A million dollars," Del said. "High roller. Maybe that had something to do with the kidnapping? Gambling debts or something?"

"These can't be all for him," Lucas said, looking at the receipts. "Every one of the hotels is different."

"Maybe it's a business thing, a convention."

"It's weird. We oughta look at it."

AT ONE O'CLOCK, with Del getting restless, Lucas was ready to leave. He turned control of the house over to Carl Driscoll, the head of the BCA crime scene crew, who said he'd get the computers to St. Paul. "If anything comes up, call me," Lucas told him. "All the routine stuff, get it in your own computer—I think Del and I are probably headed back to Custer County, and you can e-mail it to me."

The sheriff had just come back up the hill, after talking with reporters, shook his head and said, "This is gonna get goofy. The governor's statement . . . it's gonna get goofy."

"Never was gonna be any other way," Lucas said. "Not after those two people went up in that tree."

Lucas got his coat, collected Del, and as they headed for the door, saw a fortyish man in a gray overcoat walking around the line of cop cars in the driveway, closely trailed by a deputy. He was carrying a wallet-sized box, and when he saw the sheriff step out on the porch with Lucas, he called, "Hey, Brad."

"George . . . you heard about Hale, I guess." Wilson said to Lucas, "Hale's lawyer."

"My God. I was at a wedding, Ken Hendrick's kid," the lawyer said, as he came up to them. He looked back down the hill—"I got here as fast as I could, but I had a heck of a time getting through your boys down there."

"Not much for you to do, here, George."

"Yes, there is. A week ago, Hale gave me a box . . ." He handed the box to the sheriff. It was about four inches by five, an inch thick. A tough-looking lock was set flush to the polished steel surface at one edge. "He said, I swear to God, that if he should die, I should give this to the authorities. I asked him if it was anything illegal, and he said no, it's just some information that he felt should come to official attention. I thought maybe it was business, but now . . ."

"What's in it?"

"I don't know," the lawyer said. "He gave it to me, told me to file it and forget it. He said it couldn't be opened without destroying the contents, unless you used a key. He said the key was on his key ring with his car keys."

Wilson looked at the box, then handed it to Lucas. "Ever see anything like that?"

"Yeah. It looks like a magnetic-media safe, for carrying around computer Smart Cards and so on. It's bigger than most of them, and I've never seen a lock before."

"His key ring is on the bedside table," Del said. "I checked to see if there was a Jeep key on it."

"Let's go look," Lucas said.

"Maybe we ought to do it in a lab," Wilson said doubtfully.

"It's not a bomb. It's something he wanted us to get," Lucas said.

DEL RETRIEVED THE key ring, which contained one key with a circular blade. Lucas popped the top on the safe, and inside was an old-fashioned 3.5-inch computer floppy disk.

"Laptop," Del said.

They took Mary Sorrell's IBM laptop out of her briefcase, put it on the floor of the home office. The base unit had no floppy drive, but they found the drive in a separate pouch and plugged it in. Lucas brought the laptop up, slipped the floppy into the drive, and found one file. He clicked on the file. Microsoft Word began opening on the screen, and then the file itself.

A note—a brief note.

Tammy Sorrell was kidnapped by Joe Kelly, Deon Cash, and Jane Warr. Cash is a driver for the Gene Calb truck rehabilitation service in the town of Broderick, near Armstrong, Minnesota. Jane Warr is a card dealer at the Moose Bay casino near Armstrong. Warr and Cash live together in a farmhouse in Broderick. They killed Tammy on Dec. 22 and buried her somewhere nearby. The exact location is unknown. This information has been confirmed.

"Jeez. There it is," Wilson said, looking up at Lucas. "Where did he get the information? The FBI says that the kidnappers never called. The feds even started looking at Hale's background to see if he might have had something to do with Tammy . . . you know."

Lucas touched the computer screen. "He says Kelly, Cash, and Warr did the kidnapping, and that Cash is a driver for the truck place. He doesn't say anything more about Joe. I think he must've got the information from Joe. Where else would he get it?"

Wilson pursed his lips. "So Joe . . ."

"I think Joe's outa here," Lucas said. "If Sorrell was Special Forces . . . maybe he had some training with pliers and fingernails."

"You don't think Joe did this?" Wilson gestured out toward the kitchen, where the two bodies still lay on the floor.

"It's possible—but how the hell would Sorrell know about Cash and Warr? I think he probably grabbed Joe when Joe came for the money," Lucas said. He looked at the note again, frowned. "I thought all the stories were about the rich girl being kidnapped on Christmas Eve, and all the gifts around the tree . . ."

"She was . . ." Wilson shook his head. "Maybe it's a typo. Maybe he meant the twenty-fourth, and typed the twenty-second."

"Pretty unlikely," Del grunted. "That's one thing you'd get right, in that kind of note."

"Those bank draft receipts, the ones that went to Vegas . . ." Lucas had returned them to the briefcase where he found them, to have them checked later. Now he retrieved them, and looked at the dates. "They're dated December twentieth. He took a million dollars in cashier's checks to Las Vegas on the twentieth."

"What do you think?" Wilson asked.

"Could you get one of the bank managers to check on when the drafts were cashed?" Lucas asked.

Wilson looked at his watch. "It's Saturday. Maybe. Let me call somebody."

"Maybe . . ." Lucas scratched his chin and looked at Del. "Maybe he was collecting money in Vegas. He got drafts from his bank, then spent three days withdrawing the money from his Vegas accounts. He was collecting cash to pay the kidnappers."

Del nodded. "Couldn't just walk into a bank and ask for a million in cash. How else would you get it? But a bunch of bank drafts for Vegas hotels . . . He could've even passed it off as a business thing, with the banks."

"So Tammy wasn't kidnapped on the twenty-fourth," Lucas said. "They got her sooner than that. Huh." They'd been squatting next to Mary Sorrell's computer, and now they all stood up. "But there was something that Sorrell didn't get from Joe or Cash or Warr. There must be a fourth man. Or woman. Or maybe a fourth, fifth, and sixth. Somebody who knew what it meant when Cash and Warr got hanged."

"And didn't want Sorrell talking about it," Del said. "Couldn't risk it."

"Why couldn't he risk it?" Wilson asked.

Del said, "Because he didn't know if Sorrell was finished—didn't know whether or not Sorrell had his name. Didn't know what Jane and Deon might have told him."

Wilson scratched his head and said, "Shoot," and a moment later, "Goldarnit."

Lucas said to Del, "We better get back up north."

Del nodded. "But we wouldn't get up there before dark, if we left now. We should catch a nap this afternoon, leave really early tomorrow. Three in the morning. Get there when the sun comes up. Take that little town apart."

11

SATURDAY AFTERNOON, just after dark, Loren Singleton rolled along Highway 36, listening to the radio. He was tired, despite a long nap, from the overnight round trip to the Sorrells' and back. A snow squall bothered his windshield, little pecks and flecks of ice whirling down from the north.

He'd been horrified by the shooting, as he hadn't been by the killing of the little girls. The little girls just seemed to go to sleep—and he hadn't really done that. He'd just *been* there.

At the same time, there was something about the Sorrell killings that left him feeling . . . larger. Tougher. He tried to find the exact word: studlier? That embarrassed him, but it might be close.

The lights of Broderick came up through the blowing snow, the cafe, and the gas station, two dimly lit windows at the church, a beer sign in the bar—and then he noticed the light in the back of Calb's. The office was lit up, as though there were a meeting going on.

He pulled the Caddy into the parking lot, watched for shadows on the window—somebody looking to see who'd pulled in—and when he got none, climbed out of the car and walked over to the shop and tried the door. The door was locked, as it should be after dark on Saturday.

Still, the lights. He walked around the side of the building and peeked through a window, and found a meeting: Gene Calb, Ruth and Katina Lewis, and a black man that Singleton had never seen before. Both women had taken their coats off, as if they'd been there a while. The black man was leaning back in an office chair, idly swiveling a few inches from left to right.

Singleton watched for a while, but couldn't hear anything. Why had they left him out? Were they suspicious?

He eventually crunched back around to the Caddy, climbed inside, rolled back to get square with the overhead door, and punched the garage-door opener. As the door went up, he eased the Caddy inside, punched the remote again, and as the door started back down, got out of the car.

Calb and Katina were standing by the corner of the bay, Calb with a cup of coffee in his hand. "Hey, come on back. We're having an argument."

"Who's we?" Singleton asked.

"Me and Shawn Davis and Ruth and Katina," Calb said. "Shawn came up from KC. You heard about the Sorrell thing?"

"On the radio, a while ago," Singleton said. "What do you think?"

"That's what we're arguing about," Katina said. "I tried calling you but didn't get an answer."

"Been running around," Singleton said. He looked at the bridge of her nose, rather than in her eyes, so she wouldn't see the lie in his eyes. And he thought: Okay. They tried to call him, so they weren't cutting him out.

He started past her, but she caught his arm and stood on tiptoe and kissed him on the cheek and asked, "You busy tonight?"

"I sure got some time if you do," he said. She stepped ahead of him and he touched her on the butt.

Inside the office, Calb introduced him to Davis: Davis was a tough-looking forty-five, not impressed by much. He lifted a hand and nodded, and Singleton gave him his best grim cowboy look. "You got any special insight into this mess?" Davis asked him in a twangy Missouri drawl. "Gene said you knew Deon and Jane and Joe as well as anyone up here."

Singleton hurried to deflect that idea. "I have no idea what's going on. I used to stop by and talk to Deon, but that was just part of my deal, you know. Keep an eye out. I keep thinking it's Joe, that maybe they had a fight or something."

"Joe's dead," Davis said bluntly. "He never went more than five miles from his mama in his life, until he come up here. Called her every day, then he talked to her one night and the next day he was gone. She hasn't heard a word since. He's dead."

"Goddamn," Calb said. He stood up and wandered in a tight circle, his hands jammed in the back pockets of his jeans. "This kidnapping . . . if they think it's outa here, they could be all over me. You too, Shawn. If they really started pounding my books, looking at how many people I employ and how much commercial rehab we do . . . they could give me some trouble."

"Might be time for a fire," Singleton said.

They all looked at him for a moment, and then Calb said, "You're not serious."

"Take care of the book problem," Singleton said.

Calb's eyes rolled heavenward, as in prayer, and he said, "It wouldn't take care of shit, Loren. You've never been a businessman—there're records all over the goddamn place. Payroll tax receipts, workman's comp, insurance, income tax. The only thing that would happen if I burned down the shop is that I'd have a burned-down shop. Then they'd *really* get interested. If they get *really* interested, they're gonna get to all of us, including you, Loren, and the women too."

"Which gets us away from the question I want answered, and I want to know that I'm being told the truth," Ruth said, squaring off against Calb and Davis. She had her wintery fighting smile fixed on her face. "This kidnapping thing. This Sorrell girl. You didn't know about it, you didn't have any part of it, either of you. This wasn't some kind of money-making deal that went wrong."

"My God, Ruth. No. Never. I'm not nuts," Calb said. The way he said it made her believe him.

Davis was quieter, but just as convincing: "The thing is, Ruth, if these news stories are right, the kidnappers wanted a million bucks for this kid. They were gonna cut it three ways that we know of, and probably had to be four, since it seems like there's a fourth one on the loose. That'd be a quarter-million apiece, for risking the death sentence. Gene and I make that much, every year, just running our quiet little car business. There wouldn't be no sense in it."

"Some sense for somebody like Deon," Singleton said. "He was getting nothing but chump change."

"Just like you, Loren, and both of you happy to get it," Calb snapped.

"Hey—shut up," Ruth said. She looked at the two men, poked a finger at them. "We don't need a quarrel. So . . . what does Gene say to the police?"

"He plays dumb," Davis said. "That'll work, if you let it work. If you don't get smart. You go ahead and sweat, and wiggle around, and apologize—the man always likes to see that. But just be dumb. Yeah, you hired him, because I asked you to, to get him out of the neighborhood. They come to me, and I say, 'Hell, yes, it was a big favor, gettin' Deon off my back, and his old lady, too.'

"We tell them that his pay probably wasn't enough for some city boy who wants to put cocaine up his nose, and so he went off on his own," Davis continued. "I mean, this thing they did with this little girl—Deon's crazy enough, but no cop down in KC who knows me would say that I'd do it. Nobody up here would think that Gene would, either."

HE PAUSED, and in the absence of words, a full-color motion picture popped up behind Singleton's eyes: a picture of Mom getting the little bottle of drugs out of her bag, and the syringe, and sucking the fluid out, and holding the needle up, and squirting a little bit of it, then putting the smile on her face before she went in with the girl.

The older girl might have known what was going on. She'd taken the shot with a dark-eyed passivity, her eyes locked on Singleton's. She'd had a blue ribbon in her hair, with a knot in the middle.

The younger one had a stuffed toy that Jane had gotten her, a hand-sized white-mouse puppet with a pink tail. She'd said, "Okay," and had lain back on the folding bed and rolled her arm around to take the shot. Brave little kid: went to sleep with the mouse on her chest.

He'd dug her down through the clay cap and placed her in a pile of old Yellow Pages phone books, and that was that.

Wasn't hard. Didn't seem crazy; just *was*.

DAVIS STARTED TALKING again, and popped Singleton out of the mental movie. "So we play it dumb: what you see is what you got. Three dumb assholes decide to kidnap a girl because they want more money and they get killed for their trouble."

"Four dumb assholes," Calb said distractedly. "Maybe the other guy was like down on the other end of the thing, set up the girl, or something." He looked at Singleton. "They never mentioned a friend or anything?"

"No. They kept talking about all their friends down in KC."

"Whatever," Ruth said. "The thing is, I need *something* to tell the women who work with me. Some of them are afraid that somehow, everything is linked—the cars, the drugs, and the kidnapping. If somebody put pressure on them, came at them the right way, they'd probably give up the whole story. Feel morally obligated to."

"Shit," Davis said.

"Well, I agree with them," Ruth said, showing the cold smile again. "The only difference is, I know Gene." She lifted a hand toward Calb. "If I thought we had anything to do with all of this, I'd go to the police myself. But I think it was Deon Cash and Jane Warr and Joe, trying to make some money. And the fact is, even though we don't know anything about it, it could drag us all down."

"So tell them the truth," Calb said. "Tell them that we're just as scared and confused as they are. We don't know what the hell's happening, and we're desperate to find out."

"Dumb is best," Davis said again. "Believe me on that—you don't know nothin' about nothin'. If you don't know nothin', nobody can trip you up—not your friends, not the cops."

THEY TALKED FOR ANOTHER half-hour, and then broke up. Davis said he was heading back to KC that night, after eating dinner at the Calbs'. Katina walked out with Singleton and Ruth. Ruth kept going, across the highway and down toward the church. Katina held back and said, "I'd like to come over."

"You're the goddamned horniest little thing," Singleton said. He touched her face and said, "Don't worry. You worry too much."

"I just want everything to be right," she said. "You never talked to Deon about anything, did you?"

By *anything,* she meant the kidnappings, Singleton realized.

"Jeez, Katina . . ." He was insulted.

"I'm sorry, I'm just so upset."

"It'll be okay, honey."

"Not just that. I sorta need to . . . get close to somebody. After all this." She stood close to him and fumbled for his hand.

"So come over. We'll just, you know . . . hang out."

"I'll see you there," Lewis said. "I'll take my car so I can get back. Maybe we could go down to the Bird for dinner."

"Love you," Singleton said, talking down to her. First time he'd said that; no place romantic, just standing in a snow-swept parking lot in the middle of nowhere. "Love you," he said.

12

SUNDAY.

Lucas and Del went north in a two-car convoy, Lucas leading in the Acura, Del trailing in the rented Olds. They left the Big New House at three-thirty in the morning, out past the airport, around the sleeping suburbs, then northwest on I-94.

Rose Marie had called ahead and cleared them with the overnight highway patrolmen, and Lucas put the cruise control on eighty-five, with Del drafting behind him. They made the turn north at Fargo in three hours, picking up a few snowflakes as they crossed the narrow cut of the Red River. The snow got heavier as they drove north up I-29, but was never bad enough to slow them. After a quick coffee-and-gas stop at Grand Forks, they continued north, then cut back across the border to Armstrong, and pulled into the Law Enforcement Center a few minutes before nine o'clock.

Bitter cold now, but the snow had quit for the moment. More was due during the day, and Lucas wanted to get started in Broderick before conditions got too bad. The sheriff wasn't around—probably at church, the comm center man said—so they left a message that they'd be somewhere around Armstrong or Broderick, then stopped at the Motel 6. With the discovery of the bodies of Hale and Mary Sorrell, most of the reporters had gone, and they got rooms immediately.

"Like a land office in here the night before last," the clerk said. "Now we're back to Sleepy Hollow."

"All the reporters gone?"

"All but one." The clerk leaned across the desk and dropped his voice. "A black guy from Chicago. He says he's a reporter, but I wouldn't be too sure."

"Hmm," Lucas said wisely, and took the room key.

ON THE WAY OUT of Broderick, rolling through the bleak landscape, Del punched up the CD player and found Bob Seger's "Turn the Page," in the cover version by Metallica.

They listened for a while, and then Del said, "I like Seger's better."

"Close call, they're both good," Lucas said. "I go for the Metallica. Great goddamn album, anyway."

"Dusty fuckers versus metalheads; and you always leaned toward the metal," Del said. "Back when you were running around town on that bike. I remember when you went to that first AC/DC concert. You talked about it for weeks."

"They kept your motor clean," Lucas said. They were coming up on Broderick. "Tell you what—let's go on through town and find that kid."

"Letty . . ."

"West."

———

A FORD TAURUS was parked in the yard next to the Wests' Cherokee. Lucas and Del trooped across the porch, and Martha West met them at the door before they had a chance to knock.

"The state policemen," she said to the room behind her. She pushed the door open and said, "C'mon in."

The front room was too warm and smelled of wool and, Lucas thought, old wine and maybe Windex or lemon Pledge. Letty was sitting on a piano bench in front of a broken-looking Hammond organ; a short, muscular black man with a notebook was perched in an easy chair, forty-five degrees to her right, a Nikon D1X by his feet. A pillow sat on the floor at the third point of the triangle, where Martha West had apparently been sitting.

"Hey, Lucas and Del," Letty said. She got up, smiling. "Did you see me on TV?"

"All over the place," Del said. "You were like Mickey Mouse."

Martha West said, "We've been having an interview with Mr. Johnson from the *Chicago* . . ." She looked for the name but couldn't find it.

"*Tribune,*" the black man said, standing up. He wore round, gold-rimmed glasses and looked like he might once have been a lineman for Northwestern. "Mark Johnson." He reached out to shake hands with Lucas, and then with Del. "You're agents Davenport and Capslock?"

Lucas nodded. "I'm Davenport and this is Capslock. I'm surprised you're here. Your friends got out of town fast enough," he said.

"Mostly TV," Johnson said, as if that explained everything.

"We need to talk to Martha and Letty, but we don't want to disturb your interview," Lucas said. "We can come back, if you'd like."

Johnson shook his head. "I got most of what I was looking for. I'm trying to figure out how in the hell Cash ever wound up here."

"Learn anything?"

"No. The guy down in the car shop won't talk because he's afraid he'll get busted, or even worse, get sued. The guy with the dogs won't talk to me because of his American principles. And the women at the church think I'm probably a rapist because I'm black, but they're too nice to say so."

"We can't help you with Cash," Lucas said. "We'd like to know ourselves. He just doesn't fit."

"He was pure-bred city," Johnson agreed. "I called some people down in KC and they tell me there's no truck-driving job in the world that'd keep him up here. He'd rather have some cheap-ass job like robbing 7-Elevens."

"Interesting," Lucas said.

"It is," Johnson said, gesturing with his notebook. "Now you tell *me* something. Do you really think Cash and this Joe guy and Jane Warr kidnapped the Sorrell girl? If they did, why in the heck would they be out in the country where everybody could see them coming and going, and know every move they made?"

"I don't know," Lucas said. "But I think they were involved in the kidnapping. I think they did it for the money and we'll eventually nail it down. We've got a state crime scene crew taking their cars apart, looking for DNA that might tie them to the girl."

"Can you tell me precisely why you think they were involved?" The notebook was poised again.

Lucas thought it over, then asked, "Do you know Deke Harrison?"

"Yeah, sure. He's my guy at the *Trib*," Johnson said. "He runs our desk."

"He used to come through the Cities," Lucas said. "For years. We'd go out and get a drink."

"Yeah. That's my job now. He moved up," Johnson said.

"Tell him to give me a call," Lucas said. "I've got a cell phone."

———

Lucas gave Johnson the cell phone number, Johnson said good-bye to Lucas and Del, went out through the door, and then a moment later stuck his head back inside. "Find a good place to eat?"

Letty said, "The Red Red Robin."

"That's the best? God help us." Johnson said, and he was gone.

Letty put her hands on her hips and looked at Lucas. "Hey! What's that supposed to mean?"

Lucas told Letty and Martha West what they needed: any hint of an irregularity around the Cash-Warr property. "There is no body in the house—we took the place apart after we found the money and the dope."

"So they must've buried her," Letty said, crossing her lips with both of her forefingers, thinking. Martha shivered at the thought, and looked at her daughter. Letty seemed more interested than scared.

"I imagine they did," Lucas said. "But out here . . . there's ten thousand square miles of unbroken dirt and bog."

"Yeah, but even out here, there's always people going by. You couldn't just drive out somewhere and spend an hour digging a grave and be sure nobody saw you," Letty said. "People *see* you out here, because—wherever you are—you're unusual. They *notice* you. I'll be walking across the lake down by the old dump and two days later somebody'll say, 'Saw you down by the dump with your gun.' And I never saw them."

"Gives me the creeps," Martha West said. "You got no privacy."

Letty looked out the window, the white winter light picking out her blue eyes. Still not much snow. "Why don't we go look around?" she asked. "I'll come with you, see if I can see anything. I walk up and down there all the time, on my way to the crick. If we wait until tomorrow, there might be too much snow."

"Must've been snow since the girl was taken," Del said. "She was taken before Christmas."

"There's been some, but not much," Letty said.

"If you guys are gonna take Letty, could I get you to buy her some lunch or something?" Martha West asked. "I've got to run into town for a while."

"Sure," Del said. "Down to the Bird."

MARTHA WEST WAS suddenly in a hurry, and Del looked past Letty at Lucas, catching his eye, with an *uh-oh* twist of his head: Martha West needed a drink *right now.* Lucas nodded and said to Letty, "Get your coat."

"Want me to bring the .22?"

"That won't be necessary."

"Piece of crap, anyway," she said, and headed up the stairs to her bedroom.

Martha West was gone before Letty came back down. Letty came down wearing a slightly too big parka, pac boots, and carrying a pair of mittens. "S'go," she said, clumping through the living room to the door.

"Your mom's already gone," Del said.

"Straight to the Duck Inn," Letty said. She added, without irony, in a voice that sounded older than her twelve years, "It's a tragedy."

THEY DROVE BACK DOWN to the Cash/Warr house in the Acura, Letty fascinated by the CRT screen in the dashboard. "Can you play movies on it?"

"Nope—you get the information screen and the map screen, and that's it. Unless you have to eject." Lucas kept his voice flat. He was a firm believer in lying to children. "If you need to eject, you go to the information screen, and push History, and one second later, you're history. Throws you right out of the car, through the moon roof."

Letty, in the back seat, thought about it for a second, then said, "It's not nice to fuck with kids."

Del twisted and said, "Jesus Christ. Watch your mouth, little girl."

TWO VEHICLES WERE sitting in the driveway at the Cash/Warr house: a BCA crime scene van, and a sheriff's department car. Lucas pulled in behind them. They all climbed out, and a deputy sheriff came out on the stoop and said, "Your guys are out in the garage, if you're looking for them."

"Thanks," Lucas called back. They trudged up the driveway to the garage, and went in through the side door. A BCA tech was standing at the open trunk of Jane Warr's car, and said, "Hey, guys." When he spoke, another man, shorter and stockier, backed out of the trunk. He was holding a plastic bag and a pair of forceps. A magnifying hood was pulled down over his glasses, and his eyes appeared to be the size of ashtrays.

"Doing any good?" Lucas asked.

"The trunk is full of stuff—we've got hair for sure, we might have some blood, but it could be something else, too," the shorter man said. "Typical trunk."

"How about Cash's car?"

"Same thing. All kinds of stuff."

"How long before we know if anything's good?"

The taller tech shrugged. "Depends on how much stuff there is . . . a week or two. Anything we can do for *you?*"

"We're gonna look around the grounds," Lucas said. "See what there is to see."

"Uh, Dickerson called this morning, said something about a guy with ground-penetrating radar."

"Could happen," Lucas said. "But he can't do the whole place. That'd take weeks. We're gonna see if we can find a place to start."

"Good luck."

LUCAS, DEL, AND LETTY went back outside, and Lucas turned around once, looking at the house, the garage, an old dying tree line that once marked the southern boundary of the farmyard, a fence that might have marked the western end.

"If you had to bury somebody . . ." Letty said.

"I wouldn't do it here," Del said, turning like Lucas. "I'd take her someplace."

"Everybody in the state was looking for her."

"Probably not yet, when they killed her. If they killed her before Sorrell brought in the FBI . . ."

"But they couldn't be absolutely sure that he hadn't done that right away," Lucas said. "If they had her here, in that cell, they wouldn't want to take her too far. Especially if, like Letty says, everybody sees things here. Everybody would remember a black guy with a little blond girl, up here, even if they thought it was innocent."

"Keep her in the trunk?"

"Too many things to go wrong," Lucas said.

"They drove her all the way up here from Rochester."

"What can I tell you? They *did* that. Maybe. But when it came to getting rid of her, do you think they'd drive her all the way back down, and take another big risk?"

"Dunno," Del said. "I just don't know where we could start looking."

LETTY POINTED: "Out there in the trees. That's the crick. Five-minute walk. You could carry a bag. If you walked out there right at dark, nobody would see you, and you could walk back in the dark. How old was she?"

"Eleven."

"Skinny?"

"Not fat," Lucas said. "Sort of fleshy."

"Minnesota skinny."

"That's it."

"So she weighs seventy or eighty pounds. Five-minute walk."

"You'd leave footprints," Del said.

"Not in December. I remember how cold it was, but it wasn't snowing. We had hardly any snow at Christmas."

"Let's go look," Lucas said.

THE CREEK BEGAN as a swale in a farm field, narrowed into a line, not really a depression, toward the back of the Cash/Warr land, and finally deepened into a knee-deep notch in the black earth, surrounded by willows and box elders.

They started with the first tree, at the north end of the property, and followed the deepening notch into the thicker line of trees and brush, walking on the ice of the little creek itself. The band of trees was no more than thirty yards wide. They followed the creek for two hundred yards, until it ended in a bog. They saw nothing unusual—no disturbed earth, and the only tracks they found had probably been left by Letty.

They finally walked back up the creek; halfway back, three dogs began barking from the back of a house that lay down the highway from Cash's place. They were black and brown, square-faced, crazy: pit bulls. "That's the dogs I've been telling you about," Letty said.

"Scare the heck out of me," Del admitted. To Letty: "They ever let them out on you, you shoot first and ask questions later."

Lucas was annoyed. "You just stay away from there," he said. "You don't need to do any shooting."

"Maybe they fed the kid to the dogs," Letty suggested.

"Goddamnit," Lucas said. And as they came to the top of the creek, "Goddamnit. We could be standing ten feet from the Sorrell kid and not know it."

"How would you do it?" Letty asked. She looked up at Del. "If you killed a little kid, and brought her out here, where would you put her?"

Del said, "I don't think you should be here."

"C'mon, Del. Look around. What'd you do?" she asked.

Lucas looked around, then down at his feet. "Is there always water in the creek?"

"No. But most of the time, there is."

"Under the creek?" Del asked, skeptically.

"It's a possibility," Lucas said. "But if he *was* going to dig around here, I bet he'd be down here in the creek bed. Maybe digging in the bottom, or in the creek bank. Couldn't be seen, but he could see people coming."

"Unless it was at night," Letty said.

They walked up and down the creek ice, looking at the banks, but couldn't find anything unusual. Lucas probed a low cut-bank with a stick, then shook his head and threw the stick back into the trees. "We need the crime scene guys down here, and the radar guy, and maybe some dogs or something."

DISCOURAGED, THEY WALKED across the thin crunchy snow back up to the house, and Lucas looked at his watch and said, "Little early for lunch, but we could get some breakfast."

"Can I see the cell?" Letty asked. "The room in the basement?"

"Fuckin' TV," Del said. The cell had been mentioned prominently.

"Watch your mouth around a kid," Letty said, payback for the *little girl* comment. To Lucas: "I'd really like to go down there. I'm a kid, maybe I could think like a kid or something."

Lucas sighed, looked at Del, then said, "All right. Two minutes."

They trooped through the house, nodded to the deputy, and took Letty into the basement. Inside the bathroom—the cell—she turned round and round, then sat down on the floor, then lay down and looked at the ceiling, her arms outstretched as though she were making a snow angel. She closed her eyes, and a minute later, she said, "If they left me here alone—if they left *me* here alone—I would try to write my name somewhere."

She opened her eyes, found Lucas's eyes, and asked, "What do you think?"

"Sit up," Lucas said.

She sat up, and Lucas and Del sat down, and they began scrutinizing the walls. Nothing apparent. Lucas stood up, pulled the top off the toilet tank, and looked inside. Nothing visible. Lucas flushed, watched the water go down, pulled the float to stop water, and groped around the bottom of the tank with his hand. The shower stall was bare, not even a bar of soap. He pulled open the medicine cabinet, found it empty. Del looked inside the cabinet under the sink, and found four rolls of toilet paper. He looked through all the toilet paper tubes. Empty. Lucas checked the rim on the top of the medicine cabinet, and got his fingers dusty.

"I would write something," Letty said, a little defensively. "I would scratch it with something."

She crawled around on her hands and knees, peering at the baseboard. Then Del, who'd crawled over to the toilet, said, "Got something here."

"What?" Lucas got down on his stomach, and Letty crawled over.

Del was lying face up. "Something twisted around the water line . . .

it's a chain. Let me . . ." He fumbled under the tank, said, "Uhhh . . ." Then: "Got it."

He slid out from under the toilet. A silver locket, a small oval, dangled from his fingers on a short silver chain.

"Aw, Jesus," Lucas said. "Don't fuckin' move. Don't even twitch."

Lucas ran up the stairs, dashed through the house to the mudroom door, outside to the garage, and said, "You guys . . . get some shit, get some baggies and those tweezers . . . c'mon."

BACK DOWN IN the basement, the stocky crime scene guy grabbed the locket with his forceps, held it sideways to one of the overhead lights and said, "There's a partial print on the back. If it's not yours . . ."

He looked down at Del, who shook his head: "Not mine. I never touched the locket part, only the chain."

"Looks like a good print," the tech said. He turned it in the light. "It's got an inscription. The locket does."

"*What?*"

The tech's lips moved as he worked through the script. Then he frowned and asked, "Who the heck are Jean and Wally?"

Lucas scratched his head. "Maybe somebody the Sorrell kid knew. Her grandparents, or somebody?"

"Whoever, she put it down there," Del said. "The locket didn't just fall in there."

"Where'd you find it?" the tech asked.

Del explained, and the tech looked around and finally said, "Did you check the mirror? And the shower booth walls? If she used hot water in here, they'd get steamed up, and she'd write in the steam. If she had soap or shampoo or oil on her fingers, you might get the image back."

"I do that every time I'm in the bathtub," Letty said. "I write on the mirror when I get out."

Lucas said, "Worth a try, I guess."

The tech said, "Let me put this away, and get my camera. Huh. Wally and Jean."

WHILE THE TECH WENT to put the locket away, Lucas, trailed by Letty, went out to the car, got his address book out of his briefcase, and looked up the numbers for the FBI agents on the Sorrell case. He got Lanny Cole's wife on the second ring, and she said Cole was out shoveling the walk. "Just had a quick two inches," she said. "Of snow."

Lucas heard her calling her husband, then some stomping around, and then Cole was on the line. He didn't know the names on the locket. "We were told that she probably wasn't wearing any jewelry when she was taken—she was just a kid, and she had a pretty limited set of stuff. Nothing like a locket, far as I know. Sorry."

"Thought we had something," Lucas said. "It's weird."

"I'll ask around," Cole said. "I wouldn't hold my breath. Maybe the print will turn out to be something."

Lucas hung up and Letty said, "No luck?"

"Not yet."

"It's gotta be something," Letty said. "It didn't belong to the plumber."

BOTH TECHS WERE in the basement with Del, the hot water pouring out of the shower, when Lucas and Letty got back down the stairs. They half-closed the door of the bathroom, waited fifteen seconds. The mirror steamed, and showed several finger-drawn lines, but nothing they could make sense of. The tech took a picture anyway. The walls of the shower showed what looked liked sponge marks: "Somebody cleaned up," the tech said.

"Good try, guys," Lucas said.

Feeling a little morose, they all wandered back up the stairs, and the burly tech said that he'd recheck the walls with his magnifying hood as soon as the humidity cleared. "Maybe somebody wrote really small— it'd be about the only thing you could do. It was a good idea, looking for a name. It turned up the locket. That'll be something."

Lucas looked at Letty. "Maybe you *oughta* be a cop."

Letty shook her head. "Nope. I'm going to be a reporter. It's decided."

Lucas said to Del, "We could be responsible for that."

"I'll never feel clean again," Del said. "Want to head down to the Bird? My gut says it's lunchtime."

They rode down to the Red Red Robin in near silence, all thinking about the house and where the Sorrell kid's body might be. Del finally said, "If they thought they ever might be suspected of anything, they wouldn't want a body anywhere around. They *must've* driven it out into the countryside. All right, if they're seen, they're seen, but they could fix it so they weren't. Scout out a spot ahead of time, dig a hole, drop the body during the night, fill the hole—it'd only take a couple of minutes—and get out of there."

"Yeah, I know," Lucas said. "She's probably gone for good."

THE BIRD WAS AS below-average as it was the first couple of times: below-average coffee, below-average food. Below-average: Letty ate everything in sight, with the shifty-eyed compulsion of a kid who'd gone to bed hungry a few times, who was afraid the food might disappear.

"You okay with your mom?" Del asked halfway through the meal.

"Gettin' this far with her was the hard part," Letty said, working around the edges of the mashed potatoes, so the gravy wouldn't spill out of the center cup. "Now that I'm in middle school, things are smoother. I ride the bus back and forth, she can do what she needs to."

"Just checkin'," Del said. "I've had a little trouble with alcohol myself. It's a bitch to get off your back, but it can be done."

"You drink?" Letty asked Lucas, holding his eyes. Lucas shook his head. "A bottle of beer, few times a week. I never got the hang of it."

"That's good," Letty said.

THE PHONE IN LUCAS'S pocket rang, and he pulled it out. "Davenport."

"Hey, Lucas, this is Lanny Cole." The FBI man sounded like he was having a hard time catching his breath. "You said Wally and Jean on that locket. It was a white gold oval locket with a white gold chain and the names in script in the front oval. Picture of an elderly couple inside."

"We didn't look inside because of the print, but you got the rest of it, except that I thought it was silver," Lucas said. "Was it Tammy Sorrell's?"

"No."

"No?"

"It belonged to a girl named Annie Burke, fifteen, daughter of the owner of a chain of nursing homes from Lincoln, Nebraska. One of our guys downtown remembered the locket thing. She was kidnapped last April. A million-dollar ransom was paid, but she was never returned, never heard from again. The deal was, the kidnappers told Burke's father that they had an in with the FBI, and they left him a pack of papers that looked like FBI printouts. They told him that if he contacted the FBI or any police agency, they would know. He bought it, made the payoff. And get this: he got the money in Vegas, same way Hale did."

"Oh, boy."

Letty said, "What?"

"We're coming up there," Cole said. "We need that locket, we need that fingerprint. I'll talk to your boss. What do *you* need up there?"

"You got people who can look for soft spots in the ground, under the snow?"

"We got that. We have a team in California who do exactly that. They can be here in forty-eight hours."

"Bring them in," Lucas said.

13

AFTER LUNCH, they took a protesting Letty back to her house. "I can still help you."

"If we need you, we'll stop by," Lucas said. "We really do appreciate what you've done."

Her face anxious, she asked, "If I get my traps real fast, could you drop me at the dump? It's only five minutes in the car. I can walk back."

Lucas said, "We're pretty busy."

"I helped *you*," she said. "I need to get some clothes. TV might come back."

Lucas sighed. "Get the traps."

She took ten minutes, getting into an old pair of jeans, her boots and her parka. She got a can of generic-brand tuna cat food from under the kitchen sink—bait—the gunny sack with her traps, and her .22. The .22 was an old Harrington & Richardson bolt action single-shot, probably made in the 1940s. She tossed it all in the back of the Acura.

Six miles north of Broderick, on a back road, the landfill was marked by a clan of crows flapping overhead like little specks of India ink thrown against the gray sky. Lucas pulled into the entrance road, next to a sign that said "Quad-County Landfill," and stopped by a locked gate. Inside the landfill, a small Caterpillar sat at the base of a wall of garbage.

Lucas got out of the truck at the same time Letty did, and looked over the locked gate. The dump was bigger than he'd expected, covering a half of a square mile. Much of the garbage appeared to be pizza boxes, though it smelled more like old diapers. Letty walked around to the back of the truck to get her gear.

"Six miles," Lucas said, as he walked back around the truck and popped the lid for her. "How're you gonna get back home?"

"Walk, or hitch a ride," she said. She dragged the sack of traps out, stuck the rifle under her arm. "I won't have my traps. Do it all the time."

"Aw, Jesus." Lucas looked around at the weird, cold landscape, the spitting snow, the circling crows, and the piles of trash.

"I'm not asking for a ride back," Letty said. He could feel the manipulation.

"How long will it take to set out the traps? Minimum?" Lucas asked.

"Hour, hour and a half, do it right," she said.

"You got a watch?"

"No."

"Goddamnit. You need a watch." Lucas took his watch off and handed it to her. "If you lose the watch, I'll poison you. My wife gave it to me. We'll be back in an hour and a half."

"Thanks."

"Be careful."

A car pulled into the entryway, stopped, and they both looked at it. The man inside put up a hand, a *hello,* then turned and backed away. He got straight on the road, and headed back toward the highway. An old Cadillac.

Letty said, "See you," and walked away.

Lucas slammed the lid, got back in the truck. "She's more goddamn trouble than women ten years older than she is," he said.

"What're we doing?" Del asked.

"Let's start tearing Broderick down."

"Starting with . . . ?"

"Gene Calb. Go back and hit him again. Nail him down. And maybe those church women, if we can find them. Letty said they worked for Calb, sometimes, delivering cars. They're church women, so maybe they'll tell us the truth."

"Fat fuckin' chance," Del said. And a while later, as they headed back toward Broderick, "That was a nice Caddy, you know? I've thought about buying an old one myself. You see them in the Sunday paper: you can get a good one for six or seven thousand, ten years old, some old guy drove it until he died, put thirty thousand miles on it, or something. You can drive it for another ten years."

"Of course, you'd have spent ten years driving a pig," Lucas said.

"Go ahead, tarnish my dream."

CALB'S SHOP WAS locked, and Del said, "It *is* Sunday. Not everybody works."

"Yeah. There're a couple of cars over at the church, though," Lucas said. They both looked across the highway, where two '90s Toyota Corollas, both red, sat in the driveway next to the church. Electric cords ran out to both of them, firing the block heaters. "Let's check them out."

"Nuns make me nervous," Del said.

"Except for Elle," Lucas said.

"Elle makes me nervous," Del said. "I'm always afraid she's gonna start shaking and moaning and screaming about Jesus."

"Wrong religion," Lucas said dryly, as they trudged across the empty highway toward the church. "She screams about the archbishop. Jesus, she doesn't scream about."

"It could happen, though," Del said. "She's one of those skinny women with big eyes. They can start shaking anytime. That's my experience."

Elle Kruger was Lucas's oldest friend, a nun and professor of psychology at a St. Paul women's college. He'd known her before kindergarten—they had walked together with their two mothers, carrying their tin lunch boxes, on the first day they'd ever gone to school. Later, when he was with Minneapolis homicide, she'd consulted on a number of his cases; and when Lucas began writing role-playing games as a way to make extra money, she'd created a group at her college to test-play the games.

WHICH MADE THE coincidence seem even stranger—that they should be talking about Elle Kruger as they crossed the highway, and then . . .

They climbed the stoop and knocked on the door of the old church. Lucas's ears were burning from the cold, and Del said, "Fucking Minnesota" and shuffled his feet in the keeping-warm dance. Lucas reached out to knock again when the door opened, and a woman looked out. She was an older woman, in her sixties, white-haired, round-faced with little pink dots at her cheeks, wearing bifocals, and holding what looked like a dustcloth. The pink dots made her look like Ronald Reagan. When they explained what they wanted, she said, "You'd have to talk to Ruth. Come in."

When the two men hesitated, her bottom lip twitched and she said, "This isn't a nunnery or a dormitory. You're allowed to come in."

"Thanks," Lucas said, feeling a little lame. They followed her through the back of the church, which had been cut into sleeping cubicles, reminding Lucas of an old Washington Avenue flophouse in Minneapolis, except that it didn't smell like wine vomit; past a side room where two women were sitting on a couch, watching the movie *Fight*

Club; and into the kitchen. A small woman sat at a kitchen table, peering through gold-rimmed glasses into a notebook. A pile of what looked like insurance forms sat to one side. She looked up and the woman who'd met them at the door said, "Ruth, these gentlemen are from the police. They wanted to speak to somebody."

"Lucas Davenport," the woman said, closing the notebook. She showed him a thin, cool smile.

Lucas, surprised, said, "I'm sorry . . ."

She stood up and put out a hand. As they shook, her hand small and cool, she said, "I'm Ruth Lewis. I'm sure you don't remember, but I'm a friend of Elle Kruger. I once played a game with your gaming group, maybe ten years ago, when Elle was running it. I got to be George Pickett at Gettysburg."

"I remember that," he said; and he did, clearly, and with pleasure. She'd learned fast and had been determined to win. "You kept taking out Buford," Lucas said. "No matter how many times we played it, you'd kick Buford out of the way and then you'd get on top of the hills."

"And that was that," she said, dusting her hands together. "The South wins the battle and maybe the war."

"Bad design," Lucas said. "You never came back for Stalingrad."

"Nobody invited me," she said. "I thought maybe it was because I kept messing up the first one."

"No, no, no," Lucas said. "You were invited back, you just didn't come."

"Have you seen Elle?"

"Just the other day . . ."

THEY CHATTED FOR a few minutes—she'd known Lucas as a Minneapolis cop, and he told her about his move to the state; and Lucas had known her as a nun, and she told him about her migration away from the sisterhood. "I made the mistake of going to the Holy

Land," she said. "I saw that the Sea of Galilee was a big, dirty lake and that the Mount of Olives was a neighborhood. Then Jesus didn't seem divine. He seemed more real, but he seemed like another one of the guys that the Old Testament is full of. Down in my heart, I didn't believe anymore—in Jesus, I mean."

"So you quit?"

"Yup. Moved over to Catholic Charities. Got a boyfriend—though that didn't last long. I think he just liked the idea of sleeping with an ex-nun."

Lucas was embarrassed. "Some people," he said.

She smiled, letting him off the male hook, and said, "You're here investigating the lynchings."

"Murders," Lucas said hastily. "Not really—we know who did those—"

"The man from Rochester. I heard about that, the man and his wife. It's hard to believe."

"Yeah. Now we're trying to figure out who killed them. We were told that you guys sometimes make money driving cars for Gene Calb. Since Deon Cash worked over there as a driver, we thought you might have known him."

She was nodding. "I did know him, and he was a bad man. A *bad* man. Gene was going to fire him, because he thought Deon was taking dope, and Gene was worried about some insurance issues. Like if Deon was driving for him and got in an accident, driving under the influence. Gene was afraid he'd get sued for everything."

"So everybody knew about the drugs?"

"Some of us, anyway," Ruth said. "There was a woman here, Jeanette Raskin, she used to work for Lutheran Social Services down in Minneapolis and she knows a lot about drugs—she said he once had a crack pipe in his car. I wouldn't know what one looked like, but that's what she said. I have her phone number if you need it. She's back in the Cities."

"I know Jeanette," Del said, and to Lucas: "You do, too. She used to run the Love Bug place, the free clinic."

"Oh, yeah," Lucas said. "She *would* know about drugs."

"How come you guys drive for Calb?" Del asked Ruth.

Ruth shrugged. "Extra money. Pizza money. Easy money. We follow the delivery car in my Corolla. Fifty cents a mile, so we get fifty dollars for a hundred-mile round trip, and we can do that on three gallons of gas. We don't have a lot of money here."

"You did it a lot?"

"A couple of times a week," she said.

"Is Calb straight?" Lucas asked.

"Yes. He's a very nice man, in a . . . car-mechanic way," Ruth said, meeting his eyes. She had pale eyes, like the moons you could see in daylight. "His wife sometimes helps us out, when we're checking on older people, shut-ins."

"You don't think . . . if Cash and Warr were involved in a kidnapping, you don't think that Calb would have been involved?"

"Good gosh, no. I mean, the girl . . . is dead, I guess."

Lucas and Del both nodded.

Ruth continued. "Gene always wanted children, but he and his wife couldn't have any. They've been foster parents, even, for like a half a dozen kids. There's no way he'd ever hurt a child."

Lucas said, "All right. But Deon Cash could."

"Deon . . . Deon was crazy. I didn't know him very well, but you didn't have to. I once saw him kick a door for two minutes because it didn't open right. He was really crazy-angry with it. With the door." She looked away from them for a minute, thinking about it, then back, and nodded positively. "He could kill children."

"How about his pal, Joe?"

"I hardly knew him, but he always seemed to be walking behind Deon. I think Deon impressed him. Deon impressed Jane, too—she *liked* him being crazy. Like it gave her status." Again, she looked away, thinking, and then turned back. "We see that quite a bit, actually. Women taking status from the violence of their men."

"A sense of protection, if you live in a slum," Lucas said.

But she shook her head. "Not just in the slums. All kinds of women. Even nuns."

She showed a little smile and Del grinned at Lucas and said, "Ouch."

Lucas said, "Tell me one good fact. One thing that will point me somewhere. Something you know, way down in your head, about Deon."

"I've thought about this, ever since they found Jane and Deon," she said. "I keep thinking, Deon was from the big city, Kansas City. So was Jane. They hated it here. I don't think they even *knew* anybody, besides a couple of people at Calb's. But they stayed, so there had to be a reason. Something they couldn't do in Kansas City. Maybe they were selling the dope, maybe it was the kidnapping. Whatever it was, came from up here."

"Good," said Lucas.

OUTSIDE, DEL SAID, "Sister Ruth does a little dope herself."

"Yeah?"

"I could smell it on her. Faintly. Raw, not smoke."

"Brownies."

"Maybe." Del looked around at the white-on-white landscape, at their lonely car sitting in the empty, snow-swept parking lot outside the empty yellow building across the highway. "I can't blame her. It's like, it's dope or network TV. There ain't nothin' else."

"I'll ask Elle about her," Lucas said. "I'm not sure the sister was entirely straight with us."

"What'd I miss?"

Lucas shook his head. "Maybe nothing. I counted eight cots in there and most of the rooms seemed to be lived in. That's a sizable operation.

What would a hundred dollars a week mean to them? I mean, if they each worked one night in a Holiday store, they'd make three or four times as much. If they need the money that bad . . ."

"Maybe it's just easy, casual. Pin money. Take it if they have somebody around, skip it if they don't. Wouldn't be tied to a schedule."

"Could be," Lucas agreed. "She seemed pretty rehearsed . . . but then she might have expected us." He looked at his watch, and found a patch of white skin where the watch face should have been. Not having a watch was going to drive him crazy, he realized. "The bar's closed. Let's go try the cafe, and then the grocery."

"It *feels* hopeless," Del said. "Knocking on doors in nowhere."

ON THE WAY TO the cafe, Lucas's cell phone rang, and when he answered it, a voice said, "This is Deke Harrison. Is this Davenport?"

"Yeah, it is. How are you, Deke?"

"Interrupted. I was halfway through an anchovy, pepper-cheese, onion sandwich and you know what it's like to be interrupted halfway through one of those."

"So are—"

"Halfway through, when somebody called for somebody else who got a call from Mark Johnson that said you wanted him vouched for."

"You vouching for him?"

"Yeah. He's a good guy, knows what he's doing. Takes care of his sources."

"I might chat with him, then."

"Excellent. If you ever run for governor of whatever hick state you're in—Minnesota?—you'll know that the *Tribune* stands behind you."

"Far behind."

"You stepped on my line," Harrison said.

"Yeah, I know," Lucas said. "It was such an original. Go back to the sandwich."

———

SANDY WOLF, WHO RAN the cafe, told them that Deon Cash liked coconut cream pie and that Jane Warr was allergic to sulfites used as a preservative. She said that she'd never seen them argue. Every time they left the cafe together, she said, Warr would go through the door first and that Cash would reach out and squeeze her ass. Wolf also knew that Cash liked basketball and was a Los Angeles Lakers fan, and that he didn't care for football and especially hated the Green Bay Packers and the Minnesota Vikings. She once had a Vikings game on the television, and Cash asked her to turn it off. "He had a mean look in him, so I turned it off," she said.

THE CONVENIENCE STORE/GAS STATION was run by John McGuire and McGuire's sister, Shelly. McGuire was a lean man who might have been taken for a farmer; his sister, equally lean, reminded Lucas of a pool shark he'd known in Minneapolis, who eventually became a successful rug-cleaning franchisee. Both of them knew Cash, who, in addition to whatever dope habits he might have had, also was attracted to the orange Halloween Hostess cupcakes, and had bought four dozen of them last Halloween, all that the store had in stock.

They had also known Joe Kelly and said that he seemed like a shy man. Every night when they saw his car parked at Cash's place, Kelly came in and bought a twelve-pack of Budweiser. "We think he had alcohol issues," Shelly McGuire said.

"I should have offered to take him to my AA meeting," McGuire said, "but I wasn't sure he was drinking it by himself, and I couldn't get him talking. And I thought, you know, him being colored, maybe colored people can drink more than white people."

The bar was closed.

———

THE DOG HOUSE on the side street was a manufactured home, built in a factory and trucked to the homesite, where it was hammered together on a prepoured slab. The siding felt like tin. Del knocked, and a man in a sleeveless undershirt came to the door while the dogs went crazy in a back room. Lucas, without looking, could feel Del loosening up his Smith.

The man said, "Yep?" He propped himself in the door, and Lucas could smell tomato sauce and dog shit in the overheated air streaming out. The man had an American flag tattooed on one shoulder, and on the other, a skull with a dagger through its eye, and the legend, *Death From Above*.

"We're with the Bureau of Criminal Apprehension. We're investigating a series of crimes . . ."

"Got an ID?"

A woman in the house yelled, "Who is it, Dick?"

Lucas held out his ID and Dick glanced at it and yelled, "Cops, asking about Cash," and stepped out on the porch. "What can I do for you?"

"Don't want you to freeze," Lucas said. He would have liked a look inside.

"I'm fine," the man said. His arms were turning red. "Don't feel the cold."

"We understand you work at Calb's, and we're looking for any information . . ."

The man's name was Richard Block, and the woman inside was his girlfriend, Eurice. He was a prep specialist who set the trucks up for painting.

"I didn't have nothin' to do with the drivers," he said. "I was always back in the sanding booth; I ain't management. I don't think I talked to Cash more than once in my life. Never did meet his old lady, except to nod at her in the store. She never came to the bar. Talked to Joe, once or twice. He was interested in the prep business, he wanted to paint his own car. Don't know anything about him, though."

They bounced a few more questions off him, looking for an edge, and found nothing but genuine ignorance.

"You ever meet any of the nuns, er, whatever, over at the church?" Del asked.

"Never saw them, except at the cafe and maybe at the store. Call them the rug-munchers, over to the shop," he said.

"I thought they drove for Calb?" Lucas said.

"Not that I know of," Block said, his eyes shifting away, momentarily. He was lying. "You have to talk to Gene about his employees. I mean, I *ain't* in management, and I don't want to piss anybody off. I'd like to keep the job."

He had nothing more to say, except that he hoped to build a kennel and breed pit bulls.

"Nice tats," Del said, as they backed away from the door.

The man glanced at his dagger tattoo and for the first time showed a hint of a smile. "Sometimes I wished I'd gotten *Mom*. But I was in the Army, and only Navy guys get *Mom*."

THE MAN STEPPED BACK inside and closed the door behind himself. "Why would he lie about the nuns?" Del asked, as they walked away. "He was doing good up to then."

"I don't know," Lucas said. "Let's try some more."

There were a half-dozen trailer homes scattered around town. One had unbroken snow around it, and was apparently not being lived in. Of the others, three were being lived in, but nobody was home. At the other two, they talked to men who worked for Calb, but seemed genuinely confused about the killings. One of the men, who smelled strongly of beer, said, "We're sittin' here with a gun, tell you the truth."

He reached sideways onto a table, picked up a heavy-frame revolver, waggled it at his ceiling, and said, "I dare the motherfucker to come in here. He'll be walking home without a couple of pounds of meat."

"Make sure who you're shooting it at," Lucas said.

"I don't know—I think people get more scared when they think that you're crazy and maybe drunk. Tend not to fuck with you," said the man, smiling in a distinctly crazy way.

"You could be right about that," Lucas said.

As they walked away, he looked at the patch of white skin on his arm. "Let's go get Letty."

LETTY WAS OUT on the dump when they got there, a small figure in dark clothes, kicking through the trash pile. Letty was concentrating on something, and didn't see them pull in. Lucas got out and yelled, "Hey. Letty."

She turned, waved, and skidded down the side of the pile of trash, and clumped across the dirt pan between the edge of the trash pile and the gate. When she got to the gate, she passed him the .22 and the empty gunny sack, then climbed the gate. When she dropped down beside him, he got a whiff of aged garbage.

"You oughta stay out of the trash," he said. "You don't know what might be in there."

Letty said, "*Nobody* knows what might be in there. Phil gets all kinds of good stuff out of there."

"Who's Phil?"

"Drives the Cat," she said, nodding at the bulldozer. "He gets about one good computer a week."

"Won't do you any good if you die of some weird disease," Lucas said. "You better take a shower when you get home."

"Water kills cancer?"

"You're also a little stinky," Lucas said.

"Yeah? It'd be worth it, stinky, if I could get a good computer out of it," she said. "My computer is worse than this old piece-of-crap .22."

They were loading into the Acura as she said it. Del asked, "If the gun's a piece of crap, why don't you get another one?"

" 'Cause they cost money, and this one works," she said. "I mean, it's a piece of crap, but that's all I need. My computer . . . that's just a piece of crap." As they were backing out, she added, "You know what I'd do if I was a cop? I'd tell the guy at the dump to turn in all the computers he found. Most of them work, they're just old. When people throw them away, they leave all their letters and stuff on them—he finds out the neatest stuff about people, messing with the old computers. It's his hobby. One time he found, uh . . ." She suddenly colored, and snapped her mouth shut.

"What?" Lucas asked.

"Never mind."

They both looked at her, and then Del said to Lucas, "I need to get my old computer back."

14

SINGLETON COULD NOT remember feeling exactly like this: unable to breathe, unable to think. He'd driven out of the dump, down the gravel road, and straight through the stop sign onto the highway. He was heading south before he realized he'd missed the stop. He might have died right there, he thought, if there'd been a Molson truck coming through from Canada.

Goddamn Letty West. She was out there all the time, trapping the goddamn 'coons. He was *sure* that she hadn't been out there when he'd buried the girls. Except that he hadn't checked. He had the same sense of uneasiness that came when he was sure he'd unplugged the iron before leaving town, or when he was sure that he'd locked the doors before going to bed . . .

He was sure, but he wasn't *sure*.

He knew she was often out there, even late, because he'd seen her walking along the highway in the evening, carrying her rifle and her bag.

If she *had* seen him, hauling the garbage bags that held the girls' bodies, she would have assumed that he was getting rid of his own household trash. Though it wasn't legal, people did it—did it all the time, after hunting and fishing trips, to get rid of fish guts or deer remains.

But: the girl had been dragging around town with the two state cops, had apparently helped them reach the unbelievably quick conclusion that the Sorrells had been involved in the hanging of Deon Cash and Jane Warr. Now she had taken them out to the dump.

Did she know something? Were the state cops looking at *him*? Maybe he shouldn't have left so quickly, maybe he should have stopped and chatted. He could say that the dump was part of his check-route. But if they started to ask him questions, what would he have said? He wasn't ready for that.

Then: if the state cops *were* looking at him, why hadn't he felt anything at work? There hadn't been any curious looks, or veiled questions. Could the state cops be holding it *that* close, not even letting the sheriff in on it?

Or—how about this—they'd found out that he'd been hanging around Calb's, and in the process of checking on him, they'd talked to Letty and she'd mentioned seeing him at the dump, dragging the bags. Of course, putting him with Calb wouldn't get them to Deon and Jane, because he'd kept that connection very quiet.

Think.

All right, here's another possibility: it was all a coincidence. She was out there trapping, and the cops had taken her out. But why would the cops do that? It wasn't like they were a taxi service.

Think.

Better talk to Mom.

———

THE DAY HAD STARTED simply enough. He'd slept late after a strenuous evening with Katina Lewis, had then gotten up, gotten dressed, and had gone into the office to see if anything had happened with the murders of the Sorrells.

Micky James was working the comm center: "The state boys are back," James said. "They've been asked in to cover the Sorrell murders, too. They're going to be up around Broderick. What the hell you think is happening?"

"Dope dealing up at the res, if you ask me," Singleton said. "It's all gotta be tied together."

Back home, he'd decided that snooping was probably more dangerous than doing nothing—and his thoughts turned to the Caddy out in his garage. He needed to do some fine sanding on the last clear coat, and doing that kind of work always smoothed him out, along with the car. Gave him a chance to think.

In the garage, he realized that his breathing gear was still out at Calb's, and the paint he was using always specified breathing gear. That meant a trip to Broderick.

He'd gone to Broderick without a thought in his mind. As he came into town, he saw a silver SUV pulling out of the body shop, heading out on the highway, north. He pulled into the spot that the SUV had just left and found the shop deserted. Not unusual for a Sunday. He ran the door up with his remote control, went inside, and got the breather gear. Didn't feel the slightest vibration from the silver truck.

"Loren?" A woman's voice called to him. He looked back to his right, and saw an older woman walking across the highway from the church. "Hey," she called. "Did you talk to Katina?"

"Not since last night. She said she was heading back here . . ." And for a moment, Singleton thought the woman was going to tell him that

Katina was missing. If she'd gone missing, for any reason, he might be cooked.

"She *was* here, until ten minutes ago," the woman said. She was an older woman, who looked like a *Saturday Evening Post* caricature of Grandma. "She tried to call you—she's probably down at your place, now. She said if you came by, looking for her, to tell you that she'd wait."

"All right."

"Did you talk to the state policemen?"

"No . . ."

"They were just here. They've been going around town."

"Silver truck?"

The woman nodded. "Yes. You just missed them."

THEY WERE HEADED NORTH. To Letty West's? He thanked the woman, and as soon as she was back in the church, headed north out of town, after the silver SUV. He was no more than fifteen minutes behind it, he thought. He took it slow going out, looking for their car at West's house. It wasn't there—in fact, there was no car at West's. Of course, they might have come back past Calb's when he was getting the breathing gear, but he hadn't seen or heard any traffic, and the shop was quiet.

They were headed north . . .

Then it hit him. *Shit. The dump.* He denied it to himself—*Couldn't be the dump.*

He wheeled the Caddy out of the parking lot and put his foot down. The Cadillac would make a hundred and ten. He had to fight the undulating highway and the soft suspension, but he stuck with it, pushing the car as hard as he could. The dump road came up in four minutes, with no sign of the silver truck. He turned the corner, eased down the road . . . saw nothing until he came to the entry.

Turned in.

There they were, caught like deer in the headlights. The whole god-damned bunch of them, standing around the SUV.

He lifted a hand, mind gone blank, backed out, and raced away . . .

THE SCENE WENT round and round in Singleton's brain, and he couldn't stop it. There were too many permutations, but it all came back to one problem: he didn't believe in coincidence. The state cops had been out there with Letty West for a reason.

He'd put the two girls four feet down in the center of the landfill, under the clay cap. He'd dug through to the garbage layers, shoved the bodies in, refilled the holes and carefully tamped down the clay. Even if *he* went out to look for the bodies, now, he'd be lucky to get within twenty feet of them. Letty West, if she'd been back in the woods and had seen him cutting the holes, would never be able to put the cops on the exact spot.

Still: if they knew he'd been involved, they'd find a way to get him. Christ, they might hit the house. In fact, that's the first thing they'd do. If they found the money, he'd be gone.

And what else did Letty know? Had she seen his Caddy at Deon's? He'd parked it in the back, but he'd seen her walking down the creek be-hind the place. Had she seen it there? He'd been there often enough. Did she know he'd gone to Vegas with James Ramone and later with Deon and Jane?

He better get a story. He needed a story, and a good one. And he needed to think about Letty West.

Goddamnit. He looked at himself, caught his own eyes in the rear-view mirror. He'd never been like this. Could this be fear?

KATINA WAS AT his house, sitting on the back stoop in the cold, a brown grocery sack next to her leg. He pulled into his driveway and she stood up, hugging herself across the chest, jiggling up and down, trying to keep warm.

"Where've you been?"

"Had to go in for a couple of hours," he said. "Got guys running all over the place with this Deon thing." He got his keys out, unlocked the house, and she picked up the sack and followed him inside. He walked on through to the front hall, took off his coat, hung it, leaned back against the wall, and pulled off his boots.

"Something wrong?" she asked.

He didn't exactly jump, but felt himself twitch. "Huh?"

"You look a little stressed."

"Just, uh, wish I didn't have to work tonight," he said. "Anything new with the Deon thing? From Gene?"

"Not that I've heard. The state police have been going around town, talking to people. Talked to Ruth for quite a while. She didn't have much to tell them."

"Good. Be dumb."

"The Lord looks over the innocent," she said. "I brought a couple of rib-eyes and some veggies. I thought we could eat here."

"That'd be good," he said.

THEY HAD A quiet afternoon, Katina cooking, Singleton looking through car trader magazines. Calb had a computer on his desk, and he'd shown Singleton how to get online and browse car-rehab sites. Singleton did it, from time to time, but preferred paper. He trusted the magazines—he liked the color and he liked to lie on his couch and look at a photo for a long time, thinking what he might have done with the same car. He had a hard time doing it this afternoon: he kept thinking about the scene at the dump, with the two cops and Letty West.

He finally got up and went into the hall to call Mom; he got no answer. Probably at the casino, he thought—she usually was on Sunday nights. She liked her slots. Since she'd come into the money, she'd moved up to the dollar machines.

He went back to the couch and dozed fitfully, the odors from the kitchen getting better and better, almost driving the Letty West demon out of his head. Then Katina called him into the kitchen and he found a tablecloth on the kitchen table, and a couple of white candles, in fancy glass candleholders. He said, "Whoa."

"I thought you'd like it," Katina said. She blushed a little, as though she were shy about it, or maybe it was the heat from the stove. She'd made a salad with white seeds that looked like sunflower seeds, but weren't, and mashed potatoes to go with the steak.

Singleton sat down and said, "Pretty okay," then popped up and said, "You forgot the ketchup."

She said grace, as she always did, and then was quiet, until they were halfway through dinner, when she asked, "Have you ever thought about having a child?"

He said, "What?"

SINGLETON DIDN'T KNOW exactly what had happened, there, during dinner and afterward. They'd watched television and then wound up in bed, again, which was fine with him—but he'd gotten up to watch the ten o'clock news, and to get into his uniform, and she'd left, light-footed and apparently lighthearted, singing to herself.

He watched the news: they were still talking about Sorrell, and they had a quick piece of tape with Letty West, but it was old tape that he'd been seeing for a couple of days. He dozed for a while, sitting in front of the tube in the La-Z-Boy. When he woke up, he groped around for his cigarettes, found them, found the matchbox, and ripped the match down the igniter strip.

In the flare of the match, it occurred to him that the Sorrell killings had been no problem at all. He'd just gone and done it. Nothing pointed at him and a threat had been eliminated.

Truth be told, he realized as he stared into the flame, he'd enjoyed knocking down the Sorrells. Nothing to do with his mother—he'd enjoyed it for himself. Here was that king-shit Sorrell guy, all the money in the world, all big and smart and walking around in his house in silk pajamas, and here was Singleton, with his little ole mother . . .

But who had the gun, king shit? Who acted fast?

He knocked them down in his mind, knocked them down again, then swore as the flame bit down to his fingers.

"Goddamnit," he said, aloud. He lit another match, lit the cigarette.

Letty West, he thought, waving the match out. Up there in the night, with nobody but her mama.

AFTER LUCAS AND DEL dropped her at her house, Letty changed clothes and then went out to the highway and hitched a ride into Armstrong. She wasn't stupid about it. She always waited until she recognized the truck before she put her thumb out. In that part of the county, she recognized one in twenty, and they always stopped for her.

At the library, she got a computer and went online, called up the Google search engine, entered *how to* with *TV reporter* and got some strange websites.

Three boys from her class came in, two of them wearing Vikings sweatshirts and the third wearing a sweatshirt that said *Scouts,* which was the high school nickname. One of the Vikings boys was named Don, and Letty considered him somewhat desirable. She felt a pressure from them, almost like a pressure on her face. They got on computers, two of them facing her, and they all clicked along through the net.

Two hours later, disturbed by what she'd read on the websites, and carrying fifty pages of printout, she hitched back home with an eighty-three-year-old drunk who'd spent the evening with a lady friend, and couldn't keep his truck straight on the street. She flagged him down, and he let her drive. She dropped him at his house, halfway up to Broderick, and told him she'd come over in the morning with the truck, when he was sober.

As she went through Broderick, she stopped at the store and bought a bottle of milk and a box of cereal. The house was dark when she got back. She lit it up, turned down the heat, ate a quick bowl of cereal, and then went back into her mother's bedroom, to look at herself in the mirror.

She wasn't bad-looking, she decided. Actually, she was quite attractive. But she would need to soften up her face. She looked good now, but if she kept making grim lines, she could wind up looking like a crocodile. She had no makeup skills at all, but the women at the hair salon could fix that. They had a whole library of books and magazines, and an ocean of experience. Letty had never spent a dime on makeup. She'd start now.

The web sites had stressed that journalism wasn't very important, but *skills* were. That was her next assignment: print out everything she could find on TV schools.

Then she thought: *School.* Homework. Social studies. She climbed the stairs, found her textbook, and looked up the questions she was supposed to answer. Then she thought, *They can't hold it against me if I'm helping Lucas and Del* . . .

She dumped the book, went back downstairs, turned on the TV, watched for a while, reading the printouts, and every half hour or so went to look at herself in the mirror some more. She hardly ever did that—this was not a matter of vanity, but a matter of *technique*. Of *skills*. She found that if she used her mother's compact, she could hold it next to her eye and get a good right-angle profile in the dresser mirror.

One of the web sites had said that *you had to look like TV.* The site said that every female host of the *Today* show had been chosen because she looked like she'd be good at fellatio.

She'd carefully written *fellatio* on a piece of paper and carried it over to the library's *New Shorter Oxford English Dictionary* and looked the word up: "Sucking or licking of a sexual partner's penis."

She thought, *Huh,* and, a second later, *Every one of them?* Then she'd ripped the piece of paper into a hundred bits, in case one of the boys from her class might see it, thrown the tiny bits of paper into the wastebasket, and changed pages in the dictionary.

SHE WAS WATCHING LETTERMAN, and critiquing technique, when headlights swept through the yard. After a moment, they died, and she walked out to the front door. Boots clunked across the porch, the door rattled, and her mother stepped inside.

Martha West was moderately loaded—bars weren't open on Sunday so, like the old man, she'd also done her drinking privately. "Hi, honey. Whose truck is that?"

"Reese Culver. He was drinking and asked me to drive him. I'm gonna take it back in the morning."

"Okay. You got traps out?"

"Yeah, down at the dump."

"You better get upstairs, then, get to bed. It's after eleven o'clock," Martha said. Letty would have to get up at five o'clock to make it out to the dump. "You had something to eat?"

"Had some Honey Bunches of Oats," Letty said. She stood up and stretched. "There's some left, and I got a bottle of milk."

Martha yawned. "Okay. Get to bed."

Letty took the social studies book up the stairs with her, closed her bedroom door, dug a notebook out of her school pack, sprawled on the bed, and started working through the questions. If Lucas and Del didn't come through, she'd need the answers. Besides, with Reese's truck outside, she could sleep an extra forty-five minutes in the morning, and take the truck up to the dump before she returned it.

———

THE PROBLEM WITH BRODERICK, Singleton thought, was that there weren't any back roads to the place. If you wanted to go there, you went on Highway 36, or you didn't go. He took the .380. He'd have to get rid of it, he thought, and the thought pained him. He'd paid $350 for it at a gun show in Fargo, and he hated to lose it. It'd worked just fine with the Sorrells. Couldn't ask for more, not for $350, not in this world.

At eleven o'clock, with the sky black with the daily overcast, he went on the air to tell the sleepy dispatcher that he'd take a quick run down south, to show the flag—the sheriff emphasized that when nothing was going on, he wanted his deputies out to be seen. The dispatcher said okay and went away. He turned north.

Broderick showed scattered speckles of light when he crept into the south side of town. He pulled in behind Calb's shop and got out, let the wind bite at him for a moment, listening. Then, satisfied that he was alone, he pulled his parka up around his head, hunched his shoulders, and started off. He'd brought a penlight, and used it in quick flicks to guide himself along the back of the building, then past the old power transfer station, through an empty lot behind the darkened convenience store, and finally out on the open highway.

The West house was maybe six hundred yards down the road, a quarter-mile to a half-mile. Not far. Once or twice around the track at Custer High. He might have been walking into a coal pit, for as much as he could see. Not a single vehicle passed in either direction. The only sound was the wind, the scuffle of his feet on the road, and his own breathing.

When he reached the West house, he found that it was not entirely dark. Light glowed through a shade on a north-facing window on the second floor, and a variety of small lights—a TV power light, a bathroom night light, a green light that might have been on a telephone, a small row of red lights that looked like a power supply—actually gave his dilated eyes enough light to navigate.

Moving slowly, he felt with his feet for the track that crossed the culvert into the driveway. When he got close, he sensed a bulk to his right. Martha's Jeep? Too big. Pickup. Goddammit. Who was here? He moved around behind it, looked for any movement in the house, then squirted the penlight at the back of the truck.

He recognized it, all right. The dented corner panels, where old Reese Culver tended to back into solid objects, like phone poles. What was the old man doing here, with virtually all the lights out? There'd been rumors, off-and-on, that Martha West might fuck for money, but nobody paid them much attention. It was generally taken as wishful thinking in a town that *needed* somebody who fucked for money. But Reese Culver? If he was staying the night, the old fart, he *had* to be paying.

He thought about it for a minute, two minutes. Shit. He put his hand in the pocket, gripped the revolver, took it out once to make sure he wouldn't snag the pocket, put it back in, and walked up to the porch.

MARTHA WEST HAD JUST crawled into bed when she heard the knock at the door. She thought the knock was Letty, upstairs, until it came a second time. She looked at a clock. Almost midnight. Who was it, at this time of night?—and a sudden chill went through her shoulders and she thought: *Deon Cash and Jane Warr. Just at midnight.* The knock came a third time, and she picked up a ratty old terrycloth robe and threw it on, and walked through the darkened front room to the front door.

The porch light was burned out, so she turned on the interior light and looked out through the glass cut-out on the front door. The first thing she saw was the embroidered star on the parka, and then Loren Singleton's face. No ghosts, anyway. Had something happened?

Puzzled, she opened the door. "Hi . . ."

"Martha, sorry to bother you," Singleton said. "I know it's late, but Loretta Grupe called in and said she was worried about Reese—he'd been drinking some and she was worried about whether he got home. I happened to see his truck out here."

"He, uh, was drinking, and, uh, well—Letty drove him home, and he told her to go ahead and bring the truck up here, so she'd have a ride. You know how she is." Singleton kept looking past her, looking for something else. She didn't care for him, and pushed the door closed an inch or so, ready to go back to bed. "Anything else?"

"Okay. So he's home. And Letty's home, everything's all right."

"Yeah, she's asleep, everything's okay." She smiled, not her best smile. "Okay?"

No point in messing around. Singleton put his left arm out and straight-armed the door, and it flew open, bouncing Martha West straight back. She was startled, just beginning to get scared, and he pulled the revolver out of his pocket and pointed it at her eyes and said, "Tell Letty to come down here. She's under arrest."

Martha hesitated just a second, looking down the barrel of the gun, and knew in her heart that Letty wasn't under arrest, that something terrible was happening here and she thought she knew what. She mimed a turn, as if to shout up the stairs, and then instead, she threw herself at Singleton, avoiding the gun barrel, grabbing his arm, going right straight into his body, screaming and spitting at him, clawing at him; the sleeve of his coat jerked up and she got some skin, saw some blood. He fought back and she realized that she was going to lose him, and she screamed, "LETTY RUN LETTY RUN LETTY RUN . . ." and Singleton hit her and she went over a loveseat and crashed through a glass-topped coffee table, still screaming and saw Singleton coming, reaching out to her, and then she realized, just in a tiny fragment of time that she had left that he was pointing, not reaching, and she screamed "RUN LETTY . . ."

———

THE BOOM OF the gun was deafening in the small room, but the noise stopped instantly. Singleton had never liked that kind of noise, that high-emotion squealing that women did, and when he shot Martha West in the forehead and the squealing stopped, his first feeling was that of sudden relief—and he thought, *Letty,* and looked at the open door to the second floor. Martha West had been screaming at the stairway . . . He went that way, taking the stairs two at a time.

LETTY HAD FINISHED the last of the social studies problems and was packing her bag when she heard the knock on the front door. She couldn't see the front yard from her room, so she paused, listening. Was it her mother? Then she heard the knock again, and stepped toward the door, heard her mother's footsteps leaving the downstairs bedroom.

She listened, heard her mother's voice and a male rumbling—maybe it was Lucas and Del, with something important?—and then the voices went up, and her mother began screaming RUN LETTY and Letty turned and stepped across the room and picked up her rifle, which was unloaded because her mother made her swear to keep it unloaded except when she was using it, and she fumbled in the pocket of her trapping parka for a box of shells and then heard a crash of breaking glass and a RUN LETTY and she broke the gun open and there was a sudden tremendous boom and the sounds of fighting stopped . . .

Too late.

She looked wildly around the room, flipped the old turn-lock on the door, grabbed the steel-legged kitchen chair at the foot of her bed, and without thinking about it, hurled it through the east window. There were two layers of glass, the regular window and the storm, but the chair was heavy and went through. Running footsteps on the stairs, like some kind of *Halloween* movie—and Letty threw her parka over the windowsill to protect herself from the broken glass, and still hanging onto the rifle, went out the window.

She hung on to the coat with her left hand and she dropped, pulling it after her; the coat snagged on glass and maybe a nail, held her up for just a second, then everything fell. She landed awkwardly, in a clump of prairie grass, felt her ankle twist, and hobbled two steps sideways, her ankle on fire, clutching the parka in the cold, and saw a silhouette at the window and she ran, and there was a crack of light and noise like a close-in lightning strike, and something plucked at her hair and she kept hobbling away and there was another boom and her side was on fire, and then she was around the corner of the house and into the dark.

Hurt, she thought. She touched her side and realized that she was bleeding under the arm, and her ankle screamed in pain and something was wrong with her left hand. She kept going, half-hopping, half-hobbling. *Cold,* she thought. She pinned the rifle between her legs and pulled the parka on. She had no hat or mittens, but she pulled the hood up and began to run as best she could, and her left hand wasn't working right . . .

She was only a hundred feet from the house when she realized that she wasn't alone in the yard. There was a squirt of light and then she heard movement, a crunching on the snow. He was coming after her, whoever he was.

Shells. As she hobbled along, she dug in her coat pocket, and found a .22 shell, but her hand wasn't working and she dropped it. Lost in the dark. Dug out another one with the other hand, broke the rifle, got the shell in, snapped it shut. A squirt of light, then the man called, "Letty. You might as well stop. I can see you."

Bullshit, she thought. She could barely tell where he was, and he had the partly lit house behind him. And she was moving as fast as he was, because he was having trouble following her footprints through the grass that stuck through the shallow snow, and there was nothing behind her but darkness. If he kept coming, though . . . She had to do something—she didn't know how badly she was hurt. Had to find someplace to go.

His silhouette lurched in and out of focus in front of the house, and she remembered something that Bud, her trapper friend, had told her about bow-hunting for deer. If a deer was moving a little too quickly for a good shot, you could whistle, or grunt, and the deer would stop to listen. That's when you let the arrow go.

She turned, got a sense of where the man's silhouette was, leveled the rifle and called, "Who are you?"

He stopped like a deer, and she shot him.

SINGLETON RAN UP the stairs, and at the top looked around, heard the crash of breaking glass, looked back, thinking somehow that it might be Martha West, who was sprawled in the wreckage of the glass table, and realized in the next instant that it had to be Letty, because Martha was definitely dead.

He spotted the door with light leaking beneath it, stepped over to it, and said, "Letty?" and tried the knob. Locked. He kicked it once and it bent, without breaking. He kicked it a second time, a cop-kick, and it flew open. Letty was gone. Window broken, with movement—the jacket going out. He stepped on a notebook and almost fell, got right, hurried to the window and saw a dark figure on the ground, hobbling down the side of the house. He fired once, missed, and, blinded by his own muzzle flash, let go another shot, and then he couldn't see her anymore.

Think.

She was out there alone, maybe hurt. There was nobody else out there—the countryside was empty, he could shoot a machine-gun at her and nobody would hear. He ran down the stairs, realized his arm was burning. He looked at it, quickly, as he hurried through the living room and out on the porch: blood. Then he was around the house, and he got out the flash and got under the window and flicked the penlight on, and started tracking her. At the back of the house, he found blood, so he'd hit her, maybe, unless she'd cut herself going out of the house . . .

He tracked her for a minute, then called out, "Letty. You might as well stop, I can see you."

She called, "Who are you?" and he stopped, trying to focus on the direction. It was dark as a coal sack.

Then a star burst in front of him, a muzzle flash, and he felt a sharp slap on his chest and he involuntarily sat down. He could hear her running again but he paid no attention: he thought, *I'm shot. I'm shot. He couldn't believe it—he was *shot*. *Shit at and missed, shot at and hit.* He almost giggled. Had to do something about this.

He crawled back toward the house, then got on his feet, staggering, got inside, and looked at his chest. Nothing: but it hurt bad. After a second, he spotted a tiny dimple in the parka fabric. A hole, he thought, wonderingly. He unzipped the parka, found a small circle of blood on his uniform shirt. Pulled his shirt open, found a bigger circle on his undershirt. Pulled that up, and found a hole in his chest, just right of his left nipple. The skin was already beginning to bruise, and when he touched it, pain rippled across his chest.

Shit. He *was* shot.

Didn't hurt as bad as his arm, though. He took a few experimental breaths. He was breathing okay. And he thought, *She yelled, "Who are you?"*

Did she really not know? When would she have seen his face?

He began to see some possibilities—maybe he could pull this off yet. And then he thought, DNA. Goddamn DNA. Martha West had cut him up, they might find his blood anywhere . . .

LETTY FIRED THE SHOT, then stumbled away from her muzzle flash, aware that it would have given her away. The man was crunching through the snow again, and she found another shell with her good hand—*what was wrong with her left? It just didn't work*—and tried to get it in the gun. She fumbled it, found another, got this one in, stopped to listen.

Nothing. Where was he? She began to get the creepy feeling that he was right next to her, breathing quietly, and she slowly dropped to her knees, huddling into the dried Russian thistles along the West Ditch. Waited. Where was he . . .

Two minutes passed, though it took an eternity. Another minute? Where was he? What happened to Mom? She almost gagged, because she thought she knew what happened to Mom. Though Mom had fought the guy long enough for her to go out the window . . .

More light. What was that? More light, lots more light . . .

The house was burning. She was drawn to it—was there something she could do, or was the gunman simply pulling her in? Frightened, she shrank farther back into the dark, and farther back, as the flames grew.

When the first of the volunteer trucks arrived, twenty minutes later, the fire was five stories high and climbing into the night like a volcano.

15

LUCAS HAD STOLEN an old copy of *Fortune* magazine from the motel lobby and lay in bed, reading an article about how he could still retire rich, when the phone rang. Del?

He picked it up and got the comm center clerk from the Law Enforcement Center. "Mr. Davenport? This is Susan Conrad down at the sheriff's office. We've just dispatched our fire department to the West house. The call coming in said the whole house was burning like crazy. Thought you might want to know."

"Jesus. Thanks."

Lucas slammed the phone back on the hook and ran barefoot in his underwear to the door and out, down two, and began pounding on Del's door. "Get up. Del. Get up."

Without waiting for an answer he ran back to his room, left the door open, and began pulling on his jeans. He'd been outside for no more than ten seconds and he was cold—God only knew what the temperature was. He was pulling on his shirt when Del stumbled into the room, pulling on jeans, still wearing his pajama top.

"West house is burning down. Fire trucks on the way," Lucas blurted. Del disappeared. Lucas pulled on his socks and shoes, and in the distance, through the open door, could hear the siren that called in the volunteer fire department, and the roar of the truck heading out.

Shoes on, Lucas got his wallet and keys and coat and gloves and headed out to the truck, climbed inside, saw Del running toward him, popped the passenger-side door lock, and Del was inside and Lucas took off.

Del was carrying his shirt and coat and boots and dressed as they headed toward the highway. "Not a coincidence," he grunted.

"We been out with that kid all over the place, it's like we were dragging bait. I didn't even think about it," Lucas said. They were probably two or three miles behind the fire truck when they got to Highway 36, but once past the last house going out of town, Lucas dropped the pedal to the floor and left it there. Two minutes out, he pushed the button that lit his information screen, which said that it was fourteen degrees below zero. Another minute out, they could see a glow to the north, burning faintly above the closer red lights of the fire truck. "Jesus Christ, that can't be it," Del said. "We're too far away."

"Gotta be it," Lucas said, "Unless the report was wrong."

They were closing quickly on the first-responder fire truck, but didn't catch it until they were just outside of Broderick. By then, they knew the reports had been right: the fire was north of Broderick and huge, and there was nothing else out there.

Lucas, worried that some of the town residents might be in the highway, in the dark, looking at the fire, let the truck lead them through town. When the truck pulled into the house, Lucas swung past it and turned in at West Ditch Road.

Even from there, on the opposite side of the ditch, the heat was ferocious. "If there's anybody in there, they're gone," Del said. One of the firemen had jumped off the truck, slid down the bank of the ditch and began hacking at the ice on the bottom with an oversized ax. As he did that, another man was uncoiling a hose, and when he had enough of it, he rolled it down the bank, and the ax-man dragged it to the hole he'd cut and shoved it under the ice.

A minute later, a thin stream of water was splashing onto the house, but it was obvious that it was doing no good at all—it was like pissing into a welding torch. The fire was eating everything. More lights now, police cars and two more fire trucks.

Then:

"Lucas."

The voice was high and shrill but somehow weak, and might almost have been the scream of a failing joist in the fire. But Lucas knew it wasn't, and he ran down the gravel track, in the direction of the sound, and shouted, "Letty? Letty?"

"Over here. Here." He could see the pale half-oval of her face across the ditch, half of her face lit by the fire. "I'm hurt bad."

"Hang on," Lucas shouted. Del yelled, "Not that way," as Lucas went straight down the wall of the ditch, sliding, crawled halfway up the other side, slid back, tried again, slid back, and finally ran thirty feet down the ditch to where some tumbleweeds were still rooted in the side, and clambered out of it. Del had run around the end of it, and was coming toward him. "Letty?" He'd lost track of her.

"I'm hurt bad, and I think Mom's . . . Mom's in there. Somebody came and shot her." She began sobbing and Lucas came up, and he bent to pick her up and she shrank away and said, "My hand is hurt bad, and my side hurts, I think I'm shot, and my ankle might be broke . . ."

"Aw, Jesus." Del was there, and Lucas pulled off his coat and said, "We're making a sling, just . . . aw, fuck it. Del . . ." Lucas pulled his coat back on and said, "I'm gonna pick her up. Which side hurts, honey? Which side?"

HE PICKED HER UP, cradling her, and Del asked, "Where're your keys?" and Lucas told him, and Del dug them out of Lucas's coat pocket and ran back to get the truck. One of the firemen ran up and asked, "She burned?" and Letty said, "No, I'm hurt." Del was there in a few seconds, and Lucas lifted her into the back seat and then crawled in with her, and Del put the truck on the highway and they were headed back to Armstrong, running at top speed.

"You okay?"

"I'm hurt bad . . ." She began sobbing again.

Lucas got on the cell phone, found a signal, called into the sheriff's comm center. "How do we get to the hospital? We've got a hurt kid."

"You on your way back to town?

"Running fast."

"Where are you?"

"Just went through Broderick."

"There'll be a car sitting on the edge of town with its light bar flashing. Blink your headlights a bunch of times when you come up, and he'll take you right through to the medical center."

"We're coming . . ."

Lucas relayed the information to Del, then turned back to Letty. "I know you're hurt. But tell me what happened, if you can."

"I was up in my bedroom, and Mom was down in hers, and I heard this knock . . ." She told the story, and when it was done, Del muttered, "Jesus Christ, Letty," and Lucas said, "You think he was shot."

"He was shot. He fell down."

"Maybe he was . . . you know, going down so you couldn't see him."

"He was shot," she said, stubbornly. "I'd never miss anyone that close. He's shot in the chest."

"All right. Twenty-two short?"

"Yes." Her body was shaking with grief and pain. "He shot Mom.

She was yelling for me to run, and she was fighting him, and then there was a shot and she stopped yelling and he started coming up the steps . . . You didn't see her outside, in the yard or anything?"

Lucas said, "I didn't look. I was just trying to stay out of the way of the fire guys. You never saw the guy?"

"Only his outline. It was way dark. But . . . he talked to me. He knew who I was. He called me Letty. And he sounded like . . . he was from around here. He sounded like one of us."

"Did you see his car?"

After a moment of silence, she said "He didn't have a car. *He didn't have a car.* I shot him and he fell down and then he got up and walked back to the house while I was trying to reload, and then I just sat there and the house caught on fire and I couldn't get up, and then the house burned and then you came. No car ever drove away."

"You're sure."

"No car. He didn't have a car."

"Okay. Listen . . ."

He was about to say something, but she pushed a hand out of her coat sleeve and tried to look at it, and Lucas saw a huge gash that started at her wrist and ran across the palm and disappeared between her middle and ring fingers.

"Better keep your hand down," he said. "It's bleeding a little."

"Coming up on the patrol car," Del said. Lucas looked down the highway, and saw the light bar. Del clicked the high beams off and on, and the patrol car pulled out on the highway, rolled slow until they'd gotten close, and then sped up and led them through town to the medical center's Emergency Room. Three people were standing on the ramp, and then a fourth joined them, pushing a gurney, and Del pulled up next to them.

THE FOUR MOVED Lucas and Del out of the way and loaded Letty onto the gurney and pushed her inside, and Lucas went over to a plastic trash barrel and punted it out into the driveway, where it rolled around spewing its garbage.

"Her fuckin' hand," he said to Del. "Her fuckin' hand looks like it's almost cut in half."

"What about the chest? Was she shot in the chest?"

"She was pretty alert for anything deep," he said. Then: "I gotta get inside."

"I'll park the car . . ."

Lucas stopped at the door and looked back: "You getting pissed yet?"

"Yeah. I'm pissed."

A YOUNG RESIDENT had been hustled out of bed when Lucas called in, and he was looking at Letty when Lucas pushed his way into the examination room. "How is she?"

Letty tried to push up, and the doc turned, looked at Lucas over his mask: "Who're you?"

"I'm a cop. How is she?"

The resident turned back to Letty, and as an aside to a nurse, in exactly the wrong tone, said, "Get that guy out of here."

Lucas snarled, "Listen, asshole, I'm not going into all the background, but if you want to keep your license in Minnesota, don't fuck with me. Now, how is she? Is she shot?"

The doc looked at a nurse, who shrugged, and showed no inclination to throw Lucas out. The doc said, "She has what might be a gunshot wound, but it's not life-threatening. Her hand is badly cut. We haven't fully evaluated it yet. We need to X-ray her foot. It's badly swollen and she complains of pain. It might be broken—it's at least badly sprained. Is that good enough?"

"What about the hand? That looked bad."

"I cut it on the broken window," Letty said. "Did you find Mom?"

"The hand will take, mmm, take some special attention," the resident said. "There's a surgeon in Fargo . . ."

"Fuck Fargo," Lucas said. He banged back out of the examining room, and went outside, met Del, told him what he was doing, pulled out his cell phone and called home. A sleepy Weather answered on the third ring.

"Hello?"

"It's me—I've got a problem."

He told her about it quickly, and when he was done, Weather said, "Get her down here as fast as you can. We need her while the wound is fresh. I don't do hands, but I can get Harry Larson to do her. How fast can you get her here?"

"I'll have to check. Go back to sleep—I'll call you. Are you cutting tomorrow morning?"

"Not until ten. What are you going to do?"

"See if I can find a plane. If I can't, I'll drive her down, or something. Get an ambulance."

"Listen: let me call over to Regions, see what they've got. Maybe it'd be quicker to get a fast helicopter out of here, rather than messing around."

"Good. Call me back."

"Who's paying?"

"We are. I am."

"Won't be cheap."

"Call 'em."

DEL ASKED, "What're we doing?"

"We're gonna take her out of here in a helicopter—Weather's taking care of it. She's gonna call back."

"I don't think her mom made it," Del said. "When I came running around the ditch, going back to where you were . . . somebody inside the house was burning." He wrinkled his nose, then made a spitting gesture off to the side. Burning people smelled like pork barbeque, and left a stink in your nose and mouth.

"She knows it," Lucas said. "She hasn't admitted it yet. Sounds like Mama took on the asshole, whoever he is."

"Wonder why he burned the house down? If he hadn't done that, Letty might have died out there. I'd figure he was after Letty . . ."

"Why? I mean, why was he after her?"

Del thought. "I dunno."

"What if he was after Mom?"

Del shook his head. "That doesn't feel right."

"Okay. But the whole thing is pretty interesting. Why was he after her? What was he burning? Where is he now, especially if he was shot?"

"I have my doubts about him being shot. I mean, we both know cops who've emptied a whole goddamn Glock at somebody down the hall, and didn't hit shit."

"Mmm. I kind of suggested that, and she said she hit him. Said there was no way she missed. I kind of think she might have hit him."

"Better get the word out to the local hospitals."

"We can do that."

THEY WERE STILL talking about it when Weather called back. "Turns out there's an air evac service out of Brainerd, which is almost halfway up there, and they can have a helicopter on its way in a half-hour. They'll call you when they're coming, and give you a time estimate. He says there's a landing pad right there at the hospital. He said it wouldn't be much more than an hour before they're coming in up there. I can meet her when she gets down here."

"Excellent."

BACK IN THE HOSPITAL he told the doc, "We're medevacing her, sending her down to Hennepin General and a hand guy. A chopper'll be here in an hour or so. We need to get her stable."

"The hand is the only big problem," the doc said. "She's got a groove in her side where she was shot, but that's minor. So's the leg. The hand . . . the hand is a problem."

"So how soon can she go?"

"I'll start some pain medication, and she can be ready in a half-hour. If the chopper's coming in here, we're good."

Lucas said to Letty, "I told you my wife is a doctor. She's setting up everything down in the Cities, and she's gonna meet you. You'll be okay, but they want to fix your hand as soon as they can."

"Okay," she said. "Did you check on Mom?"

"We're gonna do that now," Lucas said. "I'm gonna head right back up there—you'll be okay, just ride along and do what everybody tells you. They'll take care of you."

"Mom's dead," she said.

"We'll go see what happened," Lucas said. He touched her good leg. "You take care of yourself."

BACK AT THE WEST HOUSE, the fire was virtually out— there was almost nothing left to burn, and what had been a four-square farmhouse was now a hole in the ground. A deputy, who said that he'd met Lucas at the hanging scene, shook his head when they asked about Martha West. "Nobody's seen her. Car's here. There was this . . ." He gestured at the house. "There was this smell . . ."

"I know. Letty said her mother was downstairs. She heard a knock on the door, then her mother started screaming, there was a shot, the screaming stopped, and Letty went out the window. Never saw her mother or heard her again."

"We're sure she's telling the truth? I don't want to suggest anything, but they were out here alone."

"Letty was shot herself, and it's not self-inflicted, believe me," Lucas said. "Somebody shot her from behind and above. And nobody would do to themselves what happened to her, just to cover up. Her hand—there's a possibility that she's gonna be crippled."

The deputy winced. "Okay. You know, out here on the prairie . . . strange things happen when people are alone too much."

"In the city, strange things happen when they're together too much," Del said.

"Strange things happen," the deputy said.

Lucas suspected they were about to lurch off into some philosophical black hole and hastily interjected. "We need to alert all the local hospitals and doctors that the killer may have been shot."

"That's something. Since she didn't hit him in the head, I hope she hit him in the nuts," the deputy said. "I'll call it in."

ONCE SINGLETON GOT the fire going, he'd slipped out the front of the West home and begun jogging down the highway. He'd thought about one more look around, one more quick search for Letty, but she had that gun, and she'd see him coming. He gave up on that, and jogged.

His chest hurt. Hurt a lot—but he wasn't spitting blood, wasn't having any trouble breathing. If he could just keep going . . .

Running hurt. He ran halfway back to Broderick, then he stopped, stooped over, braced his hands on his knees, and tried to ease the pain. The pain was coming in waves now, and if he hadn't been shot, he might have thought he was having a heart attack. Behind him, the fire was growing. He ran on, hurting, made it to the car, running through the dark behind the convenience store and the shop.

This was the dangerous part. This was where somebody might see him. He eased the patrol car out from behind the shop, pointed it south, and took off. No lights in any windows that he could see, but in the rearview mirror, the fire was going like crazy.

A mile out of town, two miles, four—then his handset burped, and he heard the comm center calling over to the fire station. He dropped the hammer on it. He was still two miles from the nearest road that would take him away from Highway 36.

He made it by ten seconds. He'd made the turn when he saw the light bar on the first responder truck. He continued east, and out the side window could see the huge balloon of fire at the West house; then the comm center was squawking at him and he said he was on the way back but he was pretty far south and he heard the siren come up. . . .

And he hurt. Goddamn Letty West.

He was sweating from the pain: he could smell himself. He made another mile, crossed a gravel road heading south, into the backside of Armstrong. Four minutes later, he was at his garage, running the door up.

Inside the house, he peeled off his parka, took off his shirt and undershirt, and examined the hole in his chest. It *was* a hole: a purplish, .22-sized dot on his chest, already surrounded by a nasty bruise. He pushed on the skin around it, and winced: won't do that again. Blood trickled steadily from the hole—not much, but it wouldn't stop.

He went into the bathroom, got a roll of gauze, made a thick pad, went into the kitchen, found some duct tape, and taped the pad to his chest. He couldn't help fooling with the area around the hole, squeezing gently to see if he could feel the slug. He couldn't, but he hurt himself again.

"Fuckin' dummy," he said.

The phone rang. He let it ring. Probably Katina, with news about the fire. He got enough tape on his chest that he was sure he wouldn't bleed through his shirt, then checked his arm. Martha West had scratched him, not too badly, but there would have been skin under her fingernails. Good idea about the fire. He washed the scratches with soap and warm water, smeared on some disinfectant ointment, and duct-taped it.

All right. No blood showing. He could still walk around. He got a fresh shirt, eased into it. Touched his chest, and the pain ran through him. The phone started ringing again. He ignored it, touched his chest again, gasped with the pain, and headed out to the car.

THE FIRE STATION was lit up—and empty. Every man was out at the fire. Singleton pulled into the station, pushed through the main door and called out, "Hey. Anybody home?"

Nobody answered, though a Hank Williams, Jr., song was drawling through the open truck slots.

"Hey. Anybody?"

No? Excellent. He headed up the stairs, to the sleeping loft, went straight through it to a storeroom where the medical gear was kept. The fire department was also the backup paramedic service. He pulled down a paramedic's pack, ripped off the sealer tab, and zipped it open.

Shit: no pills. He needed some painkillers, and there wasn't a goddamn thing. He'd been sure there'd be some—firefighters always seemed to have a few pills around, supposedly because of the small burns they took on the job. If so, they didn't get the pills from the paramedic packs. He zipped the pack up, replaced it.

Where else? The hospital, the drugstore. The hospital would probably be on alert, with the fire, and he didn't know how he'd get the drugs anyway. The drugstore had a safe . . .

He touched his chest. *Goddamnit, that hurt.*

He was on his way out when he got lucky. All the lockers were open and he saw a tube of pills in one of them. He looked at it: Advil. Not good enough. Then he checked all the lockers, quickly, found a dozen more bottles of pills, mostly vitamins and nonprescription painkillers. Finally, in the locker of one of the two full-time firemen, he found two tubes of Dilaudid. Twenty orange tabs, in total. Both tubes carried the notation, "One tablet every four to six hours."

Excellent. He took the tubes. Dug further through the locker and found another tube: penicillin. Good. Took that, too.

Have to think about Katina, though. He was gonna be out of action for a while, and he needed a reason. Had to think.

Made it out to the car, touched his chest. *Goddamn, that hurt.*

Then he thought, *Wonder where Letty West got to?* He'd gone out to her house to solve a problem, and hadn't. She was still out there, Letty was.

Singleton got into his car and headed for the fire. Halfway there, a new thought occurred to him: Mom was gonna be pissed.

16

THE FIRE WAS OUT, and a couple of the firemen were gin-
gerly working through the blackened jumble of burnt wood and plas-
ter in the now-open basement; it looked like a bomb crater. Lucas and
Del took turns watching the work, and getting warm in the car. Ray
Zahn showed up in his Highway Patrol cruiser, and they chatted for a
while. "The comm center called the sheriff. He told them to handle it,
and to coordinate with you guys, and then he went back to bed. I guess
this isn't important enough."

"We're not being fair to him," Del observed.

"No, we're not," Zahn said. "I'm sure we don't know all the problems and contingencies he has to deal with. The miserable twat."

Zahn left on a drag-racing call, and Lucas and Del lingered, watching. More sheriff's deputies came in, apparently working on their own
time. Zahn came back, and wanted to talk about how Rose Marie Roux
might change the Highway Patrol.

They'd been back at the fire site for an hour, when a gray Toyota Land Cruiser pulled off to the side of the highway and two women got out. Lucas recognized one of them as the woman he'd talked to at the church. He dug around in the back of his mind for a moment, then came up with her name—Ruth Lewis.

Ruth walked down to a cluster of the firemen, as the other woman popped open the back of the Land Cruiser. Lewis talked to the firemen for a moment, then two of them broke away and followed her back to the truck. The second woman was doing something in the back, then produced a carton of white paper cups, and the firemen who came back with Lewis took the cups and stepped out of sight, behind the truck.

"Coffee," Del said.

"Like to talk to that woman," Lucas said. "Want some coffee?"

"Take a cup," Del said. They got out of the Acura and walked over to the Toyota. More firemen and cops were clustering around the back of it, taking cups, and Lucas and Del edged into the line. When they got their coffee, Lucas took a sip and stepped over next to Lewis.

"You heard what happened? You heard about Letty?"

"Some of it. I heard she was at the hospital, that you took her in," Lewis said.

"She's hurt," Lucas said. "She was shot, not too bad, but when she was getting away, she had to jump out her window. She slashed her hand open, really bad—we're flying her down to the Cities so a hand guy can look at her. Her ankle is either busted or twisted so bad that she can't walk."

"That's *terrible*. I heard her mom . . ." Lewis's eyes went to the house, ". . . might still be in there."

"We're waiting, but Letty thinks she was shot to death. Right at the beginning of it. She apparently fought the guy long enough for Letty to get away."

"This doesn't happen in Custer County," Lewis said. "Somebody told me that the last murder here was fifteen years ago."

"Our operating theory is that Deon Cash, Jane Warr, and probably

Joe Kelly kidnapped the Sorrell girl and killed her, and probably another girl named Burke."

"*Two* of them?"

"Yes. We think that Hale Sorrell somehow grabbed Joe Kelly and tortured him and got the names of Cash and Warr. We think he found out that his daughter was already dead. We think he then waited until their guard might be down a little, then he came up here, took them and hanged them for the murder of his daughter. But we think there was at least one more person involved, and that person is afraid that somebody will give him away. It's a *him*, by the way, not a *her*—he spoke to Letty."

She smiled quickly, a flitting smile that was gone as quickly as it came. "Thanks for the briefing."

"I'm not just chatting," Lucas said. "Something complicated is going on around Broderick, and I don't know what it is. But it's the cause of all these deaths. And people in Broderick are evading us, they're not telling us what they know. I don't know why they're doing that, but they are."

"I more or less know everybody in Broderick. Some of the men from the body shop keep to themselves, but nobody I know well would have done this. Kidnapped those girls or . . ." She gestured at the burned-out hole in the ground.

Three firemen were standing in the ruins of the basement, and as Lewis gestured and they looked that way, one of them called up to another man, who was standing outside the hole, and he turned and trotted toward one of the fire trucks. Two more firemen dropped into the basement.

"Aw, shit," Lucas said. "I think they found her."

T H E Y   H A D .   L U C A S   A N D   D E L   hung around for another hour, watching as the medical examiner crawled down into the basement. Ten minutes later, he climbed back out.

"Martha West?" Lucas asked.

"I assume so, from what I've been told. No way to tell by looking at the body. We'll have to do DNA on the body and on her daughter, and make some comparisons. But—it's her."

"All right." They lingered a few more minutes, then headed back to Armstrong. There was actually traffic on the highway, cop cars and fire department vehicles, and maybe rubberneckers running up to see what had happened.

On the way back, Del asked, "What'd you tell Ruth Lewis?"

"I gave her something to be guilty about. Those kind of women, they guilt-trip pretty easily."

"Just gonna let it percolate?"

"Yeah, overnight. Then I'm gonna go up there tomorrow and ask Lewis if she'll go down to the Cities and tell Letty that her mother is dead."

"Mmm," Del said. Then after a minute, "Hitting her with a hammer."

"Maybe she'll break," Lucas said.

They stopped at the hospital, found it quiet. The duty nurse told them that the resident had gone back to bed, and that Letty was in the air. "They got here really quickly," she said. She glanced at a wall clock. "She should be at Hennepin in a half-hour."

After leaving the hospital, they drove over to the Law Enforcement Center, where two people were sitting in the comm center eating microwave pizza. Lucas borrowed a computer and wrote a memo to the sheriff, outlining what had happened, and what had been done about it. He made two copies, put one in the sheriff's mailbox, and kept one himself.

AT THE MOTEL, they went to their separate rooms, and though he was tired, Lucas turned on the television, found a movie channel, and watched James Woods, Bruce Dern, and Lou Gossett get wry with each other in *Diggstown*. Forty-five minutes later, Weather called.

"We've got her on the ground," she said. "The hand is not good, but it's fixable. Gonna take a while to heal. Do you know if she has insurance? She doesn't seem to think so."

"She doesn't," Lucas said. "I'm buying."

"Is this a Roman Catholic guilt thing that I've got to be psychologically careful about?"

"Yeah."

"Okay. Call me tomorrow. I want all the details. She seems like an interesting child. She's scared."

"She jumped out a window, got shot, got stalked in the dark, shot a guy, saw her house burned down, and her mother's dead. She doesn't know about her mother for sure, yet. I'm going to try to get somebody up here to fly down and tell her. Somebody she knows."

"Aw, jeez . . . All right. I'll stay with her. Call me."

SLEEP WOULD BE TOUGH—coming up to five o'clock in the morning, but he was still too cranked. He clicked around the TV channels, found nothing that he wanted to watch. Eventually, he put on his shoes and walked down to the motel office.

"That black guy from Chicago still here?" he asked the clerk.

"Yup. Said he's checking out tomorrow morning."

"What's the room?"

"Two-oh-eight. Is he gonna be a problem?"

"Naw. I called Chicago, and they say he's gonna win the Nobel Prize for reporting. I just wanted to shake his hand."

WAY TOO EARLY FOR THIS, he thought, but what the hell, reporters fucked with him often enough. He knocked on 208, waited, knocked again, and then a man croaked, "What time is it?"

"Five in the morning," Lucas said. "Check-out time."

"What?"

A crack of light appeared between the curtains in the room window, and a moment later, Mark Johnson peered out the door over the safety chain. "Davenport?"

"So, what're you doing?" Lucas asked.

"Trying to sleep."

"You're so young, too," Lucas said.

Johnson took the chain off and opened the door and yawned and asked, "What's going on?"

"Somebody just burned down the West house, murdered Martha West, and shot and wounded Letty. She's been taken to the Twin Cities for surgery."

Johnson stared, then looked back at his bed, then back to Lucas. "You're shitting me."

"I shit you not."

"Come on in. Let me get my pants on. Jesus . . . What happened?"

"I talked to Deke, and he said you'd be marginally okay to talk to."

"Yeah, margin my ass."

"So the deal is, I tell you what you want to know, and you got it from an informed source. And I've got a lot of stuff that nobody else has picked up."

"Like what?"

LUCAS TOLD HIM, and when he was done, Johnson stared down at his laptop and said, "I can see this as a story. It'll take some work."

"Christ, the best story of his life is handed to him on a platter, and he says it'll take some work," Lucas said.

"The no-attribution is the hard part," Johnson said.

"That's the deal—but I'll tell you what. You come around tomorrow, wearing your sport jacket, and I'll talk *for* attribution, but I'll also refuse to comment on some of the other stuff, like the locket. You can ask the

FBI about that. They'll be up here tomorrow, looking for the kids' bodies."

"That's great. They're like the world's worst media connections. They won't tell me anything."

"They might. Their media training's improved a lot, the last two or three years. And I'll put in a word for you."

"Appreciate it . . . Look, on my side of the deal, I sorta got a name for you." He slapped a group of keys on the laptop, saving his notes and changing programs, then reached into his briefcase for a pen and paper, scribbled on it, and handed it to Lucas.

A name, Tom Block, and a phone number in an unfamiliar area code.

"This is another guy Deke put me onto, maybe a year ago, down in Kansas City. He's sort of Kansas City's Lucas Davenport, although he's younger and better-looking."

"Could be younger," Lucas admitted. "What's he do?"

"Wanders around town. But he knows a lot about the Cash family and what that whole group does down there. You might want to chat. He told me a couple of things that I can't use, because of libel problems, but it wouldn't be a problem for you."

"Like tell me one thing."

"Like the whole Cash family—it's really more like a clan, with aunts and uncles and nephews and all that—they started out in drugs, and then, when crack came in and all the killing started, they got out. Went into other stuff. Tom says some of the brothers down there went to business school at the University of Missouri, then came back to KC and diversified."

"Yeah?"

"Yeah. One of their things now is that they steal a lot of cars. That's the rumor. Low risk, high profit. And since Calb's body shop up there is involved in this thing . . ."

"You think Calb's is a chop shop?"

"I don't know. Doesn't make sense, really. They could chop cars down there, no problem. I don't know what Calb could do out here that they couldn't do."

"Hmmp." Lucas stood up and stretched. He thought he might be able to sleep. "All right. I'll probably see you around tomorrow, one place or another. You still checking out?"

"Shit, no."

"The desk clerk thinks you're up to something. Being black, and all."

"I encourage him to think that," Johnson said. "Sometimes I can't help myself."

LUCAS SLEPT LIKE A BABY.

For almost five hours, until Del called. Lucas rolled over and picked up the phone, and Del said, "I can't lay down anymore."

"Try harder," Lucas said. Then: "I'll get up."

"I'll come over in fifteen minutes. We'll go down to the Bird and get breakfast."

LUCAS BRUSHED HIS TEETH and skipped shaving so he could stand in the shower for a few extra minutes. He was just pulling on a shirt when Del knocked. He let Del in, then sat on the bed and put on his shoes and socks, got his coat, tossed the car keys to Del. "You drive. I've got some calls to make."

He started by calling the sheriff's comm center, where he got the phone number for the church in Broderick. He called the church, and asked for Ruth Lewis.

"I'm calling to ask you to do something for me," he said, when she came on.

Wary: "What?"

"I would like you to go down to the Cities and tell Letty that her mother's dead. She knows it, but nobody's come right out and said it, yet. You know her, and she likes you. It would be good if you could tell her."

"Oh, God," Lewis said. Then, after a moment, "I could go this afternoon."

"Thanks. She's at Hennepin General, and I'll call down to make sure they let you through. If you go pretty soon, you could talk to her this evening."

THE NEXT CALL WENT to Weather's cell phone. She answered, after a moment: "I'm in the locker room cleaning up. I sat in on the operation—pretty neat stuff. The guy knows how to tie a square knot."

"Yeah, yeah. How is she?"

"She's gonna be pretty dopey the rest of the day, and they're gonna put a cage around her hand."

"The hand gonna work?"

"She'll probably need more surgery, you know, to release the scar tissue as it builds up, but yes—she should be okay. She won't be playing the piano for a while."

"How about her leg? How about the bullet wound?"

"The bullet wound isn't a problem. The guys up there cleaned it up, and should be okay—just took some skin off her rib cage and the inside of her arm. Her ankle is sprained, but it's not too bad. Since it's on the other side from the cast, she should be able to use a crutch for a couple of days, if she needs it."

"Nothing broken."

"Nothing broken."

"How's Sam?"

"He is just such a cutey. He's so cheerful. And it's pretty apparent that he's really bright . . . no, I'm serious, he's really bright. I don't think . . ."

She got Lucas laughing, all the more because she was sincere. "Talk to you later."

HE TOLD DEL about Letty's progress as he dialed a third number. A woman answered: "St. Agnes, Department of Psychology."

"My name is Lucas Davenport. I'm a police officer and I need to talk with Sister Mary Joseph."

"Just a minute, please."

Elle Kruger came on a second later. "How's the baby?" she asked.

"Probably the most intelligent kid in the Twin Cities, if not the entire Midwest," Lucas said. "I've got a question for you. Sort of a semi-official question."

"Go ahead," she said cheerfully. She'd given Lucas advice on other cases.

"You know a woman named Ruth Lewis, right? Used to be a nun? Sat in on a couple of games with us?"

He sensed a hesitation, then: "I know Ruth."

"What's going on with her?"

"What's going on with you?"

Lucas was dumbfounded. Elle was his oldest, closest friend, and he was feeling resistance. That hadn't happened before.

"I'm trying to figure out the Sorrell kidnapping. A little girl was shot last night, almost had her hand cut off, and her mother was murdered, and then she had her house burned down around her. Lewis lives just a few blocks down the highway, and she knows something she's not telling me. I can feel it. This guy, the guy who's doing the killing— he's not gonna stop if he thinks he's in danger."

Another moment of hesitation, then: "Lucas, are you on your cell phone?"

"Yes."

"Let me call you back."

"Elle? What the hell's going on?"

"I'll probably tell you, but I want to talk to Ruth first. I want to make sure there's no possibility that she's involved with your case. She won't be involved directly, but I want to make sure that there are no . . . ramifications from her job, that might create some, mmm, involvement."

Lucas was getting angry. "Elle, you're bullshitting me."

"No, I'm not. You've just got me stuck. If I tell you why, you'll understand, but I've got to talk to Ruth first."

"C'mon."

"I'll call you back, Lucas, I promise. I will tell you something about Ruth, though. She wasn't a very good nun because she was . . . too much. She demanded perfection, and she was the one who'd define what that was. The people she most admired were all martyrs. So . . ."

"She's nuts."

"No. She's not crazy, but she will do what she will do. And you won't stop her. Nobody will stop her. If she winds up martyred because of it, that wouldn't faze her. Wouldn't slow her down. In some ways, she's a throwback."

"To what, the fifties?"

"I was thinking of the crusades," Elle said. "Anyway, I'll call you back."

THEY WERE COMING UP to the Bird when Lucas got off the phone, now as puzzled as he was angry. Del asked, "What was that all about?"

"I'm getting stonewalled by Elle. She knows Lewis and she knows what's going on, but she won't tell me."

"I don't know, man," Del said. "That's weird."

"I even told her about Letty," Lucas said.

251

"Now we know one thing—something's going on and it probably ain't legal. What are the chances of two big illegal things going on in a town the size of Broderick, that aren't connected somehow?"

"Slim and none," Lucas said. "She's gonna call me back."

SHE CALLED BACK as Lucas was in the middle of a low-voiced rant about the scrambled eggs. "How in the fuck can you screw up eggs? You just scramble them in a bowl with a little milk, and then pour them in a pan. These things are like burned yellow rubber. They even *smell* like burned yellow rubber. Where'd they get the fucking eggs, from a Firestone factory? Don't even get me started on the goddamned danish. This feels like a piece of skin. Is that a prune? That looks like . . ."

"Don't say it. I'm gonna eat it," Del said.

The phone rang and Lucas dug it out of his shirt pocket. "Davenport."

"Lucas, it's Elle. Ruth is up at that church, or whatever it is. She wants to talk to you now."

"Elle, what the hell is going on?"

"I don't know the details, I only am . . . aware . . . of the outline of what she's doing. But I promised her that you were going in as a citizen, and not exactly as a cop—that your conversation would be off the record. I don't know if you'll be able to go along with it, but that's what I told her."

"Oh, boy. They're smuggling grass, right? They're using the money to regild the dome on the cathedral."

Another odd hesitation, and then Elle said, "Talk to her. I don't know what she'll say."

THEY GAVE UP on the breakfast and headed for Broderick, Del still driving. On the way out of town, they got hung up in a four-car traffic jam behind a lift truck taking down Christmas lights. For the first time since they'd come to town, there were cracks in the clouds, and hints of sunshine. The car thermometer said it was six below zero, and the air was almost still. Wherever a house was burning wood, the smoke from the chimney went straight up for fifty feet before fading away.

On the way, Lucas dialed the Kansas City number that Mark Johnson had given him early that morning. The answer was fumbled, and Lucas recognized it as a cell phone, being answered by somebody who was standing on a street corner. "Block."

"Yeah, my name is Lucas Davenport, I'm with the Bureau of Criminal Apprehension up in Minnesota—"

"Mark Johnson said you might call. He said you were the Tom Block of Minnesota. But better looking."

"That's true," Lucas said.

Block laughed and asked, "So he told me what's going on, with the lynching and the kidnapping."

"Not a lynching."

"If it was down here, it wouldn't be a lynching, either. In Minnesota, it's a lynching. Anyway, you think the Cashes are chopping cars up there?"

"No, I don't," Lucas said. "The place we're looking at—it's called Calb's—doesn't look like a chop shop. It looks like what they say it is, car body and truck rehab."

"See any Toyota trucks up there? I mean, connected to this place?"

Lucas thought—and he'd seen one. "One," he said. "Land Cruiser."

"Now we're talking. The thing is, we know the Cashes are moving hot cars. We've even caught their boys in a couple, but those were going to chop shops down here. There's a rumor that they steal new Toyota trucks. Only new Toyotas. And then the Toyotas disappear, and they're never found again. Ever. They're gone. Never get in wrecks, never sold to wrecking services. I've got some numbers of insurance companies that are interested, if you want to talk to them, but I'd say we're talking anywhere from seventy-five to a hundred trucks a year, from all over the Midwest and the plains, far east as Cleveland and far west as Denver."

"That's a lot of trucks."

"We figure about five million worth. We had one guy across the river in Kansas City, Kansas, who bought a new Land Cruiser, sixty thousand dollars, got it stolen, got his insurance check, bought another one, and they stole *that,* the second night he had it."

"Hmm."

"Listen, I gotta get a bus. If you want to talk, come down, or call me this afternoon, I'll have some open time. I can tell you all about the Cashes. I grew up with them."

"ANYTHING GOOD?" Del asked.

"That was a Toyota Land Cruiser those women were hauling coffee in, right? Last night?"

"Yeah, I think."

"They're driving for Calb for $100 a week and they drive a sixty-thousand-dollar Land Cruiser. That'll cause you to think."

"Oh, boy. Tell me about it."

Lucas told him. And as they came up to Broderick, he said, "Go on through. Let's see if there's anything going at Letty's."

As they went past Deon Cash's place, they noticed a half-dozen cars in the driveway and yard. "FBI has landed," Del said.

"Talk to them later."

There wasn't much at Letty's house: one deputy sheriff's car and one state fire marshal's car sat next to the hole that used to be the house. The deputy was in his car, writing on a clipboard, and waved at Lucas. Another man was digging carefully through the basement.

When Lucas identified himself, the man climbed out on a stepladder. He was wearing rubberized coveralls, and his face was smudged with charcoal. "George Puckett," he said.

"Figure anything out?"

"Not a thing," he admitted. "I don't see any signs of accelerant. The sheriff's deputies say the fire was deliberate, but I couldn't prove it."

"That's not nothing," Lucas said. "That means that the guy probably didn't come here to burn it down. Probably did it on the spur of the moment."

"Might not be nothing, but it isn't much," Puckett said. "Wish I could help more."

Lucas and Del walked around the scene a few minutes longer, found a patch of blood where Letty had huddled in the snow. No blood between that spot and the window, as far as they could tell, although the remaining snow was covered with soot and debris from the fire.

"Church?" Del asked.

"I guess. What else is there?"

THE MOTHERLY WOMAN met them at the door, looked hard at both of them, and without a word took them back to the kitchen, where Lewis was again working at the table. When they came in, she stood up, looked at Del, and said, "I'd like to talk privately with Lucas."

Del shrugged, looked at Lucas, and said, "I'll be out in the TV room."

When he was gone, Lewis said, "Sit down." Lucas pulled out the kitchen chair opposite her. She asked, "Want a cup of coffee?"

"No, I'm fine. So. What's the story?"

"I wasn't surprised to hear from Sister Mary Joseph. I'd been more or less expecting it." She paused, but Lucas kept his mouth shut. "Anyway," she continued, "we all talked about it, and several of our sisters have left in the past two days—people not yet too involved, so if you decide to bust us, they can pick it up later."

He kept his mouth shut.

She said, "So we talked about it, and not one of us could figure out how we could be involved in anything that had to do with the girls. We couldn't see any possible connection."

"Good," Lucas said. "The parents of the other girl are coming up here today. You could meet them, if you like."

Her hand went to her throat. "That's cruel."

"Keep going with the story," Lucas said. "What're you doing? I'll figure out for myself if there's a connection."

"We're smuggling drugs," she said abruptly. "We bring them down from Canada. We put on nun's habits so that the border people don't check too closely, and bring them across."

"Marijuana?"

"Some. But that's more complicated. Usually, it's tamoxifen and ondansetron. They're cancer drugs and we get people in Canada to buy them for us at Canadian government prices. We bring them across the border and distribute them to people who can't afford them. Because of the way the drugs are sold in Canada, they only cost about ten or fifteen percent of what they cost in the U.S. Tamoxifen in the states costs a hundred a month, or more, and you might take it for years. The poor tend to skip days or skip whole months and hope they can get away with it. Ondansetron is a really expensive antinausea drug. It costs two hundred dollars to cover the nausea from one chemo treatment—so a lot of people go with a cheap drug that doesn't work as well, and just put up with the nausea. Ever been nauseous for a week straight?"

"No."

"Neither have I, but it looks pretty unpleasant. We can buy the stuff in Canada for thirty bucks."

"Cancer drugs," Lucas said.

"And some marijuana. The marijuana is the cheapest way to fight nausea—sometimes, it's the only way—and the best marijuana for our purposes comes from British Columbia. We don't bring it across too often because of the dogs. The dogs don't care whether we're wearing habits or not. And if we have to, we can get it in California."

"Huh," Lucas said. Then: "Just, uh, for the sake of my own, uh, technical knowledge, how *do* you get it past the dogs?"

"We have a number of religious young men and women from Winnipeg who have grown out their hair. We provide them with what you might call "doper clothing," and they drive vans across the border ahead of us. If the dogs are working, they'll do the van every time, and as soon as the people see the dogs, they let us know with a walkie talkie. If there are no dogs, we'll come across."

"Okay. Cancer drugs."

"Yes."

"That's all a little hard to believe."

"Sister Mary Joseph said that if you don't believe, you should ask your wife. I don't know exactly what that means . . . is she a cancer survivor?"

"No. She's a doctor."

"Then she'll know. I promise you this, Lucas, and Sister Mary Joseph would tell you the same thing—this is only for people who might die if they don't get the drugs. People can get the standard chemotherapy, one way or another, even if they don't have money, but the ancillary drugs and the follow-up drugs . . . lots of times, it comes down to a choice between eating and taking the drugs. I'm absolutely serious about that—that's what it comes to. Our drug shipments involve about four thousand patients at the receiving end."

"Four *thousand*—"

"And we're growing."

"And you weren't involved with Deon Cash or Jane Warr or Joe Kelly."

"No. Except that we drive for Gene Calb, and they did."

"They never tried to cut in on your drug deal."

"*There is no money in the drugs.* We don't get any money. We don't buy or sell anything—the whole point is that our clients can't afford to buy it. You have to understand, except for marijuana, all these drugs are *legal* down here. We're not so much smuggling the drugs, as smuggling the prices paid for them."

They sat looking at each other for a minute, then Lucas said, "That's crazy."

"Want to know something even crazier? There probably isn't any way to make it work better. Ask your wife."

Lucas took a few seconds to think about it, then said, "My partner claims that a tiny town like this can't have two big crime deals going on at the same time without some relationship between them. I tend to agree, but if you're telling me the truth, I don't see what it could be."

"There isn't one," she said.

"So tell me one more thing," he said. "Where'd you get that Land Cruiser you were driving last night?"

She blinked. "Up in Canada."

"In Canada?"

"Yes. At an auction. We need a four-wheel drive for some of the roads here, when we're doing our regular charity work. It's a terrible truck, it has two hundred and fifty thousand kilometers on it, we're always afraid it's going to blow up. The transmission feels like . . . you're shifting through a pound of liver. It squishes," she said. Then, "Um, why did you want to know?"

He was a little embarrassed, and shrugged. "I don't know. You told me that story about raising pin money by driving for Calb."

"That's *true.*"

"But I've looked at trucks like that and they cost sixty thousand bucks or so. So . . ."

"What? We have the receipt." She was getting a little warm. "We paid one thousand five hundred dollars for it."

"Okay, okay." Lucas stood up to go. "You're going to go down and talk to Letty?"

"I'd be gone already, if Sister Mary Joseph hadn't called. I'll be going in one of our Corollas. Our expensive Land Cruiser might not make it that far."

"All right, all right. I had reason to ask."

"So what're you going to do?"

"Try to find whoever is doing the killing. I don't care about your drugs, but if you think of anything—*anything*—that might hook it all together, you've got to call me. This guy won't stop as long as he thinks he's in danger." He took a couple of steps toward the TV room, then looked back and said, "When you're taking weed across the border, you've got to be careful. My partner could smell it on you the other day. He's worked with dopers a lot, and he's pretty sensitive. The guys at the border probably are, too."

"We were repacking that day," Lewis said. "We're very careful before we go across. We have no drug abusers here—zero. That's one of our rules. The only people we allow to use drugs are survivors. Some of them are still on tamoxifen."

LUCAS LEFT THE ROOM, looking for Del, then turned around and went back to her. "Why isn't there a better way to price the drugs?"

"Because the drug companies say, and they may be right—although they lie about everything else—that they won't be able to create new drugs that everybody wants, or specialized low-profit drugs, if they don't make a substantial profit from the ones they're selling now. So they're allowed to charge what they want in the United States.

"Canada's a small part of their market, and it's got one central bulk buyer—the government, and they make the best deal they can. So the drug companies sell to Canada for a little bit more than cost, because the market's small enough that it doesn't have much effect on their overall profit."

"Why don't we just make it legal to reimport the drugs?"

"Because then Canada would essentially become a drug-wholesaling middleman for the U.S. The drug companies won't allow that. They'd start charging Canada the American price, to get the profit they say they need. The end effect would be that Canadians would pay more, or go without, and Americans wouldn't pay less."

"You know that bumper sticker about the Arabs? 'Nuke Their Ass and Take the Gas'? Why doesn't the U.S. just nuke the drug companies' ass and take the drugs?"

"Then who's going to develop the new drugs we need? The government? The people who brought you the CIA and airport security and the Bush-Gore election?"

LUCAS FOUND DEL watching *Night of the Living Dead* with the older woman who'd met them at the door. "You at a good part?" he asked.

"There are no good parts," Del said. "Everything okay?"

"Okay," Lucas said. "Let's go."

"At least you didn't open fire on anybody," the older woman said to Del.

"That's a *good* thing," Del said.

OUT IN THE CAR, Del asked, "You gonna tell me?"

"Yeah." Lucas put the car in gear, sighed, and said, "We've gotta talk to the sheriff, and the crime scene guys from Bemidji, start looking through their paper, see if there's anything. Gotta *think* about it. 'Cause it ain't these guys."

"So . . . what're they doing?" Del asked.

Lucas told him. When he was done, Del said, "I actually heard rumors about them. Down in the Cities. Never made the connection with these guys. I just thought it was some kind of feminist-wicca-earth-goddess-conspiracy urban-legend bullshit. Huh."

"Where'd you hear it?"

"My old lady."

"Yeah? You know where Lewis said I should go for more information?"

"Where?"

"My old lady."

They laughed about that for a very short time, and Lucas said, "Let's go talk to the feds."

17

ON THE WAY UP the street, Lucas got back on his cell phone and called the sheriff's office. He got the sheriff on the line, explained what he needed.

"That's not a bad idea," the sheriff said. "I've got three guys on duty at the schools, but that's not critical—I could have everybody who's in town down here in forty-five minutes."

"That'd be great," Lucas said. "We need the help. We're really stuck."

THE FBI SQUAD was led by Lanny Cole and Jim Green, the agents they'd met at Hale Sorrell's home. Cole was standing in the yard, talking to a man in an Air Force snorkel parka, the fur-rimmed snout sticking eight inches out from the man's face. Lucas and Del got out, and Cole came over with the parka and they shook hands.

"This is Aron Jaffe from Hollywood," Cole said, nodding at the parka. The parka nodded back. "He'll run the GPR search team."

"Can you hear me in there?" Lucas asked, talking at the snorkel.

"I can hear you fine," Jaffe said. "Only my legs are frostbitten."

"Is the frozen ground gonna screw you up?"

"Naw. Might help," he said. "We might see some seriously unconsolidated stuff."

They talked for another minute, then Cole said, "The second girl, Burke—her parents are driving up here from Lincoln. They want to look at the locket, although I don't think there's any doubt."

"Okay," Lucas said. "Are you all straight with the BCA crew?"

"Yeah, we're fine. You got anything going at all?"

Lucas shook his head. "Not much. You know about the fire last night."

"Went up and looked at the hole this morning."

"The girl who was hurt says the killer sounded like he was from here. His voice did, the way he spoke."

"The *Fargo* accent," said the guy from Hollywood.

"Yeah. We know that three of the kidnappers worked for the Calb auto-body place, and the whole Cash family down in Kansas City is supposedly heavy into car theft. So . . . there's a thing here."

"A nub," Del suggested.

"A nexus," said the guy from Hollywood.

"Whatever. I think it's about fifty-fifty that the killer's not more than two or three hundred yards away from us. Somebody from here, connected to Calb's."

"You wanna jack the guy up? I could come along, add a little federal heat."

"Probably. But I'm going down to the sheriff's office first. We need to talk to the deputies, to everybody that knows anybody up here. There's gotta be some kind of edge we can get our fingernails under."

Before they left, they walked Jaffe around the place, and pointed out spots along the creek, behind the house, where bodies could have been buried. "That's a sizable chunk of ground. Gonna take a while," Jaffe said.

THEY LEFT THE FBI MEN, stopped at Wolf's Cafe, found it empty except for Wolf, ordered pancakes, and asked her to name everybody she knew in every building in the town. "Please God, don't tell anybody I helped. That poor goddamned Martha West, getting roasted."

"Nobody'll hear it from us," Lucas said.

She started reciting names, and Lucas got a piece of paper from his notebook and drew an outline map of the town and slotted the names in cartoon houses. They took the map south, to the sheriff's office, and found twenty or so deputies milling around. The sheriff came out and said, "I got a courtroom upstairs. Already some people up there, I'll send the rest of them up now. Only got two or three who can't make it."

Thirty people, half of them in uniform, had gathered in the court-room. Two or three people who looked like courthouse loafers had squeezed in, curious, and Lucas ordered everybody who wasn't a sworn deputy to leave. The loafers squeezed back out, and one of the deputies closed the doors.

"I don't want anybody to talk about what goes on here," he said. "If you gotta talk to your wives, tell them to keep their mouths shut. I know it's hard, but it's only for a couple of days. What I have is a list of everybody who lives in Broderick." He waved Del's yellow legal pad. "I *think* I have the name of everybody. And we need to have a real gossipy talk about who does what up there. Who's been busted, who's been warned, what kind of trouble they've gotten themselves in, if they have—we need anything you've got. I'm telling you fellas, after last night . . . we need to nail this sucker. And we don't have a hell of a lot to go on."

"No DNA at all?" one of the deputies asked. Lucas recognized him as one of the guys who'd been at the fire.

"We're not too hopeful," Lucas said. "Mrs. West was burned beyond recognition, and those of you who've been up at the house know what *that* looks like. It's a big pile of charcoal."

"Cash and Kelly worked for Gene Calb; have you talked to Gene?"

"Yeah, but he says he doesn't know nothin' about nothin'. So what I need to know from you is, What about Gene Calb? Does he really not know nothin' about nothin'?"

"He's always been a pretty good guy," one of the deputies said. "Can't see him killing anybody."

"Ever been in trouble?"

"Traffic tickets, I guess. Maybe a DWI when he was a kid." The deputy looked around, picked out a man in gray coveralls. "What do you think, Loren? You go up there."

The man named Loren cleared his throat and said, "I rent a paint booth from him for a couple days, every year or so—I refinish cars as a hobby. The thing is . . . there are some pretty tough hombres up there. Mike Bannister or Kiley Anderson or Dexter Barnes, everybody knows them. Gene handles them, though."

"So what about these guys, Bannister and Anderson and Barnes?" Lucas asked.

The deputy said, "They're mostly just hell-raisers, but they've been known to steal a car occasionally. There's one guy out there, Durrell Schmidt, will steal a calf every once in a while. That's what we think, anyway."

"Had some marijuana around there," another man said.

"Had some everywhere, it's mostly just ditch weed," a third deputy said.

They went around for a while, told Lucas a story or two, and laughed at them. Lucas finally asked, "So who up there *could* kill somebody?" "Who up there, if he really got his back to the wall, could do that?"

Loren said, reluctantly, "You could see three or four of those guys getting drunk and maybe something happens and they get crazy with a gun and shoot somebody, almost like an accident—but if it came down to sitting around and thinking about it, and then doing it . . . I gotta say Gene Calb. Maybe Dexter Barnes. I mean, if it came right down to having to do something really tough, and then doing it, one of those two guys. I don't think they did, but I don't know anybody else up there who . . . who . . ." He scratched his chest as he looked for a word. "Who is really *organized* enough to do this. Organized isn't the right word, maybe . . ."

There was some nodding of heads, but then another deputy said, "Do we know for sure that the guy who killed the Sorrells and West had anything to do with the kidnappers? Or that the guy who killed the Sorrells is the same guy who killed West?"

Lucas smiled. *That* was a new thought, that everything was unconnected. "We believe there's gotta be some connection—if there isn't, we're *really* out in the dark."

Another deputy said, "I talked to the doc this morning, the medical examiner, and they X-rayed Martha West and she's got a slug in her head. You know about this?"

"I haven't talked to the ME today," Lucas said. "Good slug?"

"Most of it's there. So if it's the same guy who did the Sorrells, you could get a match."

"All right. Listen guys, I want you all to go out and question everybody you know. I don't mean interrogations, just ask around. Was there anything weird going on up in Broderick? Anything that's sort of undercover around Calb's place? If you hear anything, from anyone, that seems like it might be real, give me a call. The comm center here has my number."

"So what're you gonna do?" somebody asked. "Wait for us to call?"

"We're gonna go back up and walk the town again. The FBI is up there now—there are rumors about a second kidnap victim, I'm sure, and I can tell you that it seems likely that there were at least two girls, not just one. So . . . ask around. Let me know."

BEFORE THEY LEFT, Lucas asked a woman in the comm center if there was any place that they might eat a late lunch that didn't involve the Bird. She suggested they try Logan's Fancy Meats, which was down two streets and around the corner, on the right. They tried it, and found a slow-talking thin man standing behind a meat counter. He was wearing hawkish black-plastic-framed glasses, the kind that New York authors wear, and was reading a copy of *The Best-Loved Poems of Jacqueline Kennedy Onassis*. He sighed when he put the book down, and said, "What can I do for you gentlemen?"

Lucas asked, "Those pretty good poems?"

The thin man's eyebrows went up; he was skeptical. "You read poetry?"

"I do," Lucas said. "I've seen the book, but haven't had a chance to look through it."

"It's *very* good," the thin man said. "Do you know *Kubla Khan?*"

"Of course," Lucas said. "Maybe the best beginning of a poem ever written. It's wonderful."

Without prompting, the thin man lifted the book, and read, "In Xanadu did Kubla Khan a stately pleasure dome decree, where Alph the sacred river ran . . ."

When he finished, his eyes gone dreamy behind the black glasses, Lucas and Del shuffled their feet, as cops will do when caught listening to poetry, and then Del cleared his throat and said, "Could I have a cold chuck roast sandwich?"

———

THEY LEFT WITH heavy sandwiches on thick rye bread, chuck roast for Del and hot sliced chicken for Lucas, along with bottles of cream soda, and ate in the car on the way back to Broderick.

"Gonna walk the place again?" Del asked.

"No choice—things have changed since the fire. This time, we try to scare them into talking . . . if there's anything worth talking about."

WITHOUT THINKING MUCH about it, Lucas headed for the Cash house, where they could at least be inside. When they pulled up, Cole, the lead FBI agent, coatless, was walking out of the house. A black Lexus sedan was parked in the yard behind the federal cars. A fiftyish couple had apparently just gotten out and were standing passively next to a sheriff's deputy.

"Aw, man," Del said, as they pulled into the yard. "Must be that Burke kid's folks."

"Worst goddamn thing I can think of, having your kid snatched and killed," Lucas said. "You want to talk to them?"

"Maybe to see what they have to say," Del said.

"Good. Go talk to them. I don't want to. I'm gonna start hitting all the houses again. Find me when you're done with them."

"All right. We going after Calb? Looks like there are people over at his shop."

Lucas looked down the highway. There was smoke coming out of the shop chimney, and a half dozen cars were parked around the lot outside.

"Maybe wait one day," Lucas said. "Do the whole town today, and jack him up tomorrow."

18

LOREN SINGLETON HURT. The pills helped, but they wouldn't last. The bleeding, at least, had stopped, but a bruise was growing across his chest, from his breastbone to his armpit. The bullet hole looked like a black mole, clogged with hardening blood. He had a fantasy: drive to Fargo, buy some women's makeup at a Wal-Mart, paint his chest so it looked okay, then go bare-chested for a minute or so in the deputies' locker room.

Then he thought, *Why?* If they wanted to look at his chest, they'd look at it, whether or not somebody had seen it in the locker room. If they looked at it deliberately, body paint wouldn't help.

He thought about calling Katina Lewis, but dismissed that after a moment. They were falling in love, but there was no way that she'd go for the killing of Martha West, no matter how necessary it may have been. He might, in fact, have to break it off with Katina—he could fake the flu for a few days, but if they stayed together, she'd have his shirt off soon enough. He couldn't bear the idea, couldn't stand it.

He had to do something. Something to fix it all. Something that would fix the whole deal.

That guy Davenport, at the deputies' meeting, asked everybody to nose around. If everybody did talk to everybody else, they might finally figure out that Loren Singleton had been closer to the Kansas City people than anybody had really appreciated. If somebody had seen them here, and somebody else had seen them there, and if they put it with what Katina knew, and what Gene Calb knew . . .

That was the trouble with a small town: too many people knew your business, knew your *life*.

In the end he called Mom.

MARGERY SAT AT the kitchen table with her head in her hands. "You dumb shit. You *dumb* shit. What were you thinking about? Now they've got to look up here. When the Sorrells were killed, it could have come from anywhere. From Kansas City. Now . . . you're sure the kid didn't recognize you?"

"I'm still here," Singleton said. He added, after a moment, "So are you."

"What is that supposed to mean?" She didn't yell it at him—she growled it.

"It means, we need a way out."

She looked at him for a few seconds, then said, "There's only one way out. We've got to give them somebody else who did it."

"What?"

"If they look at you, with that hole in you . . . if they even suspect, all they have to say is, 'Take off your shirt.' That's it. Then you're done."

"I know it," he said, miserably. He touched his chest and tears came to his eyes. "Jeez, I hurt."

"I don't know why I help you," she said. "I just oughta go to work and forget about it."

"They'd find out what happened. You'd go to jail right along with me."

"Who's gonna tell them?"

Silence. Then: "I would. You got me into this, you . . . witch. You're the one who thought Jane was so fuckin' wonderful, you're the one who thought Deon was so fuckin' smart, you're the one who thought of stealin' the little girls, for Christ's sake. I ain't hanging for that. I ain't hanging for the little girls. I'll take them out where the bodies are, they'll dig them up, and you know what they'll find? They'll find all that shit from the nursing home that you pumped into them, that's what they'll find."

More silence. A full minute of it, the locks closing down again, just like when they lived together years ago, locks on all the doors.

"You gotta do what I tell you."

"If it makes any goddamn sense." More tears. "Goddamn, I hurt."

SHE TOLD HIM what to do, and Singleton staggered off to bed, pulling at the hair on the sides of his head. His head was burning, not from the wound, but from what his mother had said. Once facedown, he blacked out. He woke from time to time, to find Margery in the living room, watching TV, watching him.

Mom.

Finally, late in the afternoon, he pushed himself to his feet, brushed his teeth, washed his hands, went to the bedroom, opened the bottom drawer, and found the little .380 semi-auto. He checked it, put the gun in his pocket. And now a pipe.

His basement was small, dark, damp; a hole, really, for the water heater and the furnace and for a few thousand spiders and crickets and ants and mice. Singleton walked carefully down the wooden steps, pulled the string on the bare overhead bulb, dug around in an old trash rack, and eventually came up with what he'd been looking for.

A lead pipe. Lead pipes were hard to find. They'd been outlawed for decades and when a guy really needed a lead pipe, you could hardly find one. If you wanted to hit somebody over the head, you were usually stuck with a copper or iron pipe, which were really too hard to do the job right. With copper or iron, you'd break the skin, while, with a properly deployed lead pipe, you got a nice deadly rap, and no blood.

He was just lucky, Singleton thought, to have one. He carried it upstairs, walked around the kitchen a few times, whacking the palm of his hand with the pipe, then stepped down the hall to the living room. "Let's go," he said.

Margery pushed herself out of the La-Z-Boy. "You better do this right, dumb shit. This is it. If this ain't right, we're gonna die."

"I know."

"So get some different shit on. You're supposed to know how all this works—but you gotta get some different shit on."

Singleton pulled out his oldest parka, a dark blue nylon job that he hadn't worn in years. He got his heaviest gloves and a pair of boots. When he bent forward to tie his shoes, the pain in his chest suddenly flared and he gasped, a high-pitched "Yiiii . . ."

"You goddamn baby," Margery said.

KATINA HAD SAID good-bye to Ruth, and then had gone out as usual to check on a dozen elderly women living in the small towns across the countryside—women who needed food or medicine or company. Katina did it three days a week, when she wasn't scheduled to make a run. Not only did that help build a better cover for the group, she enjoyed it, and did some good, she thought.

She was south of Armstrong by the end of the day, coming back into town a half-hour after dark. She decided to check Loren's house, on the chance that he was home and awake. She swung by, found the house dark, went to the garage and looked inside. His cars were there, and she went and knocked on the door, waited, knocked again. No answer. Huh. When he went somewhere, he usually drove—Loren was not a walker.

But he wasn't answering the door. For a moment, that felt sinister. What if this killer . . .

No. There were much better answers than that. She stood on her tiptoes and tried to see inside, but there was nothing to see. After a minute or so, she went back to her car. She'd call him later, she thought, as she headed back to the church.

Only two women were left at the church, in addition to Ruth and herself, and those two had apparently gone out. There were no runs scheduled, and the other two had been making country checks like she had. She turned on the lights and found a note on the kitchen table: "5:20. Gone down to the Red Red Robin for dinner. Lucy's buying. If you make it back before six, come down."

She looked at her watch. Only five-thirty. She'd missed them by ten minutes. She could use some restaurant food, she thought. She went back out to her car, noticed that Calb's had gone dark, and headed back to Armstrong.

THE LIGHTS WERE ON at Calb's house, on in most of the houses up and down the short street. Singleton and his mother stayed in the dark as much as they could, without looking furtive. A couple of cars had gone by, and they'd leaned behind sidewalk trees as they passed. Singleton dug at the sole of his boot, trying to look as if he were doing something, if somebody looked out the window of one of the houses— though with the parkas pulled around their faces, there was no possibility that they'd be recognized.

The walk to Calb's house had taken ten minutes, and by the time they got there, the pain was fading again, as it had after he'd taken the first pill. On the other hand, his mind still felt a little disconnected, a little cloudy. That might be okay with Gloria Calb, but he'd have to be sharp for Gene.

As they came up to Calb's, Margery said, "Let's go around to the back door. Won't be in the porch light."

"Okay."

He was like a robot, taking directions. He couldn't imagine Gloria being suspicious of him—she knew what he did for Gene. They walked up the driveway, through the fence gate between the house and the detached garage, and around to the door. Knocked on it quietly. Knocked on it again, heard somebody walking around inside. Knocked on it a third time.

Gloria Calb came to the door and looked out the window, and he dropped the hood of the parka. When she saw his face, she pushed the door open.

"Loren, what are you doing?"

"Is Gene here yet?"

"No. I'm just making dinner."

"I was supposed to meet him here. We've got a real problem. The state police called a meeting today . . . Can I come in? Gene thought he'd be home by now."

She was too polite to do anything but let him in, even if she'd had a second thought. "Of course, I'm sorry, come in. Gene usually *is* here by now . . ."

He pushed the door shut behind him and she turned to lead the way through the kitchen. He had the pipe in his hand, and her head was right there, like a baseball frozen in space, and he could see the salt-and-pepper hair sweeping up past her small pink ear.

Singleton hit her behind the ear with the real, actual lead pipe.

The sound was a sharp *whap,* and Singleton could feel the soft pipe deform around Calb's skull. Calb said, "Uhhh" and dropped to the floor. Tried to push up, still alive.

Margery, who'd waited by the side of the house, came up, inside, and squatted next to her. "She's alive," she said. "Give me the goddamn pipe, you dumb shit."

Singleton handed her the pipe, and Margery straddled Calb, stooping, and hit her a half-dozen times on the head, hard, as though she were breaking rocks with a hammer.

The second or third blow probably killed her; the others were just to make sure. There was some blood, and Singleton pulled one of the plastic sacks out of his pocket and handed it to her and she lifted Calb's head by the hair and pulled the bag over it.

Still a little blood on the kitchen floor. Margery found some 409 all-purpose cleaner under the sink, cleaned up the blood with a couple of paper towels. The towels went in the garbage bag on top of Calb's head, and they dragged the body down a hallway and leaned it against the wall, in a slumped, seated position.

Margery was breathing hard. She wiped her hands together, as if dusting them off, and said, "All right. That's one. Give me that little gun—just in case. Gene's a big one, and you're hurt."

SINGLETON STEPPED INTO the living room, turned on a light, then turned on a hallway light that led upstairs, so there would be light coming down from an upstairs window when Calb pulled into the driveway. He wanted Calb to think that Gloria might be upstairs.

He told his mother and she shook her head as if it were all a terrible mistake. He went to turn off the lights and she said, "Nah, nah, leave it. Get in position." Then she slapped her forehead. "Oh, shit."

"What?"

"I gotta make a call . . . You get in your spot."

If Calb pulled straight into the garage, as he should, he'd be coming in the back door, through the kitchen. Singleton moved across the half-lit kitchen and looked out a side window toward the garage. The garage lights should come on when Calb hit his remote control. Nothing yet.

He could hear his mother muttering into the phone in the front room. What was all that about? Something at the nursing home?

Singleton leaned back against the wall, and for the first time in five minutes, noticed the pain in his chest. Not so bad right now. Not quite so bad, but his chest felt wet. He stuck a hand inside his shirt, felt the wound, felt a dampness and pulled his fingers back out. Blood. Goddamnit, he'd broken the wound open.

He had to find somebody to work on it, and soon. God knew what the lead bullet was doing inside of him. Probably poisoning him. Thinking about it sent him to the sink, where he washed his hands again, and wiped them carefully on paper towels. He put the towels in his pocket—DNA. His mother came back in the kitchen.

"What ya doing?"

"I'm bleeding again," he said.

"Won't kill ya," she said. "I seen a lot worse." She turned up her head and sniffed. "Something in the oven?" She stepped over to the stove, and looked through the glass front. "Looks like a casserole."

"Pork chops," Singleton said, nodding at the sideboard. Three thick center-cut porkchops sat on a sideboard, and one of the burners was glowing on the stove. "Turn the stove off," he said.

Margery left the burner on but put a kettle on it, obscuring the orange glow. Not bad, Singleton thought: the bubbling pot killed the silence. "Better get back in the hall," Singleton told her. "Gene doesn't miss dinner."

Calb arrived as the words came out of Singleton's mouth. Margery slunk back into the hall as the headlights swept over the side of the house and the driveway. The lights in the garage went on, and Singleton said, aloud, "Be alone." He pressed himself to the kitchen wall beside the door from the entry.

The garage door went up, then went down, and a moment later, Calb was at the back door, stomping his feet on a snow mat. "Gloria?"

He closed the outer door and stepped into the kitchen, leaning forward, groping for the light. "Gloria?"

Singleton hit him on the crown of his head and he went down to his knees. Singleton, grimacing, hit him again, and Calb stayed on his knees and one hand came up, his face turned up, and he said "cars," or something like that, and Singleton hit him across the eyes and this time, Calb went down.

Margery stepped up, took the pipe, crouched, and began hitting him as she had Gloria, the hammer swinging once, twice, three times, four, five . . .

Breathing hard, she finally stood upright, light in her rattlesnake eyes. How many times had she hit Calb? He had no idea, but Calb was dead, all right—his head was like a bag of bone chips.

"That got him," the old lady said with satisfaction.

"Did you kill people at work? The old men you didn't like?"

The rattlesnake eyes slid away. "What're you talking about? Let's get to work. Dumb shit."

Singleton looked at Calb and suddenly began bawling again. His mother muttered something and went into the living room, and Singleton wiped his eyes on his sleeves and got a bag out and bagged Gene Calb's head. Then he got a paper towel and the 409, cleaned a smear of blood off the floor, put the paper towel in the bag, and called his mother, and together they dragged Calb into the hall and left him next to his wife.

Back in the kitchen. "Goddamn, something smells good," Margery said, turning toward the stove where the casserole was still cooking, smacking her lips.

———

MARGERY MADE HIM clean the floor again; he was doing that, and she was back in the living room, "keeping an eye out," she said, when the doorbell rang. He was on his hands and knees and heard the door open, and his mother say, "Come in," and then, "Where's Loren and Gene?" and he recognized the voice and his eyes got wide and he lurched to his feet and called, "Katina?"

And at that very second, he heard the door close and remembered giving Margery the .380, and he stepped to the doorway with the towel in his hand and saw Katina looking at him, a question on her face, and Margery standing behind her, her arm pointed at Katina's head, and he shouted, *"No . . ."*

Bang!

Katina went down. Her eyes rolled and she went down on her face and she never twitched, and Singleton screamed something at his mother and started toward her, and she leveled the .380 at him and screamed back, "Get the fuck away from me, get away . . ."

EVERYTHING LOCKED UP. Then Margery said, quietly, "It's gonna take two of us to finish this. She had to go, because there was no way for you to break it off that wouldn't be suspicious. Now, you want to help, or you want me to finish you off, too?"

The gun never wavered.

"GODDAMN, THAT SMELLS GOOD," Margery said. It had taken a while, but Singleton wasn't going to hurt her. Not now—or not yet. He'd started thinking.

She went to the stove, opened the oven, took a couple of hotpad mitts off hooks beside the stove, and pulled the casserole out. She turned the top burner back on, found a pan in the bottom of the stove, and dropped in the porkchops. She found plates and bowls and silverware, dumped some macaroni and cheese from the casserole dish into the bowls, fried up the porkchops and slid them onto the dish.

"Damn, that's good." Margery said. They sat in the semidark kitchen, and talked about what to do next.

Chest hurt.

They finished eating, cleaned up the dishes and put them away, threw the cooking trash in the garbage, and began ransacking the house. Two suitcases, clothes, shoes, jewelry, Gloria Calb's purse, cosmetics, some photographs—they took two photographs out of their frames, and left the frames. Threw it all into the suitcases and carried the suitcases out to Calb's Suburban. As they went through the house, collecting things that the Calbs would take with them to Hell, they searched it, looking for money.

If Calb had left money in the house, Margery said, and the cops found it, that could queer everything. They found nothing except two safe deposit keys for a bank in Fargo. Margery took them, put them in her purse.

THEN THE BODIES.

Gene and Gloria Calb went out to the Suburban. He humped them out as fast as he could, but Calb was heavy, and he wound up dragging him. Still, the effort nearly killed him, and Margery was no help at all. Singleton's chest felt as though it were tearing apart, and he hadn't yet gotten to the hard part of the evening.

Katina, in dying, had leaked onto the carpet. They left the blood spot and carried her upstairs, got a chair from the bedroom, pushed open the access hatch to the insulation space under the roof, and pushed her body up through the hole. She was wearing a sweater, and Singleton carefully dragged the sweater across a rough spot in the framing around the hatch, so that a few strands of wool were pulled out.

Back downstairs.

Forgetting something, he thought. Hurting. He needed another pill, is what he needed. Christ, this might be too much . . .

What was he forgetting? He walked through the whole scene, and remembered the shell from the .380.

Found it in the kitchen, carried it outside, rolled it through Gene Calb's fingers, and made sure he got one good right thumbprint on the cartridge, as it would be if Gene were pressing a shell into a magazine.

Carried the cartridge back inside and tossed it on the floor.

His mother had one last idea. Gene had a home office . . .

They went through a Rolodex, and inside found a Kansas City phone number for Davis. He dialed the number and a woman answered, "Hello?"

"My name's Carl. We are asking Kansas City people for donations to the Missouri State Law Enforcement Association, which supports your local state, county, and municipal law enforcement officers—"

"We gave some," a woman's voice said.

"Our records don't show that," Singleton said. "We feel our law enforcement officers . . ."

He strung the conversation out another ten seconds, until an increasingly irate woman said, "Go away," and the phone slammed down. There'd be a record that just before the Calbs disappeared, they'd called Shawn Davis in Kansas City.

Good enough.

In the garage, he got a shovel, and they climbed into Calb's truck. He had three hours before he went on duty. Needed another pill, too.

As they backed out of the driveway he thought, *Goddamn, those pork chops were good.* Then he thought, *Katina.*

Margery said, "Watch out for the mailbox, you dumb shit."

THE REST OF THE EVENING was straight out of a horror film. By the time Singleton got home, he hurt so badly he could barely breathe. He peeled off his coat, peeled off the fleece under it, and found a three-inch bloodstain on his shirt. He took off the shirt, and his bloody undershirt, touched the bullet wound, and flinched. The scab over the hole had cracked open, and when he touched it, the pain flared through his rib cage, and ran around almost to his spine. At this rate, his arm would soon be useless.

He began sobbing as he looked at himself in the bathroom mirror. *Katina.* What about Katina? Was she in heaven? Was she looking down at him, knowing what he'd done?

He braced himself on the sink with both hands, and tipped his head down, and tried to cry, something more than the gasping sobs . . . nothing came out. After a moment, he pulled himself back together and began looking at the wound again. Something had to be done.

He carefully manipulated the bruised skin with his fingers, squeezing it, like a pimple, fighting the pain. The skin and fat wasn't particularly thick at the entry point, and he thought—could it be his imagination?—that he felt a lump. The lump didn't move, though.

Hurt. But he couldn't help himself. He went to the dresser and dug out a sewing kit, took out a needle, ran hot water on it for a moment, and then, using the eye end, probed the bullet hole. The probe hurt, but not as much as squeezing the wound. Holding his breath, he moved the needle around, then down a bit, maneuvered, felt as though he were pushing muscle aside—and hit something hard.

Didn't feel like bone. He moved the needle carefully now, judging the characteristics of the lump. Found the edges. "That's it," he muttered to himself. He found what he believed to be the center of the slug, and pushed on it. A little pain, but the lump didn't move. He found the edge of it, explored beside it. Brighter blood was coming out now, apparently from freshly pierced capillaries, and it made the exploration more difficult, the lump more slippery. But he found the side of it, and pushed with the end of the needle. It didn't move. He explored some more; he was sweating now, from the pain, but the pain was still bearable.

After a minute, he pulled the needle out and looked at it. The bullet, he thought, was stuck in a rib—hadn't gone through, but had gotten into it. Every time he breathed, or flexed, the motion was transmitted through his rib cage, and that was where the spasms of pain came from. He thought about it for a moment, then pulled on a sweatshirt and went out to the garage.

If he hadn't had just the right thing to work with, he might not have tried. But he did have the right thing, or what seemed like the right thing, in his tool box: a pair of tiny, needle-nosed pliers used to do automotive electrical work.

This was going to hurt, he thought. *But if it worked . . .*

He carried them back into the house, took two pills, scrubbed the pliers with antibacterial soap, and then, still not happy with their condition, dropped them in a saucepan, covered them with water, and put them on the stove. He let them boil for a while, then cool down underwater, as he waited for the pills to take hold. He glanced at the clock: forty-five minutes before he was due at work. He could do this.

He did it sitting at the kitchen table. Probed the lump with the needle, then slowly pushed the pliers in until he touched it. The pain had been dulled by the pills, but this hurt as bad as anything yet. His right hand, the pliers hand, began shaking, so he pinned the pliers in place with his left hand, and leaned against the table, bracing himself.

Then with his right hand, steady now, he slowly spread the pliers, pushed them down alongside the lump—or what felt like down, his hand shaking again—and squeezed. Pain flared through his body. Might have gotten some meat, he thought. Squeezed . . . and had it.

Slow and steady. He held it, pulled, pulled . . . had some meat, but then suddenly felt the lump come free. Held it, held it, pulled . . .

And had it out. It emerged like a small, gray larva, slick with blood, a .22 slug half the size of a pea.

Blood dribbled out of his chest again, but now everything felt different. The pain was changed—there'd been an ugly, corrosive feel to it, and now it just hurt. This he could handle.

He tottered off to the bathroom, looked at himself in the mirror. His face seemed narrower, sharper, wolf-like; and white, from the pain, his frown lines etched deep.

But he could touch his chest without flinching. He could manipulate the wound area without the arc of pain. He took two tabs of penicillin and a pain pill and looked at his watch. Had to start moving. He patched himself with gauze and tape, carried his bloody shirt and undershirt and fleece down to the washer, and threw them in, poured in a half-cup of liquid Tide, and started it. Climbed into his uniform.

Almost done now, he thought, as he buttoned up his shirt. There was Letty West—but if they were searching the landfill, he would have known about it, and so far, they weren't. Maybe she didn't know? Maybe he'd taken that risk for nothing?

He had the night to think about it.

And to think about the bullet. There was a sense of accomplishment with the bullet. Damn, that was a story. Maybe he could tell it someday.

THAT NIGHT WAS the longest in Singleton's life—and like most of the other nights of his life, nothing happened. He drove back and forth through town, his usual eleven o'clock grid, then headed out into the countryside, passing through a list of small Custer County towns, showing the flag for the sheriff. He tried to think about Katina as he drove, but where Katina used to be, there was a big dark box. He tried to focus on her face, and nothing came. He tried to think about what would happen in the next few days, and couldn't think of anything.

At seven o'clock, he signed off, went home, and crashed—lay fully clothed on his bed, unfeeling, until the telephone rang.

19

THEY WERE STUCK.

They'd spent the day before tramping around Broderick, talking with housewives and Calb employees, getting nowhere. The pitch Lucas had made to the sheriff's deputies hadn't produced anything yet, and Lucas began to wonder if he might be able to devise a way to pull the killer in. The problem was a lack of bait. There was Letty, but he couldn't use her. Might have been able to use her if she was a fifty-year-old asshole who'd brought the trouble on herself, but not an innocent teenager.

He worried a little that he'd even bothered to think of reasons *not* to use her . . .

HE WAS SITTING on his bed at the Motel 6, reading a *Star Tribune* story about the attack on the West house, and waiting for Del to knock. The TV was tuned to the Weather Channel, because they'd heard a rumor from the night clerk that snow was coming in. Coming in somewhere. When he looked out the window after he got up, there were a few fat flakes drifting around, but nothing serious. He was rereading the fire story when the room phone rang.

Ruth Lewis: "The sheriff called. They want to bury Martha West tomorrow and I'm going to bring Letty back up. I wanted to let you know—the sheriff said they'll provide security at the funeral."

"She can travel? Letty?"

"Your wife says so. Your wife is the admitting physician, by the way. She said you didn't know. She said they'll need Letty back here in a week, but that she could travel tomorrow."

"Has anybody figured out where she could stay?"

"Yes. She'll stay with me. I have lots of room right now, and we get along."

"All right. I wish I'd known about the funeral. I might have tried to push it a couple of days."

"I don't know about that," Lewis said. "The sheriff said the arrangements had been made . . . and that's what I know."

"Come and see me when you get up here," Lucas said. "We've got more to talk about."

"Maybe," she said.

DEL CAME BY. "We doing Calb?"

"I've got nothing else," Lucas said.

They got in the car and loafed up to Broderick, across the gray landscape, heading for Wolf's Cafe, where they'd found that the pancakes were edible. The snow had gotten heavier, and a North Dakota radio station said there could be four to six inches by evening. There were a half-dozen cars parked outside Cash's house—BCA crime scene guys, the FBI, and at least one deputy sheriff, Lucas guessed.

Wolf's was quiet, with only two other customers, both on stools at the bar, one talking with Wolf about going to Palm Springs, the other eating cherry pie and drinking coffee and eavesdropping. Lucas and Del took the furthest booth so they could talk. Through the window they could see the front of Calb's body shop, and could see people coming and going.

"Hate waiting," Del said. "We're just waiting for somebody to get killed so we've got something more to work with."

"We'd know what we were doing if we could figure out why he went after Letty. *If* he went after Letty. We're assuming that, but what if he was after Martha? We're thinking it was Letty because we've been hanging around with Letty."

"No, no. We think it's Letty because after he killed Martha, he went after Letty," Del said. "He tried to hunt her down out there, after he killed Martha. Letty says her mother was yelling at her to get out . . . Martha just got in the way."

Lucas nodded. "Okay. So what does Letty know that makes it necessary to kill her? Must be something."

"Maybe she doesn't know she knows," Del said.

"We'll talk to her again tomorrow. I keep going back to your theory that there can't be two big separate crimes in one small town without them being related, somehow," Lucas said. "We've got two big separate crimes—the drug running and the kidnappings—and they don't seem to be related."

"Could be an exception, I guess," Del said. "But . . ." He rubbed his chin, sipped at his coffee. "Maybe we ought to get with Ruth, or one of the other women, and do a whole history of how they got here. Why here? How did they get involved with Calb? Can't be just a coincidence that Calb has these ties down to Kansas City car thieves and these women . . ."

He trailed off, and Lucas said, "What?"

"What, 'what'? "

"Where were you going with that? 'Cause you gotta be right. How did they hook all this together? How did they land on Calb, out here in the middle of the prairie? There's gotta be more to it."

"That cheer you up?"

"Gives us something to think about," Lucas said. "Something to pull at."

WOLF BROUGHT THE PANCAKES OVER, and a couple of minutes later, as they were eating, a black Lexus backed out of the Cash house, rolled south, and pulled into the parking lot next to Lucas's Acura. A white-haired man got out of the driver's side, and a moment later, Jim Green, the FBI agent, got out of the passenger side. Green pointed at Lucas's Acura and said something to the white-haired man, who went back into the Lexus and fished out a briefcase.

They clumped inside and looked around, and Lucas lifted a hand. The two men came down and squeezed into the booth.

"Tom Burke—Lucas Davenport, Minnesota BCA," Green said. "You've already met Del."

"The FBI crew hasn't found anything, any gravesites," Burke said. "We don't know whether to be relieved or disappointed."

Lucas shook his head.

Burke said, "I have some paper that Jim said you may be interested in. When Annie was taken, the kidnappers told us that if we contacted the FBI or any other police agency, they would know, because they had a source inside the FBI. They sent us these papers . . ." He produced a neatly Xeroxed stack of papers and handed the stack to Lucas. "I took them to my attorney, who had worked with the Justice Department before he went into private practice, and he said they looked authentic. So we paid up, without calling in the FBI. I felt a little foolish even at the time, but I didn't think we could take the chance. We never heard another word from the kidnappers."

Lucas riffled through the stack of papers, and Burke added, "Those aren't the originals. The originals are back home, with the FBI."

"It looks like stuff I've seen from the FBI," Lucas said.

Green said, "Whoever did it had some idea of how the paperwork looks, but it's not quite right. The fonts aren't quite right, the formats aren't quite right. It's like they made them on a computer . . ."

"Cash and Warr had a computer . . ."

"Nothing on it but games," Green said. "Not even a word processor. What those are, are supposed memos inside some kind of kidnapping unit. It's all bullshit: the kidnappings they talk about never occurred. It's just good enough to convince Mr. Burke not to talk to the authorities before he paid the money."

"Because we didn't care about the money," Burke said. "One million dollars, in unmarked, nonsequential fifties and hundreds. We thought that if we paid, maybe they wouldn't kill her. It was worth the chance."

"If you didn't care about the money," Del said.

"We didn't. Not too much, anyway." He showed a quick, thin grin, dug into his briefcase and pulled out another stack of Xeroxes. "I gave one of these to Jim. They're checking the bills they got from Deon Cash's house . . . I understand one of you gentlemen found them."

"Del did," Lucas said. He took the second stack of sheets. They were legal-sized Xeroxes, each showing several fifty- and hundred-dollar bills. "What we did is, we got the money from the casinos, new bills, in stacks of sequential numbers. There were twenty bills in each stack. We Xeroxed all those stacks—the way it broke down, there were eight hundred and fifty of them—and from those, you can figure out all the serial numbers. You've got the top serial number, and the additional nineteen bills follow in order. Then we mixed them all up, so they'd appear to be nonsequential. But you can look at any bill, and tell if it came from the Vegas money."

"Pretty smart," Lucas said. "The money in Cash's place came from you?"

"Don't know yet," Green said. "The money's locked up in the bank, and we had to wait until it opened this morning. Time lock on the safe deposit. There was no great hurry anyway. We've got a guy over there now, looking."

"Did you ever have anything to do with Kansas City, or a Cash family in Kansas City?" Del asked Burke.

"We have nursing homes in the Kansas City area," Burke said. "I own six different chains of nursing homes in Minnesota, Nebraska, Iowa, Kansas, and Missouri. But when Jim told me about the Kansas City connection . . . as part of our public-relations campaigns, we donate money to various hospitals and medical schools for research on age-related illnesses. About a month before Annie was taken, we'd given two million dollars to the University of Missouri medical schools. Our public-relations people tried to get it in all the papers where we have nursing homes. They did very well—I suspect those stories were the proximate cause of Annie's kidnapping."

"Oh, boy," Lucas said.

Del asked, "Where do you have nursing homes in Minnesota? Around here?"

"Yes, in Armstrong, down in Red Lake Falls, Crookston, Detroit Lakes, Fergus Falls."

"And there was a story in the Armstrong paper?"

"Yes. I'm afraid so," Burke said. "I have to say that if I'd found out who they were, I wouldn't have done what Mr. Sorrell did, but I understand it, and I applaud it. I wish to God I could have shaken his hand. Now we've got to get this last one, or the last ones. We have to root out all of them."

"Doing our best," Green said. "We'll get them."

"Him," Lucas said. "It's one guy."

"How do you know?" Green asked.

"The feel of the killings. It's one guy." Lucas looked out the window toward Calb's shop. Little bits of icy snow were drifting across the highway.

"Cold up here," Burke said.

THEY FINISHED EATING and were pulling on their coats when Green got a call on his cell phone. They were at the door when Green said, "Hey," and waved them back. They stepped back and he said, "Numbers match. On the ransom money."

Burke had tears in his eyes, but didn't seem to know it.

LUCAS PUT THE PAPER from Burke in the car, and they rolled across the highway to Calb's. Inside, two guys were working on the truck they'd seen before, and it occurred to Lucas that there were too many people for too little truck. He stopped the closest guy. "Is Gene Calb around?"

The guy shook his head. "Can't find him. Should be here. We need the keys for the office."

"Can't find him?" Lucas said.

"No answer at his house. He's always here first," the guy said. "Don't know where he could've got to."

Lucas and Del went back outside, to the Acura, moving fast. "Please, God, let him be at Logan's Fancy Meats."

They sped back toward town, Lucas pushing the Acura hard. The snow was coming down harder now, the flakes a little smaller, but driven by a wind from the northwest. Now it looked serious. Two miles out of Broderick, a car a half-mile in front of them, and coming their way, suddenly showed the flaring red lights of a police roof rack. "Goddamn radar," Lucas said.

It was Zahn, in his patrol car. Lucas continued past him, then pulled to the shoulder, jumped out, and as Zahn swung around in a circle, waved at him. Zahn pulled up and his window rolled down and he said, "I hate to ask."

"Nobody can find Gene Calb," Lucas said. "He's not at work, not answering his phone. We're heading for his house. You know where he lives?"

"Follow on behind me," Zahn said.

They tucked in behind him and rolled down to Armstrong, and Lucas could see him talking on his radio. "Calling the sheriff," Lucas said.

A DEPUTY'S CAR was pulling up outside Calb's house when they arrived. A neighbor across the street stood by his picture window, watching, as they all got out. The deputy asked, "What do you think?"

"Knock on the door," Lucas said. They all trooped up to the stoop, pushed the doorbell, heard it ringing inside. When nothing happened, Lucas knocked and pushed the doorbell again. Del went around to the back, looked in the window on the back door, then returned to the front of the house. "Can't see anything in the kitchen—I think they're just gone."

Zahn walked over to the garage and tried the door. It opened, and he looked inside, then closed the door.

"Both cars here."

"Out for a walk?" Del asked.

Lucas said, "Let's go ask that guy." He nodded across the street, at the neighbor in the picture window. He and Del walked across, and the neighbor met them at the door. He was wearing a blue fleece sweatshirt and had a pipe clamped between large yellow teeth. "Haven't seen them," he said. "What's going on?"

"When did you see them last?"

Puff, puff, thought. "I saw Gloria yesterday evening, when she turned on the lights in the living room. That's about it."

"Haven't seen anybody coming or going?"

"Nope. What'd they do?"

"Nothing that we know of," Lucas said. They looked up and down the street. "They have any friends close by?"

Puff, puff, more thought. "The Carlsons, up in that stone-front house . . . they'd probably be their best friends. But we're all pretty friendly around here."

"Thanks."

As they were walking away, the man said, "That red Corolla in front of the house. I don't know who that belongs to." He pointed with his pipe. "It's been there all night."

"Yeah?" They stopped to look inside the Corolla, saw a clipboard and what looked like a daily diary on the passenger seat, and in the back seat, two packing boxes of canned food.

"That looks like the stuff the church women take around," Del said. "I saw a Corolla there, too."

"Been here all night?" Lucas tried the car door, and the door popped open. He reached across the seat and picked up the diary. Inside the front cover was a hand-written *Katina Lewis*.

Lucas showed the diary to Del. "Is that . . . Ruth Lewis? Or somebody else?"

Del shook his head. "I don't know. And where is she?"

They walked back across the street and talked to the deputy and Zahn. The deputy said, "Katina . . . she's the other one's sister. She's going with one of our guys. Loren Singleton. She's been sleeping over with him, but he's like a mile from here."

"Give him a ring," Lucas said. To Zahn: "Could you run down to the LEC and talk to the sheriff, and ask him to get a search warrant up here? You'll have to swear that we were looking for Calb for questioning in connection with a crime . . . which we are."

"On my way."

"Let's go talk to the Carlsons," Lucas said to Del.

———

LINDA CARLSON WAS a good-looking, blond forty-five-year-old whose husband worked as a State Farm agent. She had large eyes, slightly tilted upward, that made her looked sleepy, as though she'd just been rolling around in bed with someone. Lucas saw her and thought, *Mmm.* "I called over there last night, but didn't get an answer," she said, putting a hand on Lucas's sleeve. She was a toucher, too. "I was kinda surprised that there was nobody home, because I talked to Gloria yesterday afternoon and they weren't planning to go anywhere . . ." She was wearing a fuzzy angora V-necked sweater and her hand crept up the V until it stopped at her throat, and she said in a hushed voice, "You don't think anything's happened?"

"We're just trying to get in touch," Lucas said.

"I've got a key," Carlson said. "I can go down there anytime . . ."

Lucas spread his hands—"We can't go in without a search warrant. If you could just take a peek, if you don't think the Calbs would care. All we want to know is that they're okay."

"They wouldn't care. Let me get my coat."

She went to get her coat and Del muttered, "You've got drool dripping out the side of your mouth, marriage-boy."

"Just looking," Lucas said.

BACK AT THE CALBS', the deputy said, "I talked to Loren. He was on duty last night and didn't see Lewis. He said he thought she was coming over before he went on duty, but she never showed up. He called the church and she wasn't there."

"Okay."

Carlson's key was for the back door. She went in, as Lucas, Del, and the deputy waited on the back porch. She called, "Gloria? Gloria? Gene?"

She disappeared into the interior of the house, then came back and said to Lucas, "Maybe you better come in."

"What? Are they . . ."

"Nobody's home," she said. She was nervous, turning pink. "I don't know about these things, but Gloria's a very neat housekeeper . . . If this . . ."

She led Lucas to a hallway off the kitchen and pointed down. There was a dark spot on the carpet, about the size of a paper pie plate. Not coffee, not Coke. Heavier than that, crusty-looking.

Lucas squatted next to it, then said, "Please don't touch anything. Keep your hands by your side and carefully walk back out through the door, okay?" He followed her out to the porch and said to the deputy, "Wait out here, okay?" and to Del, "C'mere."

Del followed, and when Lucas showed him the rug, he squatted, as Lucas had, then said, "Yeah." He stood up, went into the kitchen, tore a small sheet of paper towel off a roll by the sink, tapped it under the faucet head to get it damp, then stepped back to the hallway and touched the dark spot with the damp point of the paper towel.

He held it up to Lucas. The towel showed a diluted blood-red. "That's a problem," Del said.

LUCAS PULLED OUT his cell phone and dialed the LEC, asked for the sheriff. Anderson came on and he asked, "Have you seen Ray Zahn?"

"He's here now, we're working out a warrant."

"Listen, a friend of the Calbs from down the street had a key and permission to go into the house. She went in, found blood, and invited us in. I don't know the legal aspects of it, but it looks bad. We need that warrant down here right now, before we start pulling the house apart. But we need it *now*."

"Ten minutes," Anderson said. "I'll walk it around myself."

Lucas called Green, the FBI agent, told him about the blood. "Send our crime scene guys down here, will you?" Lucas asked. "We may have another scene for him to process."

"Right now," Green said.

Lucas rang off and Del said, "Over here."

He was squatting in a corner of the kitchen, and Lucas stepped over. A pistol shell lay against a molding.

"A .380," Del said.

"Yeah. Goddamnit. Listen, let's do a walk-through. We're okay on that—the blood's fresh enough. Quick trip through the house."

THE HOUSE WAS LARGE, but they did the first pass in five minutes. No bodies, but the house had been stirred around. "Closets are halfway cleaned out," Del said. "Lot of stuff gone, and they were in a hurry."

"Whose blood is it, if the Calbs were running?"

"How did they run, if both of their cars are in the garage?"

"Taxi to the airport?"

"Do they have a taxi here? Do they have airplanes that go anywhere?"

"Shit, I don't know."

They were snapping at each other, feeling the pressure. Three people on the line—the Calbs and the church woman, Katina Lewis.

"Where's the goddamn sheriff?"

ANDERSON ARRIVED TEN MINUTES LATER—"Couldn't find the judge. He was in, but he was down in the surveyor's office, bullshitting. Took forever to find him."

"We're okay to dig around?"

"Go ahead," Anderson said. "You need more people?"

"I don't know," Lucas said. "The BCA crime scene people are coming down from Broderick. The FBI may be with them . . . First thing, we've got to figure out if the Calbs are really gone."

"Where's that blood?"

Lucas showed him, and Anderson shook his head. "That's a lot of blood."

"But whose blood is it?" Lucas asked.

HAVING GIVEN THE HOUSE a quick run-through, they checked the cars. The engines were cold, so they hadn't been used in the past couple of hours. There was nothing in either one of them that helped.

The lead crime scene guy arrived, with one of his subordinates, and with Del and Lucas trailing, they began in the basement and slowly worked their way to the top of the house. The subordinate noticed the strands of wool on the hatchway that led to the space under the eaves.

"They wouldn't hang there forever," he said. "If they were in a hurry, what were they doing up there?"

"Had something hidden?" Del suggested.

They got a chair, and then an ottoman to stack on top of it, and Lucas and Del helped him balance as the crime scene guy stood on top of the ottoman, pushed the hatch up, clicked on his flashlight, and froze. "Oh, Jesus," he said. "Aw, Jesus Christ."

"Who?"

"I don't know. Get me down."

The tech hopped down and Lucas clambered on top of the ottoman. When he stuck his head through the opening, Katina Lewis's face was four inches from his. Her dead eyes looked straight through him and he instantly flashed back to the hanging scene, the dead eyes of Cash and Warr; and he saw the face of the other woman, Ruth Lewis, in this woman.

"Lewis," he told Del. "Just like the other ones."

"Only her?"

Lucas couldn't see past her, but he could see the rest of the area, and there was nothing but pink insulation. "I don't see anyone else. I need to get a little higher . . ." He grabbed the edges of the hatch, pulled himself up a foot, but didn't have the leverage to get any farther. He could just see over Lewis's body, and there was nothing but insulation. "Nope. I think it's just her."

"I'll get something out on the Calbs," Anderson said. "You think it's Gene doing this?"

"Looks like it," Lucas said. He climbed down off the ottoman and chair. "Whoever it is, he's breaking up—he's going through a psychotic break. If it's Calb, I'd say his wife is in big trouble. He could kill anyone, now."

20

T HE CRIME SCENE CREW had suspended work at Cash's house and had moved down to Calb's. Lewis's body was still in the crawl space under the eaves and nobody knew exactly when they could move her—removing the body would be a job, and they wanted as few people as possible going in and out of the house until it was fully processed.

Lucas and Del carefully probed through the life the Calbs had left behind. Calb had a small home office, and one of the file drawers was open. Files had been taken, Lucas thought. He found income tax returns for 1996–99, but nothing newer. None of the files related directly to the body-shop business, but when they'd talked to Calb the first time, Lucas had noticed a row of filing cabinets in his office, so business papers might well be there.

Del came in after a while, with a small zippered bag. He handed it to Lucas, who said, "What?" and zipped the bag open. An insulin kit.

"Somebody's a diabetic and didn't take his or her shit," Del said.

"Unless this is a backup."

"Still."

A deputy came through, and they asked him about the airport; it was small planes only, and Calb wasn't a flier, as far as the deputy knew. Nor were there any taxis in town.

One of the BCA investigators from Bemidji, who'd been working at the Cash house, called to say that he and his partner had walked across to Calb's place and had frozen it—all the employees were there, and they were detaining any more who showed up.

Then the crime scene crew at Calb's house found a fingerprint on the .380 shell. "We'll do the Super Glue trick but it's about the best single print I've ever seen," the tech said. "We'll have something for you."

Lucas, going through Mrs. Calb's bedroom closet, found two shoeboxes that contained virtually new shoes, with perhaps an evening's worth of wear on the soles. In Calb's closet, on the floor under some shoes, he found a steel box, and inside the box, a thousand dollars in ten-dollar bills and a loaded .38 caliber Smith & Wesson revolver.

"I'm getting a bad vibe," Del said. "He might leave the gun, if he's got another one. Why would he leave the money?"

A FEW MINUTES AFTER NOON, the sheriff came back, trailing a tall cowboy-looking cop who the sheriff introduced as Loren Singleton.

"Loren was seeing Ms. Lewis," Anderson said.

"I'm sorry," Lucas said. "About your friend."

Singleton was distant, a little vague. Lucas had seen it before. "I'm, a, you know, we were . . . hell, we were sleeping together. But, I, uh . . ." A tear ran down his cheek and he wiped it with his shirt sleeve. "Goldarnit. Why'd this have to happen? You think it was Gene that did it?"

"Can't find him. Do you know any reason he'd have a problem with Ms. Lewis?"

"No, I don't," Singleton said. "I know what Katina was doing . . . I know what those women were doing, and I'm sure Gene knew . . . but how in the heck, I mean, what would that mean to Gene?"

"What were the women doing?" Anderson asked, taking a half-step back from his deputy.

"Bringing prescription drugs across the border from Canada," Lucas said. "They had a little distribution thing going, giving out drugs to the poor."

Anderson nodded, glanced at Singleton, and said, "Well, tell you the truth, half the people in town do that sometimes. No point in smuggling, though—you can order on the Internet."

"Gotta *have* the Internet," Lucas said. "Most of their clients are poor, and a lot of them are older—probably not too big on the Internet."

"How well did you know Gene Calb?" Del asked.

"I grew up here, so I knew him pretty well," Singleton said. "I didn't think . . . I don't know that he'd do anything like this. I mean, I refinish cars as a hobby, and once a year or so, I'd rent one of his paint booths to do some painting . . . That's how I met Katina. At Calb's."

"What was she doing there?" Lucas asked.

Singleton shook his head—"Just chatting, I guess. I mean, there're only forty or fifty people in that town. You tend to chat when you can."

"You know anything about Toyotas?" Lucas asked.

"Toyotas?" Singleton looked at Anderson, who frowned at Lucas.

"Toyotas?" Anderson asked.

"There are some people down in Kansas City, associated with Deon Cash—members of his family—who apparently steal a lot of Toyotas. They're never found again."

"Toyotas," Singleton said. He scratched his breast bone. "You know, I never thought about this, but there *were* a lot of Toyotas going through

Gene's shop. You don't see that many around here, but you'd see them in Gene's shop. Just about every time I went up there, when I think about it. Didn't seem strange then, but it seems kinda strange when you mention it."

"What were they doing to them? Rehabbing them . . . what?"

"Sometimes, it seemed like they had some parts off, but they weren't chopping them or anything. They were like fixing them. And painting them. Man, they painted a lot of Toyotas."

"Aw, Jesus," Del said. To Lucas: "That's where the hot Toyotas went."

"When the girls . . . the women . . . came back across the border, they were always in a Toyota Land Cruiser or maybe some old beat-up 4Runner. There's always one of them around the church, up there."

"You didn't think anything was weird about that?" Lucas said.

Singleton wagged his head. "Well, sure. But I knew what they were doing, and I . . . guess I didn't have much problem with it. I mean, gosh, everybody around here does it. Everybody's drugstore is over there."

THEY TALKED FOR a few more minutes, then Singleton went to look at Katina Lewis. He came back down the stairs two minutes later, even more shaky, sweating a bit. "Jeez . . . Jeez almighty . . ."

"Go home and lie down for a while," Lucas said.

"That's gonna help?"

"No, not much, but it's better than walking around with everybody staring at you. You look kinda messed up."

"Aw, man . . ."

LUCAS SAID TO DEL, "They bought old Toyotas across the border, brought them down here, took what they needed off the bodies, junked what was left, then transferred the papers to the ones they'd just stolen and moved them back across the border. Probably sold them out in the woods somewhere, where nobody would ever give them a second look. Even if somebody looked, the papers would match, 'cause they were legitimate papers. You'd have to take the car apart to figure out something was wrong.

"The women took them back and forth, and the body shop guys probably rigged up some kind of plug-in carriers for the drugs—a false floor, some kind of undercarriage box, that you could move from one vehicle to the next. With their tools, they could build anything. You could get a million pills into a one-inch deep false floor in the back of a Land Cruiser."

"Don't get two big crimes in a small town, without them being related," Del said.

"So the women would know about Calb's little sideline, which was bringing in a few million a year," Lucas said. Del nodded, and they both thought about it.

"Okay—I can see Calb for doing Lewis," Del said, after a moment. "But why in hell would he do the Sorrells, or Letty?"

"Because Sorrell tortured one of their guys, Joe Kelly. Who knew what Kelly told him about the whole Kansas City arrangement? That's why they had to act so fast—if Sorrell found a way to tip the cops . . . I mean, all we'd need is about three words, and we'd know all of it. If Sorrell called and said, 'Hey, a guy named Gene Calb is buying cars across the border and switching them with cars stolen in Kansas City by the Cash gang,' and if we'd called around, it'd take us fifteen minutes to put the parts together."

"How about Letty?"

"I don't know about Letty—but what if it was Letty's mother? She'd lived there for a long time. Would she know something was going on at the body shop? Maybe even knew exactly what it was, the stolen Toyotas? So then, her kid is hanging around with us, and again, all she'd have had to say was about three words, and we'd have been on Calb like Holy on the Pope."

"Gonna be interesting talking to Ms. Lewis today," Del said. He looked at his watch. "Funeral in two hours. They oughta be getting here."

RUTH LEWIS CALLED the Calb house a half-hour later. A deputy answered, and she asked for Lucas. The deputy handed the phone to Lucas and said, "Ruth Lewis."

"I'll take it."

"How did it happen?" Ruth asked, when Lucas came on. She was croaking, as though she'd spent the morning crying.

"We don't know, yet. We didn't know about the stolen car ring, so we didn't lean hard enough on Calb. Something happened here last night—we think your sister was killed here and the Calbs are gone. If you'd told me about this, we might have avoided it."

"Oh my God."

"Is there anything else I need to know right away?"

"Oh, god . . ." Ruth was weeping. Then a different woman's voice: "I don't think she can talk any more."

"Where are you? Is Letty there?"

"We're up at the church: Letty's here."

"Tell Ruth to stay there. We'll be there in ten or fifteen minutes."

THE SNOW WAS STEADY, but not getting any worse. There were a few little drifts around the edges of buildings and down in the ditches, and the highway was slick. *Maybe an inch and a half, maybe two inches,* Lucas thought. Letty was waiting by the church door with the older woman who'd watched *Night of the Living Dead* with Del. Letty was happy to see them. She held up her hand, in a fiberglass cast, smiled automatically, but then her lower lip came out and tears started and she said, "My mom's dead."

Lucas was not good around tears, even little-girl tears, and he tried to pat her on the back and she threw her arms around his waist and squeezed. "They say Gene Calb . . ."

Lucas pried her off and walked her away from the older woman, sat on a chair, and asked, "Letty, think about it. Was the guy you shot at . . . was that Gene Calb?"

"I don't think so," she said, shaking her head. "I would have known him. He was fat, and I couldn't see the man, but I don't think he was fat. I don't think his voice was right. Was Gene shot? Because I shot the man."

"There's a question about whether you hit him."

"I *hit* him."

"But if you're shooting .22 shorts, it might not even have gotten through his coat. A cold night, he might have been all bundled up."

"Then why did he fall on his butt? You don't fall on your butt if the bullet sticks in your coat."

"Maybe he was ducking."

"He wasn't ducking. He fell on his butt. Then he crawled for a while and then he ran back to the house and then the fire started."

When they finished talking, Lucas sent Letty to the TV with the older woman, who told Letty that she had to change for the service. "For the funeral," Letty said, correcting her.

Lucas wagged his head at Del, and they walked through the church to the kitchen, where they found Ruth at the kitchen table. She was red-eyed, red-faced. "Gene did this? With Gloria? That's . . . that's . . . Are you sure?" She had a brown cardigan wrapped around her shoulders.

"We're not sure. We just can't find them. There was blood on a carpet, and we found your sister hidden up under the roof."

"Why bother to hide her if she was so easy to find?" Ruth asked.

"Maybe they didn't think anyone would come looking. Or that if somebody did, they couldn't look too hard. Maybe all they expected was a head start."

"Hard to believe. Gene wasn't a bad man. I didn't think he was."

"Why didn't you tell us?"

"You know why," she said, defensively. "You could let us go, when you knew what we were doing, but you could never let Gene go."

"How did you get hooked up with him, anyway?"

She sighed. "One of our people up in Canada knew a man who bought a car from one of his . . . salesmen. We desperately needed different cars to bring the drugs across—you can't keep going back and forth, two or three times a week, without somebody asking why. So when we figured out where the cars were coming from, I came down here and talked with Gene. He wasn't too happy—but you know, if he'd done this, if he killed Katina . . . why didn't he kill me way back then?"

"Different situation," Del suggested. "No pressure then."

"Maybe. Anyway, I talked to him. I told him that we would all be committing crimes together, so nobody could talk about anyone else. He really needed people to drive the cars across, since he was starting to do some . . . some *volume*. We were perfect. Older women, forties and fifties and sixties. Who would suspect? And Gene built some special . . . things . . . for us, that fit in the Toyotas, and let us bring the drugs across. It was all very smooth."

"Did you bring a Toyota through last night?" Lucas asked.

"No. The last one was the one we had at the fire at the Wests' house. You saw it. Gene took it. It was a wreck, though. I don't think it would make another two hundred miles."

"You know what the license plates were?"

"I have no idea."

"Okay . . . You got some people killed," Lucas said. He said it in a soft voice, but a mean one, taunting, like a bully trying to pull another kid into a fight. Pushing her.

"But there was no connection between the kidnappings, between

Deon and Jane, and the car deal," she said. She said, "Listen to me: *no connection.* I knew Gene pretty well, and he didn't even *like* Deon or Jane. He didn't trust them. Deon wasn't a big shot in this thing, he was a *driver.* He was a *gofer.*"

"But if we'd had a piece of it . . ."

"It wouldn't have made any difference," she shouted, tears running down her face. "You're not listening to me. The kidnappings and all the rest of it weren't connected. They weren't."

A LITTLE LATER, Lucas spoke to Neil Mitford. "I don't think the governor necessarily would want to know about this conversation," Lucas said, as an opener.

"That's why I work here," Mitford said. "Talk to me."

Lucas outlined the situation, including the murder of Lewis, and the cover-up of the stolen-car ring. "The women covered up material information. We could bust them six different ways. The thing is, I'm not sure that if they had told us, it would have made any difference to the killer. He's operating on some other schedule—I can't figure out why Calb would kill Lewis and then run for it. As far as we can tell, she didn't know anything that all the other women didn't know. If he was going to kill Lewis, he should have been up here, trying to wipe out the church."

"And if we bust the women, that's the end of their little drug-running enterprise," Mitford said.

"That's right. I don't feel too good about that—and to tell the truth, I think we could smell a little stinky afterward. We bust them, and four or five thousand women don't get their cancer pills."

"Let me rephrase that for you," Mitford said. "Four or five thousand registered voters won't get their cancer pills and they'll complain to one of the biggest interest groups in the country, the breast-cancer coalition."

"You think we should let it slide?"

"I don't think anything. I'm not a law enforcement officer. I don't even recall having this conversation. The governor certainly never knew about it."

"So I'm working on my own book."

"Welcome to state government," Mitford said.

LUCAS AND DEL LEFT THE CHURCH, so Letty and the other women could get ready for the funeral, and walked across the highway to Calb's. The two BCA investigators were in the shop, working through the office. A deputy was sitting in the work bay, with a half-dozen employees scattered around the bay on folding chairs.

Lucas briefed the BCA guys on the theft ring, then went out to talk to the employees. "You all may be in some sort of trouble, so maybe you want to get a lawyer or public defender out here . . . but none of you will be charged with anything right away. The guys in the office will want to talk to you individually. I would like somebody to tell me one thing, which won't have any effect on you at all . . . Okay?"

The men glanced around at each other, a couple shrugged, and a stocky man in a grimy Vikings sweatshirt said, "What do you want to know?"

"You know that one of the women from the church—one of the nuns—was found dead at Gene Calb's house. Shot in the head."

"Gene didn't do it," one of the men interrupted.

"That's not what I need," Lucas said. "We're not sure what happened, but we know that both of Gene Calb's cars are still in his garage. What I want to know is . . . did one of those Toyotas come in last night, or the night before? One of the good ones?"

The men all looked around at each other again, there was more shrugging, eyes drifted away, and finally the spokesman said, "I don't know."

"Is there an old one around here? At somebody's house, or around back? I haven't looked around back."

"Not around here," the spokesman said. No more eye contact.

On the way out, Del said to Lucas, "So the Calbs are running in a wrecked Toyota. Why is that? Why not take one of their cars?"

"Because if they can get it as far as the airport at Thief River, or Fargo, and if we hadn't found out about it . . . we'd never know where they went."

"I'll get some calls out," Del said.

MARTHA WEST'S FUNERAL SERVICE was held in a non-descript chapel at the funeral home, so nondescript that it could hardly even be called nondenominational—it looked like a grade-school cafeteria without the charm, and was cold, as if the funeral home didn't want to waste energy on heating it. Seventeen people showed up, including cops. The coffin was sealed. Letty sat at the front and cried, her cast propped on the chair in front of her, her single crutch between her legs. A Lutheran minister called on Martha's friends to talk about her, and a few did, without much to say.

Couldn't say that she drank a lot, and spent most of her time at the Duck Inn.

Most talked about her songs, and how hard she worked on them, and what a good voice she had, for Custer County anyway, and let it go at that. A women's group served Ritz crackers with cheese, and sliced celery and carrots with pimento spread, in a side room, for people who weren't going to the cemetery. That was almost everybody.

Lucas and Del drove out to the cemetery behind the hearse, with Letty crying in the back seat, and Ruth trying to comfort her when she wasn't crying herself. The snow was blowing hard, and the grave looked like a big fishing hole in an ice-covered lake. The coffin went in the ground and they all left, with Letty peering back for as long as she could see the cemetery. And when she couldn't see it anymore, she rolled face-down on the back seat and sobbed.

The sheriff had made tentative arrangements for a foster home, but in the end, they didn't take her there. They left her with Ruth, at the church, with the older woman. The arrangement, they agreed, was temporary, until they figured something out. "Don't tell me you're gonna try to find my dad," Letty said. "There's no way I'd live with that sonofabitch."

As they drove away from the church, Del said, "What a wonderful fuckin' day. If there was a four-story building in town, I'd jump off it."

"There's the smokestack. There's the grain elevators."

"Fuck you."

Lucas: "Got to think of something, man."

"I *have* thought of something," Del said. He suddenly seemed comfortable, Lucas thought, which was odd, given the circumstances.

"What?"

"I'll tell you in a while. I gotta make sure I can pull it off, first."

"*What?*"

"Drop me off at the drugstore. I got things to buy."

"What're you doing?"

"Figured out how we're going to end this thing."

"*Tell me.*"

"I will—in about an hour."

21

DEL KNOCKED ON Lucas's motel door an hour later. Lucas had been watching TV news, and he got up in his bare feet to answer the door. Del had his duffel bag slung over one shoulder, and a package wrapped in brown paper under the opposite arm. He handed the package to Lucas.

"See ya," he said.

"Where're you going?" Lucas was mystified.

"Back to the Cities. Got a plane out of Fargo in two hours. Figure to get home by seven-thirty. Cheryl's gonna pick me up at the airport, and I'm gonna take her out to LeMieux's for a little French food, maybe a little wine, tell her on the way home how cute she looks with her hair that way, whichever way it is today."

"What the fuck are you talking about?"

"Gettin' laid," Del said. He ticked an index finger at Lucas. "I've got a round-trip ticket, I'll be back tomorrow by noon. Now. In that package you will find five different-colored fine-line Magic Markers and a large spiral art pad. So you get a couple beers down here, lock yourself in, and *think*. Draw your pictures on the pad, all those arrows and squares and shit. I'll come back tomorrow and you can tell me who did it."

"Jesus, Del . . ."

"We don't need to be chasing people," Del said. "We need to figure out what the fuck happened. I think there's enough information—you just haven't thought about it enough. So. See you tomorrow."

He reached forward, took the doorknob, and pulled the door shut. Lucas looked at the package, hefted it, looked at the closed door, and thought, *This is ridiculous*. He opened the door just in time to see Del slip inside the Mustang, which he'd had waiting in the drive. Del looked over at him, lifted a hand, and drove away.

"Hey!"

Del kept going.

LUCAS WENT BACK inside with the package, tossed it on the second bed, went back to the television. The woman newscaster had the most amazing lips. They couldn't be real, he thought—they must keep a bee in the studio, trained to sting them. Must hurt . . .

He fell asleep for a while, got up with a bad taste in his mouth. Del didn't understand about the arrows and boxes, he thought as he brushed his teeth. His seances with the drawing table and the arrows and boxes only worked when his head was right, when something down in the lizard part of his brain said that a solution was available . . .

He wasn't getting that message yet. He stopped brushing for a moment and looked at himself in the mirror. On the other hand, there *was* something. Not something he missed, just something about the killings that he hadn't digested yet.

Maybe he could figure something out, draw a box and a couple of arrows. Couldn't hurt.

First, get a few beers . . .

HE WASHED HIS FACE, bundled up, and walked down to the Duck Inn. The bartender had been at the funeral that afternoon, and they nodded at each other as Lucas came in. "Bad day at Black Rock," the barkeep said. "What can I do you for?"

"Six-pack of Leinies, if you got it . . . Yeah. That poor kid is the one I think about," Lucas said. "Bad goddamn thing to happen to a kid."

"She just went by—with one of them nuns," the barkeep said. He lifted the six-pack of Leinenkugel's onto the bar.

"Just now? She went by?" Lucas asked, pushing a ten across the bar.

"One minute ago. Heading over to Larson's, the way they were going. She's limping pretty good. She's gonna need some clothes, I guess."

Lucas took the change from the ten, but pushed the six-pack back at the bartender. "Hold on to this, will you? I want to see if I can catch them."

"Larson's—right down the block."

HE FOUND THEM in the women's foundations area, buying cotton underpants. Ruth Lewis saw him coming, and smiled sadly. "Have you heard anything?"

Lucas shook his head. "Not yet." He looked at Letty, who'd been looking at an underwear rack. "How are you?"

"We're both pretty sad, me and Ruth, trying to figure out what's going to happen," Letty said. Her eyes were red, with circles below. Her lip trembled. "I never even got to see Mom."

"What're you doing here?" Lucas asked Ruth.

Ruth tipped her head at Letty. "She's got nothing left. Nothing. No shoes, no underwear. We went through our stores at the church, didn't find much."

"I love to shop," Lucas said.

"Ohhh . . ." Ruth said. A skeptical smile, not the first time he'd gotten that reaction from a woman. But it was true.

"I'm serious. I really like to shop. Especially for clothes. You wanta party?"

Letty looked at Ruth, and Ruth said, "We don't really *need* that much."

"I'll let you in on a small secret, which I wouldn't want you to spread around," Lucas said. "Okay?" They both nodded, and Lucas said, lowering his voice, "I'm the richest cop in Minnesota."

"I knew that," Ruth said. "Sister Mary Joseph said you have a ridiculous amount of money."

"So I can spend a few bucks on a good time," Lucas said. "Let's go."

They bought all kinds of stuff, with Letty getting seriously involved: Jockey underpants; a couple of brassieres that Lucas wasn't entirely sure were necessary, but which he wouldn't have remotely thought of questioning; three pairs of jeans and two pairs of slacks; and four sweatshirts, which Lucas thought was too many, but Letty said "they're all I wear." They bought four more shirts at Lucas's insistence, a vest, a watch, some costume jewelry and a pair of pearl earrings, a parka, mittens, two hats, and a duffel bag that would carry everything that she didn't wear.

And though Ruth was skeptical, they spent half an hour and thirty-five dollars at the cosmetics counter.

Out on the street, Letty said, happily, "That was the best time I ever had."

Further down the street, across from an Ace Hardware, they put the packages in Ruth's Corolla, and Letty told Lucas, "I will pay you back every penny."

"I won't take the money," Lucas said. "Not a cent. You gotta learn to take gifts."

"It's charity."

"It's not charity," Lucas said. "It'd be charity if I didn't know you and didn't like you. These are gifts, because I like you."

"Would you loan me some money? Right now? If I pay back every cent?"

He hesitated, then said, "Probably. What do you want it for?"

She nodded at the Ace Hardware. "I want to go in there and get a new gun. They took that piece of crap .22, and the deputy said I wouldn't get it back. It's evidence, if they ever catch the guy I shot."

"Oh, Letty . . ." Ruth said.

"Lucas?" Letty asked.

Lucas looked at Ruth, and then said, "I'd do it, unless Ruth absolutely vetoes it. The gun would be in her house, at least for a while."

Letty turned to Ruth, who said, "I really don't think you need a gun, Letty."

"But you don't really know me very well, do you?" Letty said. Lucas estimated her working age at a quick forty-three. "I do sort of need the gun."

Ruth said to Lucas, "If you want to loan her the money, I won't say no."

ONCE INSIDE THE HARDWARE STORE, Ruth went to look at other stuff—went to be away from them—while Lucas and Letty got into the details of the gun purchase. Letty wanted a Ruger 10/22 semi-auto; Lucas suggested a bolt-action Ruger 77/22. Letty said it cost too much, and she'd be more comfortable with the lighter semi-auto. Then the store manager, a thin man with spiky gray hair, and a hunter himself who knew Letty, jumped in and said they had an even lighter semi-auto, a Browning, that split the price difference.

Lucas finally told Letty that he wouldn't buy a semi-auto, because he worried that an auto-loader was not safe enough. "I want you to know when you've got a round in the chamber, because you put it there yourself."

Then Letty got pouty: "I've been doing this for years . . ."

"Yeah, with a single-shot . . ."

". . . and I know when there's a round in the chamber."

Lucas stood firm, and the manager said, "You know, I've got a Remington pump in the back. It's used, but it's in perfect shape. I could let you have it for three hundred bucks."

Lucas and Letty looked at each other, and Letty said, "Bring it out."

They took the pump, but Letty got it for two seventy-five, with five boxes of .22 long-rifle shells thrown in as a deal-sweetener. She said to Lucas, "I've had enough of that .22 short bullshit. Next time this jerk comes around, he *better be* wearing a bulletproof vest."

LUCAS ENJOYED POETRY. Couldn't help himself. He was especially fond of haiku, the Japanese form, and in reading haiku from time to time, he'd encountered talk of Zen Buddhism, and the concept of the *koan*. A *koan* was a kind of a riddle, or paradox, without a solution. They were used by the Zen master to demonstrate the ultimate futility of logic, and to provoke—with some pupils, anyway—instant enlightenment.

Lucas heard Letty say *bulletproof vest* and took a step toward enlightenment, though later he thought the enlightenment might have been provoked by the way she'd orally italicized the *better be.*

DEL ARRIVED BACK the next day at one o'clock, knocked on the door. Lucas was lying on the bed with the door unlocked and called, "Come in."

Del pushed the door open, stuck his head in, and said, "Am I too early? Or have you figured it out?"

"I don't have a name yet," Lucas said. He held up the art pad, and the top page was covered with red and green squares and arrows. "I've got some thoughts."

Del tossed his duffel in the corner, sat on the second bed. "Give."

Lucas said, "One: We figure out in the evening that the killer was probably Sorrell. Then we drive home, and about twelve hours after we leave Armstrong, we arrive at the Sorrell house. He's dead, and he's been dead for at least a little while. That means that the killer had to hear that we'd figured out Sorrell, had to make a plan, and had to drive seven hours, at least—Rochester is more than an hour south of the Cities— and then he has to find Sorrell's house, where the phone number is un- listed, do the killing, and get away. That's pretty amazing, when you think about it.

"Two: Thirty hours after he hanged two people in Armstrong, Sor- rell lets his own killer into his house, with his wife standing right there with him. He's unarmed and is shot down in cold blood. He takes no precautions, he never thinks that the guy at the door might be con- nected to the murders.

"Three: Why did the guy attack Letty? We don't know. But we do know that Letty's mother let him in the house after midnight, when both she and Letty knew there was a killer running around loose.

"Four: Letty claims she shot the guy, but none of the hospitals in- side two hundred miles report a guy shot in the chest with a .22, that might possibly be our guy. Why is that?

"Five: I talk to Burke, Annie's dad, and he shows us stuff that looks like it came from the FBI. It looks real. How'd they know how to do that?

"Six: I talk to Letty last night after you head back to the Cities . . . Hey, did you get laid?"

"Yeah." Del nodded. "It was wonderful."

"I have fantasies about Cheryl. Maybe you could tell me . . . Never mind."

"C'mon, wiseass."

"All right. Anyway, I talk to Letty, and one thing leads to another, and we buy her a replacement rifle down at Ace Hardware. And she says to me that if this asshole comes back, quote, 'He *better be* wearing a bulletproof vest,' unquote."

Lucas looked at Del and raised his eyebrows. Del asked, "That's it?"

"That's it."

Del shook his head. "Maybe I can get a refund on some of them pens. Looks like you only used red and green."

"Think about it for a minute," Lucas said. "What are the chances that . . . the guy is a cop?"

DEL THOUGHT ABOUT IT for a minute. "If the guy is a cop, he would have heard about Sorrell really early. If he was wearing a uniform, people would let him in their house any time of day. He'd see FBI stuff, so he'd know the format. And if he was wearing a bulletproof vest . . . it would explain all of that shit."

"We know that there are at least two cops who were friendly with Gene Calb—Ray Zahn and this other guy, the boyfriend of Katina Lewis. Zahn sometimes hung out there, and the boyfriend painted his cars up there."

"How many points did you have? Six?"

"Six," Lucas agreed.

Del nodded. "Then here's number seven. If you were running a major car-theft ring, there'd be nothing more valuable than having a cop inside the only major police agency for miles around. In fact, you'd just about have to have one."

THEN LUCAS SAID, "I got another list."

"Yeah?"

Lucas said, "One: You're a friendly looking guy like Gene Calb, maybe with a spy inside the department, or maybe not—it's a small town, and word gets around. He bluffs his way into Sorrell's house, kills him, and gets back here.

"Two: He goes after Letty. We don't know the specific reason, but we do know that Letty hung around his shop and maybe he's afraid that she saw or heard something. And Calb is a friendly guy, everybody likes him, and if he knocks on the door, maybe Martha West lets him in—Letty told me one time that Martha'd had a crush on Calb.

"Three: Calb kills Katina Lewis. Why? We don't know, but suppose that Letty really did shoot him, and hit him in the chest like she said. He was hurt, but not badly. Maybe his wife patched him up or something. But suppose he bled through his shirt, or did something that tipped Katina that his chest was hurting. Heck, maybe she patted him on the chest. Anyway, the instant that she suspected, he'd have to get rid of her, because all she'd have to do is tell any cop, and we'd go straight to Calb and take his shirt off. We find a bullet hole or even a bruise, he'd be toast. So he'd have to kill her. Maybe that was done so spontaneously that he panicked, and ran."

DEL LAY BACK ON THE BED, and after a minute said, "I like the first one better. The cop."

"Why?"

"Because it all goes back to kidnapping the girls, and everybody says that Calb wouldn't do that. He might have been a criminal, but he wasn't a nut. Because if this car ring worked like we think it did, he was up to his ass in money—why'd he need to kidnap somebody? And most of all, he really seemed to think that Deon Cash and Jane Warr were stupid assholes. Would he get involved in a kidnapping with partners he thought were stupid assholes? I don't think so."

———

LUCAS THOUGHT ABOUT THAT for a while, then said, "Let's go talk to Letty and Ruth Lewis. They're up at the church. I think we ought to stay away from the sheriff's office until we've got something solid."

"I don't think Ray Zahn," Del said. "He's one of our guys."

"Yeah, well. I don't think so either, but . . . we gotta keep him on the list. And we gotta think about the possibility that it's nobody we know yet. Maybe a cop, but nobody we know yet."

"Think we'll have him by midnight?" Del said, joking.

"I don't know. If I were gonna bet, I'd say a week. Or less."

22

THE OLDER WOMAN came to the door of the church and said, "If you're looking for Letty and Ruth, they went up to the dump to shoot that gun you bought." Her tight lips suggested that she didn't approve.

"Another fan," Del said, as they got back in the car. "Dump?"

RUTH LEWIS'S TOYOTA COROLLA was parked at the dump gate, and they could hear the little .22 banging away. "You don't think they'd shoot back this way, do you?" Del asked.

"Jesus, I hope not." He hadn't thought of that. "Where are they?"

"Sounds like they're over to the left."

THEY WALKED CAREFULLY toward the sound of the shooting. A .22 long-rifle slug makes a distinctive *whip* sound as it goes by, and they didn't hear anything like that. Eventually, they crossed the high point of the dump and spotted Letty and Ruth at the far left edge of the raw dirt, shooting into a mound of clay. Ruth had the gun.

"May have been a conversion here," Lucas said. "Lewis wasn't that happy about buying the gun."

"Oughta get her an NRA membership," Del said. *"My cold dead hands . . ."*

"From what I've seen of her, she'd probably take the damn thing over," Lucas said.

LETTY AND RUTH saw them coming and stopped firing. Letty's crutch was lying on the ground, so her ankle must be feeling better. When they got close, Lucas saw that they were shooting at Campbell's soup cans, which made good reactive targets. He called, "How you doing?"

As they came up, Letty said, "The gun's not as bad as I thought."

"She hit the can every time, right from the start, even with the cast. Now she's trying to hit the gold medal thing every time," Ruth said. "I haven't hit the can once."

"I can't even see the gold medal thing from here," Del said. The cans were twenty-five yards away.

"It's sure a lot quicker than that old piece of shit," Letty said. "Even one-handed."

"Letty . . ." Ruth said.

"I know; watch my mouth." She took the gun from Ruth with her good hand, braced it over the cast on the other, and sighted down the barrel at one of the cans. She pulled the trigger and the can hopped across the ground. She turned the gun upside down with her good hand, got the pump under the upper part of her bad arm, trapped it, pumped, aimed and fired again, hit the can. She looked nonchalantly at Lucas. "So what's going on?"

"We stopped at the church, they said you were out here." He looked around. "Whatever happened to those traps you put out before the fire? Are they still out here?"

Letty shook her head. "Naw. I had Weather call Bud, from down at the hospital. He came and picked them up the next morning. We already checked, and they're all gone. I gotta get them from him."

Lucas nodded. "Okay. Listen. We need to talk to both of you about . . . mmm . . . whoever might have done all this. We were wondering specifically—do you know anything about any police officers who might have been connected with Gene Calb or with Deon Cash and Jane Warr?"

Letty looked at Ruth, and then Ruth asked, "Do you think this . . . person . . . might be a police officer?"

"There are some things," Lucas said. To Letty: "Who would your mom let in the door after midnight? We know it wasn't her boyfriend, because he was still down at the Duck Inn. Who else?"

Letty thought. "A guy? There might be a couple of guys, but I don't know. It never happened."

"How about a cop that she knew?"

"You'd always let a cop in," Letty said. "Especially since all the trouble."

"Ray Zahn? Or how about that boyfriend of Katina's?" Lucas looked at Ruth.

"Loren Singleton," she said, slowly. She pinched her bottom lip, thinking. Then, to Lucas: "I . . . oh, God."

"Look, we're interested in one thing: finding the killer," Del said to her. "We don't care about all this other happy horseshit, the cars and the drugs and all that. If you know something about a cop . . ."

"Loren kept an eye out for us at the sheriff's office," Ruth said.

Letty said, *"Really?"*

"Was that because of his relationship with your sister?" Lucas asked.

"No. They met at Calb's. Loren was being paid by Gene before

Katina got here. I don't think he'd . . ." She stopped, they waited, and then she said, "I was going to say that I don't think that Loren would hurt Katina, but when I think about it now, I'm not sure. But I can tell you one thing: I've talked to Loren since the fire at Letty's, and he certainly wasn't shot."

Lucas said, "Huh." Then, "I talked to him, too, and I didn't see any holes in him. He seemed pretty freaked out by what happened to your sister."

"He was—I talked to him that night. He was really shaky."

"Do you see him as a kidnapper?" Del asked.

"I don't . . . You know, I'm not sure he's *creative* enough, if that's the word. If he's *ambitious* enough. I didn't know Deon very well, but Deon was this ocean of *want*. He wanted money and he wanted dope and he wanted cars and he wanted clothes and he wanted to go to Vegas and LA and he wanted season tickets for basketball . . . I don't think, I mean, Loren didn't seem to want anything. He didn't seem to care about anything, or even do anything, other than sleep with Katina."

"He had his Caddys," Letty chipped in. "He was always driving one old Caddy while he worked on another one. I heard he made some good money selling them."

"A Caddy," Lucas said. He looked at Del. "Where'd we see that Caddy? You said something about it . . ."

"Right here," Del said, jabbing a thumb back at the gate. "When Letty brought her traps up here."

"Day of the fire," Lucas said. He looked around at all the raw black dirt of the dump. "If you were gonna bury somebody in the wintertime, with snow around, and you didn't want a hole that looked like a grave . . ."

Del asked Letty, "You ever see him out here? Singleton?"

"No, not that I remember."

"But you used to come out here all the time. Couple times a week, you said."

"Yeah."

Lucas to Del: "Jesus, what if he was afraid that Letty saw him? Then he sees us out here with her."

"Let's go take his shirt off," Del said.

Lucas shook his head. "Not yet. If he was wearing a vest, and that's what stopped the slug, then we'd tip him off and we wouldn't have anything. I'll tell you what: Why don't we get the California crew up here? They aren't finding anything around Cash's house. They could come up, pick a good spot, and start sweeping it. We'd know in a few hours."

Ruth said, "Loren did it?"

Lucas shook his head. "It's a possibility. Maybe one chance in three. We're really at the end of a long string here, but nobody can figure out why Letty and her mom were attacked, and why he came after Letty especially. It had to be something that she either knows, or that he was afraid she knew. And he saw us here, together, that afternoon, and then he hauled ass without a word. Turned around and took off."

Ruth looked at Letty in wonder, and Letty said, "Loren Singleton?"

23

LETTY'S HOUSE, six miles south, had been on the far fringe of the cell-phone net. The dump was out of it. "Gonna have to go get the FBI guys," Lucas said.

"I can run back with the truck, if you guys want to scrape around here," Del suggested.

"That'd be good." Lucas tossed him the keys. "The insurance certificate is in the door pocket. Don't use it."

"What am I gonna hit out here?"

Del took off, and Lucas, Letty and Ruth began walking around the dirt surface of the dump, Letty using her crutch on about every fifth step. She could feel the sprain, she said, but they'd packed her leg in ice at the hospital, and had kept the ice on it for most of the next day, and that had helped. "I'll be running in a week," she said.

"It probably wouldn't hurt to stay off it, though," Lucas said. "Much as you can, anyway."

"Drives me crazy."

"Yeah, well . . . I know. Always drove me crazy, too."

They chatted about old injuries for a while, as they wandered around. The dump was large, probably covering half a square mile, but most of the surface was covered with snow. Lucas had been to dumps before, and knew generally how they worked: the garbage and trash was dumped in the working area and was covered with a layer of dirt. Then another layer of trash went down, followed by another layer of dirt. When a predetermined level was reached, the whole thing was capped with an impervious layer of clay that would tend to sheet water off to the sides. The dump would also have a clay bottom, beneath all the layers of trash, to prevent contamination of the local groundwater.

It was, in a way, like a clay-and-garbage pie, with the clay acting as the crust, and the garbage the filling.

If Singleton was the killer, and if he'd buried his victims at the dump, he would have chosen an area already disturbed by the bulldozer, they decided. Over the rest of the area, the surface was frozen solid, and any grave-shaped hole would have shown through to the bulldozer driver.

"Do people come out here? I mean, other than the dump guy and you?" Lucas asked Letty.

"Oh, sure. Especially during hunting season. People want to get rid of deer hides and heads and so on, they'll put them in a garbage bag and bring them out and throw them in the pile. Or maybe they've got something too big to put out for the trash, they'll haul it over in their truck and throw it in. They're not supposed to, but they do."

"So it wouldn't be completely unusual to see somebody out here?"

"No. When I'm trapping out here, I probably see somebody half the time." She carried the rifle across the cast on her left arm, the muzzle pointing up at the sky. Lucas had been watching her handle the gun, and decided that she was safe enough.

"This all looks pretty raw," Ruth called. They walked over to her. She was standing on a patch of dirt thirty feet wide and fifty long, rumpled beneath the snow, softer-feeling—a bulldozer runway that led to the feeding edge of the landfill.

Lucas kicked some of the snow off, then stooped and picked up some dirt, looked at it, tossed it aside, and brushed his hands. "We oughta get the dump guy out here," he said. "Maybe he saw something strange."

After exploring the area of raw dirt, they drifted back toward the shooting range, and Lucas borrowed Letty's rifle and bounced one of the cans around. Then Letty asked about his pistol, and Lucas took out the .45 and showed her how it worked.

"Same kind of sight picture as with the rifle," he said. He stepped away from her, aimed at one of the cans, which was now about forty feet away, and fired once, missing right by three inches. He frowned, fired again, and again missed right, by only a half-inch this time, but also a little high. A third shot sent the can skittering away.

"Let me try," Letty said.

"It's gonna feel heavy, with only one hand on it," Lucas said. He gave her the pistol, showed her how the safeties worked.

She held the pistol out straight from her side, her head turned so that she was looking over her right shoulder. After a moment, she said, "Squeeze," and fired a round. She missed the can by three feet to the right, a foot low. "Holy cow," she said. "What'd I do?"

"Try once more," Lucas said. He heard truck noises back at the gate.

Letty pointed the pistol, but the barrel was shaking, and after a few seconds she took it down. "I'm not strong enough one-handed," she said.

Lucas took the gun from her, spent a couple of seconds pulling down on the can, let out a half-breath and smashed the can a second time.

"You got a string tied to the can, right?" Del called from the direction of the gate.

Lucas turned around, and saw Del with four of the California FBI crewmen walking across the dump toward them. Lucas popped the magazine from the .45, jacked the shell out of the chamber, thumbed it back in the magazine, then took a fresh magazine out of his holster and seated it in the pistol butt. The half-used magazine went into the holster.

"Good time to quit," one of the Californians said, talking through the snorkel of his snorkel parka. "If you'd kept it up, I would have been tempted to take out my piece and kick your sorry ass. No offense, ladies."

"I don't want to seem insulting, or vulgar, but none of you fuckin' FBI humpty-dumpties can shoot half as well as Del over there, and I personally can shoot several times better than Del," Lucas said.

"Au contraire," Del said. "You can hold your end up on the nice, heated, lighted range. But out here, in the real world, you can't hold a candle to me. Though you're right about the fuckin' FBI humpty-dumpties."

Ruth looked at Letty and said, "Oh, God. This is why you should never get married, honey. These people got a rivulet of testosterone running through them, and anything can set it off. A cheese sandwich can set it off."

The lead Californian was digging under his parka and produced a .40 Smith. "You are a bunch of rural people who have never seen good shooting, so you don't have to apologize for what you just said."

One of the other Californians jerked the back of his coat and he turned, and they conferred, snorkel to snorkel. Then the lead Californian turned back to Lucas and said, "Uh, are we doing this for free? Or is there some money in it?"

They spent twenty minutes banging away at cans, without conclusion, but they all felt better afterward. Lucas then showed the crew the area that needed to be surveyed, and the lead man suggested that they needn't survey all of it. "We can do stripes; we don't even have to set up guidelines, because on that thin snow, we can see where we've been . . . We can do it in a couple of hours, quick and dirty. Done before dark, anyway."

THE CREW HAD A RADAR set mounted on a wagon, which the Californians rolled back and forth over the raw patch. The radar was pointed down into the dirt, and returned echoes from lumps of differing density. The data was fed into a memory module, which was dumped into a laptop back in one of the FBI trucks. The laptop then produced a density map of the surface covered.

Striping the dirt patch took an hour and a half. Halfway through, Ruth and Letty, bored and a little cold, decided to head back to the church and eat. "Stop by when you're going back to Armstrong," Letty said. "I want to know how it comes out."

When the striping was done, the lead Californian dumped the data to the laptop, let it churn for a few minutes, then tapped a few keys and a map began scrolling up. Two-thirds of the way from the back edge of the dirt strip, toward the working edge of the landfill, he said, "Whoops."

"Got something?"

"Got a hole. We got it on the third and fourth runs. It looks like it's, uh, four feet long and three feet wide."

"Anything else?"

"Mostly what look like tread tracks from the bulldozer, both current ones and some buried ones . . . but the hole cuts through all of that. It looks like there're a few inches of packed stuff, then it goes soft." He tapped the computer screen. "You can see the edges of it."

"Better get some shovels out here," Lucas said. "Why don't you guys pin down the edges of the hole, and Del and I'll get the shovels."

"Get some sandwiches," one of the Californians said. "There's a place in town called Logan's . . ."

"Fancy Meats," Lucas said. "Give me your orders. Might as well do it right. I'll get some lights, too."

THEY WENT THROUGH Broderick without slowing down and as soon as they were within cell-phone range, Lucas called Ray Zahn. "I need to get the guy who runs the dump bulldozer. Know where we can find him?"

"Yeah, he's about three blocks from me, if he's home," Zahn said. "What do you want him for?"

"We need him to show us around the dump," Lucas said. "It's serious."

"I'll drag his ass up there," Zahn said. "When do you want him?"

AT THE ACE HARDWARE, Lucas bought four long-handled shovels and four spotlights with cigarette-lighter adapters. "Haven't sold that many spotlights since deer season," the counterman said. "Pick out a deer at two hundred yards."

Lucas thought about that for a moment, then went to the back of the store and found four two-by-four-foot pressed-board handy panels with one white side, and a roll of duct tape. "Reflectors," he said to Del. Outside, it was getting dark.

BACK AT THE DUMP, the Californians had outlined the hole, and using a long-bladed screwdriver, had determined that there were about six to eight inches of compressed dirt over a looser fill.

Lucas used a tire-iron to pop the lock off the dump gate, and they drove Lucas's truck and the two FBI vehicles into a circle around the dig site. Lucas brought the spotlights out, the Californians set up the white panels, and when the lights were plugged in, Lucas focused them on the panels, and the dig-site was bathed in a smooth reflected light.

"Cool," one of the Californians said.

THEY STARTED DIGGING, three at a time—four shovelers was one too many—and cleared out the 'dozer-compacted cap in ten minutes.

"Looks like a grave," Del said from the sidelines.

Another set of headlights swept over the dump, and a minute later, Ray Zahn had pulled in beside Lucas's Acura. Zahn and another man got out, and Zahn said to Lucas, "This is Phil Bussard. He runs the 'dozer."

"You remember seeing anything that looked like a hole, or a dug spot, right here, this morning?"

"Nothing like that," Bussard said. "Did see a bunch of truck tracks. Somebody unloaded something back here. Didn't think nothing of it."

"How did they get through the gate?" Lucas asked. "Is it always locked when you're not here?"

"Yeah, but about half the people in town know the combination," Bussard said. "All kinds of people are authorized to get in here, and the number gets around. It's ten-twenty-thirty."

"So why lock it at all?"

"For the lawyers. If somebody works the lock and gets in here, and gets hurt, I guess it's breaking and entering, or something. They committed a crime, and if they get hurt doing it, it ain't the county's fault."

"Where were you working a month ago? Around Christmas?"

"Right over on the other side there," Bussard said, pointing. "If you look at the edge, you can see some Christmas wrap. That's where it'd be."

"See any holes over there?"

"Not that I remember. See truck tracks all the time."

Zahn came back from the widening hole. "Sure does look like a grave," he said.

THE PEOPLE IN THE HOLE were slowing down, so the last Californian, Bussard, and Lucas took the shovels, and continued down. At three feet, the Californian said, "Somebody hand me that screwdriver."

He took the screwdriver, squatted, and pushed it into the dirt at the bottom of the hole, probed for a minute, then stood up. "I'd say we're eight inches off the garbage level."

"That'd be about right," Bussard said, bobbing his head.

Eight inches down, Lucas cut through a white garbage sack, and could smell the garbage inside. "Smells like old pizza," he said. "Like from a Dumpster out behind a pizza joint on a hot summer night."

"Lucky you didn't get one of them diaper bags," Bussard said. "They smell like old shit on a hot summer night."

The Californian said, "I got something here." He was probing at a dark green garbage bag. They cleared away a little more dirt, then Bussard took a Leatherman tool off his belt, flicked open a blade, and slashed through the green bag.

A woman's bare leg, flexed; her toenails were painted red.

"There you go," Zahn said. "There you go."

DEL SAID, "Loren Singleton. Here we come."

"I'm coming with you," Zahn said. "I want to see what that sonofabitch has to say for himself."

24

ALL OF IT WAS INNOCENT. Back at the church in Broderick, Letty told the older woman about the scene at the dump and the shoot-out between Lucas, Del, and the FBI. Then Letty took a pill for her hand, got a book, and found an empty bed she could lie on, to read. Ruth went to work on the phone, calling members of her network in Canada. The older woman went down the highway to Wolf's Cafe, got a piece of pie and a cup of coffee, and told Sandra Wolf that the FBI and the state were up at the dump, and about the shooting contest.

A bit later, a sheriff's deputy came into the cafe, and Wolf told him about the shooting contest, and that the FBI was searching the dump. The deputy was a little put off about it because he'd been working—well, watching—the FBI guys at Deon Cash's house, and they'd all taken off without telling him anything. He was also fairly sure that the sheriff had been cut out of the deal, so he called Mrs. Holme, the sheriff's secretary, and asked her to pass on the word to the sheriff.

The sheriff was out, but she passed it on to several other people.

The word took almost an hour to get to Loren Singleton, who was getting a Sprite out of the fire station Coke machine when he heard about it. "Up there digging holes," said the guy who'd heard it from a guy who'd heard it from Holme. "Better them than me. That place smells bad even when it's all covered up and froze."

MARGERY SINGLETON HAD JUST gotten home, carrying a brown grocery bag with a box of beef brains from Logan's Fancy Meats, flour and milk from the Kwik Stop, and a sack of potatoes, when her son burst in on her.

"The jig's up," he groaned at her. "Jesus Christ, the jig is up. The FBI and the state guys are up at the dump digging holes, and they've got all that special equipment up there. They're gonna find them. Those California guys say they can find a hundred-year-old grave, and the Calbs haven't been in the ground long enough to get cold."

Margery's eyes narrowed. "You think it's because of that kid?"

"Who else? When I took the girls up, there weren't any cars around and I took them off to the back corner and it was almost dark. So who else is up there that might have seen me? There's nothing out there, except those goddamn raccoons that the kid goes after."

"Who'd you hear this from? This isn't just bullshit, is it?"

"Naw, I got it from Roland Askew. Here's something else: they cut the sheriff out of the loop, even though they were all buddy-buddy up at Calb's house. Why'd they do that? Because I'm a deputy, and they know it's me that put them in the ground. God, Mom, I'm really scared." He jammed a knuckle into his mouth and bit it.

Margery looked at the box of beef brains on the kitchen table. Brains, sliced like bread and fried up in beer batter, were a rare treat, as long as you got the brains when they were fresh. Frozen brains got mushy when you thawed them. She thought about the possibilities for a minute, then said, "If the girl is dead, she can't testify. You've got to get up there and finish it."

"Mom, if they think it's me . . . I got a hole in my chest, and a bruise. All they have to do is get me to take my shirt off."

"So you go up and take care of the girl. By the time you get back here, I'll have it figured out: you're gonna have an accident."

"An accident?"

"A car wreck. Bruise you all up. I gotta think about it. Hurt you bad enough someplace else, like Fargo, that they put you in the hospital. You drive my car, we fake the wreck, you fake the injury. Hit something hard enough to pop the airbags. By the time they find us, the hole's healed up . . . We can figure something out. I can pretty much see what we're gonna do—but it ain't gonna work if that little kid talks."

"Aw, jeez, they're gonna get us."

"You better hope not. You know what they do to guys like you down at Stillwater? You won't have any trouble taking a shit, I tell you that. You'll be nice and loose. That's if the feds don't get you. The feds'll put you in the chair, if they get you."

"Oh, God." He stuck his knuckle in his mouth again, closed his eyes, bit on it. The pain helped clear his mind out. He opened his eyes and said, "I'm going. It's almost dark now, I still got the garage-door opener for Calb's, I can put the car in there, walk across to the church. I heard that the other women left after Katina died; there'll only be Ruth Lewis and the kid."

Talking himself into it. Margery nodded and said, "You might not have much time. Best get moving. I'll figure things out here."

THE SHERIFF HEARD about the dump dig at the same time that Loren Singleton heard. Anderson got it from an assistant county attorney at Borgna's Drugs. The sheriff was mulling over the selection of

Chap Stick products when the prosecutor came by, carrying a box of NyQuil, and said, "We gotta stop meeting like this."

Anderson said, "Especially with you carrying drugs."

"That's the darn truth. I don't know why those crazy fools mess around with meth labs when they can come down to Borgna's and buy NyQuil . . . So what'd they find at the dump?"

"The dump?" Anderson was puzzled.

"Yeah, it's all over town—the feds and those state guys are up at the dump, digging the place up. Ray Zahn's up there, they rousted out old Phil Bussard, must have him up there with the 'dozer. Must be looking for those girls."

"Aw, Jiminy," Anderson said. He walked out of the drugstore and climbed into his truck, did an illegal U-turn, and headed out of town. He got madder and madder, thinking about it, as he went north—he was smearing cherry Chap Stick on his lips when he realized that he'd just shoplifted it under the eyes of an assistant county attorney.

"These people," he said aloud, meaning the BCA, but especially Lucas Davenport. He was so arrogant, so holier-than-thou, out here in the sticks with his expensive Patagonia parka and his forty-thousand-dollar truck that no self-respecting American ought to be driving. Like to see him get that thing fixed when it blows up on Highway 36, he thought; like to see him find parts for a gosh-darned Acura out here. They'd have to tow that sucker back to the Cities.

They had their hot jobs up at the capital hanging out with that fag-got Henderson, and they didn't understand that he couldn't be cut out of this investigation—not if he wanted to keep this job, the best job he'd ever had and would ever have. *These people.*

He had a little fantasy of *arranging* a breakdown for Davenport's Acura, noticed that he'd just gone through Broderick at eighty-five miles an hour, saw lights on at Calb's and wondered if the feds might be in there, too, got even madder, and pushed the truck to ninety.

At the turnoff to the dump, he thought, *Easy does it. You're cool, now.* He continued down the approach road. There were no vehicles parked at the gate, but from the high seat in the truck, he could see over the rise of the dump to a brilliant cluster of lights off to his right. People at work.

He took the truck that way, bouncing over the ruts left by the bulldozer, saw Zahn walking back to his car, then Davenport and Capslock walking toward the fancy Acura.

The radio went, on the command frequency. "Sheriff, you there?"

He ignored it, pulled up beside Davenport and Capslock, and hopped out.

"What's going on here?" he asked Lucas.

"Take a look in the hole," Lucas said. "We think it's Mrs. Calb."

"Aw, jeez . . . How come I wasn't in on this?"

Lucas said, "I gotta apologize for that, but we got some information that, uh, the guy we're looking for might be with the sheriff's department."

Anderson had started toward the hole, but that turned him around. "My department?"

"Yeah. We think it might be Loren Singleton. Katina's boyfriend."

"Singleton? I just, I just . . . Aw, shoot." He walked over to look in the hole. They'd exposed most of the bag, and he could see a woman's thigh and lower leg. Could be Gloria Calb; about the right size.

"We gotta another bag underneath it," Bussard said, leaning on his shovel, looking up at the sheriff. He smelled like old Campbell's tomato soup. "Looks like a man's shoe. The boys here think it's gotta be Gene."

Lucas stepped up next to Anderson. "We were gonna come get you, and then go get Singleton. Since he's your guy, we figured you might want to be there to make the official arrest . . ."

Aw, shoot.

THEY ALL WENT BACK to their trucks, Anderson thinking that they'd never have called him, not until they had Singleton trussed up like a Christmas turkey. They were treating him like the village idiot, and if he hadn't gotten up here in time, everybody in Custer County would have known about it.

Anderson got in his truck and the radio bleated again, "Sheriff, are you there? Sheriff?"

He picked up the handset and said, "Yeah, this is me. What do you want?"

"We got a strange call from Margery Singleton. That's Loren Singleton's mother. She said she's afraid he's done something awful and that he might hurt some more people. I don't know, she sounded a little overcooked, but I thought I'd call you . . ."

ZAHN WAS LEADING the parade out of the dump, Lucas behind him, Anderson in the third truck, and as they pulled out of the approach road, Anderson began honking his horn and flashing his lights. They all stopped and Anderson ran up beside Lucas's truck.

"Loren Singleton's mom just called in. She said she thinks Loren's done something awful, and he's headed up to Broderick and thinks he might hurt some more people. She said he mentioned that Letty kid."

"Aw, shit," Lucas said. He shouted "Tell Ray," and accelerated away, barely giving Anderson time to jump back from the truck.

Anderson watched as Lucas swerved around Zahn and out onto the approach road. Zahn had stopped with all the horn honking, and had gotten out of his car when Anderson had gotten out of his. Zahn yelled, "What?"

"Loren's on his way to Broderick; he's after that Letty kid."

Zahn didn't say anything—just got in his car and tore out after

Lucas. Anderson got back in his truck and followed, onto the approach road. Then he picked up his handset, called the dispatcher and said, "You gotta get the phone number of that church up in Broderick. Tell them that they're in danger, that Loren's coming after them. Tell them to lock their doors."

The call was, he thought later, the only good thing he'd done all night—but it was *very* good.

25

LOREN SINGLETON HAD JUST gotten his truck in Calb's garage when another truck went through town at high speed. He heard it, didn't see it—but its urgency carried a message. Something had happened north of Broderick, and the only thing north of Broderick for a long distance was the dump.

In his heart, he knew they'd found something. He sat slumped in his truck, the radio muttering at him, and then, distantly, playing an old Wayne Newton tune, "Danke Schoen." He, turned it up a bit, and the song hit him emotionally, and he began to weep, thinking about Katina, but also about himself. The chances of Mom getting anything together were just about zero, he thought. He was toast.

He finally wiped his eyes with the heels of his hands, pulled on his gloves, got the .380 out from under the car seat, put on his cop hat, took a deep breath, and headed out to the church.

———

RUTH LEWIS HAD FINISHED her calls north. Letty was sleepy from the pain pills, and had given up her book and was watching one of the nuns' DVD movies, *Thelma and Louise,* her injured leg up on a pile of pillows. The older woman was in her cubicle, doing her afternoon prayers. Ruth, restless, thought about collecting Letty and walking over to the diner, or getting back in the car and checking at the dump, to see if anything had been found.

Thelma and Louise was starting to show noise—either that, Ruth thought, or the DVD machine was breaking down. She leaned against the doorway, watching the movie over Letty's head, when the phone rang in the kitchen. She hurried back, picked it up. The sheriff's dispatcher, talking all in a rush: *"Loren Singleton's mom says he's coming up there with a gun he might hurt you and you're all supposed to get out of there quick, the sheriff's on his way right now but Loren may be ahead of him . . ."*

The doorbell rang.

RUTH DROPPED THE PHONE and ran toward the front of the church, stopped in the doorway of the TV room, and said, quietly as she could, but with urgency, "Loren Singleton's on his way. Get up in the loft and hide."

The doorbell rang again and Letty, not asking questions, limped past Ruth, and Ruth went to the front of the church and peeked out the small window at the front. Loren Singleton, hands in his pockets, shoulders hunched against the wind, was standing on the concrete stoop.

She backed away. Silence was best, she thought. Then the older woman, interrupted at her prayers, called, "Ruth? Did you get the door?"

The doorbell rang again and then the doorknob rattled, and she heard Singleton yell, "Sheriff's deputy. Open up."

The older woman came out, puzzled, and asked, "What's going on?" Ruth grabbed her by the arm, saw Letty disappearing into the loft at the back, and dragged the older women toward the back of the church. "Loren Singleton . . . the sheriff says he might be here to hurt Letty."

"What?"

They were at a window, and Ruth looked out—but there was nothing out there except a few snow-whipped buildings, hundreds of feet apart, and the plains. If they ran out the back door, and if Singleton saw them, there'd be no place to go, or to hide.

"I don't . . ." she began, and at that moment, Singleton kicked in the door. He did it like a cop, a quick heavy kick at the doorknob, and the door buckled, without quite breaking clean. Then he kicked it again, and Ruth said to the older woman, "Hide. Anywhere." She turned toward the door to confront Singleton.

Singleton loomed in the doorway and Ruth shouted at him, "The sheriff's coming. They just called and they know!"

Singleton had a gun in his hand, but the message got through to him and he stopped, breathing hard, maybe thinking and then Letty, from up in the loft, yelled, "You killed my mom, you sonofabitch."

Ruth's heart sank.

Letty added, "I shot you once and I'll shoot you again if you don't get out of here."

Singleton saw her up in the loft, and shouted, "You little . . ." He lifted his gun hand as though he might shoot at her, and Letty shot him and he fell down.

"Letty," Ruth yelled. "Stop. Stop!"

"Get up and I'll shoot you again, you sonofabitch," Letty yelled.

Ruth walked carefully toward the front of the church, where Singleton was trying to roll over on his stomach. Ruth could see a gun lying on the floor off to the side. He couldn't see her coming as he tried to push himself up, and she stepped around him and kicked the gun off to the side and waved at Letty, who shouted, "Get away from him, Ruth."

Singleton got his feet underneath himself, and he looked sideways at Ruth and said, "Little bitch shot me right in the stomach. God that hurts."

"We can get you to the hospital."

"Fuck that," Singleton said. "How did you know I was coming?"

"Your mom called, I guess. She was afraid you'd hurt somebody. Was it . . . did you . . . are you the one who hurt Katina?"

Singleton was puzzled. "Mom?"

"Called the sheriff," Ruth said. "Did you hurt Katina?"

From the back of the church, Letty shouted, "Get away from him Ruth. Get away from him."

Ruth waved at her. "Did you . . ."

"But, Mom . . ." Singleton was puzzled.

"What?"

He looked at her, his eyes rolling a little. "But, Mom . . . I mean, she did it all. She had the idea. She gave the shots to the girls. She got the money. She shot Katina . . ." He managed to focus on Ruth, and tears started. "I wouldn't hurt Katina. I didn't, I didn't . . ."

There was a scuffling, sliding gravel sound outside, cars pulling into the graveled lot, and Singleton pushed himself to his feet and said, "You better get out of here."

He pushed his parka back and slipped a service revolver out of a holster and said, "Better back away . . ."

She backed away and he lurched into the doorway and Letty yelled, "Watch out, watch out," and shot him again in the back, and he lurched forward and lifted the pistol and Ruth heard men yelling outside and Letty shot him in the back again, and Singleton pulled the trigger on his pistol once and then buckled under a volley of pistol shots, taking two steps back and falling into the church.

Then she heard somebody shout, "Del . . . Del . . ."

THE ACURA COULD GO a hundred and five, but didn't like it: didn't like the tar joints on the county highway and Lucas felt like a pea being rattled in a tin can. Del was shouting, "Go, go," and in the rearview mirror, Lucas could see Zahn slowly closing on them. Within a minute or two, Zahn was fifty yards back, and he hung there; they were only two minutes out of town.

They were still more than a mile out when they saw somebody walking across the highway far ahead. At that distance, he was the apparent size of a flea seen from across a room, but Del said, "That's him: that's gotta be him."

They were a little more than a mile out when they saw him kick in the door of the church, and Del pulled out his pistol and said, "Put me right on the door."

Lucas said, "Going too fast. I don't know where I can put us. That's all gravel in there."

Seconds later, they were skidding across the gravel, Zahn fishtailing into the lot right behind them, trying to keep from colliding. Lucas stopped a little beyond the church door and Del was out and then Lucas was out and he saw Zahn drawing his pistol and aiming over the roof of the cruiser and then Singleton was in the door and Lucas leveled his gun at him and started shouting—didn't know what he was shouting, he was shouting a *noise,* and he heard what sounded like gunfire—and then Singleton, who'd been moving in a slow jerking motion, suddenly and spasmodically lifted one hand and there was a gun in it and he fired and Del went down and Lucas and Zahn opened fire and Singleton slumped back into the church.

Lucas ran around the truck. "Del . . . Del . . ."

RUTH LEWIS CAME to the door, cautiously. Letty was right behind her with her gun. Lewis stopped to look at Singleton, but Letty came through and saw Del on the ground and said, "Oh, no, is he hurt bad? Is he hurt?"

Lucas was kneeling beside him, Zahn standing over them both, and Del asked, "How bad?"

"Your leg is fucked up," Lucas said. "Doesn't seem to be pumping blood. You want to wait for an ambulance or you wanna go for a ride?"

Zahn, above them, said, "I called for an ambulance, it'll be here in seven minutes. I've seen a hell of a lot worse. If you wait, you'll have a comfortable ride."

"I'll wait," said Del.

"Let's get some blankets under him," Ruth Lewis said. "Loren's dead."

"We found the Calbs out at the dump—Loren killed your sister, and the Calbs, and Letty's mother, and the Sorrells, and probably the two children," Lucas told her. "Guy's done a lot of damage."

"Mmm," she said, distantly. Lucas thought she might be going into shock. Then, "I'll get the blankets. The ground's so cold." She hurried back into the church.

Letty squatted next to Del. "I shot him three more times," she said. "I heard you coming and he went to the door with his gun, and I shot him three times but he kept going."

"Aw, man," Lucas said. "This is awful."

"Guy committed suicide," Del said. "Just wish . . . just wish . . ."

Ruth Lewis ran inside, saw the .380 kicked against the wall. Blankets. She needed blankets for Del. She went to the closest bed, stripped off the blankets, then got some more from the next cubicle. And she thought: *Mom?*

On the way back out, she saw the cluster of people around Del, and she stepped sideways and picked up the little .380 and put it in her pocket.

RUTH CAME BACK with the blankets, and they pushed them under Del's butt and back and good leg, and Del asked everybody, pain in his eyes, "I won't lose the leg, will I?"

Zahn said, "With our hospital, you never know," and when Del did a kind of eyeball double-take, he said quickly, "Just kidding. Hang on, there. That fuckin' Loren."

26

DEL WAS STABILIZED in Armstrong and then flown back to the Cities, where he was met by Weather, by Rose Marie, and by the governor himself.

Lucas stayed behind for a hard two days after Singleton was shot. They brought Margery Singleton in, a bird-like woman shocked by what they were saying. "It can't be my boy; it can't be my boy," she said. "He's dead? You say he's dead?" The sheriff eventually patted her on the back, thanked her for the phone call, and sent her on her way.

They debriefed Ruth Lewis, who was accompanied by an influential Minneapolis attorney who did the heavy lifting for the archdiocese of St. Paul and Minneapolis. The drug runs weren't mentioned, but she told them what she "suspected" about the car theft ring.

All of Calb's employees were interviewed, except for three who'd departed for parts unknown. All of those interviewed professed to have been mystified by the number of Toyotas they'd been painting. They'd all heard that it was a deal with some insurance company to fix slightly flawed new Toyotas.

Letty was interviewed and sent down to the Cities with the older woman from the church. She was scheduled for more work on her hand.

THE FBI CREW FOUND first Tammy Sorrell's grave, led there by the Christmas wrap at the edge of the dump cut, and then, later the same day, Annie Burke's.

Lucas turned the details over to the crew from Bemidji, and on the third day, left Custer County. An Alberta Clipper was coming through, and he stayed close to the front all the way down, driving through the feathery snow, listening to the FM stations come and go.

HE ARRIVED HOME to find his wife putting her coat on.

"Going to Subway. I thought I'd be back before you got here," Weather said, after kissing him hello.

"I can go if you want," Lucas offered.

"No, I'll go. Back in fifteen."

"Talk to Del today?"

"Yes. Went over, talked to him, looked at the films. I'm no ortho-pod, but I think what you heard is right," Weather said. "The break's a bad one—some of the bone got blown back into his calf. Twenty years ago, before they got so good with bone grafts, he'd be stuck with a pretty bad limp. Now, it'll be a while before he's out jogging, but I don't think he'll limp."

"Cheryl's pissed at me," Lucas said. "That happens. The wife always gets a little pissed at the partner when somebody gets hit."

"You feel bad about it?"

"Some," Lucas said. "But I don't know what else I could have done. We thought he was in there killing them."

The phone rang, Weather picked it up, listened, said, "Yes, just a second." She covered the mouthpiece with her hand, said, "It's Sheriff Anderson from Armstrong," and, "I'm going to Subway."

THE KID WAS IN BED, the housekeeper was in her apartment. Lucas went up and took a quick shower, and got back downstairs just as Weather arrived with the sandwiches. They sat at the kitchen table, eating them and splitting a bag of potato chips. "I thought things would go easier, with the new job," Weather said. "I think Cheryl thought so, too. Del's been in some scrapes, but nothing bad since that deal with the pinking shears."

"That was more . . . grotesque . . . than really bad," Lucas said. "I mean, it wasn't like he couldn't work for months and months."

"SO WHAT'D THIS Anderson character have to say? The sheriff?"

"About what?"

"About the autopsy, for one thing. You said they were going to do them today."

"Singleton had eight bullet holes in him. Two were mine, two were Zahn's, and four were Letty's, from two different guns. She said she shot him, and she had—he had a hole in his chest, but somehow he got the slug out."

"Jeez."

"Yeah. The two little girls were killed with injections. They're not sure what the agent was, but when I heard that, it kind of weirded me out. I don't know what to think about that." He frowned, contemplated his sandwich, and added, "The Calbs were killed with the same gun used on the Sorrells, but it wasn't Singleton's service revolver. He probably ditched it somewhere. His mother said he had another, smaller gun, which sounds right. But the injections . . . that kind of worried me. Doesn't sound like Singleton.

"But then, the sheriff tore apart Singleton's place—actually, it was the guys from Bemidji and a couple of deputies—and they found a load of cash in the basement. More of the kidnapping money. A lot of it's missing, but they probably just spent it. If the Burke guy wants, he could probably bring an action against the Calb estate and the Cash estate and get some of the money back from the sales of their houses, and so on. I don't know if it'll come to much, now—the Cash house, anyway. With Calb out of business, I think Broderick's probably gonna sink back into the prairie."

"Huh." Weather took an unladylike bite out of her sandwich.

"DID YOU SEE Letty today?" Lucas asked.

"Yes," Weather said, talking with her mouth full. "They took the cast off to have a look, put another one back on. They think that they might do some revisions next week. She's going to be a hurting little kid for a while."

"Huh. She was pretty unhappy when I talked to her last night," Lucas said. He half-grinned. "Anderson took her new gun away from her, for one thing. I don't think she's gonna get it back."

"She's gotta be traumatized," Weather said. "Her mother might not have meant to do it, but that little girl has been abused. That's what it amounts to. Taking care of a drunk when you're twelve years old? And she's done it for years. She was the adult in the family. And then she's shot and shoots back, and her mother's killed . . . It's amazing that she hasn't gone catatonic."

"Yeah . . ." They chewed for a moment, then Lucas said, "Anderson said that Ruth Lewis took off. He's trying to find her, but the older lady up there, at the church, said Ruth crossed into Canada, something to do with her network. Said she'd be back in a few days. Sheriff said he checked, and the border people have a record of her crossing this morning. So . . . I suspect she's rearranging things. They'll be bringing the dope across somewhere else."

"Hope she pulls it off," Weather said. "She seemed like she was trying to do the right thing."

"I don't know," Lucas said. "I'm not smart enough to figure out all the what-ifs."

THEN LUCAS SAT tapping his fingers on the table for a minute, inspecting an olive that had squirted out of his sandwich, and finally, Weather said, "What?"

He put the sandwich down and made his face sincere, like when he wanted to do something that Weather might not like. "You think, uh, Letty might be able to move in with us for a while? Until things get figured out?"

Weather ripped open the nearly empty sack of potato chips, and dumped the last four chips on the table. She took two of them. "I wondered if you were going to ask. I think we could, though I would predict some trouble. She's tough, she's gonna do what she wants to do, and she doesn't mind giving you a hard time."

"Which reminds of us who?" Lucas asked.

Weather was puzzled. "Who?"

"Jesus Christ, Weather, you just described yourself perfectly." He took one of the remaining chips.

"I *did not*." She was amazed. "I'm the most flexible person I know."

"Aw, man . . ." He gave up. "But you think we can do that?"

"I think we could. I like her a lot," Weather said. "We've got plenty of room. Even if we have another child, the two little ones could sleep together until Letty went off to college . . ."

"Another . . . hmm."

"I'm not pregnant, dummy," she said. "I'm just talking theory, at this point."

Lucas looked at the table. "You gonna eat that chip?"

THAT SAME NIGHT, Margery Singleton was surprised to find her back door open when she got home. She always locked it. Or almost always—though, it being a small town, she sometimes forgot.

She pushed inside, trying to recapture the feeling of the morning. Hadn't she gotten the key stuck in the door that morning? Or was it yesterday?

She pushed the door closed, flipped the light, took a step into the kitchen and stopped. A woman was sitting at the table and Margery took a step back. "Who the hell are you?" Then she saw the pile of money on the table. "That's my money, there."

Ruth Lewis picked up Loren Singleton's .380.

"You killed my sister, Mom. And you killed those little girls with needle injections. And God only knows who else. Something has to be done about that." She was pointing the pistol at Margery's chest.

The pistol, which Ruth had picked up at the church, had been surprisingly simple to work. She'd done a little practice before she'd sent another one of the sisters across the border with her driver's license. Ruth would cross herself later that night, with that sister's ID. A simple-enough alibi—she'd learned to think like a criminal.

"Well, you can't just shoot me," Margery said. She was thinking ahead two squares, like she had with Loren. Loren had been dead and gone before he'd left her house that night, and she'd known it. But Loren was screwed up in the head, and if the cops had gotten a handle on him, he would've spilled all the beans. And when they found the little girls at the dump, and found those needle pricks . . . who would have thought they could do that, after all this time?

"You can't just shoot me," Margery was saying. If she could get close enough to the table . . .

Ruth said, "I don't see why not."

She flinched with the blast, deafeningly loud in the small room. But she showed that cold, wintery smile when Margery Singleton went down.